Uncle Seth
Fought the Yankees

Uncle Seth
Fought the Yankees

James Ronald Kennedy

PELICAN PUBLISHING COMPANY
GRETNA 2015

The word "Pelican" and the depiction of a pelican are
trademarks of Pelican Publishing Company, Inc., and are
registered in the U.S. Patent and Trademark Office.

Library of Congress Cataloging-in-Publication Data

Kennedy, James Ronald.
  [Short stories. Selections]
  Uncle Seth fought the Yankees / by James Ronald Kennedy.
    pages ; cm
  ISBN 978-1-4556-2121-7 (hardcover : acid-free paper) -- ISBN 978-1-4556-
2122-4 (ebook) 1. United States--History--Civil War, 1861-1865--Fiction. I.
Title.
  PS3611.E5634A6 2015
  813'.6--dc23

                              2015011919

Printed in the United States of America

Published by Pelican Publishing Company, Inc.
1000 Burmaster Street, Gretna, Louisiana 70053

*Some folks are lucky to go through life and have a good friend.
Others are lucky to find someone who truly knows how to love.
Some are happy to settle for a mate who tolerates their unique ideas.
And occasionally a person is lucky enough to know
someone whose passion for life is equal to their own.*

*But I am the luckiest of all because I have someone who is all the
above and more. And to her I dedicate this book:
my wonderful wife, Shelly Cape Kennedy.*

Contents

Acknowledgments

I wish to acknowledge the following artists for their creative contribution to this work.

The late C. "Jim" Whittington of Louisiana, who worked on the first Uncle Seth stories published in 2000; Charles Hayes of Texas; Betty Kennedy of Louisiana; and Jerry McWilliams of Mississippi, who did Uncle Seth's portrait used on the book cover. Their willingness to use their creative talent, in this age of leftist political correctness, to promote our Cause is a living testament to their honor and courage.

Also a special thanks to my twin brother, Walter Donald Kennedy, for his review, suggestions, and encouragement. As always, all of our books have been a mutual effort driven by our passion for freedom and love of the South and *all* of her people—a people who deserve to be free, to be the masters in their own homes.

About Uncle Seth

There once was a land in the New World populated primarily by hardy descendants of Scottish, Irish, and Welsh immigrants. These people carried with them a common distrust for big and powerful governments; of government, they only asked to be left alone. In the Old World, their ancestors' lands had been routinely invaded by the armies of strong, centralized English governments. Big governments always brought wars, invasions, foreign occupation, taxes, and a type of slavery similar to European serfdom. These people were by blood and culture rugged individuals; their loyalty was to the clan (tribe) and to friends and neighbors who were allied to their clans—often referred to as "kith and kin." A man's value was not measured in material things but in things of the spirit: honor, loyalty, veracity, trustworthiness, and, most of all, bravery. A man's word was his bond. No written document was necessary among such people. For these folks, an un-witnessed handshake was more binding than a signed and witnessed document under royal seal. They were a warrior people, quick to take offense and quick to remedy said offense with blood. They loved weapons as both a symbol of manhood and a symbol of their personal liberty. Knowing this, they spoke slowly and in a respectful manner when dealing with strangers and each other. They knew that being offensive, dishonest, or impolite among a well-armed people could be a deadly matter. They brought this rich heritage of rugged individualism to the new world as they flowed over the Cumberland Gap and the mountains of Kentucky and Tennessee. While the Puritan descendants of their vowed English enemy were settling New England, these folks came to Virginia, the Carolinas, and Georgia and began to push westward toward the Mississippi River and eventually places that would be called Texas, Arkansas, Missouri, and Oklahoma. They settled the vast interior of America, finding its solitude to their liking and asking of government only to be left alone.

(Jim Whittington)

During the American Revolution—when the Thirteen American Colonies seceded from Great Britain—the English ordered that these hardy people living on the westward slopes of the Appalachian Mountains return to the English-controlled side of the mountains and surrender their guns. They came with their hunting rifles and met the English at Kings Mountain, the Cowpens, and Guilford's Courthouse in the Carolinas. But they did not surrender their guns; those rugged Southerners pointed them at the hated English and destroyed the English Army sent to disarm them. The English began a steady retreat until, at last, the American "Rebels" had the English commander Charles Cornwallis surrounded at Yorktown, Virginia. American independence was assured with Cornwallis' surrender there. In many respects American independence was a result of the bravery of those Southerners, armed with their own private weapons, who only asked to be left alone.

Uncle Seth's great-grandfather was one of these heroes. He was a yeoman farmer who had no part in the fight on the eastern side of the Appalachian Mountains. But when the English government—the same government that had caused his father to flee Northern Ireland—decided to dictate how he would live, the fight was on! Fighting tyranny was a part of Uncle Seth's Celtic heritage—a heritage Uncle Seth was determined to pass on to his children, his grandchildren, and, in the last days of his life, to his great-grandchildren.

Uncle Seth's South was inhabited by other peoples who combined their cultural heritage with the Scotch-Irish to create a unique population—Southerners. The second-largest group in the South comprised descendants of Africa who had been kidnapped, sold into slavery by their fellow Africans, and shipped to the New World by New Englanders. This shipment of human cargo was called the "middle passage," and it is estimated that at least half of the human cargo carried in New England Yankee slave ships died while in the "care" of the self-righteous sons of New England. Many of those captives who survived and were "lucky enough" to be sold in America instead of in the Caribbean islands found a new home in the South among a people who, though different in skin color, were of a clannish/ herdsman culture similar to their own tribal/ herdsman heritage.

Germans were also a part of Uncle Seth's South, coming early to the area and creating "Germantown" upriver from New Orleans and even in the hill country of North Louisiana and in other Southern states. Port cities such as New Orleans, Louisiana, Charleston, South Carolina, and Savannah, Georgia, gladly received immigrants from Ireland, Italy, England, and other European nations. Louisiana, Florida, and Texas enjoyed a rich Spanish heritage, and in Louisiana a large population of

French-speaking Acadians populated the southern part of the state. Their ancestors had been driven out of their homes in Quebec, Canada, by the English. Added to this mixture were numerous Native Americans of the Creek, Cherokee, Chickasaw, Choctaw, and Seminole tribes who contributed their folk ways and hardy genetic stock to the blood that made up Uncle Seth's beloved South.

These were a religious people who viewed God as a loving and merciful Heavenly Father who would eventually judge all. The religion of the backwoods, hills, and mountains was mainly of Protestant denominations, while "high church" Episcopal and Roman Catholic churches held sway in the river cities of the South. Amazingly, there were also a number of Jewish Synagogues across the old South. Religion was important to Southerners; it was personal and private, which encouraged a tolerance of personal religious views as opposed to the intolerance and conformity practiced in early New England. The Southern preacher, priest, or rabbi simply announced the word of God; the faithful accepted it and were comforted in their pilgrimage through this life, and the fools rejected it and suffered the eternal consequences. The local church was the center of the community, used for both prayer meetings and social gatherings.

Uncle Seth viewed the world as an American patriot—in the original meaning of the word: loyal to family, extended family, friends, neighbors who make up the local communities, and finally to his state. A patriot looks beyond the nation's borders and sees peoples with differing ideas regarding the type of government they want to live under. A patriot looks at different people as potential trading partners but is quite willing to allow them to develop their society and government as they see fit. A patriot is willing to leave other people alone as long as they return the favor and leave our nation alone. This is the original concept of American patriotism in which each person is the citizen not of the nation but of his state. The nation exists for one primary purpose—to protect the states from foreign people who refuse to leave us alone.

Nationalism, on the other hand, is very different, although in modern times it is often mislabeled as patriotism for political purposes. Nationalism looks to a strong, indivisible central government, capable of enforcing its will on people at the local level and enforcing the national will on foreign nations. Nationalists look outward from the nation to see other peoples and nations as possible resources to be exploited for the benefit of the nation's ruling elite. Patriots see government as a source of persecution and an enemy of individual liberty; conversely, nationalists see government as a source of power, perks, and privileges for the ruling elite and those closely allied to the nation's ruling elite.

When Uncle Seth and his fellow countrymen answered the call to arms to defend the South from Yankee invasion, they acted as a family of patriots working together to protect their families, their homes, and their communities—to defend those they loved from the invader's torch, the pillaging, raping, and murder that always follow nationalist armies as they seek to dominate a people who only ask to be left alone. Uncle Seth and his generation understood that New Englanders were seeking to do to the South what their English brethren had done to Scotland, Ireland, and Wales. The great Southern patriot Patrick Henry warned the people of the South in 1787 that the day would come when the commercial interest of the North would control the federal government and use the vast powers of that government to impoverish, enslave, and ultimately destroy the South. Patrick Henry warned them that liberty was more important than the union under the proposed constitution, but unfortunately too many Southerners put their trust in the false promises of the habitually deceptive merchants and bankers of New England.

In his many stories about the war, Uncle Seth uses the terms "Federal Empire" and "Yankee Empire" interchangeably. The reference to the United States of America as an empire as opposed to a republic may offend some modern Americans, but it must be understood that Uncle Seth was born and raised in an America in which the term "nation" was rarely used. He was born and raised in a constitutionally limited Republic of Republics—a form of government handed down to his generation from America's founding fathers that is based on the consent of the governed. This government, this Republic of Republics, died with the invasion of the South. Because of his frame of reference, Uncle Seth could see and understand the radical change that came about as a result of South's defeat and the Yankee-imposed Reconstruction that followed the war. The states in Lincoln's new Union are no longer sovereign; now the federal government is supreme; controlled by power-hungry politicians and their cronies, its rulings are final. The Federal Empire now decides whether or not the federal government is violating the limitations imposed on it by the Constitution—in other words, the federal government, its ruling elite, and those associates closely allied with the ruling elite are free to do as they like. "We the people" of the states no longer control the federal government; the federal government now controls the people. Uncle Seth witnessed the perversion of the original and legitimate American government. He saw how the people of the South, who were once citizens of their specific sovereign state, were violently compelled to accept their new status as subjects of the newly created Federal Empire. Nationalism was in the ascendancy and true American patriotism was dead.

About This Book

The Northern and Southern readers of this book will discover truths about themselves that may be very unpleasant. This book is like a mirror of the soul and the reader, when looking into it, will see unknown, unspoken, or unrealized parts of themselves. This book brings to light secret things that the ruling elite and those closely connected to the ruling elite hope to keep secret forever—indeed, their tenure in power requires that they keep such unpleasant matters secret. The misnamed "Civil War" is not shown as a glorious campaign to save the Union and free the slaves but instead as an aggressive effort of Lincoln, the Northern war governors, and their commercial or radical ideological supporters to create a supreme federal government. This new Federal Empire would then be used to expand and protect their commercial and financial empire—an empire that cost the deaths of more than six hundred thousand Americans to establish. It has also provided the ruling elite and their supporters with a worldwide commercial empire while allowing them to impose their worldview on lesser peoples. Rather than a war to free the slaves, it was a war to enslave the free people of the South, to deny them the right to live in a country founded on the consent of the governed, a war to deny "we the people" of the once sovereign states of Dixie the simple right to be left alone.

An apologist for the Federal Empire looking into this mirror will, with great disgust, send the mirror crashing to the floor. It is not easy to see the ugly, blood-stained spots on your soul, especially when you were raised to believe that you are so much better than those evil folk of the South. Yankee propagandists have worked diligently for more than two hundred years to create and maintain a false image of themselves. They view themselves as a people who are the chosen of God or destiny, specifically elected to build a "city on the hill" and appointed by destiny to send busybodies the world over to instruct lesser peoples of the evils of local cultures—cultures that stand at variance to the Yankee ideal. They then offer Yankee salvation by converting all the earth via word, bribe, threat, or sword to Yankee ideals; most importantly, as second-class Yankees we are to serve the commercial

17

and political interests of those who live in that "city on the hill." They are, and always have been, an arrogant, self-righteous, and self-centered people who hold in contempt those who refuse to accept Yankee ideas and rule.

Southerners who look into this mirror will see their souls bound head to foot by the chains of political, economic, social, and spiritual slavery. They will begin to understand that a people cannot survive and prosper if they continue to imbibe their conqueror's toxic philosophy. For Southerners who have been taught all of their lives that they belong to a cruel and evil people—a people who, being motivated by racial hatred, wanted to enslave an entire race—this mirror will provide an uncomfortable challenge. The knowledge that those antagonists made war against our Southern homeland, unapologetically attempted to *exterminate* the people of the South who refused to accept Yankee domination, and for political and economic purposes perverted the original, constitutionally limited Republic of Republics where individual liberty was protected from centralized tyranny by *real* States' Rights causes many uncomfortable questions to arise. Shall we continue to accept foreign domination? Shall we continue to go along to get along? Shall we continue to reject principles of liberty in exchange for the security of slavery? Or shall we, like our ancestors in 1776 and 1861, demand for ourselves and our descendants the right to live under a government ordered upon the free and unfettered consent of the governed, the right of self-determination, the right to have a government that "we the people" of the sovereign states control—in short the right to be left alone?

For some Southerners the answer will be easy and natural: resistance to tyranny is obedience to God. The current supreme federal government controls our society as completely as any cruel overlord ever controlled the sugar plantations for absentee landlords in the Caribbean. Resistance to such tyranny will be the obvious reaction to some. Others will find the challenge a bit unnerving, but these may yet gain the courage needed to stand for principle and resist tyranny. Some, though, will recoil as if from a venomous serpent. Every conquered nation has had its share of loyalists (saps, weaklings, Tories) who found it more convenient to serve the king rather than take the chance on freedom offered by the patriots; or scallywags who were willing to betray their own people in order to gain the perks, privileges, and power offered by the foreign rulers of their erstwhile free states; or Vichy men and Quislings (World War II Nazi collaborators in France and Norway) who gladly cooperated with their country's invaders rather than risk joining the resistance. It can be seen every day here in the South, where the Federal Empire's establishment will greatly reward any self-hating Southern educator (or news media agent, clergyman, or politician) who parrots the official "Civil War" party line. Southern educators or news media moguls will be rewarded by the establishment when they re-enforce the standard line that the "evil" South fought for slavery while the "virtuous" North fought to free their black brothers from the bondage of Southern slavery. But woe be unto those who dare to question the official party line! Their careers will be short at worst or, at best, be limited to some backwater area of the still-impoverished South. A Southerner who understands the truth of his country's history faces the choice of remaining silent and being rewarded by the establishment dedicated to the advancement of the Federal Empire or speaking up and receiving career-destroying punishment typically by being publicly ridiculed and held up as a racist or advocate of slavery. If Hitler had won, the Vichy men and Quislings would have enjoyed the benefits of their hero status but they would have been morally wrong nonetheless. Might does not make right—temporal success is not a proper criterion for morality and virtue.

There is yet another group who may read this book: foreigners, people who have only read the official United States-endorsed version of the American "Civil War." For these individuals, this book will not be a mirror but a philosopher's stone that will turn the base metal of Yankee lies into golden truth. Uncle Seth would often tell the story of a Southern soldier standing picket duty early one morning. This Confederate soldier knew he and his comrades were fighting a foe who had almost unlimited resources at his command. This Confederate soldier, however, felt that the people of the South would still win the struggle to maintain their independent Southern nation. His hopes were suddenly crushed when he heard rumblings in the Yankee army's camp and a loud voice shouting an officer's command: "Nations of the world, forward into the line of battle." For too long the South has faced the Federal Empire alone, without a single friend in the entire world of nations. Perhaps Uncle Seth's stories will eventually convince the people of the world to abandon their tacit support for the Yankee Empire and recognize the right of the South to be a free and independent nation.

About the Truth in Uncle Seth's Stories

Oral history has played a major part in the creation of human cultures the world over. It played an especially important role in the heritage of the Celtic peoples—a people who placed a high value on personal honesty but were never hesitant to improve a story, just a little, for the dramatic impact while leaving the essential truth untarnished. Uncle Seth may have taken poetic license in order to fill in unknown troop movements and such, but each of his stories and comments on the skirmish line or in rebuttal to anti-Southern spokesmen are drawn from the words of former Confederate soldiers, civilians, Southern scholars, or writers. Uncle Seth could have supported each story with footnotes, but footnotes are not a part of oral history. Uncle Seth knew that those who hate the South would not be dissuaded even if provided with thousands of footnotes and that those who love the South do not need footnotes—a man's word is his bound.

The characters in Uncle Seth's family are fictional; any similarity to actual individuals is purely coincidental.

§ Deo Vindice[1] §

ON THE SKIRMISH LINE WITH UNCLE SETH
"I have been reproached for not asking for a pardon, but pardon comes after repentance, and I have never repented. If it were to do over again, I would do exactly as I did before."

—Jefferson Davis, former president of the
Confederate States of America, March 10, 1884

---

1. *Deo Vindice:* "God Shall Vindicate," the Latin motto of the Confederate States of America.

1

Why Do the Yankees Hate Us?

Uncle Seth and Billie Jean were walking down the dusty lane toward the creek and their favorite fishing hole. They each had their cane fishing poles over their shoulders and Billie Jean had a tin can filed with crickets to bait their hooks. Uncle Seth loved to take the young children to the same fishing hole he enjoyed when he was a child. It also gave him time to visit with his great-grandchildren and share one of his many war stories

"You know, Billie Jean," the old Confederate veteran began, "during the war, when the Yankees would come through a community they would often not only burn homes but also destroy all the food in the area. They were trying to force starvation on the South as punishment for resisting the Yankee Empire. You recall what Yankee General Sheridan said about Southern women and children who dared to resist Yankee invasion: 'Leave them nothing but their eyes to cry with!' Not exactly the thing you would expect from a Christian, but I don't think those people were doing God's work—more likely Satan's work."

Billie Jean stopped for a moment, looked up at Uncle Seth, and innocently asked, "Uncle Seth, why do the Yankees hate us?"

Uncle Seth realized that this question demanded an answer he was not sure he was capable of providing, but he knew that Billie Jean would remember and one day tell her children. He wanted the answer to go on from one generation of his kin to the next. As the two reached the creek bank and settled down next to a large water oak tree, baited their hooks, and set their fishing poles into the creek, the old man decided to answer her question the only way he knew—by telling her a story about an incident he witnessed during the war. "Billie Jean, during the war a Yankee soldier shot a six-year-old girl playing in front of her house. I recall coming upon the terrible scene after the Yankees had left the town. When the girl's mother heard the gunshot she rushed out of her house, and to her horror she found her young daughter screaming in pain with blood gushing from her neck. The mother begged the Yankee soldiers to get a doctor before the girl died, but the Yankees refused to do anything to help the child. The reason they gave was that the young girl's father had refused to take the pledge of allegiance to the United States—the loyalty oath as it was then called. Her father was later arrested by the Yankees and forced to sign the oath of loyalty to the indivisible Union. Fortunately for the young girl, there was a Union officer from Kentucky present who took pity on her and called a doctor who saved her life. As this six-year-old was lying in a pool of her own blood she looked up at the Yankee officer and, with tears running down her young cheeks and mingling with her blood, she innocently asked, 'But what did I do wrong?'

"Billie Jean, this is the picture of the entire South under the heel of Yankee invasion and tyranny. What did we do wrong? All we asked was to be left alone. Shooting an innocent child is not a 'normal' thing to do; a 'normal' human being would naturally tend to want to protect an innocent child. You have to train or condition a human being in order for him to allow himself to do such evil. And the Yankee world had spent generations training their people to hate Southerners. Therefore, when they invaded the South they viewed us as less than human and deserving any ends that better men from the North determined to fix upon us.

"Billie Jean, you know that hate is bad but man by his very nature—according to the Holy Bible—is naturally prone to do evil. And left to his own devices, man will do great evil to his fellow man. That is why we need God and religious training; man needs Divine help to overcome his natural tendency to do evil. Thomas Jefferson and James Madison recognized this when they noted that men were not angels and that if we gave men the use of unlimited governmental power men would use the power of government to enrich themselves and oppress others. That is why they advocated the establishment of a constitutionally limited Republic of Republics that could be controlled by 'we the people' of the sovereign states via *real* States' Rights. Sen. John C. Calhoun wrote in his book *A Disquisition on Government* that man by his nature tended to be more self-centered or selfish in his dealing with others and, therefore, we must not give man access to the unlimited power of government because it would allow him to do unlimited evil to his fellow man. So you see, the people of the South viewed government as a potentially dangerous agent that had to be carefully controlled. But the people of the North had a vastly different view.

"Men of the North such as Alexander Hamilton viewed government as an active agent for the expansion of a large American commercial empire. Hamilton and his fellow travelers desired a 'vigorous' federal government that would be a partner in the development of a vast commercial and banking empire—an empire that would eventually be controlled by political and economic elites in Washington, DC, Wall Street, and some Northern states. It is not a mere coincidence that the first meeting of the United States Supreme Court under its first Chief Justice, John Jay, met in New York City on Wall Street and that John Jay wanted to use the power of the court to compel states to submit to federal rule. Nor is it surprising that Alexander Hamilton, who wanted to use the federal government to support Northern industry and commerce, had his law office on Wall Street. Remember what I told you about how the *New York Times* warned that if the North allowed the South to go in peace the North's prosperity would end and grass would grow on Wall Street without Southern tariffs. Remember what a Northern newspaper said, 'We were confused until our pockets were touched, no we must not let the South go.' You see, for those people, commercial, financial, and economic concerns are more important than things of the spirit such as principles of fairness, justice, honor, or civility. They will do whatever it takes to maintain and expand their commercial empire. For them, material wealth overrules spiritual values. For such people, doing evil is absolutely permissible if it furthers the pursuit of wealth and power. But before you can do evil to your neighbor, you must first brand your neighbor as someone so evil that he deserves no consideration due a normal human being. Once you dehumanize him, his people, and his society, it is not only acceptable to exterminate him but it would be evil not to do so.

"Lincoln's consul to Argentina before the war wrote a book in which he described 'the shame, poverty, ignorance, tyranny, and imbecility of the South.' He noted that the South 'is now weltering in the cesspool of ignorance and degradation' and was eager to describe Southerners to all who would listen as 'the stupid masses of the South.' The New England intellectual hero and transcendentalist Ralph Waldo Emerson said the average Southerner was a 'spoiled child, good for nothing, dumb, and unhappy, like an Indian in church' and only a little more civilized than the 'Seminole' Indians of the South. Another New England hero, Charles Sumner, described Southerners as being 'perverted, beastly, illiterate, bullies' and 'hirelings picked from the drunken spew and vomit of an uneasy civilization.' This type of Yankee anti-Southern insult, slander, and propaganda had been going on from the very beginning of the United States. By the time Lincoln's blue-clad invaders set foot on Southern soil, they had been primed to believe the worst about us and to do their best to exterminate us as a people—all in the name of Yankee materialistic virtue—glory, glory, hallelujah.

"Yankee General Sherman wrote, 'If need be, take every life, every acre of land, every particle of property, everything that to us seems proper; that we will not cease till the end is attained; that all who do not aid us are enemies, and that we will not account to them for our acts. If the people of the South oppose, they do so at their peril; and if they stand by, mere lookers-on in this domestic tragedy, they have no right to immunity, protection . . . make them so sick of war that generations would pass away before they would again appeal to it.' During the 1860 election, Lincoln and his Republican Party published articles describing the South as 'an inferior part of the country; that she was a spotted and degraded section.' And we should never think that these sentiments ended at Appomattox. At the closing of their war of Yankee conquest, a Yankee soldier, T. R. Kennan of the 17th Massachusetts Volunteers, wrote home, 'I am sorry the war is ended. Pray do not think me a murderer. No; but all the punishment we could inflict on the rebels would not atone for one drop of the blood spilled. I would exterminate them root and branch.' Recall that during Yankee-imposed Reconstruction Pennsylvania representative Thaddeus Stevens declared that they planned to turn Mississippi into a 'frog pond.' Recently a Harvard professor wrote that 'the Southerner had no mind; he had temperament. He was not a scholar; he had no intellectual training; he could not analyze an idea.' Such is the current view of a Northern intellectual about the South. The evil those people did and continue to do to us could not have occurred and would not continue to occur to this very day if it were not for the hate and slander they have heaped upon our people since the very beginning of these United States of America. And what was our crime? Our crime was that we asked to be allowed to go in peace and be left alone.

"Billie Jean, those people were taught to hate us. They could not have committed the raping, pillaging, murder, and lynching of innocent civilians; burning of homes; and the attempted extermination of an entire people had they not believed we were evil and ignorant folk bent upon destroying *their* Union. And from their point of view, we deserved to be invaded, punished, and impoverished because we stood in the way of their expanding commercial and political empire. Their values are not our values, but we are today compelled to support and pledge allegiance to an empire that wears the trappings of the old Republic while in reality bearing no actual resemblance to our once-free Republic of Republics.

"The sad truth is that as long as 'we the people' of the South accept our assigned position as second-class Yankees and are willing to pass on to each successive generation an inheritance of poverty and peonage to the Federal

Empire, the world will always know us as evil men who wanted to destroy the Union in order to keep our slaves. For the Yankee Empire to survive, it must continue to promote this myth. If our people are ever allowed to know the truth it would spell the beginning of the end of the current Federal Empire. The people of the South are being urged to forsake our traditional spiritual values in exchange for the crumbs that fall from the table of the wealthy Yankee Empire. We are invited to join those who sold their souls for filthy lucre's sake. Will our hungry and famished people accept a bowl of Yankee pottage in exchange for our birthright? I hope they will remember the warning that Jesus gave us when He asked, 'What doth it profit a man if he gains the whole world but loses his soul?' Will the South remember? It's up to your generation and those following yours to answer."

Uncle Seth reached down and hugged the young girl close to him. Was he hugging her or future generations yet to come—generations that one day would need courage even greater than he and his comrades demonstrated on so many battlefields in the War for Southern Independence if they are to ever be truly free?

§ Deo Vindice §

ON THE SKIRMISH LINE WITH UNCLE SETH

Sherman's war against women and children—an eyewitness: "I saw with my own eyes the destruction visited upon the innocent; their only crime was that they were Southerners. I am witness to the devastation made by the United States army under the command of General Sherman. I saw ladies with children in their arms driven out of their homes and everything they had destroyed. For miles and miles, I found nothing to eat, no hogs, no cattle, no sheep, not even a chicken. Some of our ladies were seen in abandoned Yankee camps where cavalry horses had been fed, picking up grains of corn that had dropped from the horses' mouths to appease their hunger." What honor could there be for the people of the South if we would so easily forget?

2

A Brave, Barefoot North Carolina Tar Heel

Uncle Seth was sitting on an old empty barrel watching the boys as they ran around the backyard barefoot and enjoying the warm Mississippi summer weather. The boys began a tussle; one boy trying to push the other backwards over an imaginary finish line. The loser was bitterly complaining that his opponent had cheated, but actually he had been outmatched. "Hush your complaining, boy. You were beat fair and square. Next time you need to let me put some tar on your heel to make you stick," Uncle Seth said trying to console the smaller boy.

"What do you mean by that, Uncle Seth?" the boys asked almost in unison.

"Well come over here and I will tell you all about being a good tar heel," Uncle Seth said as he beckoned the boys to sit next to him. "Some say they got that name back during the war when the Yankees made a determined attempt to break General Lee's line, which was held by a group of North Carolina soldiers. They held that line even though the Yankees outnumbered them four or five to one. After the battle, General Lee came over and commented that the North Carolina boys must have tar on their heels because they stuck to their positions so well. In Colonial times, North Carolina's pine trees provided pitch and pine tar to waterproof ships. It was General Lee's way of complementing the fighting spirit of the brave lads from the Old North State.

"Captain W. H. S. Burgwyn of the 35th North Carolina once told me about a sixteen-year-old barefoot North Carolina boy who earned a pair of spurs and the right to ride as a courier for his unit. It happened when Gen. Stonewall Jackson asked the colonel of a North Carolina unit to try a second assault on the Yankee artillery unit on their front. The colonel said he would try again and felt that he could take it, just like he had done on the last attempt, but he feared he would not be able to hold it because of the large numbers of Yankee infantry behind the artillery position. General Jackson was skeptical and asked if there was a man close by who could scale a tall oak tree next to where they were standing. Immediately a young boy of sixteen volunteered to scale the tree. That boy was Pvt. William S. Hood of Company H, 35th North Carolina Infantry. Hood had his shoes off in a jiffy, and before General Jackson could turn around Hood was up to the top of the tree. Now the Yankees could see the young lad going up the tree and they knew what his intentions were. They sat their sharpshooters to work trying to bring young Hood down. But thankfully for Hood the Yankee sharpshooters were more shooters than they were sharp.

"General Jackson shouted up to Hood, asking the boy to tell him what he saw. Hood replied that he saw Yankees, a whole ocean of Yankees! Well, this was not quite specific enough to be useful. General Jackson instructed Hood to count the flags. Knowing the number of flags would tell Jackson the approximate strength of the enemy behind the artillery position. Hood began counting—one, two, three—and continued until he had counted thirty-nine, at which time General Jackson announced that Hood could stop. The general agreed with the colonel that it would not be feasible to hold the artillery position.

"Sometime later that day, after the firing had ceased, the colonel asked for a volunteer to go on a one-man scouting mission to find out what the Yankees were up to. Once again Hood jumped up and volunteered to go. You boys know why I said that Hood jumped up? It is because we learned early on that you never run if you can walk, you never walk if you can stand, you never stand if you can sit, and you never sit if you can lie down. Hood got up, volunteered, and struck out at a 'turkey trot,' holding his rifle at trail arms. Trail arms, you know, is when you grasp your rifle in the middle, balanced with half of the weight of the rifle forward and half behind your path of travel, and hold it down beside your leg, relaxed, arm fully extended, and at knee level. It was one of General Jackson's favorite marching commands for 'Jackson's foot cavalry.' You could see General Jackson watching the boy and could tell that the general was proud to have such a fine young man under his command.

"It was several hours before Hood returned; the general and his fellow soldiers were afraid that something had happened to him. But he did make it back safely to our position and gave the officers a full and accurate report of the enemy's strength, position, and movements. Hood explained that he took so long because he heard the cries of a wounded Yankee begging for water. He found the man, who happened to be an officer, and gave him water from his wooden canteen. The officer offered to give Hood his gold watch and all the money in his pockets if Hood would take him to Federal lines. Hood told him he could not do that but left his wooden Confederate canteen with the Yankee officer. However, the thought of leaving a wounded man to die alone on the battlefield was more than

Hood could bear. He eased his way up close to the Yankee picket line and began a private soldier's truce negotiation—something most officers on both sides frowned upon. Somehow Hood managed to convince two of the pickets to leave their post and accompany him back to the wounded Yankee officer. He then helped the Yankees carry their wounded officer back to the Yankee line. By all rights the Yankees could have made Hood a prisoner, but instead they rewarded his act of kindness with food and coffee and then released him. The boy seemed to have a charmed life.

"When Hood returned he took off his shoes. His feet were sore and covered with blisters. You see a lot of us did not have shoes and many times when we did have shoes we didn't have socks. This resulted in a lot of blisters and, eventually, infected feet. We were constantly out of the basic necessities, and it was not uncommon to find a barefoot Southern soldier walking around a battlefield looking for a dead Yankee about his size who no longer had need for shoes, socks, or other accoutrements.

"Shortly after Hood returned from his scouting mission, one of the officers who witnessed Hood's feats of heroism sent word for him to report to the officer. The officer gave Hood a horse, a pair of spurs, and made him his courier. The next time the boys of the 35th North Carolina saw Hood, he was galloping past them riding an officer's horse, carrying a dispatch to the front. He waved his kepi in the air and hollered greetings to his old unit, but the unit could not reply because they were all laughing at the site of Hood's bare feet in the stirrups with riding spurs tied securely on both heels.

"Hood rejoined the 35th in time to participate in the assault on Fort Steadman on March 25 of 1865—a mere fifteen days before General Lee was compelled to surrender at Appomattox Court House on April 9. Hood died in that assault. He was only one of the many brave North Carolina tar heels."

Uncle Seth looked around to see if the boys were still listening to his story. He looked down at the barefoot boys around him and thought back to the days when he, too, would run around these same hills and hollows barefoot as the day he was born and happy as a lark. The old Confederate veteran knew that it would be different with these young Southerners. They were destined to grow up in a South impoverished by war, Reconstruction, and a national government that viewed the South as a useless backwater. Somehow he felt guilty for the loss of their birthright. He and his generation had been given an economically strong South, a South that was slowly beginning to solve the question of slavery. But alas, all of that was now gone. He could only wonder if there would ever be a day in which Southerners would realize their loss and take the necessary actions to reclaim liberty.

(Courtesy Betty Kennedy)

§ Deo Vindice §

ON THE SKIRMISH LINE WITH UNCLE SETH

A son's description of his Confederate father: "My father was wrapped heart and soul in the South. Out of six brothers who rode to the war, one died at Shiloh, two died at Vicksburg, one died at Rock Island, one was shot at Gettysburg. The youngest, my father, came out of the struggle with an arm gone—not a bad argument for one family to put up in support of their convictions. Father was just simply a Southern soldier fighting for a principle. That's what he asked to be carved on his gravestone."

3

Colonel Mosby—the Gray Ghost of the Confederacy

"Uncle Seth," shouted Curtis, "one of the older boys at school said that there was never any such Confederate general called the Gray Ghost. But I told him he was crazy because the Gray Ghost was Col. John Singleton Mosby."

"Well," Uncle Seth began slowly, not wanting to dampen the young boy's enthusiasm, "you know, I don't ever recall hearing anyone refer to Colonel Mosby as the Gray Ghost during the war. I think that may have been thought up by someone after the war. Perhaps they were trying to link Mosby to his idol—the Revolutionary War hero Francis Marion, who was referred to as the Swamp Fox. You know, Mosby was one of our most successful partisan raiders during the war.

"I recall being told by C. C. Hart from Elkins, West Virginia, about one of his unit's action near Winchester, Virginia. Mosby had sent Colonel Lang with around one hundred men and one piece of artillery to guard Berry's Ferry. It was rumored that the Yankees would attempt to cross there and attack our troops. By the time Colonel Lang arrived, he found the Yankees had already made it there and crossed the river. Well, Colonel Lang knew what to do: without even the slightest hesitation he ordered his troops to charge the Yankees. And with a shout of the Rebel Yell coming from one hundred determined Confederates, the charge was on! They drove the Yankees back across the river. By then our artillery boys had enough time to set up their cannon and open on the Yankees who had, by now, reached the other side of the river. The intense and accurate fire from that one piece of artillery forced the Yankees back up the mountain on the other side of the river and out of range of our cannon.

"Once the Yankees got to the safety of the mountain, they set up their cannons and began firing at us with six pieces of artillery. That went on for some time. Their six against our one—Yankee odds! Colonel Lang's cannon was running out of ammunition and began to slow down their reply to the Yankees. The Southern cavalry moved behind some chestnut trees at the edge of the mountain out of sight of the Yankees who must have thought our men had pulled back from the fight. The Yankees sent a regiment of cavalry over the river to attack and take our cannon and any Confederate cavalryman left behind. Our artillerymen had anticipated their move and had set grapeshot and canister shot out ready for quick loading should the Yankees venture an attack. The boys in gray waited until the Yankees were within forty yards of the cannon and then our boys let loose a round of canister shot directly into the their cavalry. The artillery boys fired at least three or four rounds in rapid order. It was sheer carnage—dead and wounded Yankees mixed in with dead or wounded horses. The Yankees' bravado instantly changed to panic as they broke rank, turned, and fled back toward the river, each man determined to put the other between himself and the Confederates. By that time, our men came out from behind the chestnut trees about one hundred strong and began to attack the fleeing invaders—pushing them from the rear to encourage their panic. Colonel Lang's skirmishers had made it to the ford before the Yankees returned and began shooting the oncoming Yankees, who must have thought we had gotten behind them—more panic. As the Yankees rushed past our skirmishers, our boys did not have time to reload and began clubbing the Yankees as they passed. Several of the boys climbed up the side of the ridge and began throwing sandstones at the fleeing Yankees. Only about twenty-five Yankees escaped with their lives, though they were wounded by cannon or rifle fire or clubbed or stoned by our boys.

"Unbeknown to the Yankees, Colonel Mosby was on the way with his unit of men and had directed reenforcements be sent from General McCausland with six pieces of artillery. The Yankees were no doubt greatly embarrassed by the way we had treated their superior numbers—not to mention their self-assumed superior intellect. They were determined to show our boys what happens to people who dare to resist the loving embrace of the Yankee Empire. They came back in full force and crossed the river. As they were crossing the river and just before our boys were about to open up with our artillery batteries, they heard a loud Rebel Yell and saw Colonel Mosby as he led his unit in a daring charge into the middle of the invading force. They ran the Yankees back up the mountain beyond their original position and spiked all of their cannons and returned to our side of the river in safety. As the Yankees turned back to see what had become of their artillery units, our cannon opened fire on them.

"Yes, Curtis, Mosby was one of our best Partisan Raiders. You know that Lt. Gen. Ulysses S. Grant issued an edict in 1864 that any of Mosby's men captured would not be treated as prisoners of war but immediately hung. Yankee honor, boys! As a matter of fact, old Yellow Hair of Little Big

Horn fame—you know, Brig. Gen. George A. Custer—even hung seven of our boys. Mosby immediately hung a few Yankees and the Yankees decided that maybe it was not a good idea to hang prisoners of war. But they did it all over the South nonetheless.

"You know, one time Colonel Mosby conducted a daring raid far behind the Yankee lines at the Fairfax County courthouse in 1863. His aim was to capture the Yankee officers in charge of the occupied area, including the head Yankee for the area, General Stoughton. Late one night Mosby slipped into Stoughton's bedroom, where he found the Yankee peacefully snoring away. Colonel Mosby awoke Stoughton with a slap to the Yankee's backside. Upon being so rudely aroused, the general exclaimed, 'Do you know who I am?' Mosby loudly questioned the Yankee, 'Do you know Mosby, general?' 'Yes!' Stoughton exclaimed. 'Have you got the rascal?' 'No, but he has got you!' And the Yankee general became a prisoner of his nemesis, Colonel Mosby." Uncle Seth ended his story with a self-satisfied chuckle.

§ Deo Vindice §

ON THE SKIRMISH LINE WITH UNCLE SETH

"Can any historical fact be more demonstrable than that the States did, in the [Articles of] Confederation and in the Union [under the Constitution], retain their sovereignty and independence as distinct communities, voluntarily consenting to federation, but never becoming fractional parts of a nation? He must be a careless reader of our political history who has not observed that, whether under the style of the 'United Colonies' or 'United States,' which was adopted after the Declaration of Independence, whether under the Articles of Confederation or the compact of Union, there everywhere appears the distinct assertion of State sovereignty, and nowhere the slightest suggestion of any purpose on the part of the States to consolidate themselves into one body."

—Pres. Jefferson Davis

4

Outnumbered Rebels Rout Yankees— 1865 and Still Fighting

Uncle Seth was keeping himself busy feeding the chickens out by the corncrib. The boys were having a great time engaging in corncob warfare—throwing cobs at each other. Barry came over to Uncle Seth and asked him to join with him in the battle against Curtis and Joe William. It seemed that the older boys had teamed up on the younger boy.

"Well, I don't think a corncob soldier in his late seventies would do you much good, Barry," the old Confederate veteran replied. "But you know you can win a battle even if you are outnumbered. We did it a lot during the war. Sit down and let me tell you about a time when I was attached to the 51st Alabama Partisan Rangers and we won against a much larger and better-equipped Yankee army."

Barry settled down next to Uncle Seth as the other two boys came around the side of the barn, corncobs at the ready. Uncle Seth informed them that he had declared a temporary truce. Now that Uncle Seth had a proper audience, he began his story.

"It was March of 1865, only a few months before General Lee was compelled to surrender. We were all but exhausted from four years of hard fighting, but we refused to yield to Yankee-imposed rule of our country. We were part of General Wheeler's army that was attempting to hold in check Yankee General Sherman's much larger and well-equipped army of Yankee invaders. General Wheeler had around 4,700 hungry and exhausted men left in his army. General Sherman, on the other hand, must have had close to 100,000 well-feed, well-equipped, and well-rested Yankee soldiers, cavalry, and artillery units at his command. He could instantly deploy against us at any point along our thin defensive line. Sherman had so many men on the line of battle in front of us that we had to stretch too thin in order to meet him.

"At about 2 pm, the 17th Federal Army Corps charged us at our weakest point, which could have been anywhere along our line! We had dismounted in order to give our worn-out horses a rest. We had no breast works or anything to provide protection. All of a sudden we looked up to see at least 20,000 blue-clad invaders with bayonets gleaming in the sun rushing toward us! The 8th Texas had been posted on our left and were mounted. When the 8th Texas's colonel saw the situation developing, he wisely withdrew to a more defensible location farther to our left and hid his unit in a pine thicket. When the head of the Yankee column was within firing distance of our dismounted unit, we began firing and sent every fourth man back to bring forward our horses. We were all mounted before the Yankees reached us. The 8th Texas let loose with a Rebel Yell just about the time we mounted our horses and made a vicious flanking attack against the Yankee column. We then made our frontal charge firing our guns and raising our own Rebel Yell.

"Now, the Yankees outnumbered us at least five to one, but that did not matter. The 8th Texas's spirited flanking attack combined with our frontal charge broke their cohesion and they began to fall back. We pursued them for more than a mile, and as we continued to press them their retreat turned into a Yankee rout similar to the one at the beginning of the war at the Battle of First Manassas—sort of ironic that the Yankee invasion of our young Southern nation started with a Yankee rout and even at this late point, when they were so close to exhausting the South, the Yankees still knew how to turn and run from the fury of Dixie's soldiers.

"We killed and wounded a large number of them before we were recalled. In the entire engagement, we did not lose a single man or horse. That shows you what audacity can accomplish—the odds against you are not always the most important factor in battle. While the odds may influence, they do not determine the outcome. The South's army and navy did more with less against a much larger force than any army and navy in history. Yep, boys, we just wore ourselves out whipping Yankees!

"Oh yes, I must tell you about an interesting incident that occurred as we were returning to our lines after the fight. The ground over which the Yankees had charged was boggy with so many small pools of stagnant water that we had to ride around carefully seeking dry ground on our return. Of course, when we charged the Yankees we just rode through them without slowing down. And when the Yankees first charged toward our weakened line of battle, they just waded through them and of course they decided to run back through them seeking the safety of even more superior numbers of their fellow blue-clad invaders with frenzied yelling and firing Rebels in hot pursuit.

"As we carefully picked our way through the boggy area we noticed a wounded Yankee lieutenant leaning against a tree. He appeared to be badly hurt. We checked our horses and turned back and approached the wounded man. The water in the pool next to the tree on which he was leaning was red with his blood. We offered to put him on one of our horses and take him to our surgeon. His answer demonstrated the degree of hatred that so many in the North had for Southerners before, during, and long after the war, even now. The wounded Yankee declared, 'You go to hell, you damn Rebel. I'd rather die and go to hell than have your polluted hands touch me.' My comrades immediately attempted to reason with the Yankee by assuring him that he would be taken care of and most likely would survive. We even told him that short of a miracle, the war would soon be over and he could go home a conquering hero. But to no avail— he refused to accept help from filthy, evil, slave-owning Southerners. One of our boys asked if we should inform the poor man that none of us ever owned nor desired to own slaves. My un-Christian response was that we were wasting our time trying to rationally reason with a Yankee and that we should leave the man in peace and hope he soon entered the infernal regions below." Uncle Seth concluded his story and tossed a red corn cob out toward the stomp lot. The boys looked up at the old soldier. His story left them a little confused. They could not tell if he was ashamed or proud of what he said about the poor dying Yankee.

§ Deo Vindice §

ON THE SKIRMISH LINE WITH UNCLE SETH
"When the Constitution was adopted by the votes of States at Philadelphia [Constitutional Convention 1787], and accepted by the votes of States in popular conventions, it is safe to say that there was not a man in the country, from Washington and Hamilton, on the one side, to George Clinton and George Mason, on the other, who regarded the new system [the Federal government] as anything but an experiment entered upon by the States, and from which each and every State had the right peaceably to withdraw, a right which was very likely to be exercised."
—Sen. Henry Cabot Lodge Sr., Massachusetts

Yet in 1861 Massachusetts and the rest of the North discarded constitutional principles of limited federalism and *real* States' Rights in order to maintain their hold on the riches they were exploiting from the South. Empires always find convenient excuses to invade and conquer people holding riches coveted by the empire's ruling elite.

5

Young Girl Makes a Paul Revere Ride to Call Out the Militia

"Uncle Seth," called out Billie Jean, "look at me riding the mare—I'm part of General Forrest's cavalry."

"Yes, but you be careful, you are a green recruit and haven't completed your training yet," warned the old Confederate veteran. "You are doing real good here in the corral. How would you like to ride fifty-six miles on horseback with Yankee cavalry hot on your trail?"

Billie Jean pulled on the reins and jumped down from the saddle. "I don't think I could go that far—I don't think anyone could," she said, knowing that Uncle Seth would soon tell her about someone who did.

Uncle Seth eased himself down on the side of the haystack and arranged himself as if he would take a nap. Looking up into the clear blue sky he began, "I read an article that was reprinted from the *Roanoke Times* about a young girl of twenty, just a few years older than you, Billie Jean. Well, she had to make a ride similar to Paul Revere's ride, except instead of telling the folks the British are coming she had to tell them the Yankees were coming.

"Yankee Colonel John T. Toland of the 34th Ohio Mounted Infantry was in the area around Wytheville, Virginia, doing the usual Yankee thing of making war upon the innocent civilian population, robbing and burning both public and private property. They had spent most of the days before July 18, 1863, destroying as much of the Virginia and Tennessee Railroad track and trestles as they could. On the 18th it was learned that the Yankees would move toward the town of Wytheville with the purpose of looting and burning the place—of course they called it a military operation. On the way to Wytheville, Toland's unit marched through Tazewell County and made camp on the farm belonging to Confederate Captain W. E. Peery, who, of course, was not home but doing service with the Confederate army. Toland threw out pickets to protect his encampment from Confederate partisan rangers. One of the picket stations was close to Rocky Dell, the home of our heroine, twenty-year-old Mary Tynes.

"When the Tyneses heard that the Yankees were close by, they gave all of their valuables to Jim, a loyal servant, and told him to 'head to the hills and don't come back until you know the Yankees are gone.' They told Jim that if the Yankees burned their home they would come into the hills and find him. The only other people in the house were Jim's elderly wife, Mary's aged mother, and Mary's crippled father. All the other young, able-bodied men folk, two brothers, were on active duty with the Confederate army.

"Word had reached them that Toland planned to move the forty-four miles to Wytheville. The Tyneses knew that, just like the Yankees had done in other places, they would be burning and looting all along their path of invasion. The Yankee invaders had cut all communication in that direction and therefore no one between the Tynes' home and Wytheville—some forty-four miles—knew that danger was approaching. Mary volunteered to ride to Wytheville. She planned to give warning of the approaching Yankees to anyone she saw along the way. She knew that if she were caught, the Yankees would execute her as a spy. She also knew the dangers facing a young woman riding alone through open roads. But she was determined to get the warning to her people and she knew her horse would not let her down. She rode a small mare almost like the one you were riding, Billie Jean." The old man looked down at his great-granddaughter just to make sure she was still listening to his story.

Satisfied that he still had her attention he began anew. "Early the next morning, before first light, Mary saddled her mare and began her Paul Revere ride to warn her people—fellow Southerners she did not personally know, but to whom she felt a strong bond of kinship. She rode through Burk's Garden, over and through what seemed to be endless mountain passes and steep inclines of the mountain road; down into the forest wilderness so thick that the morning sun could not break through; through Sharon Springs; and on to Wytheville. All along the route she would shout out the warning about the approaching Yankee invaders. When at last she reached Wytheville—she had traveled forty-four miles—the folks there were not willing to believe this young girl. No one there even knew her! In desperation she rode another twelve miles—six miles south of Wytheville to her mother's cousin's home plus another six miles back to Wytheville. She returned with her cousin, who vouched for Mary's honesty and credibility. By now the exhausted Mary had ridden fifty-six miles.

"Now it was time for the people of Wytheville to act. The call went out for the militia to form up in the town square. With most of the men at war the militia consisted of old gray beards and young boys between twelve and sixteen years old. Working with great haste, they fortified the town. When the invading Yankees arrived they found a fortified town protected by Confederate Major Thomas M. Bowyer and the local militia armed with their own private weapons. Colonel Toland ordered a full attack on the town, and in the process he was killed along with several of his troops. His one–eyed comrade Major Powell was taken prisoner along with some of his troops.

"So you see, Billie Jean, even young girls and teenage boys were an important part in our effort to turn back the Yankee invaders. Because of Mary's Paul Revere ride that day, the town was spared the invader's torch and the railroad trestle and miles of valuable railroad track were saved. And don't forget, the Virginia militia, composed of old men and young boys with their hunting rifles in hand, were instrumental in delivering Colonel Toland his just reward, at least on this earth. The devil is taking care of him now! I know that sounds harsh, but if they had simply stayed at their own homes and left us alone none of the horrors of war would have been vested upon us all. You have to remember, Billie Jean, empires cannot leave people alone."

§ Deo Vindice §

ON THE SKIRMISH LINE WITH UNCLE SETH
While occupying Williamstown, North Carolina, the United States cavalry used several of the fine homes as horse stables. On Sunday morning, as they were leaving, the Yankees set the town on fire. No attempt was made by Yankee officers to prevent such outrages. On the contrary, they endorsed and encouraged it—it was part of their plan and some private Yankee soldiers bragged that they were ordered to set the town on fire. This was Yankee punishment for Southerners who merely asked to be free. Yet the great strategic failure of the post-war South was its failure to maintain the struggle for the *principle* of Southern Independence. It then appeared to the world that once slavery was abolished the South was no longer interested in independence. This allowed Yankee propagandists to establish a false narrative—that the South fought for slavery and not independence. And our political leaders, who are more interested in their careers than our freedom, have never challenged this false Yankee narrative!

6

Uncle Seth's Reply to Self-Hating, Yankee-Educated Southerners

"Yes, the South loved the Union their Colonial forefathers had fought to create," the Yankee schoolteacher argued, "but the Confederates sought to withdraw from the very Union those patriots' blood had created. The South tried to destroy the Union."

Uncle Seth replied, "The Union or Federal government you speak of has none of the sacredness of patriots' blood attached to it. The original Union was a confederation, first under the Articles of Confederation and then under the Constitution. It was formed by the states for the common benefit of each individual state. No patriot in 1776 fought to create this new Federal government or Union. No blood of 1776 was shed in its creation. The original Federal government or Union was formed the way a contract would be used to create a business corporation—an agreement among equals.

"Our fathers, in 1776, took up arms against Great Britain, not to establish the American Union but to establish the independence of each individual state. This they won. And they bequeathed liberty to their children in each state, not to an aggregate group of Americans. Southerners were fighting to maintain the independence handed down to them by their forefathers, while the armies of the United States invaded the Confederate States in order to deprive us of that independence. The Southern soldier was fighting to preserve what his Colonial forefathers had fought to establish."

§ Deo Vindice §

ON THE SKIRMISH LINE WITH UNCLE SETH
"Why not let the South go? O that the South would go! But then they must leave us their lands."
> —Henry Ward Beecher, Yankee Radical Abolitionist
> speaking at Exeter Hall, London, England, 1863

7

Confederate Humanity—Testimony of a United States POW

Uncle Seth stood at the front of the classroom. As he looked across the room he could see the faces of the students. He knew each one; each one had a grandfather or other close relative who had worn the gray in the War for Southern Independence; each one had the blood of Southern heroes flowing through his veins; each one had a relative who had sacrificed his life defending the South against Yankee invasion; and even though these young people did not know it, through Yankee invasion and conquest they had lost more than blood relatives.

The school's history teacher had asked him to come by and give the South's reply to the charges made in the school's New York-published textbook. The "Yankee textbook," as Uncle Seth called it, made numerous erroneous claims against the South. For instance, it stated that the South intentionally mistreated United States prisoners of war during the war. And to add insult to injury, it insisted on incorrectly calling the War for Southern Independence the Civil War. This was a term that Uncle Seth avoided like the plague. The schoolteacher was a nice-enough lady, but she was one who had been thoroughly indoctrinated in the Yankee version of history—a version that served as an excuse for Yankee invasion, conquest, and occupation of the South. She knew that Uncle Seth was her most-outspoken critic, but she consoled herself with the knowledge that she was teaching progressive ideas to a new generation of Southerners, ideas that she knew would one day eclipse the outdated views of the few remaining Confederate veterans. She thought, or perhaps hoped, that men like Uncle Seth would soon pass from this world, taking with them all of their outmoded and socially embarrassing ideas. But since he was one of the last Confederate veterans, it seemed only polite to allow him to say a few words to the children, especially since they, most likely under the influence of Uncle Seth's stories, had challenged so many of the textbook's anti-Southern accusations. After all, she wanted to at least appear to be fair to the old man. So, with the spirit of condescending politeness, she had allowed him five to ten minutes before lunch to speak to the class.

The students were quiet and respectful. They all knew and loved the old man, and he returned their love. He had put on his United Confederate Veteran's uniform for the occasion. Many of the students thought it was his war uniform, but Uncle Seth corrected this misconception. "No," he explained, "when I came home from the war my uniform consisted of a torn and tattered battle shirt, a slouch hat, a pair of cotton pants with both legs torn and repeatedly stitched, and no shoes. But I tell you this: my gun was still in perfect working condition when I turned it over to the Yankee invaders at the surrender." The students could tell by the defiance in his voice that there was still fight left in the old Confederate veteran and that if given a choice he most likely would love the chance to pick up that old Enfield rifle and give the Yanks another "what for." They had often heard the old man resolutely declare, "General Lee surrendered; the government of the Confederate States of America did *not* surrender; and, by God, neither did I!" This would usually produce an almost nervous outburst of laughter because somehow all who heard it knew that to Uncle Seth it was not a joking matter. Somewhere deep down inside, they all repressed the painful thought that the old man was right! It was too painful to admit such a thing. What good is it to admit something so true but so impossible to publically express: a love of their Southern homeland that had no means of expression? To do so would bring down the wrath of the Yankee establishment—even the possible re-establishment of Reconstruction. No, it was better to repress such feelings and not bring such painful thoughts to conscious acknowledgment. Why acknowledge them publically and then not have a way to deal with the political, social, and economic reality of Yankee invasion and occupation? Though they did not know it, Southerners were learning to be good subjects of their Yankee masters. Uncle Seth knew it, though, and was determined to equip the rising generation around his feet with the truth needed to overcome the reality of Yankee lies.

"Well, your teacher has asked me to tell you about the treatment of United States POWs, as prisoners of war are called today. Now, I know that your Yankee textbook claims that we Southerners treated our prisoners with malicious cruelty. And I know you expect me to come here and say that it's not true. But me doing that would not accomplish much. After all, you all know that is what I would say, don't you?" Uncle Seth asked almost rhetorically. The class all smiled in agreement, although the teacher had a rather perplexed look on her face; she was wondering where the old man was going with his explanation. "Better that I let Yankee soldiers who were held captive by us tell you about how we treated them," explained

Uncle Seth as he slowly began to outflank both the Yankee textbook and the youngsters' "progressive" teacher.

"I have here a copy of a letter," he said as he slowly pulled a crumpled paper from his vest pocket. "It is dated February 23, 1862, and is from Columbia, South Carolina. During that time, a group of United States POWs were held there. The document is addressed to Capt. William Shiver, Confederate States Army, and others of the 'Rebel Guards.' It begins:

> Gentlemen: The officers of the United States Army, now held as prisoners of war in Columbia, South Carolina, being about to return to their homes after their captivity of several months, deem it appropriate and due to you to express their grateful feelings for the uniform kindness and consideration with which they and all the prisoners of war have been treated while in Columbia, South Carolina.
>
> It gives the undersigned committee, appointed unanimously on behalf of the officers, the greatest pleasure to bear testimony to the care you have exercised to deprive our imprisonment of as many as possible of its unpleasant parts, and in all respects to render our situation as comfortable as was in your power, and we feel that whatever enjoyment we have received while under your charge has been wholly owing to yourselves. During our incarceration as many privileges as were consistent with our safekeeping have been allowed us by you and those who constituted our guard. Whilst occupying the peculiar relations towards you that we have during the past two months, you have exhibited the traits of true soldiers in being just and considerate to those placed in your power; and the recollections of all the manliness and courtesy shown us by you and the Rebel Guards will constitute pleasant moments in our future lives. We earnestly hope that we may meet again under more favorable auspices, when our intercourse may be free and unrestrained and when we can associate together in all relations of life as men and brothers.

Attached are the signatures of the officers from various Northern states," announced Uncle Seth as he held the document up for the entire class to see and remember.

"As most of you know," he continued, feeling an emerging moral victory, "when the United States government put Confederate Captain Wriz on trial alleging numerous murders of Yankees at the Andersonville POW camp that he commanded, the Yankees could not find one man who would testify to actually witnessing these alleged murders. After the trial and execution of Captain Wriz, the United States government's key witness confessed to having been paid by U.S. agents for his testimony!

But of course your Yankee textbook doesn't tell y'all about that little bit of history or that Captain Wriz's Yankee-appointed defense counsel quit the case because of how unfairly the Yankee judges were treating them and their Confederate client. And by the way—do y'all know how the United States army repaid the people of Columbia, South Carolina, for their humane treatment of the Yankee POWs? On February 17, 1865, United States general Sherman's troops entered Columbia. The city was defenseless because all Confederate combatants had evacuated the city. By the end of that terrible day, the invading Yankees had burned to the ground all property, both public and civilian, in that defenseless city. Defenseless women and children and sick and wounded men and women were left with nothing

Maj. Henry Wirz, Swiss-born Confederate hung by the US, which used purchased testimony to obtain a verdict (Library of Congress)

but the clothes on their backs and the ashes of their ruined city. Their only crime was that they were Southerners!

"Young folks," continued Uncle Seth in a quiet voice, yet still full of passion for his people, "you all have the blood of Confederate veterans—Southern patriots—flowing in your veins. You must always remember that we are a conquered nation and our conquerors write the history you are taught. They write it in order to justify the innumerable crimes they committed against our people. Remember the victor always writes the history—he writes it to cover his crimes—and he enforces it, if need be, at the point of a bloody bayonet! I want y'all to remember that it is Southern blood on the tips of those Yankee bayonets."

A hush fell on the classroom as Uncle Seth left the room. The teacher did not know exactly what to do. The ringing of the dinner bell saved her from the utter embarrassment of the moment. As she dismissed her class she made a mental note to never make such a mistake again.

Uncle Seth understood the value of this "living history" and was determined to use it to resist the slanderous lies the victorious Federal Empire continues to spew forth to justify its naked aggression against "we the people" of the once-sovereign states of Dixie.

§ Deo Vindice §

On the Skirmish Line with Uncle Seth
What the civilian population of the South endured in the Yankee sacking,

robbing, and pillaging of towns, homes and churches, finds no parallel in history of civilized peoples. The *New York Tribune* celebrated the punishments inflicted upon the people of Fredericksburg, Virginia, by noting that beautiful mansions were freely entered into by Federal troops seeking plunder regardless of whether these homes were empty or occupied by the owner or his family. Every room was searched, torn apart, and riddled with gun shots; all the elegant furniture and works of art broken and smashed by United States soldiers; fine mirrors were removed and thrown out of windows.

The records of the Spanish and Moorish struggles, the Wars of the Roses, and the Thirty Years' War in Germany may be safely challenged for comparisons with the acts of barbarity of the Yankees. Soldiers of the United States army did not commit these acts of barbarism while under the intoxications of wild combat but in cold and cowardly blood. Their acts were directed not at an armed adversary but at non-combatant civilians composed of old men, women, children, and babies whose only crime was that they were Southerners who asked to be left alone to live in a country of their own—one that would no longer be dominated by Yankees.

8

Lincoln Saved the Union but
Destroyed the Constitution

Uncle Seth was slowly walking down the rows of dried corn stalks. It was early August and time to begin pulling corn from the dried stalks, putting them in heap rows, gathering the dried ears of corn on to the ground slide, and taking the harvest to the corn crib. Some of the dry corn leaves would be gathered to use a fodder for the cows and mules in the upcoming winter. "For everything there is a season," the old Confederate veteran mused to himself as he walked down the rows of corn stalks, rustling the dried leaves as he moved past each stalk.

"Uncle Seth, these rows of corn look like butternut-clad Confederate soldiers," observed Joe William, who had been silently walking beside the old man.

"Yep," replied Uncle Seth, "by late war just about all of us Southern boys were wearing ragged homemade butternut uniforms. But that did not stop us from resisting with all our might Lincoln's well-feed and well-equipped blue-coated legions."

"My teacher says that it was a good thing that the South lost the war because otherwise Lincoln would not have been able to save the Union." Joe William's response was apologetic in tone, as if deep down inside he knew what he had been taught was not correct.

"Well," began Uncle Seth, "Lincoln did manage to save the Union, if by Union you mean the geographical territory in which the North could enforce its will through political and military might. But remember what Patrick Henry of Virginia said back in 1787 when the states were debating the proposed Constitution: 'The first thing I have at heart is American liberty, the second thing is American Union.' You see, liberty always trumps government. Lincoln and his henchmen were intent on saving their lucrative system of government—a government that leached taxes from the people of the South for the benefit of the Northern power elites and their friends. A president is sworn into office by an oath to protect the Constitution, not the Union. The constitutional Republic of Republics devised by the founding fathers was destroyed by Lincoln, and

45

it was replaced by a supreme federal government controlled by powerful men in Washington, DC and the financial houses of New York.

"One of my Confederate comrades, Berkeley Minor of Charlottesville, Virginia, wrote a letter to a Northern friend in which he tried to explain what Lincoln and his henchmen did to our once-free Republic of Republics. He told his Yankee friend that it is true that the world now claims Lincoln made the United States of America a government of the people, by the people, and for the people. But this was not the United States of America that the founding fathers created. Their creation was formed by the free and voluntary consent of the people of sovereign states. Lincoln's creation was one of force, compulsion, military conquest, and the destruction of Southerners' right to live under a government based upon the consent of the governed.

"Lincoln inherited a republic of sovereign states, which he immediately set out to destroy. He changed that republic by force and against the will of the people of Dixie. Up to 1861, the federal government was a republic of sovereign states of such wisdom and power as to win the respect and love of all true lovers of political liberty. That federal government was wise enough not to coerce sovereign states. That government was murdered by Lincoln—murdered in order to save the Yankees' Union.

"Now, since 1865, the United States of America is a nation with once-sovereign states reduced to provinces. States' rights are gone—for what rights have they who dare not strike for them? Today the United States is not admired by the world but feared and mistrusted as a nation boastful and overbearing, ready and willing to regulate, if not to rule, the world like Rome of old. 'O what a fall was there, my Northern friend,' was Berkeley's final comment to his Yankee friend.

"Joe William, you were born into a sad time, a time when the majority of Americans prefer an American Empire over American liberty. Patrick Henry would be sad indeed if he could see what became of American liberty. But Joe William, you must remember that as long as even one Southerner remembers why we fought the War for Southern Independence, there is hope yet—hope that liberty and Southern freedom will rise again." Uncle Seth was a true unreconstructed Southerner who would never take the oath of allegiance to Lincoln's Federal Empire. The old Confederate veteran walked down the rows of corn stalks gently touching each one as if touching gray-clad Southern warriors standing in ranks facing the hated Yankee invader.

§ Deo Vindice §

ON THE SKIRMISH LINE WITH UNCLE SETH
"I hope to see the Union preserved by granting to the South the full measure of her constitutional rights. If this cannot be done I hope to see all the Southern States united in a new confederation . . . if the stars and stripes become the standard of a tyrannical majority, the ensign of a violated league, it will no longer command our love but will command our best efforts to drive it from the State."

—Gen. Patrick Cleburne of Arkansas

9

Louis Napoleon Nelson—Black Confederate and Loyal Friend

It was a late fall morning in rural Mississippi and Uncle Seth was enjoying his morning coffee on the back porch. While no one was around to correct him, Uncle Seth loved to pour his hot coffee into a saucer, blow across the thin layer of liquid, and then slurp down the stimulating brew. These were perfect mornings for the old Confederate veteran—alone with his thoughts, coffee, and a flawless scene of cold, crystal-white fall frost crowning beautiful orange pumpkins in the fall garden just sitting there waiting to be harvested. But it was not to last because his grandchildren were beginning to stir. Uncle Seth picked up the latest issue of his *Confederate Veteran* and began reading, but his quiet was shortly broken when Carroll Ray sat down next to him.

"What are you reading, Uncle Seth?" asked Carroll Ray, more as an announcement of his arrival than a request for information. But Uncle Seth never let an opportunity to "tawk" go by without using the moment. "I'm reading about one of my Confederate comrades from Lauderdale County in Tennessee," Uncle Seth replied. Without pausing, thereby preventing the youth from interrupting, he continued, "He is one of the many black Confederate soldiers who suffered and endured the privations and dangers of military life during the War for Southern Independence."

"Did you say he is black?" asked Carroll Ray in a tone of voice that indicated to Uncle Seth the boy had more than a little interest in Uncle Seth's story. Before Uncle Seth could continue, Carroll Ray blurted out, "My school teacher says that there were no blacks in the Confederate army, that they all ran away and joined the Union army."

Uncle Seth's eyes fixed on Carroll Ray with such intensity that the boy was afraid to move. "Your self-hating Southern schoolteacher is an example of how Yankee lies, masquerading as education, can ruin a good mind!" exclaimed Uncle Seth. Carroll Ray was not surprised; the young boy realized what Uncle Seth's reaction would be as soon as he had inadvertently allowed the words to roll off his tongue.

"Look at this picture of Louis Nelson in his United Confederate Veteran uniform," implored Uncle Seth, almost as if he was imploring the world to see the truth through the eyes of one young Southerner. Continuing, he explained, "Louis Nelson joined Company M of the 7th Tennessee Cavalry and served as cook and body guard. He stayed with the unit through the entire war and mustered out with the rest of the company. He was well-known and respected by his fellow Southerners. He regularly attends the meeting of the John Sutherland Camp of the United Confederate Veterans there in his home." Uncle Seth was fighting modern-day Yankee education with the same passion he channeled when he fought the Yankees during the war. He knew that one day he would not be around to correct such lies about his people and denounce the Yankee slander against his Southern homeland. "See, Carroll Ray," he softly intoned in an effort to gain the boy's complete attention, "the picture is of Nelson at the National Confederate Veterans Convention where he was one of the delegates from his UCV camp there in Lauderdale County. It says here that when the delegation arrived the host camp suggested they should set up separate quarters for the black member of the Sutherland Camp. The white boys would not hear of such a thing—they fought together as a unit during the war, they meet together as a camp, and they threatened to go home if the host tried to separate Nelson from the rest of the delegation. They said that 'they bivouacked together then and they will bivouac together today.' You see, Carroll Ray, the enemy who invaded, conquered, and even today occupies our Southern homeland knows that if the truth about why the Yankees fought that war is ever truly understood by Southerners there would be a new revolt—empires don't like refighting their evil conquest!" Uncle Seth slowly sat back against his chair, more in an effort to regain his composure than to rest, and then continued, "I see here that Nelson is drawing a Confederate pension—paid for by the people of Tennessee to their soldiers and sailors who fought for the South during the war. Brave men deserve to be honored, especially by those for whom they fought. Tell that to your Yankee-miseducated teacher!" Uncle Seth exclaimed with a certainty in his voice that promised to transcend time and generations.

The morning sun was just over the horizon. The old red rooster had been atop the chicken house for some time now, crowing as if he thought he was responsible for bringing up the morning light in the east, and Uncle Seth slowly sipped the last of his now-cool coffee. He felt strangely satisfied this chilly Mississippi morning—this beautiful God-given day in Dixie—with yet one more skirmish won in the continuing struggle for Southern Independence.

White and black (two on right) CSA veterans, Huntsville, Alabama, reunion circa 1928

§ Deo Vindice §

ON THE SKIRMISH LINE WITH UNCLE SETH

The love, loyalty, and respect between white and black Southerners confounded the Yankee invader during the war. Many black Southerners, free and slave, joined with their white neighbors in the struggle to repulse the Yankee invaders. Ben was one such black Southerner. Ben rode with Harvey's Scouts of Gen. Nathan Bedford Forrest's cavalry. During one of the engagements, Ben was captured by the Federals but managed to reject Yankee freedom by escaping and rejoining his unit of Forrest's cavalry.

10

CSA Cotton-Clad Navy Defeats
USA Navy Warships

Uncle Seth and the boys were admiring the cotton bales lined up at the cotton gin at Rockport awaiting shipment to New Orleans. Cotton prices were depressed this year, but their crop promised to provide the cash needed to carry them through the coming year. Cotton was the family's cash crop, but just like all of the plain folk of the South they used their hogs and cattle, grazing on the open range, as a major source of cash and food. In essence the family was almost self-sufficient. The land provided for most of their wants while the cash received from the occasional sale of hogs, cattle, and a small cotton crop supplied the cash to purchase those items they could not produce for themselves.

"Now you boys be careful, a-climbing up there on those cotton bales," the old Confederate veteran admonished his youthful companions.

"Uncle Seth," exclaimed Joe William as he pushed against one of the cotton bales, "how can something as light as cotton be so heavy?"

"Well, those cotton bales are made by compressing a lot of cotton," the old man explained. "You know that during the war we often used cotton bales on our ships as a protective shield against Yankee cannons."

The boys settled around the old veteran as he began his story. "One time, at the beginning of the war when the United States navy was blockading the mouth of the Sabine River, we used cotton-clad ships to capture two Yankee ships. It was in January of 1862, or maybe '63, when the Confederate steamers *J. H. Bell* and *Uncle Ben* captured the Yankee sailing ship *Morning Light* (which was about 1,100 tons with more than one hundred and twenty men on board) and the Yankee schooner *Velocity* (of about 100 tons and with twenty men on board). The *Morning Light* was equipped with eight 32-pound cannons and the *Velocity* had two small guns. On our side the *J. H. Bell* had one 64-pound rifled cannon forward on the main deck and the *Uncle Ben* had two 32-pound smoothbore cannons. What a matchup, boys! The newly organized and ill-equipped Confederate navy, with converted river steamers and three cannons and foot soldiers as marines, against the long-established, trained, and equipped

United States navy with seasoned sailors and ten cannons.

"At that time, we had around twelve hundred Confederate soldiers about five miles from Sabine Pass. When we heard that the Confederate cotton-clad ships had arrived and needed men to help with the attack against the invaders—well, every man there wanted to be part of the action. Unfortunately, the two small Confederate ships would only hold about 150 men. So we were all given a ticket and lots were drawn. The lucky winners got to be part of the Confederate navy—as Confederate marines! All the men, except for the ones detailed to operate the cannons, were assigned duty as sharpshooters. It was our job to use our Enfield rifles to silent Yankee marines and to sweep the enemy's decks clear of all sailors.

"We were marched to our boats around midnight. At about 4:00 in the morning, while it was still dark, we got under way. We were about eight or nine miles away from the enemy ships. We did not have any coal to fuel the fire box under our boilers so we had to improvise by using pine knots, several barrels of pine rosin, and bacon fat. Now, as you boys know, pine knots will burn very hot. But man, did we make a black smoke; you could see and smell us from miles away. I went down to see the steam engines and quickly returned. It was so hot down there that the men had to take turns coming up to cool off and get some fresh air. While down there I noticed that the engineer, in order to get all the steam pressure he could, had used a monkey wrench to tie down the safety valve on the steam chest! I just knew that at any moment the whole boat would blow up, killing all of us before we even had a chance to fire one shot at the Yankee ships.

"The *Bell* led the way and the *Uncle Ben* followed. When we left before dawn there was no wind; we had hoped it would not pick up before we got within range of the invader's blockading ships. But when we were nearing the enemy a light breeze picked up. The U.S. ships had already spotted us and were setting their sails, ready to battle us or—more likely—ready to run. They started moving away from us as soon as they had weighed their anchors. It looked like they would escape us because the light breeze had turned into a good wind. The Yankees were taking no chance even in a fight when they out-gunned us better than three to one. But the steam chest held and our boat was able to close the distance before the U.S. navy could make its escape. We fired our first shot at the *Morning Light,* which fell just forward of the bow under the bowsprit. We were about a mile and a half away from the enemy. The *Morning Light* turned her side to us and replied with a full broadside. Man, what a noise that made. I expected any moment to be riddled by Yankee cannonballs, but all of her shots fell short. Now it was our turn to reply. We fired another shot and were greatly pleased with the results. It seemed as if we had dismounted their forward gun and wounded a number of their sailors. Well, we knew what was coming, because it was now the United States navy's turn to answer us. She gave us a second dose of her broadside but, saints be praised, in the excitement of battle the Yankee gunners had overcorrected for their last failure and this time instead of undershooting they overshot! Yep! Every shot sailed harmlessly over our ship, although it made quite a hissing. I'm not sure, but it may have been a cursing-noise as it passed over our ship. We all burst out in laughter as one of the newly commissioned Confederate marines declared loudly, 'Look, our Confederate Battle Flag is waving goodbye to the Yankees.' We all knew that the next broadside would not be solid shot but grape and canister—it would be like a broadside of giant shotguns and anyone caught on open deck would certainly be killed or wounded. But, once again, thanks to our great head of steam, we were closing the distance so fast that the Yankee gunners were having trouble adjusting for the distance. Our captain managed to maneuver our ship to the *Morning Light*'s stern and thereby avoid another broadside. It was then our turn as Confederate marines to use our Enfield rifles to clear the enemy's deck—and that we did with a vengeance.

"This running battle continued with all four ships engaged for about an hour and a half. The Confederate marines had run all of the Yankee sailors below deck, where they could do us no harm. Well, except for one brave U.S. naval officer and one poor sailor who was up in the rigging. The sailor had managed to save himself from our shots by staying high up in the riggings behind the largest mast. During the fight one of our men— Andrew McClug, a second sergeant—was injured. When we had gotten within fifty yards of the *Morning Light*, Sergeant McClug stood up and took aim on the U.S. officer bravely standing on the deck of his ship. One of our officers saw what McClug intended to do and, just as he fired, the officer knocked the rifle up and the shot fired harmlessly into the air. By that time we were up against the *Morning Light* and McClug, rifle in hand, jumped from the top of a cotton bale down onto the deck of the *Morning Light*. When he landed he twisted his ankle—that was our only injury!

"The officer on deck was the *Morning Light*'s captain; his last name was Dillingham. We later found out that he had relatives living in Houston, Texas. He stood on the poop of his vessel holding his naval sword by its blade and waving the hilt in the air as a token of surrender. Shortly after that, he ran a white flag up and all firing ceased as both U.S. naval ships surrendered to our makeshift Confederate navy."

The old Confederate veteran enjoyed telling and retailing his stories about the war. He wanted his kin to know why he and the other men who wore the gray in the War for Southern Independence were so willing to fight against such overwhelming odds. The old man hoped that one day they would pass these stories on to the generations of Southerners yet to come. He hoped that his people in the South would always love and respect their Southern heritage. The old man knew that his generation, despite heroic efforts, had not been able to secure their freedom, but as long as the next generation remembered, there was still hope for eventual liberation. The old Confederate veteran knew this to be true, but he shuttered when he considered the fact that the Yankee invaders also knew this and would do everything in their power to crush the truth. The old man took comfort in the thought that the truth, though crushed to the earth just like his South, would yet rise again.

§ Deo Vindice §

11

Kelly's Brigade and Other Confederate Fighting Irish

"Saints and begorrah, if it's not another St. Patrick's Day," announced Uncle Seth as he shook the bedstead trying to awaken the boys. "You all had better get up, get dressed in some green, eat your breakfast, and head to school." The old Confederate veteran's enthusiasm for a new day was not generally shared by his young grandchildren. The old soldier was waiting for the boys in the kitchen, where their breakfast of eggs, grits, ham, and hot biscuits with gravy and molasses was waiting on the boys. "Come on in boys, sit down. Someone say grace, and while you all are eating I want to tell you all about the Irish Confederates we had fighting with us during the war," Uncle Seth told the boys as a warning for them to keep quiet while eating and listen to his story.

Capt. Joseph Kelly (Courtesy Wilson Creek NB National Park Services)

"I know that your Yankee history books like to tell about all of the Irish who fought for the Yankees when they invaded the South, but they never tell you all why so many Irish joined the Yankee army. But I will tell you. It was because the first cousins of the New Englanders—the English— had invaded, occupied, and impoverished the Emerald Isle. It was so bad in Ireland that many of the native Irish were starving. Of course, that is generally what happens when an empire invades free people and imposes their exploitive rule in place of local self-government. Many of the young Irish would immigrate to America, and as soon as they got off the boats the Yankee recruitment officers were there promising them all sort of benefits after the war if they joined the Yankee army. Well, it was a far better offer than they had gotten from the English back in Ireland, so many joined up on the spot and were formed into Irish units. And of course, due to the Yankee blockade of Southern ports, only Northern ports of entry were open to the Irish. But despite this, we still had a large number of Irish fighting with us.

"Many recent Irish immigrants to the South saw the war being waged against the South by the North as similar to the age-old struggle of the Irish to gain their independence from the English. In St. Louis, Missouri, an Irish immigrant became so alarmed about the violent raids conducted by Unionists in Kansas that in 1857 he organized a local militia company. It was so well-drilled that he would charge admittance fees for the privilege of watching the company drill. He gave most of the money to Fr. John Bannon's Catholic Total Abstinence and Benevolence Society and helped to raise money to build St. John the Apostle and Evangelist Church, which still stands in St. Louis today. In late 1860—this was before the war—his unit was sent to western Missouri to drive out the anti-Southern invaders from Kansas. When the war broke out and Missouri's legislature tried to pass a bill of secession, the Yankees sent troops to disrupt the state's legislature—just like they had done in Maryland and Kentucky. Capt. Joseph Kelly's militia was mustered into Confederate General Sterling Price's Missouri State Guard, and in 1861 they participated in the battles of Carthage, Wilson's Creek, and Lexington. The unit was known as Kelly's Fighting Irish and was well-respected throughout the South.

"We had many other 'native' Southerners who were of Irish decent. For example, Brig. Gen. John McCausland had Irish parents and was born in St. Louis. He was one of the cadets who accompanied General Lee to Harper's Ferry to put down the infamous John Brown insurrection prior to the war. When war came he raised the 36th Virginia Infantry for Confederate service and was commissioned its colonel.

"Brig. Gen. Patrick Theodore Moore was born in Ireland. Prior to the war he was elected as captain of the local militia. He was in command of the 1st Virginia Infantry at the Battle of First Manassas, where he received a severe head wound that ended his active military service, but he continued as commander of a brigade of the Richmond, Virginia, defense force.

"And boys, let's not forget about Fr. John B. Bannon from St. Louis. He was born in Roosky, Ireland, and served as a Roman Catholic priest for the Irish community around St. Louis until the war. When his fellow Irish parishioners departed to serve in the Confederate army, he appointed himself as the chaplain of the 1st Missouri Brigade. The Confederate staff soon made the position official, and he became known as the Confederacy's Fighting Chaplin. During the siege of Vicksburg, Mississippi, he manned artillery pieces. His loyalty to the Southern Cause was so well-known, he was sent to Ireland to discourage Yankee recruitment of young Irishmen to serve as Lincoln's cannon fodder. He was later sent as a representative of the Confederate States of America to the Pope in an effort to gain recognition of our new nation.

"And you all remember when I took you to see the Confederate Memorial Hall on Camp Street in New Orleans, Louisiana? Do you remember me showing you the mural of Fr. Abram J. Ryan, the poet priest of the Confederacy? He is remembered more for his poetry in which he described the post-war South—defiant even in defeat. Who could forget his poems "A Land Without Ruins," "The Land We Love," or "A Prayer for the South"? But his poem "Erin's Flag" is equally as defiant.

"I could go on and on, but I think you get the idea that even though we were not able to recruit native Irishmen to our cause, those who lived among us and knew the truth about the Yankee invader were proud to serve the Confederate States of America." The old Confederate veteran had so much more to tell the boys, but they were finished eating and he was ready for another cup of coffee.

§ Deo Vindice §

ON THE SKIRMISH LINE WITH UNCLE SETH

John Baker was an Irishman and member of Gen. William L. Jackson's Confederate cavalry. As a good Irishman he was rather fond of whiskey. During a lull in the fighting, John decided to venture into territory that was not controlled by either army in search of a local distillery. Finding one and remaining a little too long and consuming a little too much of the local flavor, he was taken by surprise as he left the establishment. The solitary Yankee ordered John to surrender, which he did. He handed the Yankee his carbine as token of his surrender but kept his canteen full of drinking whiskey. On the way to the Yankee's line John discovered that the Yankee was also an Irishman and offered his countryman a drink from his canteen. At first the Yankee refused, but he gladly accepted when he learned of its contents. As the Yankee turned up the canteen and attempted to empty it, John reached into his boot and pulled his backup pistol and informed the Yankee that he was now a prisoner of the Confederate States of America.

12

John Brown—One of Many South-Hating Yankee Fanatics

"What are you reading, Uncle Seth?" asked Joe William as he bounded up the steps to the front porch with the natural exuberance of any boy coming home after a day at school.

"I'm reading a book review about one of your Yankee-educated teacher's heroes—John Brown," Uncle Seth explained as Joe William moved over next to the old Confederate veteran to get a view of the newspaper in Uncle Seth's hands. "Maybe we will get this book so you can do a book report on it next month," the old man said with a chuckle.

"I don't think my teacher would give me a good grade on a report about John Brown unless I made him look like a hero," Joe William said in a matter-of-fact tone.

"Well, the author of this book, a fellow named Hill Peebles Wilson, published it six years ago, back in 1913. His personal story is really more enlightening than the story he eventually writes about the infamous Yankee abolitionists. You see, Mr. Wilson was a member of the Kansas legislature and was part of the majority of that legislature who voted to erect a monument to honor the works of John Brown. After his vote, he decided to write a heroic history of Brown's efforts to end slavery. But being an honest man he wanted to use original sources; in school he had been taught the usual Yankee propaganda line about how John Brown loved the black man and willingly sacrificed his life in the effort to free slaves.

"But the problem was that when Mr. Wilson began to look at the facts he discovered the Yankee history about John Brown that he had been taught in school was at great variance from the actual historical record. As he searched archives and original records of those who personally knew John Brown and personally witnessed his raids, Mr. Wilson

John Brown, Yankee terrorist, (Courtesy Charles Hayes)

changed from an admirer of Brown to one who was ashamed of what Brown and those who supported him had done. Mr. Wilson was shocked and surprised that this Yankee hero turned out to be anything but heroic. Mr. Wilson describes Brown as

> not merely a sanctimonious hypocrite and philanthropic fraud, but a ruthless robber, a persistent and very successful horse thief, and, more, a heartless fiend, who, to get rid of witnesses to his infamies, had murdered in cold blood five inoffensive and innocent men. His deeds were deeds of an utterly depraved scoundrel and in entire keeping with the rest of his career. His aim through life was to acquire a fortune, not by work, which he disliked, but by barefaced robbery and bold plundering; and he was unscrupulous enough to believe that the fanatical hatred of all Southern whites by Northern abolitionists would afford him the opportunity, by posing as a philanthropic rescuer of the blacks from slavery, to fill his own depleted coffers with the wealth that would be within his grasp when the South was invaded by the hordes of savages he hoped to lead.

Not a typical Yankee view of John Brown!

"In May of 1856 the fanatic Brown lead a party of his followers on a raid along Pottawatomie Creek not far from Osawatomie, Kansas. He killed five people. I have here a copy of a letter sent to John Brown while he was awaiting execution after his failed Harper's Ferry raid. The letter is from Mrs. Mahala Doyle, who lost her husband and two of her sons to Brown in that raid. Listen to what she told Brown in her letter: 'You can now appreciate my distress in Kansas, when you entered my house in the middle of the night and took my two boys and husband out into the yard and in cold blood shot them dead. This was in my hearing. You can't say you did it to free slaves; we had none and never expected to own one. You made me a disconsolate widow with helpless children. Oh, how it pained my heart to hear the dying groans of my husband and two children.' Another letter from a J. J. Veatch of Washington County, Kansas, a Republican and former Union soldier, wrote this about John Brown: 'John Brown allowed his men to sharpen their swords and kill five unarmed men by cutting them to pieces in the presence of their wives and children, and therefore he is guilty of murder.'

"This is just a small part of John Brown's legacy. Don't forget that Brown's men's first victim at Harper's Ferry was a free man of color! What crime did these people commit? What evil did they possess that they should be judged as deserving death by this agent of the North? They were not slave owners; indeed the one at Harper's Ferry was not even white!

Their crime was that they were Southerners—evil Southerners who stood in the way of an expanding Yankee Empire.

"You know, Joe William," Uncle Seth said as his eyes fixed on the young lad to make sure he was hearing every word, "John Brown was a fanatic who sought to use a supposed good cause to enrich himself, but he would not have been able to do this if the North had not been primed for years with anti-Southern propaganda. And make no mistake, they still pump out their anti-South propaganda even to this day. The general attitude among a large and vocal group in the North was that we Southerners were innately evil and not only needed to be destroyed but deserved to die in order to bring Yankee salvation to America—a materialistic salvation devoid of spiritual value and principles. This fanaticism among the radical abolitionists destroyed the efforts of Southern abolitionists and caused all Southerners to rally together against the radical abolitionists as a matter of self-defense. All hope of finding a way to peacefully end slavery ended when these radical, fanatical Yankee abolitionists became the vocal leaders in the North. Even though they were not in a majority they were the squeaking wheel that got the political grease from Northern politicians like Lincoln.

"Look, boy! Look at the famous and prominent men of the North who were financing John Brown's murderous plans and activities. Northerners such as William Lloyd Garrison, Wendell Phillips, and U.S. Senator Charles Sumner—all three were from Massachusetts. But these are just a few of the noble race of New Englanders who were more than willing to finance and support the efforts of their fellow fanatic in his efforts to murder white Southerners and any stray black who might get in the way. You can include in this list Henry David Thoreau, Rev. Theodore Parker—a so-called reverend, mind you—and Ralph Waldo Emerson. These were the type of Yankees who would one day happily unleash the military might of the United States of America in an effort to exterminate the people of the South and the principles of limited, constitutional government enforced by real States' Rights that we Southerners held as first principles of true American government.

"Yankee arrogance and hypocrisy know no bounds. I recall reading the other day about how many New England newspapers were decrying the brutalities of the Germans in Belgium and France in the recent Great War. But not long ago, New England had men of high social, intellectual, and political status who were secretly plotting to destroy not only the fortunes but the lives of their fellow countrymen of the South! No people can create a truly free nation who can admire men who were cowards, frauds, and above all murdering fanatics who did their evil work in order to accumulate personal wealth and political power." Uncle Seth slowly released the newspaper as if its weight was too much to hold. As it fell to the porch floor, Joe William eased toward the door and the tea cakes he knew his mom had waiting for him. The old Confederate veteran closed his eyes to rest for a moment—weary from yet another of the endless skirmishes with the Federal Empire.

§ Deo Vindice §

On the Skirmish Line with Uncle Seth

In the winter of 1863-64, Governor Moore of Confederate Louisiana, in his official message, published to the world the appalling fact that more Negroes had perished in Louisiana from the cruelty and brutality of the public enemy (Yankees) than the combined number of white causalities of war in both armies.

13

Fourteen-Year-Old Confederate
Tried as a Spy

Uncle Seth was in the backyard giving the boys a lesson on shooting a black powder pistol. It was an old flintlock pistol that had been his grandfather's. He hoped to give it to one of his great-grandchildren with instructions to pass it on to one of their sons. "Now, Joe William," the old Confederate veteran explained as he carefully handed the loaded weapon to the excited youngster, "this pistol is only loaded with powder, no ball in the barrel, but you treat it as if it is fully loaded, ok? You remember what I have always told you about weapons?"

"More people are accidently killed by empty guns than any other kind," Joe William replied.

"That's right. Treat all weapons as if they are loaded; always control the muzzle by keeping it pointed away from people; and point it only at the target that you have first identified," the old man sternly instructed the boys.

Joe William followed the instruction as he slowly squeezed the trigger; the hammer holding the flint was released and struck the frizzen, causing sparks to fall into the pan—the "flash in the pan" was followed by a loud boom as the black powder-charge in the barrel was ignited. The report of the pistol was almost drowned out by the excited shouts of the boys as they each begged to be the next one to shoot the pistol.

"You boys know that during the war a fourteen-year-old boy joined Mosby's Rangers and used a pistol smaller than this to capture a Yankee cavalryman?" Uncle Seth asked. Before the boys could answer, the old Confederate veteran began, "John McCue was the youngster's name. He was only twelve years old when the war began. He lived in Northern Virginia. The boy wanted to join the Southern army but his father, Capt. John McCue, Sr. of the Confederate States army forbade the boy from joining at such a young age. He knew the boy was determined to do his duty for his country. So, in hopes of keeping the boy out of trouble, the father sent young John to VMI to study. You boys know that VMI is

Virginia Military Institute, don't you? You had better or else I will thump your hard noggins with the hilt of this pistol," the old man teased as he retrieved the weapon from Joe William's hands.

"Well, the war dragged on for the next two years and each year a graduating class of young Southern patriots would march off to join the Confederate army. Then the beautiful Shenandoah Valley of Virginia was invaded by the Yankees; United States troops were burning and killing almost at will. In those days—days of their country's distress—young teenage boys became men overnight. The cadets of VMI were called upon to march to the Battle of New Market. They were clad in parade dress uniforms, wearing low-cut shoes and armed with old, almost useless military rifles. But the Yankee invaders would hear from the boys of VMI on that day! When the cadets charged toward the Yankees, they had to cross a newly plowed wheat field—the damp ground pulled the shoes off of many of the boys' feet, yet they never stopped the charge. They continued toward the Yankees in sock feet. Those young cadets carried the enemy lines and planted their flag on the spot that the hated invader had previously occupied.

"Unfortunately, John and several of the other youngest cadets were not allowed to march off with the oldest cadets. This was the last straw for the fourteen-year-old. He took the only weapon left and found a young pony almost too small to carry him and left in search of General Mosby's command. John found Mosby's men and told them he wanted to join. The hardened Confederate soldiers could not help but laugh at the sight of this small boy on an even smaller pony—carrying what amounted to a popgun used as a noisemaker at a Fourth of July celebration—wanting to join Mosby's Rangers. But Judge Dorsey of Howard County, who was one of the Rangers, declared, 'My boy, if you shot me with that pistol I would think that I had been bit by a mosquito, but if you are that determined then come on board.' You see, boys, you should always remember that it is not the size of the dog in the fight—it is the size of the fight in the dog! Judge Dorsey and the other Rangers could see fight in the boy.

"It was not long before the first engagement took place, and as the Rangers charged upon a group of United States cavalrymen, young John, mounted on his small pony, was in the fore of the charge. He rode up to a huge Yankee cavalryman and pointed his small pistol up toward the Yankee's face and demanded his surrender. John captured his man and became the owner of the Yankee's horse and other military equipage—including a fine new rifle and pistols.

"Shortly after that, John and other Rangers were on patrol behind

Yankee lines trying to determine what movements the invader was planning. They unexpectedly ran into a larger group of Yankees, and in the ensuing fight John was knocked unconscious. He was taken by the Yankees to Baltimore, Maryland, and charged as a spy, which meant he would be hung—something the Yankees were notorious for doing to any Confederate soldier caught behind their lines. You have to remember that if someone is willing to break into your home—and the South is our home—and burn and kill innocent noncombatants then you surely should not be surprised when they ignore the other rules of civilized warfare. In other words, boys, the Yankee invaders were not civilized soldiers; they were invaders of a people who only asked to be left alone. That is a request that a civilized people would honor, but the Yankee Empire knows no such limits on its ambitions.

"John was being held in Fort McHenry awaiting his trial as a spy (if you could call a court martial held by the United States of America against a soldier of the Confederate States of America a trial—certainly not a fair trial—more like a show trial). A lady friend of the McCue family begged the Yankee commander to allow her to hire a lawyer to defend the Southern youth. The United States officer declared he would allow it but she would not be allowed to hire a pro-Southern lawyer! She was able to find a lawyer acceptable to the United States but the lawyer thought the case was hopeless. The lawyer obtained John's father as a witness— Capt. John McCue, Sr. was at that time a prisoner held at Fort Delaware. The only reason he called Capt. McCue as a witness was that the lawyer thought it would be the father's last chance to see his son.

"The so-called trial was short, and during the defense's closing remarks, John's lawyer asked the court to have mercy on the boy because he had been conscripted into the Confederate service. John jumped to his feet and declared his lawyer's claim was false. The young Southern patriot declared in open court, 'I was not conscripted. I ran away from school to join the army. Take me out and shoot me now, but don't tell my people I said I was conscripted.' That ended the trial and the lawyer sat down in despair, all hope of saving the boy's life lost. As John was being led out of the courtroom he had but one last request of his lawyer: 'Ask them not to shoot me in the face. My mother hasn't seen me for so long she would not know me.' With his last request made known, the lad was taken back to his prison cell.

"The next day the court martial reconvened and announced their verdict. By a margin of only one vote, John was spared the death sentence. The invader's court sentenced the Southern youth to life in prison. He remained in prison even after the war, until friends of the family in Baltimore convinced President Grant to issue a pardon. While in prison, the boy was put to work making nails. He became so good at the task that, when he was released from Yankee prison, he set up his own nail business at Iron Gate, Virginia." The old man enjoyed such stories because it taught the boys important lessons about honor, courage, and faith. "Such things are important but are no longer taught in modern New South schools," the old Confederate veteran thought to himself as he looked around to see which of his boys would be the next to fire the old flintlock pistol.

§ Deo Vindice §

ON THE SKIRMISH LINE WITH UNCLE SETH
The characteristics of the war made by the Yankees upon the innocent people of the South are precisely those actions one would expect from a people whose core values are based on the never-ending love of materialism: treachery dignified as genius and cruelty set up to dazzle the world as examples of the Yankees' grander and power. The stained fabric of treachery and the scarlet threads of lies have been carefully woven by skilled Yankee propagandists into the official garment of American history. It is a self-congratulatory garment that artfully conceals naked Yankee aggression.

14

Uncle Seth's Reply to Self-Hating, Yankee-Educated Southerners

One of Uncle Seth's great-grandchildren came home from college and told him his history professor claimed that before the war the South was composed of three classes of people: aristocratic plantation owners, poor whites, and slaves. In addition, the poor whites had been pushed off fertile lands by rich plantation owners and were forced to seek refuge in the hills and mountains with poor and barren soil. Uncle Seth lived in the South before the war and he knew the truth.

Uncle Seth replied: "The early history of the South was written mostly by Northerners traveling through the South. These travelers made assumptions about Southern people, culture, and economy that were developed and distorted as a result of their Yankee worldview and values. These Yankee assumptions were then widely published in Northern newspapers and often quoted as absolute truth even though they had never been tested or validated. But these negative assumptions fit well into the prejudices Northerners held toward Southerners and were therefore readily accepted. These outside visitors would see a backwoods, non-slaveholding Southerner plowing a small patch of corn and observe that the man would stop his work to come over to the road to talk with any visitor who came by. To the industrious Yankee, this was a sign of absolute laziness; thus books have been written by Northerners about the lazy South. But the Yankee visitor was making a uniquely Yankee economic interpretation of the South. They analyzed the economic man but failed to understand that Southerners placed a greater value on the social, gregarious, kith-and-kin family man. These small farmers were the plain folk of the old South. The Yankee visitor could not understand why a man would stop productive economic activity merely to converse at length with a stranger. But the Southerner was interested in news of the world that a stranger may bring; or news about his neighbors, or his kin. His small patch of corn could wait, but an opportunity to "visit a spell" came only rarely in the near-pioneer conditions of the old, rural South.

"The contrast between the mansions of the plantation owners and the rather humble cabins of the plain folk allowed the Yankee observer to make the illogical leap that the plain folk were poor—thus the origins of the concept of "poor whites" of the old South. But, in fact, the majority of these folk were land owners, with large herds of hogs and cattle. The Yankee observer, upon seeing a Southerner in the hill country or mountains cultivating a small patch of corn or vegetables, would naturally assume the individual's primary occupation was that of one engaged in agriculture; in reality the plain folk's primary occupation was that of a herdsman. Small patches would provide some cash-crop money, but it was chiefly a source of food for the family and its domestic livestock, especially milch cows— today referred to as milk cows. And, of course, the corn could also be used as an excellent tool for the distillation of alcoholic beverages.

The value of Southerners' livestock can be seen in the fact that in 1829 more than two and a half million dollars' worth of livestock was sent from Kentucky over the Cumberland Gap to markets in the east. This livestock was hidden from the view of a casual Yankee observer because the hogs and cattle were roaming freely on the open range. The plain folk allowed their stock to increase naturally while grazing on the bounty of nature: hogs would feed on mast—acorns and nuts that fell to the ground from trees that were plentiful in the so-called barren soil of the hill country and mountains of the South—while the cattle would find abundant grazing in bottomlands and canebrakes. The plain folk's primary economic assets required very little work. The livestock fed themselves on the open range; thus, the folk avoided the work of building and maintaining fences, except for the fences around their small cultivated patches. The winters were relatively mild, and once a year the community would work as a group to gather the herds in, crop their ears to identify the owners, select a few for home consumption and a few to go to market, and return the rest to the open range. The 1850 census ranked Florida and Texas as the two highest per capita valuations of livestock in the United States. The plain folk's economic system was much less labor intensive than that of the Yankees' and, as such, allowed greater time for leisure, socializing, hunting, fishing, and developing a strong sense of community.

"The plain folk of the old South were a strong, self-reliant, and industrious people who found in the hill and mountain country of the old South a place perfectly suited to their folksiest temperament—a temperament that was strongly influenced by the folkways of Scotland and Ireland. Unlike the Yankee observer, whose cultural values were strongly influenced by England, plain folk of the old South were not primarily motivated by materialism. They were spiritual in that the local church was the center of the community. And unlike the religion of the strict, bluenosed Puritans of New England, the religion of the plain folk was one of joy—a joyous celebration that proclaimed a loving and forgiving God. Especially forgiving, because the plain folk understood their need for mercy when, after death, they would stand in judgment before God. Their conception of God was of one who watched over the lives of all His earthly creatures with such care and loving understanding that He knew when even a small sparrow fell to the earth. As a group, they expected a lot from each other but little of government. And, most of all, they expected the government to leave them alone. Such ideas were totally alien to the Yankee—then and now."

§ Deo Vindice §

On the Skirmish Line with Uncle Seth
Miss Mary Waring of Mobile, Alabama, writes on April 15, 1865, from Yankee-occupied Mobile that Yankee officers came to her home asking if she would rent them a room. She was astounded at the audacity and arrogance of foreign men who had invaded her country, killed and wounded so many of her kin, and who were actively pillaging her homeland. Yet they actually acted surprised that neither she nor any of her neighbors would voluntarily provide them with room and board. What Miss Waring did not understand is that the Yankee mindset is one of a superior; Southerners—and indeed all other peoples—are inferiors who should be honored to be in the presence of such superior human specimens. The Yankee, after all, is that special form of man elected by destiny to be what the New England Transcendentalists referred to as those intellectually superior men destined to bring proper enlightenment to the world—even if it meant bringing it at the point of a bloody bayonet. The thinking of the Yankee officers in Mobile was no different than the thinking of Yankee General "Beast" Butler, who ordered that all females in New Orleans who refused to exchange polite and courteous formalities with Yankee officers be treated as prostitutes plying their trade, and that Southern religious leaders who refused to pray for Lincoln be treated as criminals and thrown in jail. Even as late as 1865, Southerners had not yet learned their proper place in the Federal Empire. Southerners still needed to be taught that they were a conquered and humiliated people, a second-class people who owed eternal obedience to their Yankee superiors. The invading Yankee found Southerners to be a stiff-necked people who had to be taught by the Yankee taskmaster's whip the new art of supplication. For years, Southerners had stood up to the arrogant Yankee. But now, like whipped slaves, they would be taught to bow down to their Yankee masters.

15

Rebel Fist Against Yankee Saber

Uncle Seth was on the front porch almost asleep, rocking slowly in his favorite rocking chair, when the peaceful silence was broken by the noise of the boys. Uncle Seth could tell that it was more than normal play—it sounded like a fight to him. "Better go see what they're up to," he thought as he gave his chair one great rock forward to help propel himself from it.

"What's all the noise about?" the old Confederate veteran shouted.

"Curtis and Barry are in a fight," explained Carroll Ray.

Surveying the two boys, it was plain to see that the fight was out of both of them. "Well, you both gave as good as you got—so sit down over here and cool off," admonished Uncle Seth. Though he tried to pretend that he was irritated at having to deal with such petty matters, the boys knew better. For more years than most could remember, it had been the old man's responsibility to look out for the youngsters around the place.

"Now you boys settle yourselves down. I saw enough fighting during the war to last the rest of my life. I don't want to see my own kin acting like this," he lectured, trying his best to sound stern.

"But Uncle Seth," piped in Carroll Ray, "I bet you never saw a fist fight like this one during the war."

"Well, boy," began Uncle Seth, "I once saw a brave fellow from across the Pearl River over in Simpson County take on a Yankee major—Southern fists against Yankee saber. Sure enough, the Rebel's fists won!"

"That's not surprising, Uncle Seth. I always heard that we Southerners could beat the Yankees with cornstalks," laughed Curtis.

"Yeah, but they wouldn't fight like that," joked Carroll Ray as everyone joined in laughing at an old joke that somehow never seemed to lose its pithy humor.

"Uncle Seth, please tell us more about that fist fight you saw during the war," begged Barry, who had nursed his Irish pride back to the point where he was ready to face off any challenger again—if necessary—but now was eager to hear Uncle Seth's story.

"Well, I was asked to take communications to Cleburne's division near Triune, Tennessee, just before the Battle of Murfreesboro." Uncle Seth eased himself into position on the end of an oak chopping block and began his storytelling. The boys quickly settled down around him, each taking a mental trip along with Uncle Seth—a trip so real to them that it would remain vivid in their minds for the rest of their lives.

"After delivering the documents to Cleburne's headquarters, I attached myself to a group of good fellows from Company A of the 45th Mississippi. I went out on the skirmish line in the company of a first corporal by the name of J. T. McBride. McBride was from near Westville, which was the county seat of Simpson County, Mississippi, at the time. Everyone said he was a devout Methodist; I had no occasion to question that, but I tell y'all that Methodist could fight like the devil," laughed Uncle Seth.

"Now where was I—oh, yes, skirmish line, that's right. We were deployed against a group of Yankee cavalry from Michigan, General McCook's corps, as I recall. Well, we were outnumbered, as usual, but it's the skirmishers' job to slow the advance of the enemy, not defeat it. So when the fighting got too hot, the command was given to withdraw the skirmishers. Well, everyone heard the order except McBride and Captain Cook. The rest of us scurried back to the safety of the main body. I looked back and saw the predicament that McBride and Cook were in. Major Rosegarten, the leader of the Yankee cavalry, saw McBride and Cook out there unsupported and determined to make them prisoners. McBride had other ideas. He waited until the Yankee was within twenty yards; Rosegarten was coming on in full charge, drawn saber in hand, raised over his head ready to cleave the Johnny Reb like a piece of old cheese. McBride stood his ground, in the clear, facing the charging major with the calmness of a man shooting squirrels. He raised his rifle, took careful aim, and slowly squeezed the trigger," Uncle Seth paused to gauge the boys' reaction.

"Did he get his man?" they asked in almost perfect unison.

"Nope," replied Uncle Seth as he gazed quietly at his audience.

"Uncle Seth, how could he have missed?" complained Barry.

"He didn't miss. His gun didn't fire—must have been a bad percussion cap," explained Uncle Seth. "In an instant, the Yankee was riding over McBride, bringing his huge saber down toward McBride's head. But McBride was as cool as the north wind in February. He clubbed the Yankee with the butt of his Enfield rifle. His blow landed just under the Yank's left collarbone and rendered the dazed cavalryman horseless. The brazen Yank had ridden twenty to thirty yards ahead of his supporting cavalrymen. This gave McBride the time he needed to attempt his escape.

As he turned to run toward our main body, he was faced with a ten-rail worm fence. It had been raining the past several days, causing the fence rails to become slick. Every time he would try to grab ahold of the top rail and climb over, his hand would slip and down he would fall. He made three attempts, each with the same disappointing results. On his fourth try he felt the major's saber across his back and shoulders. Lucky for McBride the leather strap on his cartridge box and heavy coat took the force of the first several blows. Well, this infuriated McBride, who turned to meet his foe face-to-face. McBride sprang at the Yankee major like a bulldog, caught him around the body, threw him down, sat on top of him, and, with his fists, began to beat the life out of the poor Yank. Before long the other Yankee cavalrymen arrived, but that didn't stop McBride—he had his Irish up! The Yankees gathered around and began shouting to shoot the rebel, but they quickly changed their mind for fear of hitting their major. All this time, McBride kept pounding the poor fellow. Finally, after great effort, they pulled him off their major. Without hesitation, McBride then turned his rage on his new captors. Finally Captain Cook, who had also been captured by that point, ordered McBride to surrender or else 'the Yankees will kill both of us.'" Uncle Seth slowed down to see if the boys would prompt him to continue.

"What happened to McBride?" asked Carroll Ray.

"The Yankees took both prisoners back to their camp and placed McBride under heavy guard. They even put shackles on him both to shame him and for their own security. Numerous Yankees would come by to see the Johnny Reb who killed Major Rosegarten with his bare hands. We never found out if the Yankee major was actually killed in the incident, but that was the rumor in the Yankee camp," Uncle Seth declared.

"Corporal McBride was sent to Camp Douglas as a prisoner of war and was eventually exchanged. He immediately returned to the 45th Mississippi and received a hero's welcome. The brave lad saw action with his unit at the battles of Missionary Ridge and Ringgold Gap. He became their color-bearer and carried the flag fearlessly at Resaca, New Hope Church, and Kennesaw. His last brave act was to place the flag on the invaders' breastworks on that dreadful November evening in 1864, at the Battle of Franklin, Tennessee. There he willingly sacrificed his life for you—fighting to rid our country of the hated Yankee invader." Uncle Seth's voice had assumed a tone of importance the boys knew well.

The boys enjoyed the old Confederate veteran's stories. To them it wasn't history they were learning; it was the legacy of their community, their kith and kin, and their fellow countrymen. To them the War for

Southern Independence was as real as Uncle Seth and their country as close as the soil beneath their bare feet.

§ Deo Vindice §

On the Skirmish Line with Uncle Seth
"That the cause we fought for and our brothers died for was the cause of civil liberty, is a thesis, which we feel ourselves bound to maintain whenever our motives are challenged or misunderstood, if only for our children's sake."

—Basil Gildersleeve, "The Creed of the Old South,"
Atlantic Monthly, 1892

16

The New Nationalism and the
Expanding Federal Empire

Uncle Seth and several of his older friends were huddled around the potbelly stove at Little's general store in Rockport, Mississippi, listening to the war stories of one of the local youths who had participated in the Spanish-American War and had served an extended tour in the Philippine Islands. The old veterans were comparing notes about the difference between their war and the modern war with Spain, which had ended before the turn of the twentieth century. And now Teddy Roosevelt, who won great recognition in that war, was president of the United States. While most Mississippians—like most Americans of the day, with their strong military heritage—had supported the war with Spain, Uncle Seth had been cautiously concerned. He warned his neighbors not to let their sons become cannon fodder for the Federal Empire. He could see the Federal Empire using Southern blood to expand their commercial empire just like the British used Scottish, Welsh, and Irish blood to expand the English Empire. Uncle Seth knew that occupied territories had always been useful to empires as a source of cheap blood to spill in strange, foreign lands.

"You know, folks," Uncle Seth took control of the conversation, "some of us here today remember back in 1861 when the leaders of the Federal government used the patriotic zeal of the common folk in the North to gain support for the invasion of our newly established Confederate States of America. Politicians are not above appealing to popular emotions in order to further their political careers and win rich contracts for their friends in industry, commerce, and banking. That is exactly what Lincoln and the Northern War Governors did back in 1861—they appealed to the common man's sense of patriotism by telling them that the South was trying to destroy their Union. By the end of the war the constitutional Union was destroyed and replaced with a supreme Federal Empire—a government that is the sole judge of its own powers. War is the politician's best friend; it allows him to increase the power of government; it allows him to increase taxes to bring in more revenue for his big government; it allows him to pay off those commercial, industrial, and banking interests that are the base of his support; and it allows for expansionism into foreign lands. Patriots fight defensive wars to protect their homes and loved ones from foreign invasion, while nationalists who falsely claim to be patriots fight foreign wars that expand the nation's powers and commercial influence.

"There was a time, before the war, when people were citizens of their states. They owed their allegiance to their state. The Federal flag was flown over Federal buildings such as courthouses, post offices, and Federal military posts. Most people seldom had contact with the Federal government. But today the Federal government is everywhere and constantly increasing its intrusive powers—the Federal flag is superior to the state flag even on state property! It serves as a demonstration to the conquered population that the Federal government is their supreme ruler. There is no longer a sovereign state to interpose its sovereign authority between a defenseless people and the usurped powers of the supreme Federal government.

"Teddy Roosevelt's 'New Nationalism' is just another example of the never-ceasing expansion of Lincoln's national government. The United States is becoming an international commercial, if not colonial, power. The South was the first colonial prize seized by the Federal Empire; then followed the Hawaiian Islands. Now we have Cuba, the Philippines, and numerous Pacific and Caribbean Islands that we control directly and others that we command by virtue of military threat. And who gains by all of this nationalist expansion? The politicians, the ruling class, the war industries, and the trading and banking class, but not the common man!

"No, boys, I tell you I have seen it before—great words of humanity and freedom for black or brown people. But in the end, the common man's sons die and black, brown, and non-ruling class people are left with a ruined economy, unable to understand what happened to make them poorer and less able to sustain their society. Beware of politicians who ask you to pay more taxes to help protect the nation and to send your sons fighting to defend the nation in wars that you do not understand against an enemy that has not invaded your state or any other American state."

Uncle Seth rocked back in his chair and decided it was time for him to be silent. He knew that his words were not well appreciated because so many of his people were willing to accept simple answers—almost as if it pained them to think seriously about such subjects. He especially did not want to insult the young man standing there in his Yankee military uniform—all U.S. military uniforms were Yankee uniforms as far as Uncle Seth was concerned. But he remembered talking to so many young men proudly wearing their blue uniforms during the war. Most were sincere and actually thought they were fighting to preserve the Union of their fathers—but they were sincerely wrong. Whether they knew it or not they were fighting to establish a supreme Federal Empire that would rule their states and the people therein.

"Too many people are willing to accept simple answers," the old man thought to himself. The Spanish-American War was a good example. If asked, most people would say that the United States went to war because the Spanish sunk the USS *Maine* at anchor in Havana harbor. But what logic would cause the Spanish to attack an American warship when the U.S. was closer to the potential field of action and had a much stronger navy? And at the end of the day, whose empire was lost and who came away with new, rich colonial positions? It reminded Uncle Seth of the way in which Lincoln and Seward managed to force the South to fire on Fort Sumter to prevent it from being reinforced. But by doing so they made the South appear to have initiated the war. It made the old Confederate veteran sad to see his own people blindly accepting the simple answers offered to them by the ruling elite of the Yankee Empire. The old man could never understand why his people could not see that the Yankee Empire was using them as pawns in their game of political and economic expansionism. And while the ruling class and those closely associated with the ruling class enrich themselves, the common man becomes the poorer. It is just like the war—rich man's war but poor man's fight.

§ Deo Vindice §

ON THE SKIRMISH LINE WITH UNCLE SETH

By the late 1890s, the Federal Empire had turned the United States government into an instrument for the aggrandizement of the ruling elite and those commercial and moneyed interests with close connections to the ruling elite. It had become an instrument for the advancement of commercial and moneyed interest to the detriment of those who pay the taxes and whose sons are sent off to fight in the empire's ever-increasing foreign wars. The South was trapped in Yankee-imposed poverty while Northern cities and interests grew rich. Government became the exploitive source of ill-gotten wealth. Prior to the war, Federal government expenditures never exceeded sixty million dollars. But by the late 1890s that number had reached more than four hundred million dollars and was growing. The Federal Empire uses the almighty dollar as a lever by which to raise the affluence and influence of the ruling elite and to intimidate those who would dare to question its divine right to expand and increase its power and control.

17

Sinking the USS *Cairo*

The spring rains had swollen the creeks and word had gotten around that the new bridge across the Pearl River at Rockport was in danger of being swept away. Uncle Seth had the boys hitch the mare up to the old family buggy. Together they all headed off to see the sights at Rockport. Uncle Seth liked to load up the buggy and take what the boys called "the slow way" to town. Somehow this form of transportation seemed better in keeping with the display of nature all around their Southern home.

Sure enough, they found the water splashing up between the road timbers that ran over the bridge. Uncle Seth had never seen the river quite so high.

"Uncle Seth, where does all that water come from?" asked Billie Jean, the old Confederate veteran's great-granddaughter.

"Yeah, and where is it going in such a rush?" laughed Joe William.

"I don't know, but it's been flowing long before I was here and will most likely be flowing long after all of us are gone," answered Uncle Seth.

"Have you ever been out on the river when it was that high, Uncle Seth?" asked Joe William.

"The Yazoo River was almost that high when I helped sink the USS *Cairo* during the war," replied Uncle Seth. His purposeful silence gave him time to judge his audience's interest in his story.

"Really, Uncle Seth," exclaimed Joe William, "you sunk the *Cairo*?"

"Now, I wouldn't go so far as to lay claim to sinking it myself, but I was there along with our former neighbor, John Wesley Kennedy, over on Paradise Road in the Pearl Valley community. He was serving with the 38th Mississippi Infantry. John and I were with H. Clay Sharkey, who was a member of the 3rd Mississippi Regiment. There were about twenty-five of us in all. We were all detached from our units and sent about ten miles above Vicksburg to where the Yazoo River meets the Mississippi River. Thomas Weldon, a young engineer, was one of the first to develop what we now call underwater mines to use against warships. It was our job to take these underwater bombs out in rowboats and string them across the river—sort of like an explosive trot line, but instead of catfish we were trying to catch Yankee gunboats," he explained with a laugh.

"How did Mr. Weldon make those mines?" inquired Joe William.

"Now, we didn't call them mines at that time; we referred to them as torpedoes. But they weren't like the torpedoes that the Kaiser's U-boats are using. They were what we now call mines. They had never been used to sink a warship, but this Southern engineer knew he could bag one of those Yankee mechanical monsters." Uncle Seth stop to catch his breath—the thought of battles past caused his heart to race and his "wind" to come faster the more he remembered.

"Mr. Weldon," continued Uncle Seth, "had us fill close to a hundred five-gallon demijohns with blasting powder. He placed wires with firing caps on the end into the blasting powder. The demijohns were then sealed with corks and wax. On the outside there was a casing of light wood and the whole thing was so balanced in the water that it would sink no more than two feet under the surface. The torpedoes were secured to a line out in the river while the blasting wire, which was a little longer, was secured also. When the warship broke the shorter line the torpedo would float free, tightening the longer blasting wire and causing the percussion cap to ignite and blow up the entire thing." Uncle Seth seemed to be peering into the distance as he strove to remember every detail. The boys knew this look and knew to keep silent and let the old Confederate veteran gather his thoughts. Soon he did just that.

Uncle Seth shifted his weight self-consciously, realizing his audience was waiting on him. "Oh, well, now let's see—oh yeah—we then were detailed as sharpshooters along the river bank. Our job was to try to force the boats over against the opposite bank where most of our torpedoes were located. We were at that time commanded by a Capt. W. H. Morgan. On the 12th of December two Federal gunboats came up the river. The river was high and the swamps were full of water because at that time there were no levees. That kept our small force safe from the Yankee marines. The two gunboats steamed up the river firing indiscriminately—they couldn't see us but they knew we were out there. So they just wasted powder, shot, and shell trying to force us away from the river bank. These two passed through without triggering any of our torpedoes. But soon the USS *Cairo* followed with more than five hundred Yankee troops on board and it set off at least one of our torpedoes. The boat's prow was lifted into the air while the back of the boat sunk under the huge wave made by our explosion. Most of those poor fellows on board never had a chance to get off—it went straight down. Some Yanks could be seen struggling in the water. We tried to reach them in our small rowboats but the other gunboats opened fire on us! The very few who reached the east bank were captured by our pickets. The other gunboats cautiously eased back down the river, passing our trap with no incident.

"Something most people don't know about the construction of those torpedoes is that Mr. Weldon was assisted by a black craftsman. He was a carpenter and craftsman—one of the best ever seen in those days. Yes sir, if it had not been for the loyal and efficient support of this slave, the South would have never sunk the USS *Cairo*," Uncle Seth concluded with a note of satisfaction in his voice.

§ Deo Vindice §

Confederate infantryman

ON THE SKIRMISH LINE WITH UNCLE SETH
Southern ingenuity during the war produced new weapons such as ironclad gunboats, cotton-clad gunboats, underwater torpedoes, and semi-submergible and submergible crafts. But one idea that was a little too far ahead of its time was recalled by W. G. Jackson of Yuleville, South Carolina. He recalls an attaché of the Confederate War Department begging the department to allow him to develop a balloon that he said would be large enough for him to float over the Yankee lines and drop explosives on the invaders. His idea was discussed in Richmond papers, but he was dismissed as a crank. Today [1910] it does not appear that he was a crank, just ahead of his time.

18

Choctaw Indians as Confederate Soldiers

Carroll Ray had left his Mississippi history school book next to Uncle Seth's chair because the boy knew how much Uncle Seth enjoyed thumbing through history books. Uncle Seth eyed the book as he rocked back and forth in his rocking chair. But before he could pick it up, Carroll Ray came in, hurriedly grabbed the book, and opened it to a page he had marked. "Look, Uncle Seth," the boy was eager to show Uncle Seth what he had discovered in his new book, "there's a picture of the Choctaw War Chief Pushmataha in my new history book! Too bad we didn't have him around to help us fight the Yankees."

"Yes, Carroll Ray, Pushmataha was one of the greatest Mississippi Choctaw warriors. You know some of those stone arrowheads we occasionally find in our plowed fields could have been used by Pushmataha—I know for sure they were made by the Choctaws who lived on this land before the white man settled this part of Mississippi. Yep, ole Pushmataha was both a warrior and a diplomat—we could certainly have used him. But you know we did have quite a few of his kinsmen fighting beside us during the War for Southern Independence." Uncle Seth rocked back in his chair, enjoying the company of his young great-grandson. The aging Confederate veteran knew that his days on this earth were very limited, and he wanted to make sure that the next generation of Southerners would understand the truth about why the men in gray fought the Yankee invaders of our Southern nation.

Uncle Seth began rummaging through a stack of newspapers and United Confederate Veterans newsletters and then announced, "Ah, here it is. Look, Carroll Ray. Here is an article by Major Spann, commander of UCV Camp Number 1312 in Meridian, Mississippi. He tells about how brave and loyal to the Confederacy the Choctaw Indians were during the war. Yes, he quotes an official document stating that, while other Indian nations had a few individuals who were disloyal to the Cause of the South (and of course this is also true of some individuals in several white communities), the Mississippi Choctaw Nation fully supported our efforts to expel the Yankee invaders from our Confederate homeland. Listen to what the Confederate government official said: 'The Choctaws alone, of all the Indian nations, have remained perfectly united in their loyalty to the government of the Confederate States of America. It was said to me by more than one influential and reliable Choctaw during my sojourn in their country that not only had no member of that nation ever gone over to the enemy but that no Indian had ever done so in whose veins coursed Choctaw blood.' How about that? I hope we always remember that, as Confederate soldiers or civilians, the Choctaws never betrayed the trust we placed in them, nor did one ever desert the flag of the Confederate States." Uncle Seth rocked forward in his chair again, looking for something in his stack of papers next to his chair.

"Here, Carroll Ray," Uncle Seth began anew. "I have an article about how Major J. W. Pearce in Hazlehurst, Mississippi, organized the First Battalion of Choctaw Indians in 1862. Some of the Choctaw Confederates were sent to Camp Moore in Tangipahoa, Louisiana, where we had a Confederate training camp. Unfortunately, a Yankee raiding party came up from New Orleans, then occupied by the Yankees under Gen. Benjamin Butler from Boston, Massachusetts. We all called him 'Beast Butler' because he ordered the hanging of a young man who pulled down the Yankee flag

when it was first raised over New Orleans. During the raid on Camp Moore, several Choctaws and white officers were taken prisoner. Most escaped before arriving in New Orleans. But those poor Choctaw Confederate soldiers who did not escape were taken to New York and were daily paraded in the public parks as curiosities for the sport of Yankee sightseers."

"Uncle Seth," Carroll Ray interrupted, "that is not the way you are supposed to treat prisoners of war!"

"You are correct, Carroll Ray, but the Yankee has never allowed dictates of honor, or rules of civilized warfare, to interfere with his pursuit of power or the puffing-up of his arrogant and conceited

Pushmataha, Mississippi, Choctaw war chief whose grandson served in the CSA army (Courtesy Mississippi Department of Archives and History, Jackson, Mississippi)

self-image." Uncle Seth's voice betrayed a deep dislike for the invader. "You know, during the war the Yankees would build large observation towers close to the prison camps where Confederate soldiers were held and charge admission to the local Yankee population for the privilege of viewing ragged and emaciated Southerner soldiers. During another, earlier war, when a young lieutenant by the name of Jefferson Davis held a prisoner of war, the treatment was much different. Lt. Jefferson Davis treated his former adversary with the honor and respect that was due a prisoner of war. It was in 1832 and the prisoner was Indian Chief Black Hawk. Black Hawk wrote about his treatment as a prisoner, explaining that Lieutenant Davis treated him with much kindness; when the boat they were traveling on landed at towns, Davis would not allow the local people, who crowded around the boat, to enter the holding area or to look upon the captured warrior. Black Hawk said that Lieutenant Davis treated him the same way Davis would have wanted to be treated had the situation been reversed. As you know, boy, that very same Lt. Jefferson Davis would eventually become president of the Confederate States of America." Uncle Seth's voice was full of pride.

"Now compare the treatment that Black Hawk received while under the care of Lieutenant Davis to what happened when the Indian chief was delivered to the tender care of the Federal government. In St. Louis, Missouri, Chief Black Hawk was forced to wear a ball and chain, more as an effort to humiliate him than to prevent his escape. Black Hawk described the degradation. He wrote to Davis and expressed the hope that 'you may never experience the humiliation that the power of the American Government has reduced me to.' It is indeed ironic that these words were written to a young lieutenant who would one day, after the fall of the Confederate government and as a prisoner of war, suffer the humiliation of being forced to wear chains and leg irons by this same arrogant Yankee government." Uncle Seth sat in silence as he spent a moment quietly paying tribute to the memory of his last president.

"Oh, yes, Carroll Ray," Uncle Seth suddenly remembered his original intention when he started his storytelling, "You know that while we did not have the Warrior Chief Pushmataha we did have his grandnephew fighting alongside us. His Choctaw name was Eahantatubbee but our white tongues could not properly pronounce it. So he used his white name of Jack Amos. I met him in early June of 1863 while stationed up around Newton County in central Mississippi. While up there I had a chance to see firsthand just how brave Jack Amos and his fellow Choctaw Confederates were.

"It was when the siege of Vicksburg, Mississippi, was just beginning and Confederate troops were being rushed to the defense of the city. Before I arrived, rain had been falling in torrents, causing local streams and the Chunkey River to overflow their banks. The railroad bridge across the Chunkey River was submerged. A troop train was headed to Vicksburg in all haste. The train engineer was under military orders, and his long train of cars was filled with Confederate soldiers who, like the engineer, were animated with but one impulse—to Vicksburg! To victory or death! Even though the raging waters of the Chunkey River had over-topped the railroad bridge, the engineer, with the loud encouragement of the troops, decided to hazard the crossing. Onward rushed the train. All cars passed safely over the rickety bridge except for the very last car. The last train car full of Confederate soldiers fell into the rushing waters of the river when the railroad bridge collapsed. Nearly one hundred Southern boys were trapped and drowning at the bottom of the Chunkey River. The cry for help reached the Choctaw camp and was immediately answered by Jack and a great number of his fellow Choctaw Confederates. It was here that I witnessed Choctaw courage and devotion to our Confederate nation in action. Led by Jack Amos, every Indian present stripped and plunged into that raging river to rescue their drowning Confederate comrades. Ninety-six young boys were pulled out by the brave action of their Choctaw comrades. Twenty-two were brought out alive and returned to the troop train as it continued on toward Vicksburg. The bodies of the dead Southern boys were interred next to the railroad track, where, as far as I know, they remain.

"I met Major Spann at a UCV reunion in New Orleans not long ago. He told me that, as fighters, the Confederate Indians had no equal. They were at their best on the skirmish line and as sharpshooters. Spann said that the Indian fears nothing. But their best service was as scouts and pilots through pathless swamps and jungles and over boundless prairies; his instinct for courses and geographical precision is equal to the bee and surpasses the horse or other animals. The Indians that we served with were obedient to authority as long as they respected the bravery of those in charge. None but the truly brave and purely honest at heart can command Indian soldiers. But for such who are lucky enough to have them under their command, the Indian soldiers would die in the execution of a command.

"Oh, by the way, I see here that the UCV Camp Number 1312 was organized in Meridian, Mississippi, with sixty-eight white veterans and eighteen Choctaw veterans enrolled. As I recall, Jack Amos was at the

1903 UCV Reunion in New Orleans. He was celebrated by the ladies and lauded by the press and honored by other Confederate veterans every day," Uncle Seth concluded.

Carroll Ray stood momentarily in silence. Somehow he knew he had just received more than merely a great story, but his young mind did not know what to do with it. Like with so many of Uncle Seth's stories, the young boy would unconsciously store it in his memory and recall it many years later as he regaled his grandchildren. This was, after all, Uncle Seth's purpose: he would do his part to move the Cause of Southern Freedom forward from one generation to the next—who knows, perhaps the South may yet rise again.

§ Deo Vindice §

19

Stealing a Yankee Locomotive

Click-clack, click-clack, click-clack—Uncle Seth was lulled to sleep by the rhythm of the train wheels as they rolled along the train tracks. The smooth rocking back and forth of the train car was almost as comforting as his favorite rocking chair. The Gulf Mobile and Ohio Railroad was the primary connector for traffic between New Orleans and Memphis. His car was packed with families traveling with their grandfathers to the United Confederate Veterans reunion in Memphis. Most of the veterans were even older than he was. As the train pulled away from Georgetown, Mississippi, an old veteran took his seat next to Uncle Seth.

"Sure wish we had some of these fine cars to ride in during the war," he commented as a way of opening up a conversation. "Yep," replied Uncle Seth, "I can remember riding on top of the car because we did not have room inside. It was quicker than marching."

"Well, yes," the old vet continued, "but marching was a lot safer! I can remember several times when the roadbed was so poorly maintained that the weight of the train would cause the rails to separate from their crossties. When that happened you could count on the train and car rolling off the railroad tracks and landing upside down in the ditch."

"You know," said Uncle Seth in an agreeing tone of voice, "I remember that during the first years of the war we rode on trains a lot more than we did toward the end. The supply of locomotives, rolling stock, and maintained railroad tracks was running short in the last two years of fighting."

"The supply of locomotives was so slim by '64 that we had to steal one from the Yankees!" declared Uncle Seth's fellow traveler. Uncle Seth sat there rocking back and forth keeping time with the rhythm of the wheels on the tracks. The inquisitive look on his face naturally invited the older veteran to continue with his tale.

"Yep, it was late in '64. The Confederacy did not have the means to buy or build new locomotives to replace those that had been destroyed by the Federals who had invaded our country. Well, if we could not buy or build, we had only one alternative—we decided to steal one. A group numbering a little more than one hundred men were selected from General Lee's army and placed under the command of a big, six-foot-four Georgian. I can't recall his name but I was one of the one hundred selected to go on the adventure. The Georgian was skilled in the use of derricks, block and tackle, pulleys, and other such equipment used to lift heavy loads. Prior to the war he had been a foreman of a stone quarry. He took us along with plenty of rope and logging wagons. We silently slipped across our lines, passed through the Yankee lines, and moved into Maryland. When we got there we went to an isolated section of tracks belonging to the Baltimore and Ohio Railroad. We made ourselves comfortable and waited for the next Yankee-owned train to come down the line. It did not take long. They were so sure that they were safe there in Yankee-occupied Maryland that all we had to do was flag them down. They just rolled to a stop in front of our camp. You should have seen the surprised looks on their faces when we told them that we were requisitioning their locomotive to be used in the defense of the Confederate States of America! We put our prisoners under guard and with nothing more than the tools and equipment we had brought with us we began to disassemble that brand-new Yankee locomotive. We loaded the sections on our wagons and began the long haul back to Dixieland. It was fifty-two miles over hills, across streams, and through bogs and woods until we struck a line serving unoccupied Dixie. We reassembled the locomotive, fired it up, and ran it down the tracks back to General Lee's army.

"When Robert Garrett, the president of the Baltimore and Ohio Railroad, heard about us stealing one of his locomotives, he could not believe it. He came down to where we captured his locomotive just to see

for himself. He personally went over the route we used and declared it to be the most wonderful feat of engineering ever accomplished. After the war was over he delegated a man to go down to Georgia and find that six-foot-four Confederate soldier who successfully commanded such a bold mission. Garrett sent for him and on the strength of that single feat made him rail master of his entire system of railroads," the old vet exclaimed, demonstrating his great satisfaction with a loud slap of his knee.

(Jim Whittington)

Uncle Seth peered out the window at the array of farmland, houses, and new towns passing before him. It always thrilled and saddened him to hear and tell such stories of Southern adventure, gallantry, dedication, and heroism. It thrilled him because he was there; he shared in that great struggle for Southern Independence; he knew that by consideration of morality, justice, and honor the South was due its right of self-government. He was saddened not because of the unparalleled suffering and sacrifice freely made by his people but because he knew that unless something changed very quickly the next generation of Southerners would never understand the justifiable logic for Southern Independence. "How sad," he thought, "that our great history will one day be completely told by our enemies—those people who have a vested interest in distorting and denying our heritage. And in so doing they will assure that our descendants remain loyal subjects of the newly created Federal Empire."

§ Deo Vindice §

ON THE SKIRMISH LINE WITH UNCLE SETH

A constitutionally limited Federal government enforced by *real* States' Rights might not make for an efficient form of central government, but it was the price of maintaining social, economic, and political freedom in a diverse country. It was the price of bringing into one Union or Federal government so many different groups and interests. It was thought to be the only means by which the larger Northern element could be prevented from seizing the Federal government and using that government to exploit the smaller Southern element. When real States' Rights died at Appomattox, the legitimate United States of America died and was replaced with an illegitimate supreme Federal government—a Federal government similar to the one that the founding fathers and the sovereign states had specifically *rejected* in 1787. The original United States government was founded on mutual respect and consent of the sovereign states; the current United States was created and is maintained by the immoral persuasion of bloody bayonets. It is a perverted government in which consent was replaced with coercion.

20

Humanity in the Midst of Hell

Uncle Seth sat on the porch quietly listening to the pitter-patter of raindrops as they fell on the white-oak shingles of the roof over his head. When he was young, he and his twin sister, Sarah, would climb into the attic and watch during the first twenty to thirty minutes of a rain as the attic filled with a wet mist. This happened because after a long dry spell the oak shingles would shrink. When rain finally did begin to fall, the shrunken shingles would allow a wet mist into the attic. After a while the oak singles on the roof would become water-laden and swell up, creating a water-tight roof. He and Sarah would call these childhood events "attic fog times."

Sitting on the porch while the rain pitter-pattered on the white oak shingles also reminded Uncle Seth of the steady cadence of a well-trained cavalry unit moving into a canter. He was surrounded by his "boys"— those numerous great-grandchildren, great-grandnephews, and various cousins that either lived in the house or were constantly dropping by to visit and socialize. He was loved and respected by his kinfolk as well as the entire community. Unknowingly to all, he served as a bridge from an almost-forgotten era to a new, yet-to-be-born era. Cousin Barry was there, and everyone knew that just like his Irish ancestors he loved a good fight. When he was around Uncle Seth, Barry would always find a way to "get Uncle Seth's Irish up." It was Barry's way to jokingly pick a fight with Uncle Seth—a fight he never expected to win. "Uncle Seth," shouted Barry. Everyone hushed their conversations and waited to hear Barry's question—all anticipating a verbal skirmish. "My history textbook says that General Sherman was one of the best generals in the war. It says that he made Georgia howl and taught the South that war is hell."

Now, Uncle Seth knew what Barry was up to, but the old man wanted to play along with him and use the opportunity to defend the honor of his fellow Confederates, especially in front of these youngsters who would, one day, inherit the responsibility of defending the Cause. "You know, Barry," Uncle Seth calmly began, "when civilized folk use their intelligence to

develop instruments for killing their fellow men and send young men off
to shoot and kill other young men just because one group of old politicians
refuses to honorably settle its differences with the leaders of another
country—well anything can become hellish. But it does not have to be
as bad as General Sherman allowed and encouraged it to become during
the war. Evil men take advantage of war to unleash their hellish nature
on innocent and defenseless civilians. Good men will use their position
of leadership to try to protect the innocent even during the hell of war
and even if the leader does not agree with those civilians—civilians who
may be supporting the nation the leader is invading or fighting." Uncle
Seth slowed his cadence and looked off into space as if trying to recapture
distant memories.

"I remember," he continued, "when I was riding with General Forrest
shortly after the Battle of Corinth. We got word of the activities of a Union
cavalry unit, the 6th Tennessee. It was composed of pro-Union folks:
people who were fighting for the United States against their own people
of the Confederate States. The U.S. 6th Tennessee Cavalry was composed
of folks from Purdy, Tennessee, over in the western part of the state. The
folks in the town were about half pro-Union and half pro-Confederate.
The commander of the U.S. cavalry unit was also from Purdy. He and his
U.S. unit had recently left the town, but before they left they burned the
homes of all Confederate soldiers and left the pro-Southern women and
children with nothing to keep them warm but a burning hatred for such
evil men. General Forrest headed for Purdy, and God help the United
States cavalry if he managed to catch up with them! Many of our men
had wives and children in Purdy and the general knew that they would
be naturally eager for vengeance. So when we were about five miles from
town he sent six of us ahead to guard the U.S. cavalry commander's home
and family. On entering the town, blackened walls, lone chimneys, and
charred remains of buildings gave abundant evidence of the U.S. cavalry's
cowardly vandalism. I went directly to the cavalry commander's home and
tapped lightly on the door with the hilt of my saber. In a moment a lady
opened the door, and I asked her if she was the U.S. cavalry commander's
wife. Trembling, she answered in the affirmative, and from the terror
expressed on her face I surmised that she judged all soldiers to be morally
no better than those U.S. soldiers under her husband's leadership. I
hastened to relieve her of her apprehensions and told her that neither she,
her family, nor any of their possessions would be harmed and that General
Forrest had sent me there to post a guard to assure their safety. I tipped
my hat to her and turned to remount. Before I could leave, she declared in

a tone of voice that betrayed both relief from impending destruction and a sense of shame for her husband's criminality, 'Please, sir, say to General Forrest, for me, that this is more than I had any right to expect of him, and that I thank him from my heart for this unexpected kindness. I shall gratefully remember it and shall always believe him to be as generous as he is brave.'" Both his voice and the expression on his face betrayed Uncle Seth's admiration for General Forrest and the general's "horse critters," as they were fondly called.

"General Forrest," continued Uncle Seth, "had by now arrived in town and was approached by a delegation of citizens who informed him that the U.S. sympathizers were fearful of reprisals. The general's reply was characteristic: 'I have issued orders to my command that no unionist citizen of this town will be insulted, much less harmed, and I am sure that my personal order will be obeyed by my command. But one thing the U.S. 6th Tennessee cavalry and their supporters can rely on—if we ever are so fortunate as to find them just once in my front, I will wipe them off the face of the earth. They are a disgrace to this state and to humanity!'

"So you see, Barry, war is hell, but hellish men make it even worse than it has to be. General Forrest was, and still is, the most maligned, slandered, and hated of all our Confederate generals. Yet this general, who the Yankees despise even to this day, demonstrated humanity in the midst of the hell of war. I daresay you cannot find such honor in the record of the Yankee General Sherman," declared Uncle Seth firmly.

Gen. Nathan Bedford Forrest, Confederate States of America (Library of Congress)

§ Deo Vindice §

21

Yankee Crimes Against Women and Children

It was early in the day and Uncle Seth had already made his way out to the workshop. The prior day's calm had been broken mid-afternoon by the ringing of a neighbor's dinner bell. Usually the dinner bell was only rung at noon to signal those working in the fields that dinner was ready. (Dinner in the rural South was the noon meal, while supper was the evening meal.) If the dinner bell is rung more than a few times, then it was a signal of an emergency requiring all who heard the bell to come to the neighbor's assistance. Yesterday, when Uncle Seth and the boys heard the bell, they looked toward the sound to see a horrifying column of black smoke. In an instant all knew that the house of their neighbor, Theodore Kennedy, was on fire. The house and most of its contents were a complete loss, but at least no one was injured. While the ashes were still smoldering, Uncle Seth and the other neighbors began the work of restoring the Kennedy home. Arrangements were made for the younger children to stay with relatives and neighbors. The women in the community began collecting household necessities while the men decided who would work Theodore's field and who would work with Theodore to help him build a new house. Mr. Ben Page offered to fire up his sawmill to cut the timbers need to frame the house, and Mr. Mike Guess offered a number of fine pine logs to feed the sawmill. Uncle Seth and the boys volunteered to supply the white oak shingles needed for the roof.

Uncle Seth began talking without waiting to see if anyone was paying any attention to him. "You know, boys, that column of black smoke reminded me of the many homes that were purposely and needlessly burned to the ground by the invading Yankees during the war. Of course during the war we often saw not one but many such columns of smoke rising from Southern communities."

"Uncle Seth," intoned Carroll Ray as he began stacking the shingles that Uncle Seth was removing from the two-foot white oak block, "my history teacher said that the destruction that occurred during the war was merely the type of damage that occurs in any war."

"Now, Carroll Ray," Uncle Seth's voice was firm, "how many times do I have to tell you that you cannot trust history teachers who are educated out of Yankee textbooks? They don't even realize that they are being used by the invaders to secure Yankee domination of the South!" Uncle Seth knew that if Southern children continued to be educated out of textbooks written by those who serve the "national" interest of the Federal Empire then one day Southerners will accept their assigned role as second-class Americans and impoverished subjects of the Yankee invaders.

"Let me tell you about what happened around Stevenson, Alabama." Uncle Seth paused from the task of shingle making, holding the froe in one hand and the wooden mallet in the other. "A Yankee captain by the name of Gates went to a house near the place where the invaders' supply train had been fired on and ordered his men to search the house. They found only women and small children in the home. Captain Gates had already instructed his men to go upstairs and set the bedrooms on fire while he kept the women and children downstairs so they would not be able to save any of their possessions. When the house was full of smoke, the Yankee officer left the women and children to fend for themselves."

"But Uncle Seth, the women and children did not have anything to do with the attack on the Yankee supply train," lamented Carroll Ray.

"That didn't matter to the Yankee invaders. They hated us and wanted to do everything possible to exterminate us as a people. For example, Yankee Colonel John Beatty of the 3rd Ohio Infantry warned the non-combatant civilians of Paint Rock, Georgia mainly women, children, and old men—that every time the telegraph wire was cut the Yankees would burn a house; every time a train was fired on they would hang a man; and they would continue to do so until every house was burned between Decatur and Bridgeport, Georgia. Just to make sure they believed him, the Yankee invader ordered the town to be burned to the ground. Things like that were happening all over the South. Another Yankee, Colonel Turchin, who was from Russia and had helped to crush revolts in Poland and Hungary, told his men who had just re-occupied Athens, Alabama, 'I shut my eyes for two hours—I see nothing.' Athens, Alabama, and its people were pillaged by this mob of Yankees. Later a court martial was convened but the Yankee officer presiding, Brig. Gen. James A. Garfield, was less than sympatric to the rules of civilized warfare. Garfield declared, 'Until the rebels are made to feel that rebellion is a crime, which the government will punish, there is no hope of destroying it.' By the way, that same Yankee invader was later elected the twentieth president of this Yankee Empire." Uncle Seth turned and spit on the ground for no reason other than to demonstrate his utter contempt of the government that still occupies and rules his homeland.

"But Uncle Seth," Carroll Ray cautiously inquired of the old Confederate veteran, "did we do the same things to Yankees during the war?"

"No, we did not!" Uncle Seth was emphatic. "You know that when General Lee invaded Pennsylvania he gave strict orders that no private property should be harmed and, if any was taken, a receipt for full value would be given to the owner. But more importantly, General Lee's officers enforced his command not to harm private property. This respect for the enemy's private property was followed even on the high seas. Admiral Semmes of the CSS *Alabama* reminded us about the difference between the way Southerners treated non-combatants and the way the Yankees treated Southern civilians. He declared that 'no prisoner of mine was ever disturbed in the possession of his strictly personal effects. Every boarding-officer had orders to respect these, nor do I believe that the orders were ever violated.' Admiral Semmes challenged the world to compare this conduct with the shameful house-burnings, robberies, and pilferings by both officers and men that accompanied the march of the enemy's armies through the Southern states." Uncle Seth sat motionless for a moment— the work of making white oak shingles seemed to increase with the passing of each year.

After catching his breath and collecting his thoughts, the old Confederate veteran began again, "Carroll Ray, the one thing that bothers me the most is that too many of our Southern countrymen are willing to accept their assigned role as second-class and impoverished subjects of the Yankee Empire. We are the descendants of the men who drove the English back at Kings Mountain and who accepted Cornwallis's surrender at Yorktown! Why should we be forced to accept a government controlled by folks who hate us and don't have our interest at heart? It just does not seem right! Why should we accept the decision of Appomattox as if it were the final word on the South's right to be free? Did the decision at Appomattox rewrite the Declaration of Independence by removing the promise that 'we the people' have a right to live under a government ordered on the consent of the governed? Why should we be less willing to struggle for our country's freedom than our Irish cousins? Recall the Irish declaration 'Whereas for seven hundred years the Irish people have never ceased to repudiate and has repeatedly protested in arms against foreign usurpation.' If the Irish can fight for seven hundred years, why can't we? Why should we become subjects to those who hate and slander us? Did the bloody pond of Shiloh drink not only Southern blood but Southern courage as well? I just don't know, Carroll Ray." Uncle Seth slowly picked up the froe and mallet and began anew the work at hand. Carroll Ray silently studied the old Confederate veteran's demeanor. Somehow he understood; but, like his fellow countrymen, he felt completely helpless. What could they do against the powerful Federal Empire?

§ Deo Vindice §

ON THE SKIRMISH LINE WITH UNCLE SETH

It was a midsummer day in 1864 near Shepherdstown, West Virginia, when Yankee soldiers came to burn homes of non-combatants. The date was July 19, and the home of Confederate Colonel Boteler was burned by Yankee invaders from the 1st New York Volunteer Cavalry. As the home was burning, the women and children were outside begging for mercy from the heartless hordes of United States troops. No one noticed that the colonel's youngest daughter had re-entered her burning home. However, they soon learned that someone was inside when they all heard the piano playing and a young girl singing the South's national anthem, "Dixie," at the top of her lungs. She was pulled from the fire before the roof collapsed upon her. Just one more reason to stand when you hear "Dixie"!

22

Stampede of Yankee Cavalry

The boys were getting ready (or "fixing," as Southerners would say) to open the barn's stall door to let the young calves out for their first venture in the barn lot. It was customary to put the calves in the large stall until they were ready to be weaned. Uncle Seth knew from experience that the calves would be timid at first but that once one left the stall, the rest would follow in rapid succession. "Now watch out, boys," the old Confederate veteran shouted. "After the first one comes out the rest will bolt for the open door."

Shouts of excitement and laughter made it evident that the boys were not taking the old man's advice. After the first calf left, the other three came out almost at once knocking two of the boys to the ground as they jumped over the stall's ground sill. The second calf knocked the boys down while the other two calves jumped over the boys who were attempting to get up and out of the way. Uncle Seth could not help but join in the laughter.

"Oh boy, that was like a Yankee cavalry stampede I saw just before the Battle of Atlanta." The boys had regained their composure and slowly circled around the old man as he began his story. "It was in 1864. The Yankee General Sherman was busy making war on innocent women and children and had decided to try to break the Confederate communications by sending out a massive cavalry force of nearly ten thousand men. As always these Yankee invaders were well-mounted, well-equipped, well-fed, and, of course, they outnumbered us more than two to one. Sherman's objective was to destroy the railroad track and junction station of the West Point and Macon Railroad. It was the main supply route for Confederate forces under General Hood. But even though we were outnumbered, we were still better soldiers with better generals. General Wheeler's Confederate cavalry met and defeated this huge Yankee force in a number of engagements, completely foiling General Sherman's plans.

"General Wheeler captured as many Yankees as he had men under his command! Among those captured were Major General Stoneman and more than half of his command, somewhere around two thousand Yankee prisoners. Because we had so many prisoners—too many to guard—several hundred escaped. A small force from Breckinridge's Kentucky Brigade pursued and captured about three hundred of the Yankees near the Jug Tavern at what is now Winder, Georgia.

"The reason we called the escape a stampede was because of what we found as we followed the Yankees. It reminded us of what happened at the close of the first Battle of Manassas. It wasn't a retreat or any type of orderly military withdrawal—it was a disastrous rout in which the Yankees lost all military order, composure, and self-control. It was every man for himself with no thought of anybody or anything except of putting distance between the individual Yankee invader and his Confederate opponent. They all seemed to be herded together and headed in the same direction, but no thought

Confederate cavalryman

was given to command or control. The first escapee took off in a direction opposite the main Confederate forces, and all the rest—just like sheep following the leader—followed in that same direction. They went through fences, thorn patches, brush, woods, swamps, hills, and hollows. There wasn't a road in front of them but there certainly was one behind them.

"After following the newly made Yankee roadway for about two miles we came upon a most unpleasant scene. In their rush to get away from their just punishment at our hands, many of them inflicted an even harsher punishment on themselves. We found an old field of about twenty acres that had grown up with young pine saplings no bigger than broomsticks and about ten feet tall. The Yankees had trampled it flat to the ground, but as the leading elements approached the pine thicket they could not see that immediately beyond the thicket there was a gulley of about ten to twelve feet deep and at least twenty feet wide. When the leading element of the escaping Yankees cleared the pine sapling thicket, they and their horses immediately tumbled head first to the bottom of the gulley. The mind of a man seized with fear and panic thinks naught of safety of himself or those around him. So with no thought but to escape from the Confederates behind them, each successive rank plunged down into the gulley.

"By the time we reached the spot, the gulley was full of men and horses. It was a terrible sight to see—and even though we hated the invaders for what they were doing to our women and children and their effort to destroy our country, no one rejoiced over the fate of those men and beasts as we surveyed the horrific sight before us. As best as we could tell, many of those in the rear of the stampede were able to pass over on top of their fallen comrades and continue their hasty retreat. A little beyond that point we found several others who had died when a small pole bridge they had attempted to ride over collapsed, taking both the Yankees and their horses to the bottom of the creek.

"On closer inspection it appeared that the clothes and flesh of both man and horse had been torn by the metal horseshoes of those in the rear, who rode over their fallen comrades. I tell you it was not a pleasant sight to see. I've seen dead Yankees strewn over the battlefield. I hate to admit it, but I have rejoiced at the sight of the dead invader lying on Southern soil whose bloated body had been made heavy by Confederate shot and shell. But this was different; it seemed so pointless—indeed, it was inhuman. Boys, war is not glorious, as General Lee said when one of his officers spied the Yankee army and declared that he wished God would strike them all dead. General Lee corrected the young officer and told him he wished 'no harm to any one of those people'; he 'only wished that they would return to their homes, tend their business, and leave us alone.' Unfortunately, that is just too much to ask of the arrogant Yankee.

"Several of us were detailed to help collect the discarded equipage and bury the occasional dead Yankee we found still lying over the stampede route. We came to the Sunshine Church, which had been converted to a hospital. The pews had been removed from the Church and the floor was covered with injured Yankees. Our surgeon, with limited supplies, was doing the best he could to easy their sufferings. We deposited the military hardware the Yankees had so graciously contributed to our Cause and left the area hoping never again to see such a sight."

The boys were a little confused. They had often listened to Uncle Seth as he told them stories about the South's struggle against the hated invader. He never seemed to mind telling them about the struggle or about the Yankees who fell under withering Confederate fire. But this time the old man seemed sadden by the tale. Strange, they thought, how you can have compassion for an enemy—for someone you would quickly kill in battle. But perhaps it is a testimony to humanity that there is no real joy in killing, even if it is in defense of one's county, home, and family. Uncle Seth hoped the boys would remember what Confederate General Robert

E. Lee said: "I wish no harm to any one of those people, I only wished that they would return to their homes, tend their business, and leave us alone."

§ Deo Vindice §

ON THE SKIRMISH LINE WITH UNCLE SETH
Official Yankee reports of the action stated that the Yankee regiment had been attacked by two thousand Confederates in Northern Missouri, but here is how it actually happened. We were on a recruiting mission in Northern Missouri but the country was so full of Yankees that we had to do our work at night. One dark night near Platt and Clay Counties we pulled up suddenly when we heard a large group of Yankee cavalry approaching us. We tied knots in our bridle reins, pulled two pistols each, and separated, putting about twenty yards between each of us. We waited until the Yankees got within forty yards of us and then, very loudly, each Confederate ordered, "right front into line of battle double-quick, march, fire, and charge." The Yankees fired one round in our direction, turned, and began to retreat. Then they broke and ran as fast as any Yankee at First Manassas. We followed after them in the darkness, firing every pistol and carbine we had. We chased the entire regiment of fleeing Yankees until we got about a mile from Liberty, Missouri. There were three of us!

23

Brave Soldiers in the Heat of Battle
and the Horror of War

Uncle Seth was waiting in the lobby of the hotel in Little Rock, Arkansas. He and many of his comrades had assembled for the 1911 annual reunion of the United Confederate Veterans. Each year it seemed that there were fewer of the old veterans left to attend such meetings. But those who remained were having a great time in Little Rock. The local citizens were doing their best to show the heroes of yesterday a good time. Several of the good ole Rebels had joined Uncle Seth and were chatting when one of the old soldiers mentioned, "I have often been asked by my grandchildren to tell them about the worst battle I was in during the war. I tell you, it is hard to answer that question because there were so many."

"Yes," replied Uncle Seth, "most people nowadays think about the big battles, but the small battles, engagements, and actions were just as tough for the men who were there."

"I tell you, Seth," W. P. Helm began (his friends always called him W. P.), "the battle at Iuka, Mississippi, was the most frightful and bloody engagement I saw during the war. I was with Company I, 3rd Texas Cavalry. By the time we reached Iuka, our horses were spent. We became dismounted cavalry—that took a little training—and we sent our horses to Holly Springs to graze and recuperate. The entire Confederate army was footsore, hungry, and ill-clad from months of hard campaigning. We were part of General Sterling Price's army. The Yankee General Rosecrans' army outnumbered us and was well-equipped and well-fed. They had been in that part of Mississippi doing their usual Yankee thing: insulting the women and burning and looting civilian and public property. Even though we were exhausted, the tales of Yankee abuse of our people had us all fired up and anxious to get at the invader.

"When we approached Iuka, we learned that the Yankees had departed in haste. It was received as welcome news because the entire Confederate army needed a rest and the warm springs around Iuka promised to be just what the doctor ordered for our exhausted army. Chasing Yankees will wear you out!" W. P. and Seth chuckled at the old joke about how the

South was forced to end the war because "we wore ourselves out whipping Yankees."

"Well, as all Southern soldiers knew, during the war good news did not last long. Just about the time we were relaxing and learning how to be infantry soldiers—man we missed our horses—we got the surprising news that the Yankee General Rosecrans had received reinforcements and was marching on us! Gen. Sterling Price ordered our colonel to advance the dismounted cavalry several miles toward the Yankees' advance. We were told that there were no Yankees in our area, so we began our advance at quick trot, as we cavalrymen would say, but at the double-quick as the infantry would call it. Because we thought there were no Yankees around we did not throw out a skirmish line in the advance of our unit—big mistake! In the haste of preparing for battle, officers often are forced to give orders based on limited information, and soldiers in the line of battle are the ones who have to pay the price.

"We had gone only a short distance when we came to a valley overlooked by gentle, rolling hills. We quick trotted down the slope of the valley and onto the flat valley floor when all of a sudden, a line of nine Yankee cannons about one hundred fifty yards in front of us opened fire on us! The cannons had been concealed at the crest of the hill. They were firing almost at point-blank range with canister shot and grapeshot. The horrible fire mowed down many of our men. I will never forget it—like a lightening crash out of the blue, our clear, beautiful morning was turned into a death pit. It happened so suddenly that we were not able to tell where the shots were coming from and we were not able to protect ourselves. We were out in the open and being mowed down like grain before a harvesting blade. We fell prostrate on the ground and tried to determine the direction of the attack. Captain Green, of Company I, rose on his knees and shouted to us, 'Steady, boys, steady,' and before the brave man could utter another word he was decapitated by a Yankee cannonball. One of our men broke and rose to run away when Lieutenant Ingram stood up and grabbed the hysterical man. Lieutenant Ingram was a good officer and he knew that if one man turned and ran it might initiate a general rout. He also knew that the poor soldier stood no chance of surviving if he remained upright. Unfortunately, both men were struck by grapeshot before the lieutenant could wrestle the frightened soldier to the ground. Literally in the blink of an eye, our ranks were decimated.

"We knew that we could not retreat. This short action had already cost Company I twenty-seven of the forty-two men in our already depleted Company. Nearly every one of our field officers was slain or wounded.

But on our own, we began a slow advance toward the field artillery. The Yankee invaders had taken away many of our comrades, but they had not taken away our desire to destroy the hated invaders. We found what cover we could, behind trees and logs. From our position we began a steady and accurate sniping fire at the Yankees as they worked their guns.

"We hoped that we would get some help from the troops coming up behind us. But then again, in the heat of battle, hope can turn to despair in a flash. General Whitfield's men were sent to support us, but they were raw recruits who had not been seasoned by battle. When they arrived at our rear, they mistook us for the Yankees and began a deadly fire on us. One of our last living officers, Lieutenant Hunt, saw the developing disaster and bravely stood and shouted, 'Boys, if we are going to die, let it be by Yankee bullets, not by our friends.' Lieutenant Hunt was a good officer. He quickly realized that if General Whitfield's file closers and officers saw us advancing toward the enemy they would correct the firing of their raw recruits. He also had determined that the Yankee cannons were placed slightly behind the crest of the hill and that once we started up the hill slope, the Yankees would not be able to lower their cannon tubes and bring them to bear on us. The Rebel Yell was heard over the cannon and musket fire as those of us who could still stand surged forward over the crest of the hill. For a while it was bloody hand-to-hand fighting, as swords, Navy Colt pistols, and bayonets were used by both sides. The Yankee artillerymen spiked their cannons as soon as they saw us coming up the slope of the hill and shot all of their horses. We captured all nine of their cannons and collected the trace tack from the dead horses. The Yankee infantry was putting up a fearful resistance, and it appeared for a while that their overwhelming numbers would do us in. But relief was on its way.

"Gen. Louis Hebert of Louisiana attacked the Yankees with a flanking movement and his Louisiana, Arkansas, and Mississippi troops carried the day. My company, Company I, and the other companies of our group had a total of around sixty men left out of our original number. Even though we were exhausted and depleted in numbers, we formed up and wheeled right, advanced at the double quick, and captured the remaining elements of the 1st Iowa Regiment. The Yankee invaders had been pushed off the field of battle and retired to a defensive position. Both armies sleep on their arms that night, expecting to renew the fight the next morning.

"The cries of the wounded and dying lying out on that blood-soaked battleground filled the night. Men from both sides were begging for just a single drop of water. But such is war that no one dared to go to their rescue—all humanity was dismissed that night. If anyone from our side tried to go to the aid of any man, blue or gray, the Yankee sharpshooters would drop him immediately; our sharpshooters were equally as determined to drop any Yankee seen on that moon-lit field.

"All the suffering on both sides could have been avoided. That war was not destined by eternal providence. It was made necessary by an evil empire that was determined to keep the Southern people under its control! The South asked nothing from the North other than to be left alone, to live in peace and mind our own business. But those Yankee captains of industry, commerce, banking, and politics who had been made rich by their close association with a Federal government controlled by Northern politicians were determined to keep the South and its tariff tributes flowing into Federal coffers and eventually into their bank accounts. The effusion of blood assured the North's economic ascendancy at the cost of the impoverishment of our people. The Holy Bible says that the love of money is the root of all evil, but I tell you that the love of money and power is the root of all Imperialist wars." Helm sat back in his chair, totally exhausted.

These old soldiers had fought their battles and, even though they had right on their side and even though all they had asked was to be left alone, their efforts had been in vain. The constitutionally limited Republic of Republics bequeathed to them by their fathers had been destroyed by the Yankee invader, and these old Confederate soldiers felt a keen sense of failure in that they could not bequeath the same government to the children of the South. They felt a sense of duty to make sure the next generation understood what had been taken away from the people of the South. But they struggled on just as in the war, with no friend in the world to recognize their legitimate right to be a free and independent country, with no one in the community of nations willing to challenge the increasingly more aggressive Yankee Empire. Outnumbered and undersupplied with necessities of war, they still hoped that the next generation or the one following that would remember and that once again the South would rise and break the chains of Yankee bondage.

§ Deo Vindice §

ON THE SKIRMISH LINE WITH UNCLE SETH

"You have no right to ask, or expect that the South will at once profess unbounded love to that Union from which for four years she tried to escape at a cost of her best blood and all her treasure. Nor can you believe her to be so unutterably hypocritical, so base, as to declare that the flag of the Union has already surpassed in her heart the place which has so long been sacred to the Southern Cross [the Confederate flag]."

—Lt. Gen. Wade Hampton, CSA

24

CSS *Arkansas* Defeats Thirty Yankee Navy Ships

The boys were down by the frog pond enjoying the cool water on a hot Mississippi summer day. They were taking turns jumping from the flat bottom jon boat into the cool spring-fed pond. Uncle Seth had a visitor who had served on the CSS *Arkansas,* and he wanted him to tell the boys about the great naval battle between the *Arkansas* and thirty Yankee gunboats.

"You all bring that jon boat over here," Uncle Seth shouted to the boys. "I want you all to meet my friend John Lafayette Martin from Blytheville, Arkansas."

The boys settled down around the edge of the pond next to where Uncle Seth and the stranger were standing. "John, I want you to tell these boys about how you all manned the guns on the CSS *Arkansas,*" Uncle Seth said, looking over the group of boys to make sure everyone was paying attention.

"Well," John began his account of those exciting and dangerous days as part of the hastily organized Confederate navy, "a group of us were on our way from Missouri to join General Price at Tupelo, Mississippi, in April of 1862. While in Memphis, Tennessee, our unit received orders from the secretary of the Confederate States navy instructing us to report to a gunboat fleet that had been assembled in Memphis. The fleet of gunboats had been developed by putting some iron sides on seven fine side-wheeled steamboats and equipping them with rams. These new warships were named the *Bragg, Beauregard, Price, Thompson, Van Dorn, Sumter,* and the *Paul Jones,* which served as our flagship. We also had a small dispatch boat named *Little Rebel.* The group I was

CSS Arkansas (Courtesy Charles Hayes)

with was assigned to the *Sumter*. We engaged the better-equipped United States navy river gunboats that were lying off Plum Point, in the Mississippi River, on May 10, 1862. We managed to sink one of the Yankee gunboats and smash another so bad that it had to ground itself on the opposite bank to keep from sinking. Because of our experience as navy jacks—that was a joke boys—we were assigned to go to Yazoo, Mississippi, and man the CSS *Arkansas,* which was being constructed in a flooded cornfield. We did not know it, but this group of country boys was about to be engaged in one of the most lopsided naval battles ever fought. At that time, the *Arkansas* did not have a full complement of crew, only officers—Captain Brown, Lieutenant Stevens, and three or four midshipmen. The men with me—Captain Brown, Captain Harris, and Captain McDonald—were assigned to man the *Arkansas*'s guns.

"The Confederate government built a damn across the Yazoo River to prevent the Yankees from coming up to where the *Arkansas* was being built. Now, boys, stop and think about what we were doing—we had no more experience than you have on jon boats. We flooded a cornfield and used local carpenters who had never built anything bigger than that jon boat you all are playing on. We were now building a warship to challenge the forces of the invading United States navy. What chance did we have against such odds? But I tell you, boys, when your homes and families are threatened by a cruel invader hell-bent on enslaving your young nation, you do what you have to do to defend home and loved ones." John stopped, apparently to catch his breath but actually to remember the bitter reality of the war.

Regaining his composure, John continued, "When the *Arkansas* was completed we manned her and cut the dam that had kept the Yankee invaders away. Now we began the search for our country's enemy fleet. It did not take long because the invaders had posted two of their best gunboats below the dam to give warning to the rest of the Yankee fleet should the *Arkansas* sally forth ready for battle. The Yankees had the *Tyler* and the *Carondelet* on picket duty that day. We opened fire on the nearest one, the *Tyler*, and damaged her so badly that she had to go ashore to keep from sinking with all hands on board. The *Carondelet*, showing typical Yankee bravery, refused to give battle man-to-man and instead beat a hasty retreat. The noise of the short-lived battle did give warning to the rest of the Yankee fleet, and they began to prepare to meet the Rebel monster *Arkansas*. The invader's fleet numbered between thirty and forty gunboats—good Yankee odds—that were ready to do battle as we steamed downriver. Our goal was to reach Vicksburg and then move toward Port Hudson in Louisiana, sweeping the invaders' fleet before us. The Yankee

fleet lined up to meet us, each of the gunboats planning to rain death
and destruction down on a single Confederate ship. Each Yankee gunboat
opened fire on us as we came within range. We, of course, returned the
favor. The Yankees' job was to prevent us from breaking out and reaching
Vicksburg, Mississippi, which was, at that time, under siege. We had our
choice of targets—a target-rich environment as they say! We fired right
and left, front and back—we did not know the proper nautical terms port
and starboard, bow and stern. We knew more about plowing clay hills
than we did about being sailors, but with typical Southern tenacity we
were quickly learning. I do not recall how many, but we must have sunk
a number of their gunboats and damaged many others. Thirteen of our
men were killed while going through the Yankee fleet. But nothing was
going to stop us. One of our inexperienced men—in the exhilaration of
battle—poked his head out one of the gun ports to get a better view of the
battle and had his head removed by a single cannonball. His decapitated
body fell back into the ship and had to be removed in order to service the
gun at that gun port. The officer ordered one of the gun crew to throw the
body out into the river. That seems rather disrespectful but it was what
we had to do if we wanted to survive and defeat the United States navy
armada that was attacking us on both sides. The young soldier-turned-
sailor refused the order because he said he just could not do such a thing.
The officer demanded to know why he was refusing a direct order during
the heat of battle. The young lad replied that the dead man was his brother!
The officer then had someone else remove the body.

"Another of the Yankee shells went through the pilothouse, killing the
pilot and wounding Captain Brown, one of our Missouri soldiers. Dick
Brady, an old steamboat pilot, took the wheel and steered the *Arkansas*
safely to Vicksburg. I do not believe that history has another story to equal
that of the outnumbered and outgunned *Arkansas* as she broke through
the barricade of more than thirty enemy vessels and left destruction in her
wake." John completed his story and stood there looking at these young
men who would one day be responsible for passing to the next generation
the story of the South's struggle against the Federal Empire during the
War for Southern Independence.

§ **Deo Vindice** §

25

Yankee Gunboats Invade and Conquer Hawaii

It was an unusually cold and windy February morning in south central Mississippi. Uncle Seth decided to spend the morning at the village store in Rockport. He pulled his chair close to the wood-burning potbelly stove and occupied the morning visiting with neighbors as they came to "trade" for household and farm supplies.

"Oh man!" exclaimed Mr. Jeremiah, the owner of the general store who was busy restocking the empty shelves behind the counter. "I sure wish I was where this came from," he announced to anyone willing to listen as he held up a can of Dole pineapples. "I understand that Hawaii is a virtual paradise—a modern-day Garden of Eden," he paused momentarily from his reshelving as he held the can over his head for all to see. He was facing the shelves with his back to those in the store and remained strangely silent for a few moments as he dreamed of a vacation that he knew would never happen.

"Yep," declared Uncle Seth with a voice loud and firm. His voice warned all who knew him that he intended more than mere agreement with Mr. Jeremiah's wishful declaration. The center of the store's activities suddenly changed from Jeremiah to Uncle Seth. All eyes were on Uncle Seth as a hush filled the small store. "It was a paradise—that's why the Damn Yankees invaded it and stole it from the people of Hawaii." Uncle Seth's voice was indicative of a man who had deep sympathy for a stranger who had been grievously wounded by a common enemy.

The folks from the communities around the village of Rockport knew and respected Uncle Seth because he was one of the last of the surviving Confederate veterans in their communities. They also knew that his view of the current United States was particularly different from the

(Courtesy Betty Kennedy)

105

views of most "modern" Southerners. But he was highly respected, and somehow—in ways the modern Southerner could not explain—they knew he was right. But what could they do but get along from day to day as best they could? Uncle Seth would often remind them that they were children of an invaded, conquered, and occupied nation. This was too painful to accept, and therefore they tried to ignore such reminders of the South's impoverished second-class place in the Federal Empire.

Uncle Seth knew this to be part of the invaders' plan to complete their conquest. The Yankee invader wanted to turn future generations of Southerners into pacified and obedient subjects of a sovereign central government and its expanding empire. Uncle Seth understood that the victorious Yankee wanted Southerners to become a subservient people who would supply sons to fight its wars—just like the conquered Scots who provide cannon fodder for the British Empire. He understood that the battle was no longer one of swords and bullets but one of ideas. Once again, the South was outnumbered—without a single friend in the world to aid in its struggle for survival as a distinct people. But for the honor of those who wore the gray in the War for Southern Independence, he would fight on until the bitter end, always hoping and praying that future generations of Southerners would once again rush to the defense of their true country's flag, its honor, and its right to be free.

"Now, Uncle Seth," Mr. Jeremiah responded with a questioning tone of voice, "I don't recall ever reading about Lincoln sending any blue-coated Yankees to invade the Hawaiian Islands."

"Well," began Uncle Seth in a slow and contemplative pace, "who do you think writes the history of such aggressive acts? The victor does, and he does it in such a way that masks his true intentions and makes the invaded people appear to be evil villains, deserving the wrath of the invaders' terrible, swift sword." Uncle Seth paused to see several of the men smiling because of his disparaging reference to the "Battle Hymn of the Republic"—a terrorist hymn in the same vein as "John Brown's Body" and "Marching Through Georgia" that was used by the Yankees to celebrate their destruction of the South, to mock Southerners, and to slander Southern heritage. "Of course, you have never heard the truth about how the Hawaiian Islands became the property of the United States." Uncle Seth was setting the stage for one of his impromptu lectures.

Uncle Seth looked around to make sure he had the attention of his recently acquired audience as he began his explanation. "After the defeat and occupation of the Confederate States of America in 1865, the Federal Empire was free to reduce Indian resistance in the American West. By the end of the nineteenth century, most Indian lands had been seized and the inhabitants 'reconstructed' by way of the reservation system. With the American continent 'settled,' the Yankee Empire cast its eyes even farther westward—toward the island nation of Hawaii.

"The Kingdom of Hawaii was formed by native islanders as early as 1810. Its strategic location in the Pacific Ocean made it a target of early European colonialists, especially from Spain, Russia, Great Britain, and France. In an effort to resist colonial attempts to dominate the Hawaiian nation, King David Kalakaua proposed an alliance with Japan and other nations suffering from colonial expansionism. New England 'missionaries' had early on established a company in Hawaii that would eventually become the Dole Food Company. Yankee intentions were made clear in 1875, when the United States demanded that the sovereign nation of Hawaii cede to the US control of Pearl Harbor, Ford Island, and around five miles of coastline. In 1893 Americans and Europeans lead a revolt against Hawaii's queen, Queen Liliuokalani, and demanded a new government, which would eventually disenfranchise most native Hawaiians. During this revolt, the USS *Boston* sent marines ashore to 'protect' American interests—just like Lincoln did when he sent Federal ships and troops to Fort Sumter to 'protect' Yankee interests. The landing of American troops helped to remove Hawaii's queen and replace her with a government that would eventually be dominated by non-natives. After disenfranchising native Hawaiians, a new government was established and Sanford Dole became the occupied nation's first president. He was the cousin of James Dole, founder of Dole Foods, which supplied the can of pineapples that Jeremiah was holding up. Hawaii was then annexed to the U.S. in 1900 and Sanford was eventually appointed to a federal judgeship. You see, there is always great reward for those doing the Federal Empire's bidding.

"This is a pattern of behavior used by New England 'missionaries' to agitate for federal intervention in the affairs of a Sovereign nation. The use of high-sounding principles as the excuse for war, all in order to protect or expand Yankee commercial interests, is not new to those who know the history of

Sanford Dole (Library of Congress)

Lincoln's initiated 'civil war.' Perhaps this is why standard American history—better described as Yankee propaganda—labors so hard to prevent modern-day Southerners, as well as people all over the world, from knowing the truth about Lincoln, the War for Southern Independence, and other acts of Yankee aggression," Uncle Seth concluded with a note of finality.

Uncle Seth always felt a kinship with those who had endured the "loving" embrace of the Yankee Empire. During the War for Southern Independence, he had seen firsthand how evil, brutal, and corrupt empires are and how easy it is for them to rationalize aggression against people who wished only to be left alone and live under a government of their own choosing—one ordered on the principle enshrined in the American Declaration of Independence, a just government based upon the "consent of the governed." Uncle Seth could hear the wind outside; it was picking up and getting even

Confederate officer

colder. Uncle Seth pulled his coat tightly around him as he prepared to face the cold, harsh winds of reality—it reminded him of his battle coat that kept him warm during the war. It also reminded him of battles past and battles yet to come.

§ Deo Vindice §

ON THE SKIRMISH LINE WITH UNCLE SETH

On November 8, 1861, the United States naval ship USS *San Jacinto*, in violation of international law, stopped, boarded, and forcibly removed three Confederate citizens from the British steamer RMS *Trent*. The British government demanded the return of its passengers and sent eight thousand troops to Canada and began efforts to strengthen its fleet. Lincoln reluctantly released the Confederates and apologized to the British government. He justified the apology by telling his inner circle, "One war at a time." This was not an idle comment. We know that General Sherman observed that he wanted to use Southern soldiers in "future wars." Republicans in Congress expressed an interest in obtaining certain islands in the Caribbean and the Russian-possessed areas of Alaska, as well as a desire to push the French under Maximilian I out of Mexico. The efforts to seize American Indian lands were already well in place even during the war. Lincoln's comment was an outward expression of American nationalism that was, at the time, creating the new Federal Empire—an empire that emerged from the ashes of the original constitutionally limited Republic of Republics.

Uncle Seth's Reply to a Yankee Social Worker

"Reconstruction that took place after the war was a time in which the people of the North tried to help newly freed slaves and create a New South that would never again threaten the Union," argued a Yankee social worker.

"As you say, Reconstruction was an effort to remake the South from the ground up—not just repair the roof but remake the entire structure from the groundsill all the way to the roof," began Uncle Seth in response. "It was a fool's errand; it was a time when Northern hatred of the South was turned loose on a defeated and impoverished people, a people who had no official means to resist the vindictive Yankee hatred aimed toward them. This Northern hatred is evidenced in the declaration of the leading Radical Republican in Congress who boasted that he planned to 'turn Mississippi into a frog pond.' Reconstruction-era Louisiana is an example of what was happening across the South. The Reconstruction (Yankee-controlled) state legislature passed confiscatory taxation and, in many parishes, tracts of the richest land were being sold under the tax collector's hammer at a dollar an acre. Even then buyers were hard to find because of the extremely high rate of taxation. Economic malaise and the resulting poverty were plentiful and fell on both white and black Southerners. Ruin was everywhere—ruin instigated by Northern-created scallywag and carpetbagger state legislatures, ruin enforced by Federal marshals, ruin backed by Federal bayonets. All of this vindictively heaped upon the South by our Northern masters as punishment for asking to be left alone to live in a country of our own.

§ **Deo Vindice** §

She Gave Her Shoes to a Barefoot Confederate Soldier

Mary Carolyn was Uncle Seth's granddaughter's youngest daughter. She and her mother traveled over from Shivers Hill in Simpson County to visit him. Word had reached them that Uncle Seth was under the weather, but by the time they arrived the veteran was feeling much better. Mary Carolyn knocked on the door to Uncle Seth's room and waited to see if he was awake and ready for visitors.

"Is that you, Mary Carolyn?" the old man asked.

"Yes it is, Uncle Seth," the young girl announced with great formality. "Can I come in and show you the new shoes mama bought for me in Georgetown?"

"Come on in. I would love to see you and your new shoes." The old man seemed to draw renewed strength and energy from the many youngsters that would gather around him. Uncle Seth showed great interest in his great-granddaughter's new shoes and assured her that he had never seen such a fine pair of shoes or a lovelier young lady. In reality, the old man's eyesight was getting so bad he could hardly make out Mary Carolyn's form in the dim room. "Come over here and sit next to my bed and let me tell you about a young girl, a little older than you, who gave her new shoes to a young Southern boy who was marching by her house on the way to fight the Yankee invaders," Uncle Seth said as he pointed to the old goatskin straight back chair next to his bed.

As Mary Carolyn settled into the chair, Uncle Seth began his story. "The young girl is old today and lives in Florida. Her name is Mrs. Enoch J. Vann of Madison. It seems that a young drummer boy named Nelson Mosby had worn out his only pair of shoes and was marching barefoot while drumming. He was with the 23rd Georgia Infantry. Nelson's company was passing through the town on the way to Olustee, Florida. The Confederates had 5,000 troops and the invading Yankees had 5,500 troops. Our men met the Yankees at the Battle of Olustee and routed the Yankee invaders.

"As young Nelson passed in front of this girl's home, he was on his way to help defend her and her neighbors from the Yankees, who would surely burn their homes if they were not turned back. Well, this young girl saw the young boy marching on bloody feet. She was about the same size as the drummer boy, so she called out to the company's officer asking him to stop, but the officer could not stop the entire army—they had Yankees to contend with and no time to stop for a visit. The young girl asked the officer to send the drummer boy to her so she could give him a pair of shoes and socks for his bloody feet. The officer ordered the drummer boy to fall out and go to the girl. Now, everyone thought the girl had shoes from her brother or another male who had outgrown them and no longer needed them. But no, as soon as the drummer boy reached the young girl, she sat down on the ground and began removing her new shoes and socks. The drummer boy resisted the offer, but the young girl would not hear him. She insisted that he put her socks and new shoes on and rejoin his unit. She shouted to him as he ran back to his unit wearing her shoes, 'If you can march with bloody feet to defend me, I can walk barefoot to the church to pray for you and your friends. God preserve you and give you victory.' I tell you, Mary Carolyn, the men in that army had been in the field since the beginning of the war, and it was February of 1864 by then. Those veterans were hardened soldiers who had seen much death and destruction. They knew the horrors of war and had been toughened by years of struggle with an evil invader who would do anything to destroy the South and stamp out our free country. But when these veterans saw that young girl's gift to this small drummer boy—well, I tell you, there was not a dry eye in the entire army."

The old Confederate veteran looked at Mary Carolyn sitting there next to his bed. She reached over and touched his hand and sat there with him without speaking—no words were needed. The soft touch of the next generation of Southern youth was a comfort to the old soldier. He hoped that one day her children would grow up in a better country—a country where the people of their state controlled the federal government, a country where people were left alone to enjoy life, liberty, and the property they honestly earned. "That's not too much to ask," the old man thought as he slowly closed his eyes.

§ Deo Vindice §

ON THE SKIRMISH LINE WITH UNCLE SETH
Of all the tragic and terrible things I witnessed during the war, the most heartbreaking sight was viewing the lifeless body of a young Southern

drummer boy shortly after the battle at Savannah, Georgia. The lifeless body was there with other bodies awaiting burial. The lad must have been between ten or twelve years old. His uniform was exceptionally neat and well embroidered—signs of loving hands of a mother who sewed each stitch with fine needle, thread, and a prayer. He lay there with his hands across his breast and soft, blond, curly locks of hair tinged with his own red blood. His waxen face gave the appearance of a child sleeping, soon to be awakened with a mother's kiss. He is only a faded memory now. Who is left to remember this young Southern child-patriot? But of course—as the Yankees would have us to believe—he doesn't deserve to be remembered because he was only fighting to keep his slaves.

United States Army General Murders
Southern Prisoners of War

Uncle Seth was busy out in the tack room repairing a bridle and was surprised to hear Billie Jean calling his name. His young great-granddaughter always tried to keep a close eye on him and had used the excuse of gathering eggs at the hen house to come by and check on Uncle Seth.

"Come on in the tack room," the old Confederate called out, "I'm just trying to be useful."

As Billie Jean came in the room she noticed the old scar on Uncle Seth's arm—a reminder of the war, as Uncle Seth would say. "Uncle Seth," she said as she reached out to touch her great-grandfather's arm, "how could you find the courage to stay in the army so long and face so many dangers? I don't think I could have done it."

The old man instantly stopped his tack repair, recognizing a wonderful teaching moment, and began to explain, "You know, Billie Jean, when your country is invaded by a people who have no respect for your rights or the rights of your kin, it is only natural to want to defend the people you love—even if it means facing death.

"A while back I was talking to John T. Fitzpatrick. He lives in Royse City, Texas, today but back in May of 1861 he joined Company E, 17th Tennessee Regiment, under Colonel Taz W. Newman, Zollicoffer's Brigade. He fought in an engagement around Rock Castle, Kentucky, and then the Battle of Shiloh. When his enlistment was up he reenlisted in Company K, 4th Tennessee Cavalry. While serving in middle Tennessee, he was detailed to check on a raid the Yankee General Payne had ordered in and around Tullahoma, Estill Springs, and Decherd.

"During the Yankee raid, a Confederate soldier by the name of William Green, who was a member of Confederate General Forrest's escort, was murdered by the Yankee soldiers after he had surrendered. The Yankees then killed Capt. Bill Davis, who was a scout for General Braggs—he was killed about a hundred yards from the spot where Green had been killed. Two non-combatant civilians named Brown and McKnight were killed about a mile from the Lutheran church, and a very old man, Joel Van Zandt, was killed on the road leading from his mill to his house on the bank of the river. All of the bodies were left out in the open as a warning to all Southerners that Yankee swift justice had arrived—glory, glory, hallelujah.

"The Yankee invaders made their terrorist rounds throughout the countryside looking for Southerners to murder. On the first night in the area the Yankees found Frank Burrough at his grandmother's home recovering from a broken arm. They took him and about fifteen other discharged Confederate soldiers—all of whom had proper papers—as prisoners. When the Yankee raiders and their prisoners reached Fayetteville on the next day, these men were marched out onto the public square, put in a line, and, on orders directly from Yankee General Payne, shot. These Southern soldiers were not spies; they were men who had proper discharge or furlough papers. But niceties such as rules of rules of warfare, civility, and honor have never been a hindrance to Yankee ambitions.

"The Yankee is indeed a strange creature—he is either fish or fowl as his needs may require. He will be an ardent defender of rules and regulations as long as said rules and regulations promise him profits, but he will vehemently denounce and ignore those same rules and regulations if they threaten to impede his progress toward worldwide commercial, economic, and political dominance. He both loves and hates the written constitution crafted by the founding fathers and ratified by the various sovereign states. He loves and respects it when he can use its words to his advantage and hates the same constitution when those same words protect the rights of those whom the Yankee wishes to exploit. He sees no inconsistency in his actions because to him he is the master and all others must bend to his will. He interprets the constitution, rules, and regulations to his advantage and his decisions are not to be challenged. As Thomas Jefferson warned, the constitution has become a thing of clay to be molded in whatever fashion suits them.

"So you see, Billie Jean, when a man is faced with such people he has no real option—that is, if he is a real man. You and, one day, your children must always remember what Chief Joseph of the Nez Perce American Indian tribe said when a white man asked him why he fought the United States government: 'A man who will not honor his father's grave is worse than a wild animal.' After the defeat of his tribe, Chief Joseph learned what it meant to be the conquered possession of the United States government. In the Yankee Empire there are two basic concepts. One is rammed into the heads of the conquered people's children until they eventually embrace it and become well mannered, self-hating, second-class Yankees. The other is the concept of American rights that is twisted and warped by Yankee politicians to fit the circumstances and the occasion. The Yankee Empire did it to the American Indians of the West and they did it to the South." Uncle Seth reached behind his stool and picked up another piece of tack and began inspecting it. Billie Jean sat next to the old man as she pondered these things and wondered what she would do with all the stories Uncle Seth had told her. Uncle Seth felt a warm sense of contentment because he was still doing his duty in defense of his country—the Confederate States of America.

§ Deo Vindice §

ON THE SKIRMISH LINE WITH UNCLE SETH
Recall the last words of Edmund Ruffin (1794-1865), who upon hearing of the South's defeat wrapped himself in a Confederate flag and committed suicide:

"I here declare my unmitigated hatred to Yankee rule—to all political, social and business connection with the Yankees and to the Yankee race. Would that I could impress these sentiments, in their full force, on every living Southerner and bequeath them to every one yet to be born! May such sentiments be held universally in the outraged and down-trodden South, though in silence and stillness, until the now far-distant day shall arrive for just retribution for Yankee usurpation, oppression and atrocious outrages, and for deliverance and

Edmund Ruffin (Courtesy CivilWarPhotos.net)

vengeance for the now ruined, subjugated and enslaved Southern States!

. . . And now with my last writing and utterance, and with what will be near my last breath, I here repeat and would willingly proclaim my unmitigated hatred to Yankee rule—to all political, social and business connections with Yankees, and the perfidious, malignant and vile Yankee race."

29

The Confederate Flag—Brave Men Carried It and Died Defending It

It was January 19 and Uncle Seth and the boys had hung out his old, faded Confederate flag in honor of Gen. Robert E. Lee's birthday. It was a tradition that Uncle Seth kept religiously. The boys did not understand why he wanted to display the flag, because very few people would see it. But Uncle Seth knew that it was necessary for him to demonstrate to the boys the importance of honoring both the flag that so many of their kinsmen fought under and those who died fighting to protect the flag and the country it represented—and even now still represents.

"Come over here, boys," Uncle Seth said as he beckoned the boys to his side, "and let me tell you about a young boy who died during the war defending his unit's flag. His name was Thomas J. Dingler. He was maybe twenty-one years old. He belonged to Company E, of the 44th Georgia. He was from Spaulding County, a farm boy, very likely a part of the plain folk of the old South. He was not a plantation boy but a simple farm boy, typical of the volunteers who answered their country's call to defend our people's right to live under a government based on the consent of the governed. His bravery and dedication to duty earned him the respect of the entire 44th. His comrades said that he would stand in line of battle and shoot at Yankees as calmly as if he were back home shooting at squirrels. Eventually, he was asked to give up his rifle and become the unit's flag-bearer. As you boys know, this is a task that only the bravest can handle; it is the flag-bearer's responsibility to take his assigned post even under direct enemy fire and with only his bravery to rely on for protection in order to give his fellows the point on the battlefield where they are to form up. When the captain wants to move the entire unit, he can't tell each man where to form up but he will tell the flag-bearer to move to a certain point. Then he orders his men to form up. In the heat of battle, with guns firing at you and all around you, it only requires a quick glance to your left or right to know if you are where you are supposed to be. We called this 'falling in on the colors.' If the flag goes down, the unit will become disorganized, an easy target for a cavalry or infantry charge. Only a brave man will face the enemy armed with only a flag—and you know that the enemy knows that if they take the flag away it is more than just a prize of battle—it destroys the opponent's unit cohesion.

"It was late in May of 1864 when the flag of the 44th was captured by the Yankee invaders during the Battle of Spotsylvania Court House, Virginia. The Yankee invaders had selected ten of their best regiments and hurled them at the 44th Georgia. The massed Yankees overran the portion of the Confederate line defended by the 44th and held that portion of the line for a few minutes. Seeing the danger, the Confederate commander rushed reinforcements to aid the 44th and soon was able to push the Yankees out of our line of battle.

"When the Yankees overran the position of the 44th and before our reinforcements arrived, the Yankees surrounded the 44th's flag-bearer with the intention of capturing the flag. Young Thomas Dingler fought them back using the hickory flagpole as his only weapon. But eventually the Yankees managed to plunge their bayonets into the young Southerner and he fell to the ground, still clinging to the Southern flag, fighting with his last ounce of energy to protect it. When his body was found by the reinforcements, they counted more than fourteen Yankee bayonet wounds in the young boy's lifeless body. His hands tightly grasped the torn shreds of his unit's flag. Even in death, this young Southerner refused to surrender to the Yankee invaders.

"With these precious fragments of the emblems of Southern rights, this young hero was laid to rest. His earthly remains are now entombed in the soil of the country he died defending, still grasping the remains of his flag and forever demonstrating his love of the South, something that the Yankee invader is incapable of understanding. You boys always honor that flag and honor the hope that one day we may yet again live in a country of our own."

The old Confederate veteran knew that Yankee-trained school masters were doing all they could to teach young Southerners that the war was fought over slavery. Uncle Seth understood that they did this in the hope that, eventually, all Southerners would become self-hating, obedient, second-class Yankees. The old man silently shook his head and thought, "How could any Southerner be so simple-minded to believe that a man like Thomas Dingler was fighting to keep his slaves?" The very thought angered Uncle Seth. Unconsciously, the old Confederate veteran picked up his walking cane, holding the crook with his right hand and slowly extending his left hand toward the end of the cane. His right thumb moved over the top of the cane's shaft as if trying to find the hammer of his old Enfield rifle.

§ Deo Vindice §

ON THE SKIRMISH LINE WITH UNCLE SETH

The North viewed the South as its property. In 1856 when a Southerner asked Lincoln what he would do if the South left the Union, Lincoln replied, "We won't let you. With the purse and sword, the army and navy and treasury in our hands you could not do it." The South began to realize that the Union of once-sovereign states had become a Yankee-controlled prison in which Southern resources were exploited for the benefit of the Yankee majority. No, the Yankee majority would not let their property— the South—go.

30

Prince de Polignac, Major General, CSA— Dixie's Lafayette

"Uncle Seth," shouted Joe William as he bounded up the front porch steps. He was obviously excited to be home from school and eager to share some new information with his great-grandfather. "We had a lesson in history about the French general Lafayette and how he helped General Washington defeat the British. I told the teacher that you had been talking about a French Confederate general who was known as the Lafayette of the South. She asked me to write a paper about this man—will you help me?"

"Well," Uncle Seth hesitated slightly, "I never actually met Major General de Polignac, but we all knew about him, especially after the Battle of Mansfield in Northwest Louisiana. I have been reading about the dedication of a monument to him at the battlefield in Mansfield this past April. Here we are in 1925 and the memory of this fine Frenchman is still being honored by the United Daughters of the Confederacy and the Sons of Confederate Veterans—that is good to know because there are fewer and fewer of us good ole Rebels left with the passing of each year.

"Now, let me see," the old Confederate veteran rummaged through the stack of newspapers and magazines he kept on a small table next to his rocking chair. "Yes, here it is," the old soldier exclaimed as he grabbed a recently arrived magazine, opened it, and began reading. "His full name was Camille Armand Jules Marie, Prince de Polignac. He rose to major general in the Confederate States army. He was born 1832 in Millemont, Seine-et-Oise, France, to a family that was a prominent part of French society. He was an outstanding student who studied math at St. Stanislaus College and was chosen to represent France in a continent-wide math competition and won first place. During the Crimean War—1853 to 1856—Prince de Polignac served as a lieutenant but resigned after the war and began a tour of

Maj. Gen. Prince de Polignac (Courtesy David M. Rubenstein Rare Book and Manuscript Library, Duke University)

Central America and North America. While in New York, he met Pierre Gustave Toutant Beauregard, a Creole Frenchman from Louisiana, who would shortly become the Confederacy's first brigadier general and hero of the First Battle of Manassas. The Yankees call that battle the First Battle of Bull Run—which the men in gray like to refer to as the First Battle of Yankee Run." The old soldier chuckled at his own joke and continued, "When the war broke out, Prince de Polignac wrote to Beauregard and offered his services to the cause of Southern independence. The offer was accepted and the Confederacy soon had a prince commissioned as lieutenant colonel of infantry. The commission was issued on July 16, 1861, and he was immediately attached to Beauregard's staff. He served with Beauregard at the Battle of Shiloh and Siege of Corinth. He later served with General Bragg during Bragg's invasion of Yankee-occupied Kentucky. During the Battle of Richmond, Kentucky, at a critical moment during the fight, the flag bearer of the 5th Tennessee was killed and the unit's flag fell, causing the unit to lose its fighting cohesion. Polignac rushed forward, picked up the unit's flag, called to the men to rally on the flag, and then carried it forward. His gallantry won him promotion to brigadier general on January 10, 1863, and he was transferred in March to the Trans-Mississippi Department—you know that department was composed of all the Confederate States west of the Mississippi River. It was in this department that he would play a critical part in our victory over the Yankee invaders at the Battle of Mansfield, Louisiana.

"During the Battle of Mansfield, Polignac was attached to Gen. Alfred Mouton's division. It was early April 1864 when our heroes in gray, outnumbered and ill-equipped, moved forward toward the Yankee invader. Our men were under the overall command of Gen. Richard Taylor. (Richard Taylor's father was Zachary Taylor, who was elected U.S. president in 1848.) General Taylor was assisted by General Mouton, Polignac, and others. They met the Yankee invaders in the hills of Northwest Louisiana. The Yankees broke and began a disorderly retreat when Mouton's division charged into them. Many Yankees had thrown down their rifles and surrendered, and their lives were spared according to the rules of war. But as we all know, Yankees follow rules only when it is to their advantage. When a group of the surrendered Yankees saw Confederate General Mouton riding by where they were being lightly guarded, they rushed past the guard, seized their rifles, and shot and killed General Mouton. General Mouton's staff immediately shot the Yankees, but their brave general was dead. This meant Polignac had to take command. This is what General Taylor, who had overall command of Confederate forces during the battle, said about the effect on the troops when they heard about the murder of General Mouton: 'Can we forget that the news of his [Mouton's] death drew scalding tears from his brave soldiers' eyes?' In a flash, Polignac was in command of the division.

"When Polignac took over, he rode to the front of the division and proclaimed, 'Follow me, my brave men, and I will lead you to victory.' With a shout the division moved forward.

"Prince de Polignac often wrote about the war and why he felt compelled to support the cause of Southern independence. In an effort to gain an even greater victory for the Confederate States of American, Prince de Polignac volunteered in late 1864 to run the blockade and travel to his native homeland and plead the cause of the South before Emperor Napoleon III. Prince de Polignac embarked on a slow sailing vessel and crossed the Atlantic to urge his countrymen to uphold the right of constitutional government, self-government, and the consent of the governed by recognizing the Confederate States of America. But alas, time had already run out for our poor, beleaguered country and it was crushed by the overwhelming power of the Yankee Empire.

"Look here, Joe William." Uncle Seth held the magazine open to a photograph. "This is a photo of Prince de Polignac's son and widow, who were present at the unveiling of the monument to General de Polignac at the Mansfield Battlefield. It says here that the erection of the monument was a joint effort of the Major General de Polignac chapter of the United Daughters of the Confederacy of Paris, France, and the Louisiana Division of the United Daughters of the Confederacy. You can see the monument is decorated with both French and Confederate flags. And look at the name General de Polignac chose for his son—Prince Victor Mansfield de Polignac. It says here that many gray-clad Confederate veterans attended the dedication as well. The monument was unveiled by General Taylor's grandson, Dick Taylor Stauffer, and the band played 'Dixie' accompanied by loud and enthusiastic Rebel Yells.

"Now, Joe William, that should give you plenty to write about." The old Confederate veteran seemed especially pleased that his great-grandson was eager to tell the story about the South's Lafayette. But more importantly,

Prince de Polignac's son and wife circa 1925

it also confirmed to the old man that his efforts to tell the true story of the South were not in vain. Perhaps the next generation of Southerners would remember and pass on to the future South the dream of liberty, the hope for freedom, and the knowledge that the men who wore the gray in the War for Southern Independence were honorable men fighting for the right of the people of the South to be free of the Federal Empire, to live in a country of their own and simply to be left alone.

§ Deo Vindice §

On the Skirmish Line with Uncle Seth
Col. John W. Gray of the 8th Georgia Infantry, CSA, was an ardent opponent of secession prior to the war. When the votes were counted in Bartow County—his county—the vote was 60 percent against secession while the state of Georgia as a whole voted overwhelmingly in favor of secession. When the Yankees invaded the South to prevent us from becoming an independent nation, John Gray joined in the defense of his people and country. He understood that if you cannot leave, then you are not really free. It is a lesson that Southerners still need to learn and understand.

31

General "Stonewall" Jackson—A True Southern Leader

It was late winter in south central Mississippi, where Uncle Seth was born and, except for the war years, where he had spent his life. The winters here were mild with only an occasional night during which the temperature would drop below freezing. It would almost never remain below freezing beyond noon the next day. Ice storms were infrequent and snow was a novelty that occurred maybe once every two or three winters. This morning was one of those rare occasions when winter's rain and low temperatures had turned the pine trees into ice trees. The boys were up early and enjoying this novelty of nature.

"Uncle Seth," called out Barry, "I bet you saw a lot of this up north during the war."

"Yes, I saw a lot of this way up north in Virginia." The old Confederate veteran laughed at the thought that a Southern state could be considered way up north. "Now be careful boys, the ground is slippery and the creek bank has ice spewing out of it. You might find yourself wading in that cold water like Gen. Stonewall Jackson and I did one day during the war." The old man felt it his duty to keep the boys as safe as possible and to make sure they understood why he and his comrades wore the gray in the War for Southern Independence.

"What happened, Uncle Seth? Did you and General Jackson fall in the creek?" teased Joe William as he and the other boys burst out laughing at the thought.

"No, it was a little more serious than that. We were busy fighting the

Gen. Stonewall Jackson, CSA (Library of Congress)

124

Yankee invaders. As always, we were outnumbered, but General Jackson could defeat any Yankee army, even when they were better equipped and outnumbered us three or four to one. We were somewhere around Rye Cove up in Scott County, Virginia. It was in the dead of winter, and winter up there would have made this seem like an easy spring day.

"The general was executing one of his famous rapid flanking movements. His army would be facing the Yankee invader in one place and before the United States military experts—if you could call them military experts—would realize it, we would be behind them or on an exposed flank and ready—eager, really—for battle. You know, back then they called us 'Jackson's foot cavalry' because of how fast we could move. It was more than good generalship though; the common soldiers who wore the gray in the War for Southern Independence, we were fighting to protect our homes and families from a cruel invader; we were fighting to be free from the Yankees. The Yankees, on the other hand, well they were fighting to maintain their control over the South—a territory that they were determined to keep as part of their empire.

"Well, anyway." Uncle Seth realized he was losing his audience's attention so he returned to his war story. "It was a cold winter's day and we had come upon a large stream with ice flowing in it. The banks covered with ice and snow. Now, you have to remember that our uniforms were less than ideal for the cold and our shoes and boots were shoes and boots in name only. They were worn and torn from so many marches, countermarches, and battles. As we approached the stream, it was obvious that the only way across was to jump in and wade across—with no hope of a warming fire or dry clothes on the other side and many more miles of marching ahead. Our officers ordered the front ranks into the water but they refused to budge. More officers from the rear came up to find out what was wrong, but a general revolt seemed to be taking place. One officer shouted that if we did not follow his command to wade the icy stream he would bring up a cannon and fire on us! Boy, that had the exact opposite effect that he had hoped for and a general shout of 'no, no, no' was heard.

"All of a sudden the ranks became silent as we saw General Jackson riding up to find out what was delaying his army's progress. Seeing their superior approaching, several of the officers rode to meet him, hoping to explain what was happening. As Gen. Stonewall Jackson approached us, many of the men uncovered their heads in respect for him. Now think about the irony of it all, boys: just moments before, these same men were ready to shoot these other officers, but now they were removing their slouch hats and kepis in this freezing weather out of respect for their general. Jackson waved those other officers away as he approached us and leisurely rode to the front as if he were on parade. At the creek bank he observed a young soldier not much older than you, Joe William. The general noticed that the boy's feet were almost bare and so footsore that he was limping and almost unable to stand. General Jackson pulled up close to the boy and asked him, 'Son, why are you not back at the hospital?' The young boy-soldier straightened up in the most professional military bearing a soldier could have and looked at the general as he replied, 'General, I did not join the army to fill a hospital bunk but to do a soldier's duty.' General Jackson immediately dismounted and told the boy to mount his horse and swim it across the creek's icy waters. The boy declined, declaring that he did not think it fitting for a soldier in the ranks to mount and ride an officer's horse—especially the general's horse. But there was no denying General Jackson; he ordered the boy on the horse and across the creek. General Jackson then turned to us and in a loud voice shouted, 'Well, boys, who wants to take a swim with me?' and with that, he stepped into the icy waters and began the crossing. It seemed as if every man in the entire army wanted to be the next man into the creek. The other officers were busy following the general's example as they dismounted and gave their horses to lame soldiers." Uncle Seth turned away from the boys as he pulled his handkerchief from his pocket pretending to blow his nose; actually he was wiping the tears from his eyes. The boys around the old Confederate veteran also pretended—they pretended not to notice. They understood in ways they were unable to explain.

"Now, boys," Uncle Seth said as he regained the situation, "you need to understand that the Southern soldier could not be driven like a mercenary or a hired killer. But we would go to sure death in obedience to the commands of a leader whom we respected—a man who would willingly face the same dangers that he expected his men to face. I guess it is part of our Scotch-Irish tradition—it is in our Celtic blood.

"Gen. Stonewall Jackson was a very religious man. Each month he would send part of his military pay back to a black church near Lexington where he had often taught Sunday school. He believed that in the end God would judge us all and evil would not triumph. *Deo Vindice* is our country's motto, and it was General Jackson's as well. *Deo Vindice,* "God shall vindicate" (roughly translated, that is). Once, during a discussion with a close friend, the friend observed that the South may not be able to maintain its freedom. General Jackson's only reply was that he did not wish to outlive his country's freedom.

"Boys," Uncle Seth's voice indicated that he had something very serious to say, "you see all these pine trees, see how they are weighted down with all the ice and how some of them have lost branches and others have broken tops? But look around; there are generations of pine trees out here. They are all are covered with cold, heavy ice but not all will die. One day the sun will come out and the ice will slowly melt away. It will melt slowly at first but soon the heat from the Southern sun will cause all the ice to fall to the ground. When that happens, these pine trees will straighten up and reach for the sun. Being covered with ice is not their natural destiny—their destiny is to grow and flourish and give us new and stronger generations of pine trees."

The boys were looking around at the trees with bewildered looks on their faces. What on earth was the old man talking about? What did pine trees have to do with General Jackson? "Boys," Uncle Seth almost whispered. "I'm telling you something I want you all to remember and tell your children and grandchildren and then tell them to tell their children for as long as it takes! Today our country is like these pine trees covered with a heavy load of ice. Today the South is bent over carrying the load of poverty frozen upon us by our enemies. The United States military destroyed our armies but they did not destroy our natural destiny to be free. The Federal Empire is convinced that we will forever accept its political, social, and economic domination; they think we are broken as a people—unable to rise or to remove ourselves from the stool of eternal repentance on which they have placed the South. But I tell you that one day the Southern sun will shine again in all its brightness and the ice of Federal tyranny will melt away. It is your job to keep the memory and hope of freedom alive."

The old Confederate warrior felt the cold in his bones as he turned and headed back to the house. He was old now and it seemed that he was always cold. He knew that he was in the winter season of his life. He knew his time was short, but with his fading sight he could still see hope for the future—if only they know the truth.

§ Deo Vindice §

ON THE SKIRMISH LINE WITH UNCLE SETH
Confederate General "Stonewall" Jackson was a Christian believer of a very direct and simple character. His religion had taken hold, deep and lasting, of his whole being. He was devout and reverent, humble, steadfast, prayerful in spirit, and faithful in duty. He lived his own life strictly according to the will of God, which he sought to know, yet he respected the views of others. Although he was a Protestant, he nonetheless was personally interested in securing a Catholic chaplain for a Louisiana regiment largely composed of men of Roman Catholic faith.

32

A Southern Lady Becomes a Confederate Spy

Uncle Seth was taking his evening stroll in the backyard, admiring the peach trees that had recently put on fruit. "Looks like we're going to have a good crop of peaches for you and your mother to put up this year," the old Confederate veteran said to Billie Jean. Billie Jean was busy hanging the wash on the clothesline and stopped long enough to reply to her great-grandfather. "Yes, it will be even more work for the women folk, but that's the way it always is, you know. I wish I had been born a man. Then I could have done something important like you did," the young girl said with a tone of disappointment in her voice.

"Now, Billie Jean." The old man was particularly partial to Billie Jean—she always looked after him now that he was well into his late sixties. "What you do is very important—this family could not function without your mother's and your help. Besides, do you know that during the war there were many women who served not only on the home front but actually worked with the army to help defeat the Yankee invaders on many a battlefield?"

"Really, Uncle Seth?" Billie Jean responded as she sat the white oak wash hamper down on the ground and paused to hear the old soldier's response.

"Yes, I recall reading about a lady who died recently in Santa Fe, New Mexico. It was last year, 1910. I believe her married name was Georgia Dietz, but during the war she was Georgia T. Read. She was born in the Yankee state of Indiana just across the Ohio River from Louisville, Kentucky. When she was only six months old, her mother died. Her father moved her and her older brother to New Orleans, Louisiana, where he established a wholesale drug store. The family prospered and soon became a favored part of New Orleans society—a society that was fond of parties and balls. Then the war broke out and their idyllic life would soon end forever. Her brother joined the Confederate army and was killed in one of the first battles of the war. In May of 1862, New Orleans was occupied by the Yankee invaders, and Yankee General Benjamin "Beast" Butler took over the occupied city. Just like so many of the Yankee invaders of Dixie,

Beast Butler took advantage of the occupied South by 'legally' looting private property for his own use. Butler took Georgia's father's drug store and the impoverished family had to live off the small amount of money that Georgia earned by giving private school lessons in New Orleans. Eventually, Georgia managed to escape from New Orleans and joined the Army of Northern Virginia as a nurse. She was with General Lee's army at Gettysburg and several other major battles. But she wanted to do more to help the cause of Southern freedom and she soon found an opportunity.

"The life of a nurse had not provided her with the opportunity to do real damage to the Yankee invader, so she hit upon the novel idea of cutting her hair short and disguising herself as a Union soldier. She would then calmly stroll into and about the Yankee army camp and gather information about troop strength, morale, and possible upcoming troop movements. She would then leave camp, cross the Yankee picket line, and make her way back to either General Lee's or General Price's camps with the intelligence she had gathered. At other times, she would disguise herself in a black dress and pretend to be the grieving widow of a Yankee officer seeking to reclaim some personal effects belonging to her dead husband. The Yankee pickets never stopped her. But one day, while on a mission for Confederate General Price, she was captured due to information sent to the Yankees from one of her Indiana relatives. She was arrested and sent to prison in St. Louis, Missouri.

"After the war, she became a teacher in Fredericktown, Missouri. But when some of the Yankee loyalists found out about her Southern sympathies, they demanded that she take a loyalty oath—you know, like the pledge of allegiance to the United States of America. This she refused to do. She knew that she owed no loyalty to the nation that invaded, conquered, and occupied her homeland. Her reward for maintaining her loyalty to her Southern country, the Confederate States of America, was to be known as the only female to ever be ordered out of the state of Missouri and the only female to suffer banishment because of her love for the South and disdain for the Yankee Empire. She served her country faithfully during the war. She met and became friends with many great Southern generals and partisan fighters—men such as Lee, Price, Mosby, Jessie James, and the Younger brothers.

"After being banished from Missouri, she met and married Mr. A. W. Dietz, a wealthy miller who owned several large flour mills near Lincoln, Nebraska—oh, how it pained her to live in a town named after the hated president of the Yankee Empire. After her husband's mills were destroyed by fire, she moved to Santa Fe, New Mexico, where she recently died.

"So you see, Billie Jean," the old soldier was becoming tired and moved slowly toward the back porch to find a chair, "it was not just the men who fought and struggled for our Southern nation during the war. The struggle for freedom is not reserved just for men. You are just as important as any man—we all have our purpose in God's great plan. And remember—you will have to keep fighting for the South long after I am gone on to my eternal reward. If the South is to ever regain her liberty it will be because of men and women like you who know the truth and are willing, just like Miss Georgia Read, to show your loyalty to the South and to stand up for your country's right to be free."

§ Deo Vindice §

On the Skirmish Line with Uncle Seth
The record of the brave daughters of Fredericksburg, Virginia, stands as testimony to the dedication of the Southern people to the cause of Southern freedom. As the Yankee invader moved into their town, the ladies of Fredericksburg declared that they would rather see their homes reduced to ashes than polluted by Yankees and used by the invaders. These women went forth in the cold blast of winter, risking the invaders' guns and worse. They met their sons and husbands in the Confederate army and while speaking nothing of their want and encouraged their loved ones to resist with all their might the evil, blue-clad hoards of the Yankee invaders. As recognition of their bravery, the ragged and hungry men of the Confederate army collected several thousand dollars from their pittance of pay to relieve the sufferings of these civilians.

Confederate infantryman

33

He Fought for the South and He Had No Slaves

Uncle Seth walked slowly along the newly plowed cornfield. His grandson had hitched "Ole Jeff," the family's gray mule, to the harrow and had been plowing since sunrise. He knew his grandson expected him to bring a cool jug of spring water to quench the plowman's thirst. Uncle Seth sat on the ground beneath a crabapple tree on the fencerow.

"Boy!" shouted Uncle Seth. "Here's your water." Carroll Ray uttered a sharp "get-up" to encourage Ole Jeff to quicken his pace. Carroll Ray made the turn at the end of the row and hollered "whooaaa" to Ole Jeff, a command the mule had been taught that meant he should stop. "Come on over here and let Ole Jeff take a breather," Uncle Seth declared as he held the water jug up as if he would have to tempt Carroll Ray to stop his labors. Carroll Ray quickly tied the plow reins to the fence, strode over to the crabapple tree, and took the jug from his grandfather. He hoisted it upon his strong shoulder and gulped down almost half of its contents. "Don't get so excited, boy," laughed Uncle Seth. "That's just water, you know, not good ole Kentucky whiskey." A cooling, late-morning breeze rustled the green corn stalks and carried along with it the sweet smell of freshly plowed earth.

Looking up at the crabapple tree, Carroll Ray commented, "Uncle Seth, you planted this old tree before the war, didn't you?"

"Yes, I did. I planted it just before I left to muster into the Confederate army there at the county courthouse in Hazlehurst," replied Uncle Seth. Carroll Ray was in deep thought. Uncle Seth could tell that he was composing a question of some importance.

"Uncle Seth, why did you and so many of the boys from around here volunteer to fight for the South? I mean most of y'all didn't own slaves," questioned Carroll Ray.

Carroll Ray was right in that very few of the folks around had owned slaves. Uncle Seth and his community were part of the plain folk of the Old South—that vast community of Southerners who made up the larger part of the white Southern population. They were folks who were not a part of the plantation system that most people now think of when they think of slavery in the pre-war South.

"Well," Uncle Seth began slowly as if to take a little extra time to gather his thoughts. "We fought because our homeland was being threatened by outsiders who knew little about our people and cared even less about us. The vast majority of those of us who wore the gray in the War for Southern Independence had no direct financial interest in slavery. But slavery did provide the invader with the perfect excuse to convince the world that the Yankees had a right to invade, conquer, destroy, and occupy our homeland. Let me tell you about a Southerner who owned no slaves and was not even in the army yet fought to defend his home from Yankee invaders.

"James Keelan was his name," Uncle Seth began. "He lived near a railroad bridge in Strawberry Plains, Tennessee, early in the war. The Confederate government had sent troops to defend the railroad bridge, but demands for troops were so great that they had been recalled for other, more pressing duty. James had accepted the task of guarding the bridge day and night. He slept in a bunkhouse at one end of the bridge and kept a single-shot pistol and a rifle with him there. James was small in stature, with a ruddy complexion, blue eyes, and light brown hair. He had a wife and three children at the time. The attack on the bridge came on a cool and frosty night when the moon was covered by clouds.

"It seems that the United States had hired a Colonel Carter to destroy all the bridges from Hiwassee River at Charleston, Tennessee, to Bristol. The United States paid Colonel Carter ten thousand dollars to attack the various bridges on the night of November the 8th. About midnight, they reached the bridge James was guarding. He was asleep but the noise woke him. He noticed that a group of about fifteen men was approaching in his direction and that several of them were attempting to start a fire at the other end of the bridge in an attempt to set it ablaze. As they set their matches to the pine kindling, James fired a shot from his single-shot pistol and dropped one of the incendiaries. James was then fiercely attacked by as many as could get around him to land a blow—there not being enough of him to allow all the incendiaries to get in a punch! James was shot and struck with clubs, knives, and heavy timbers. He managed to get off a shot with his rifle and then manfully defended himself with a small dirk—you know that's a small Celtic knife. Lights were lit in nearby homes after the first shot. This and the fact that the attackers thought they had killed the little man caused them to beat a hasty retreat," Uncle Seth looked up to see if Carroll Ray was following his story.

"James crawled to Mr. Elmore's home. When the neighbor, who had been awakened from a deep sleep, first saw James, he exclaimed 'Jim, you've been drunk or asleep and let the train run over you!' 'No, Mr. Elmore; they have killed me but I have saved the bridge.' Mr. Elmore immediately called for a surgeon and no effort was spared to preserve the hero's life. James' head was cut open six to seven inches, and the brain was oozing from the dreadful gash; his left hand was cut almost completely off and hanging by a mere shred of skin, and the right hand was also badly cut. He had been shot at many times but had been hit only once. When the surgeon informed James that he would no longer be able to use his rifle because his hand had to be amputated, James responded that he would still be able to brace a gun on the stump of his remaining arm." Uncle Seth's voice was full of admiration.

"Carroll Ray, that's just one example of the unnumbered Southerners who were not slave owners but who were willing to risk everything in order to defend their country from the Yankee invader's torch. I tell you, those people who claim we were fighting for slavery don't understand honor and truth any more than Ole Jeff over there," lamented Uncle Seth as he pointed toward the gray mule.

"Yep," piped in Carroll Ray, "and they're not nearly as smart either!"

§ Deo Vindice §

ON THE SKIRMISH LINE WITH UNCLE SETH

Lamenting the numerous compromises the South was being forced to make as a result of slavery, Thomas Jefferson wrote to a friend, "But as it is, we have the wolf by the ears, and we can neither hold him safely nor let him go. Justice is in one scale, and self-preservation in the other." Slavery was a social issue that required calm reflection to resolve, but it was being used by Northern agitators and politicians as a fiery propaganda tool to fire up their base in order to advance Northern commercial and political interests. What recourse did that leave for the people of the South—a people who valued honor, justice, personal liberty and asked simply to be left alone?

34

Large Slaveholder Opposed Secession

Uncle Seth watched as the young children came marching in from school. He made sure he was always around to count the heads to make sure everyone made it home safely. He would call each by name as they came up the steps and onto the front porch. Peggy Joyce, his oldest granddaughter, was the last to come up the stairs—she would always bring up the rear just to make sure the younger ones did not fall out of rank on the walk home. "Well, Sister," Uncle Seth followed an old Southern tradition of calling the eldest girl in the family "Sister," "what did you learn at school today?"

"Uncle Seth," Peggy Joyce responded, "our new history book called our country the Slaveholder's Confederacy. I told everybody in the class that the book must have been written by a Yankee or a Scallywag Southerner!"

Uncle Seth laughed loudly at Peggy Joyce's defense of her country—the old Confederate veteran felt both pride in his descendent and satisfaction in his efforts to teach them the truth about the War for Southern Independence. "You did good, my child," the old soldier said in a tone of voice that conveyed his love for her, more than a mere acknowledgement of her correct response to the purposeful insult. Peggy Joyce stood there next to his rocking chair because she could tell that the old man wanted to continue his conversation with her.

Uncle Seth held up a small journal he had been reading as if he was presenting evidence to a jury and declared, "So many people in the North—really in the entire world—think we fought for slavery. That is a lie—a damn Yankee lie—used by our oppressors to justify their invasion and conquest of the people of the South. Yet, because they control all the news and educational outlets, the Yankees are able to control the narrative about the war. The Yankee villain in that war can tell the world that the invaded people, who only asked to be left alone, were evil and that the Yankee invaders were crusading for human freedom, justice, and their version of the American way. It's just not fair, Peggy Joyce. I tell you it's just not fair." The old man's voice trailed off to a stern whisper as he lowered the wrinkled journal and dropped it to the floor.

"Take it easy, Uncle Seth," warned Peggy Joyce, "You can't re-fight the war."

"Peggy Joyce," the old Confederate veteran said while looking deeply into her blue eyes as if searching for his past in her future, "I just read about the death of Mr. William M. Doxey of Cameron Parish in Louisiana. Prior to the war he was one of the largest slaveholders in the state of Louisiana. Now, if you believe that our Southern nation was a Slaveholder's Confederacy, then you would think he would have been a rabid secessionist. But not so! He was against secession prior to the war and did all he could to promote pro-Union sentiment in Louisiana. Many large plantation owners were opposed to secession—

William M. Doxey circa 1890

they belonged to the Whig Party and wanted to maintain the Union, even if the Southern people were forced to continue paying a larger cost in taxes and tariffs to do so. That is why ole Abe Lincoln first offered to pass an amendment to the United States Constitution protecting slavery in those states in which it existed, provided those states renounced secession and peacefully returned to the Union. But it did not work—we wanted no part of a Yankee-controlled Union in which we would continue to be the Yankee's cash cow!

"When the war came, men like Mr. Doxey demonstrated that their true loyalty was not to a political party or advantageous economic policies; they demonstrated their loyalty to their people, to the blood and soil of the South. He was too old to join the army, but he promised each volunteer who joined the Cause that their families would never suffer want as long as he had the means to supply their wants. In those days a man's word was his bond. He and his wife kept their word. Colonel Breau, the enrolling officer of the district, put Mr. Doxey in charge of relief for the families of military personnel from the district. Even during the dark and gloomy days of the war when all seemed lost, he maintained his vigilance and stayed true to his post to the very last. No small number of Confederate soldiers from southwest Louisiana—now living and dead—had reason to bless the name of this true, Southern, Christian gentleman."

Many people thought the old Confederate veteran was lost in the past. But Uncle Seth knew that the past—a past full of destruction, oppression, poverty, and slander—will be the South's future if current and rising generations do not understand their country's true history. The old man knew this and he also knew that the Yankee invader who now controls the South knew this as well. That is why they insist on continuing their campaign of lies and slander against a people who only asked to be left alone.

§ Deo Vindice §

35

General Forrest Fights Yankee Jack Ass Raiders

Uncle Seth sat in a comfortable chair in the hotel lobby. He had made the trip from Hazlehurst, Mississippi, to Little Rock, Arkansas, for what he thought would be his last UCV annual reunion. He was still active for a man of eighty-five years, but he knew he could not make many more extensive trips. Billie Jean, the old Confederate veteran's constant companion—he called her his overseer—had been sent to find Capt. James Dinkins of New Orleans, who had promised to meet with Uncle Seth during the reunion. Captain Dinkins had been a member of Gen. Nathan Bedford Forrest's command, and Uncle Seth wanted to get a full account of General Forrest's capture of Yankee General Streight. Eventually Billie Jean returned with Captain Dinkins.

"Captain Dinkins," Uncle Seth stood and extended his hand, "I have been looking forward to meeting you. I understand that you are one of the last surviving officers of General Forrest's command."

"Yes, Seth, I sometimes feel like the last leaf on a mighty oak tree in late fall with a strong, cold wind blowing," Captain Dinkins said as he and Uncle Seth sat down.

"Captain," Uncle Seth began, "I have always been impressed with the action against General Streight. Why don't you tell Billie Jean and me about that action?"

"It was a prolonged running battle in which we were as usual greatly outnumbered by the Yankee invaders. At the end of the running battle, all we had was around five hundred men and the Yankees had more than fifteen hundred men. Colonel Streight was at Tuscumbia, Alabama, and had orders to march toward Rome, Georgia, destroying everything in between, capturing Rome and destroying all railroads.

"The Yankees outnumbered us, but this time they were short on horses so they stole all the mules from the surrounding country and mounted many of their men

Gen. Nathan Bedford Forrest (Library of Congress

on mules. Now, this was the origin of what we called the Yankee Jack Ass raid. We could always tell where the Yankees were because every morning the mules would begin braying—as mules tend to do when they expect to be fed. You should have been there. It was something to hear, more than a thousand mules braying for their breakfast each morning." Captain Dinkins could not restrain the humor and began laughing loudly while slapping his knee with his right hand.

"Now, Billie Jean," Uncle Seth interrupted the jovial moment, "you need to understand what it means when an invader steals all the plow mules. It means starvation for the civilians who are left with very limited means to grow food. Mules are essential for an agricultural people, and without them there is no way to grow enough food to keep the people alive. And don't ever doubt the fact that the starvation of the Southern people was just what the Yankee invader had in mind."

After catching his breath, Captain Dinkins began again. "We began our efforts against them in the rugged mountains of northern Alabama and ended just outside of Rome, Georgia, a distance of around 125 to 150 miles. By the time we got to Rome, we had ridden close to one hundred and fifty miles almost without stopping. Some of our men were going to sleep while still in the saddle and falling to the ground. We had almost no food but we had put the fear of God in the Yankees and we were determined to keep the fear of God in them until they surrendered.

"I recall our first attack against the Yankee Jack Asses, as we impolitely called them. It was night and General Forrest ordered us to dismount; the Yankees did not know we were close. We detached the horses from our artillery and pushed the cannons by hand. We got within 150 yards of the invading United States forces before we said 'hello.' We opened with cannon and rifle fire as fast as we could fire and reload. The United States army broke and fled the field in wild disarray. They left many of their dead and wounded behind and never even returned fire. We had put the scare in them and General Forrest knew that once we did that all we needed to do was to keep the pressure on. Eventually the scare would make their superior numbers meaningless.

"General Forrest ordered us to mount and pursue the enemy. Their trail was littered with discarded supplies, broken equipment, and wounded and dead Yankees. That was the way ole Abe Lincoln supplied us with our food and much-needed military supplies. It was around three o'clock in the morning and the civilians nearby were terror stricken by the sound of the battle. Many fled their homes and sought safety in the heavy underbrush and thick forest of the mountains. The civilians knew that if the Yankee invaders came close to their homes, the Yankees would burn them out and kill as many as they desired. General Forrest halted us and told us to grab a quick nap before we renewed the pursuit. While we were getting some much-needed rest, the general had ammunition brought up to us so we would be ready to begin the work again as soon as dawn began to break in the eastern sky. When daylight dawned, we had been without food for more than two days, but we began the pursuit with renewed vigor.

"General Forrest took his escort and one squadron of the 4th Tennessee Regiment and, moving rapidly, reached Blountsville around eleven that morning. Imagine our surprise when we found Yankee Jack Ass raiders who had halted to rest, thinking that they were safe. We drove the Yankee pickets in and as the Yankees fled they set fire to their supply wagons. The Yankees headed off toward Gadsden, without offering to put up a fight and with General Streight at the head of the column. He wasn't running—no, he was leading a parade toward Gadsden!" Once again, Captain Dinkins was enjoying the humor of his enemy's humiliation.

"Now, never one to waste an opportunity to resupply at Lincoln's expense, General Forrest ordered a group of his men to put the fire out and save the supplies in the wagons the Yankees had so thoughtfully left for us. When General Forrest saw that the Yankees were not intending to make a stand, he returned to see about 'his' supplies. A number of men were working feverishly to extinguish the fires and collect the supplies—all except for their lieutenant, who was sitting on his horse observing his men at work. General Forrest rode up to the lieutenant and inquired why he was not helping the men. The lieutenant replied, 'Because I am an officer.' General Forrest's face turned bright red as he drew his sword and loudly declared with numerous oaths, unspeakable in polite company, that he would show him what he thought of a man who was more concerned about his status than 'my supplies.' To avoid the general's sword, the lieutenant leaped from his horse and ran to help extinguish the fire and save the General's supplies.

"After resupplying, with the loss of very little time, General Forrest renewed the pursuit. We were relentless in our pursuit—every time we passed a burned home or civilians who had been robbed by the army of the United States, we were even more determined to deliver justice to our country's invaders. We overhauled the Yankees before they reached the Black Warrior River; about ten miles from Blountsville, and a running fight began. The ford at the Black Warrior River was rocky, steep, and rather dangerous even when time was of no matter. But with us at their rear and closing fast, time was of essence for the Yankees. Before all had crossed the river, we were upon them and captured a number of them, causing many of their pack mules to drown. Poor creatures, it was a shame. I'm a-talking about the mules of course.

"Oh, I forgot to tell you about the teenage girls who captured several Yankees and brought them to us. We were about a mile from the Black Warrior River, pushing the Yankees hard, when we noticed three or four blue-clad soldiers, unarmed and walking toward us. Behind them were two young girls riding two of the Yankees' horses and leading the other horses, Yankee rifles slung over their young shoulders and each with a loaded Springfield caped, cocked, and ready to fire. All pointed directly at the Yankees—who were marching meekly toward us. The very sight caused us all to halt and burst out in loud laughter—no doubt adding even more humiliation to the heretofore proud and arrogant Yankee invaders. It seems that the Yankees came to the young girls and told them that they could not continue fighting night and day and would prefer to surrender to any Southerner who would accept their surrender—'we just want to rest' was their reasoning. These brave little girls were dressed in homespun clothes and were barefoot but clean, neat, and well mannered. General Forrest relieved them of their prisoners and told them to keep the horses they were riding—which looked as if they could hardly hold the weight of young girls. The horses were probably as glad to surrender as the Yankees.

"After the fight at Black Warrior River, General Forrest ordered another short rest, five hours, to allow food to be brought up to the horses. See, General Forrest knew we soldiers would not let exhaustion or lack of food stop us, but our horses needed rest and food. Without them we could not keep the pressure on the invaders. The general was everywhere looking after the provisions of food for horses and ammunition for his men. I don't believe he slept at all during this entire running fight. Shortly after midnight, he ordered us to begin our pursuit again. The Yankees destroyed every bridge they crossed in an effort to slow us down, but it had little effect. We were in hot pursuit, headed toward Wills Creek, which is about fifteen miles at the far end of Wills Valley. This was where the Yankees were resting and feeding their mules and the few horses they had. They had no food for the men because the blue-clad invaders, in their haste to avoid Confederate justice, had abandoned most of their food. We were more than glad to receive it. Unfortunately, it was being picked up by the units following behind us—we were too busy pushing Yankees to stop and pick up abandoned Yankee food. When Colonel Streight realized that we were attacking him yet again, he left without ceremony; he, his command, and his troops just grabbed what they could and headed in the direction opposite from the sound of that damnable Rebel Yell. We captured twenty-five Yankees and a hundred negroes—some of whom were dressed in Yankee uniforms—an abundance of forage, and ten pack mules.

"By this time we were all but worn out after three days and nights of constant moving and fighting. We were beginning to show signs of exhaustion and perhaps a desire to stop the pursuit. General Forrest would not for a moment consider letting his quarry off so easy. But he knew the limits of human endurance—even Southerners fighting to protect their homes and families could reach those limits. But the general knew us well and he judged us yet able to go the last mile. Then providence gave the general the perfect opportunity to encourage us. Several ladies whose husbands and friends had been seized and carried off by the Yankees appeared and filled our camp with their sad wails and appeals to restore their kinsmen. Their appeals had the desired effect on us—which the general knew it would—and we were all immediately filled with a burning desire to get at the Yankee enemy and rain down on him the justice he deserved. The general called us together and told us he intended to put an end to this group of Yankee invaders, and he knew we were just the men he needed at this crucial moment to do the job. He called for all who were willing to follow him to come forward, and we all rushed to his side. The women shouted encouragements and thanks to us as we rode in pursuit of our Yankee enemies. We moved off at a gallop, five hundred strong with only two artillery pieces to support our attack against more than fifteen hundred Yankees.

"We overhauled the Yankees again. It was around ten o'clock when General Forrest called for fifty volunteers of the best mounted men, with whom he and his escort charged headlong into the rear of the Yankee column. Facing hot Yankee fire, we pressed the Yankees. This turned into another running battle for around ten miles. When the Yankees decided to make another stand, I think it was around Black Creek, and after a heavy skirmish, Colonel Streight crossed the creek and burned the bridge. It was a deep, fast-flowing creek and no doubt the Yankees thought they would be safe. It was here that yet another young, sixteen-year-old Southern girl came to her country's defense. Over her mother's objection, she took General Forrest's hand as he helped her up onto his horse behind the general and began to guide the Confederate forces to a ford that would allow us to get safely across the creek. The girl's mother was not concerned about Yankee retribution—everyone faced that threat—but she was more concerned about what people would say about her young daughter riding away with strangers. General Forrest calmed the mother's anxiety and promised to return the young woman safely to her mother. Yes, she did her country a great favor. Her name is Emma Sanson, and the State of Alabama gave her a reward of several acres of public land, several years ago, in recognition of her service to the Confederate Cause.

"After fording Black Creek, we rode hard and soon reached Gadsden, which was about three miles from the ford. General Forrest sent couriers ahead to Rome, Georgia, to warn the people there and tell them to call out all available militia, which was mostly old men and young boys, and hold the Yankee invaders in place until he arrived. General Forrest rushed forward with three hundred men; the other two hundred, along with two artillery pieces, were following some distance behind us. The enemy, however, after being checked before Rome, Georgia, knew we had to be coming up behind them. They set up a very well-arranged ambush, and had it been sprung on any other commander it might have worked. But not with General Forrest. The general led his escort in a vigorous flanking attack that caused the Yankees to fold and the remaining Yankees fled. They left some fifty wounded and dead on the field. We had six wounded and lost two men.

"During the engagement, Sgt. William Haynes of the 4th Tennessee was captured and taken before Colonel Streight, who demanded to know how many men Forrest had coming against him. The Confederate prisoner, without hesitation, conjured up several phantom brigades that had supposedly been attached to Forrest's command for the purpose of capturing the Yankee Jack Ass Raiders. When Streight heard the news, he exclaimed, "Oh my God, he has us now!' During the night, Sergeant Haynes made his escape and returned to inform General Forrest about his phantom army. By sunrise on May 3, the Confederates from Gadsden, two hundred men and two artillery pieces, had re-united with the main force—giving General Forrest five hundred men and two artillery pieces to face off against more than fifteen hundred Yankees and a battery of artillery consisting of six pieces. But we had put the scare in them and we had General Forrest leading us.

"The invaders had been in full flight all night; and by sunrise on May 3rd they were pretty much spent—their fighting vigor all but gone, worn out by a handful of hungry, ill-clad but patriotic Southerners. We had to ford the Coosa River because the Yankees had burned the bridge. We dismounted and hand carried the ammunition chest across just like we did at Black Creek. When the horses pulling the two artillery pieces across went into the river, the pieces went completely underwater, but our horses pulled them through. Before long, we were once again hot on the trail of our blue-coated enemies. We once again overhauled the Yankees. It was around 9 a.m. and they were busy eating their breakfast and drinking their coffee—thinking, of course, that they were safe because they had burned the bridge across the Coosa River. With shouts of Rebel Yells and well-placed gun fire, we convinced the Yankees to abandon their dining experience and try out their running shoes. They left us hot coffee, a number of mules and horses, saddles, and other spoils. Their commander rallied his men on a ridge in an open field, but his men were greatly demoralized. It was at this time that General Forrest demonstrated that a bluff in the hands of an expert can take a straight." Captain Dinkins again chuckled at his own joke.

"General Forrest sent forward his men as skirmishers on the left and right, while he and his escort threatened an attack on the center of the Yankee line. He ordered a ceasefire and sent Capt. Henry Pointer forward under a flag of truce offering Colonel Streight an opportunity to surrender and avoid the 'needless destruction of [his] command.' Colonel Streight requested a meeting with General Forrest, and in the meeting the Yankee insisted that he be allowed to see for himself that he was indeed hopelessly outnumbered. General Forrest replied that he would not insult his men, who had bested the Yankee invader at every encounter during this lengthy running engagement, by having them reviewed by a Yankee. During their conversation General Forest's men would come up and report the arrival of another phantom unit and ask him where he wanted them placed. Colonel Streight was also counting the arrival of each new artillery piece, but in reality it was the same two pieces that would make a wide circle and come back into the colonel's view. The artillery maneuver was done so well that Colonel Streight asked General Forrest how many artillery pieces he had at his disposal, to which General Forrest replied, 'Enough to destroy you and your command in thirty minutes. It would have been sooner than that but the rest could not keep up.' While Colonel Streight continued to hesitate, General Forrest ordered his men to prepare for a full assault to commence in fifteen minutes. Hearing this, the Yankee colonel asked to return to his command and consult his officers. On his way back to his line, Colonel Streight was shocked to see several of his officers coming toward him under another flag of truce. They quickly informed him that his men were exhausted and had no desire to continue the struggle. Colonel Streight then surrendered. The Yankees surrendered six artillery pieces, two colonels, one lieutenant colonel, four majors, and around fifteen hundred men with their captains, lieutenants, and non-commissioned officers." Captain Dinkins finished his story with the enthusiasm and pride of one who had been there and knew the horrors of war and the dedication of the men who wore the gray in the War for Southern Independence.

§ Deo Vindice §

ON THE SKIRMISH LINE WITH UNCLE SETH
Yankee General Sherman compliments Southern fighting skills: "War suits them, and the rascals are brave, fine riders, bold to rashness, and dangerous subjects in every sense. They are the most dangerous men which this war has turned loose on the world. When the resources of *their* country are exhausted, we must employ them. They are the best cavalry in the world" (Emphasis added).

Notice how the Yankee, during the war, was already planning to make use of his conquered foe as soon as the war was over. Even before the end of his efforts to incorporate the Southern people into his newly created empire, the arrogant Yankee looks forward to the day when he can use Southern blood in his future conquest. This is the way of empires—they eventually pacify the conquered peoples and use the sons of the conquered people as cannon fodder in future imperialistic wars. The Federal Empire has followed the same path.

36

Choosing Slavery in Mississippi Over Freedom in Pennsylvania

Uncle Seth leaned on his hoe and slowly wiped the drops of perspiration from his brow. The early spring had brought new weeds to his garden and he was determined to keep them out of his patch in the family's garden. Looking up the lane running beside the house, he noticed a large, dark form of a man. "Who's that a-coming down the road, boy?" Uncle Seth asked his great-grandchildren who were pretending to help in the garden.

"That's Jessie," Carroll Ray announced before taking the opportunity to drop his hoe and wander over toward the road and wait for Jessie's arrival. Jessie frequently came over to borrow Ole Jeff, the mule, when he needed an extra to hitch with his mule to pull his wagon. Jessie turned in toward the barn and gave Uncle Seth a wave.

"That young man sure looks like his father. He carries himself just like his father did," declared Uncle Seth. "I should know. We walked many a mile together during the war," the veteran said as he lifted his hand and waved toward Jessie.

"But Uncle Seth," exclaimed Billie Jean, "Jessie is a black man! You said that his father was a slave on the Page farm before the war. Why would his father want to fight with the Confederate army?" asked Billie Jean.

"Billie Jean," began Uncle Seth, "that's a story that few people—black or white, Northern or Southern—can understand. The more time that passes, the harder it is even to tell the story—tell it and have those who weren't there understand it, that is.

"I recall talking to a young man during the war named C. C. Cumming—we called him C. C. He lives in Fort Worth, Texas, the last I heard from him, but he was originally from here in Mississippi. His father owned a large plantation north of here. C. C. had a body servant by the name of George. They were about the same age and actually grew up together hunting and fishing on and around the plantation. When war came, C. C. volunteered. George refused to stay on the plantation if his master left for war. By law and custom, they were master and servant, but in reality, they were the best of friends. So C. C. and George went off to war together. This was not that unusual—as a matter of fact, quite a few former slaves are still today drawing state pensions earned by their service to the Confederacy during the war. Well, George stayed with C. C. at First Manassas, Leesburg—where he helped capture several large guns—Chancellorsville, Sharpsburg, and, at last, Gettysburg. At Gettysburg, C. C. was wounded during the second day fighting in the Peach Orchard. George located an ambulance in which he loaded C. C., a sergeant major and Colonel Holder of the 17th Mississippi, and an officer of the 21st Mississippi. The retreat was so slow they were able to cover only a few miles that first day. The Yankees were bearing down on them and C. C. feared George's capture by the Yankees more than his own. George and C. C. had already heard that the Yankees were separating all black Southerners from captured white Southerners. You see, they knew the Yankees would treat a loyal black Southerner much harsher than they would treat a white Southerner. Many times captured black Southerners would not be given rations in the POW camps. So C. C. insisted that George leave them and move on with the withdrawing Confederate army. But George refused to leave his friend. Soon they were cut off from the main body of Confederates and knew it would be only a short time before they were captured. On their march into Pennsylvania they marched through a settlement of free blacks located a short distance from where they were then hiding. C. C. advised George to declare his freedom and make his way to the settlement of free blacks. 'No sir! I'd stay 'iffen I could, but least I can do is catch-up with our army and cross the river [the Potomac]. When you get exchanged, I'll be there to meet you on the other side of the river.' Those were the last words George spoke to C. C. as he turned to make his escape. He paused and returned to give C. C. his only canteen of water and the last bit of hard tack he had. Thus, this faithful friend gave all he had and departed for the Potomac and, hopefully, Mississippi." Uncle Seth's voice seemed to waiver—something his great-grandchildren had never before heard.

Uncle Seth cleared his throat, regained his composure, and continued. "On his way back to catch up with the rest of our army, George was stopped by a lady who inquired about one of the wounded that George had assisted as he left Pennsylvania. In spite of the danger of roving Yankee cavalry, George stopped and gave what little information he had to the distressed lady. While he was talking to her, a group of Yankee cavalry spotted him in his gray uniform. George turned and attempted to escape, only to be killed by Yankee bullets. The lady had him buried and then found her son just as George had told her she would."

Uncle Seth turned away from the children to wipe the moisture from his eyes and, with his back to them, slowly walked away. The children did not understand but knew not to follow him. Uncle Seth knew that this generation—nor any other, black or white—could understand the relationship between so many of both races who wore the gray in the War for Southern Independence. Uncle Seth wasn't sure about his feelings either. He was glad that Jessie was born and reared never knowing human bondage, but he remembered many a good day before and during the war when he and Jessie's father worked and enjoyed life together. How odd that, in all of the stories about the sacrifices of his fellow white Confederate soldiers, he had never been forced by tears to interrupt a story, yet this story about a black Southerner who preferred his natural friends over freedom was almost more than he could tell. Jessie was a good neighbor and his father had been a good friend. More than that Uncle Seth could not explain—or maybe it was that he simply felt that such tender connections between natural friends just did not need an explanation.

§ Deo Vindice §

ON THE SKIRMISH LINE WITH UNCLE SETH

After the Battle of Gettysburg, a group of 250 wounded Confederate prisoners of war were forced into manure-encrusted cattle cars and shipped off to prison. The train made a short stop in York City, Pennsylvania. Numerous locals crowed around the cattle cars, offering the wounded Southern soldiers an opportunity to avoid prison camp and future fighting. All they had to do was to sign an oath of allegiance to the United States and they would be paroled, given a place to stay until the end of the war, and then provided passage back home. Of the 250 half-naked, half-starved, and wounded Confederate soldiers on that train, not a single one accepted the enemy's offer. Our Yankee masters would have Southern children and the world believe that these men and thousand like them were fighting to keep their slaves. The truth is that they were fighting to keep their children and their children's children from becoming slaves to the Yankee Empire.

37

A Gallant Saber Fight

The rocking chair squeaked its familiar sounds as Uncle Seth rocked back and forth. Sitting on the front porch in the still of the evening was the old Confederate veteran's "remembering time." He had much to be thankful for: a full life, many years of watching his children, grandchildren, and now even his great-grandchildren grow. Like his beloved Southland, the mere fact that he had survived and, in some small measure, prospered, was enough to make him happy. But, like the South, the totality of his existence seemed to have been molded, marred, and measured by the experiences and consequences of the War for Southern Independence. Therefore he remembered. He remembered not for himself but for those around him who would not understand unless he told them why. Why he found it necessary to remember, why he and his comrades fought, why it was important that each succeeding generation of Southerners should remember, why the fight continues with each new generation—a fight to uphold honorable principles of constitutional government and a fight to deny the invader the ability to slander the Southern people in order to justify the invader's aggression. He remembered in order for his people to know the real reason why he and his comrades wore the gray in the War for Southern Independence.

The sudden slamming of the screen door announced the presence of one of his "boys"—the term he used to refer to all of his youthful male kinfolk.

"What you doing, Uncle Seth?" asked Joe William.

Now Joe William's inquiry was more in the way of a conversation starter than an attempt to determine what his great-grandfather was doing. Everyone knew and followed the routine, which was rather common in the South in the early 1900s. After supper the men and boys would gather on the porch. The younger ones would engage in youthful banter while keeping an ear tuned to Uncle Seth. They knew that sooner or later he would regale them with one of his war stories. Everyone, from the youngest boy to the mature men, respected the old Confederate veteran. He had earned respect long before most of them were born. It only seemed right that they should accord a man of his age and experience great respect. Without knowing it, the grown men were setting the example of how they expected their youngsters to treat them when they too became elderly. The extended family, with no compulsion other than a sense of duty to one of their own, was engaged in maintaining a social security system based on blood ties, honor, and Christian ethics.

Joe William pulled out his pocketknife, opened it, and drew a large circle on the ground in front of the porch. He then issued a challenge to all the other boys to a game of "mumble-peg." To his dismay, none of them accepted his challenge.

"Uncle Seth," he cried out, "no one wants to accept my challenge!"

"You must be too good for them," chuckled Uncle Seth. "It reminds me of the day that Capt. John G. Ballentine of the 7th Tennessee Cavalry accepted a Yankee's challenge to a saber duel," Uncle Seth declared. The boys quickly settled down around the old Confederate veteran, eagerly anticipating another exciting war story from Uncle Seth. Even the men on the porch stopped talking and quietly turned a curious ear to the beloved old man's story.

"It was around the spring of 1862, shortly before the Battle of Shiloh. Major Schaeffer, commander of a battalion of United States troops, came down from occupied areas around Paducah, Kentucky, and had set out on a raid to harass the civilian population in West Tennessee. I was with the 7th Tennessee Calvary and we were sent out from Jackson, Tennessee, to intercept this U.S. force. We managed to catch up with the Yankees just as they were going into camp. Most of them had dismounted and were in the process of making camp for the evening. Col. W. H. Jackson sized up the situation in an instant and immediately gave us the order to 'charge-em boys!' The United States Calvary's first hint of their impending doom was when they heard us, as if with one voice, giving the Rebel Yell as we charged amongst them like redeeming angels sent to destroy demons from the infernal regions. We caught the Yankee invader flatfooted. They only had time to mount their horses, point them north, and skedaddle. Many of the Federals were captured on the spot. That action began a four-mile-long flight and fight. The Yankees were trying to put distance between us while we were trying to put Southern steel into them! Many unfortunate Yanks were killed and more were captured, including Major Schaeffer. Likely, all of them would have suffered a similar fate but for the lateness of the evening and coming darkness. Just before dark, I was riding next to Captain Ballentine. He and I were well mounted and had managed to overtake the head of the Yankee stampede. Captain Ballentine was riding down on a Federal cavalryman who had emptied his cavalry carbine and both of his pistols. The captain pointed his Navy six-shooter at the Yankee and ordered him to surrender. Instead of surrendering, the Yankee threw down his empty guns and, while looking directly into the captain's eyes, the Yank tapped his saber. Now, boys, this was a challenge that honor would not allow the captain to ignore. He returned his loaded revolver to its holster and drew his sword, which was only a small officer's saber. Now all of this was done while both horses were in full gallop! The captain was only about 135 pounds and had only his small officer's sword. The well-fed Yankee must have been around 180 pounds and was armed with a much larger cavalry saber. During the fight, the captain's hat was sliced through to the brim and his coat was pierced through by a thrust of the Yankee's saber. The captain ended the contest with a well-aimed thrust into the U.S. cavalryman's back.

"Captain Ballentine," continued Uncle Seth, "was raised in Pulaski, Tennessee, and educated at Yale. His father had been a British army officer and taught his son to be an expert swordsman. After the war, Captain Ballentine was elected to the U. S. Congress twice." Uncle Seth reached into his pocket, pulled out his pocket-knife, opened it, and expertly threw it into Joe William's circle.

§ Deo Vindice §

ON THE SKIRMISH LINE WITH UNCLE SETH

On September 22, 1862, Mr. Lincoln issued another proclamation in which he declared that the object of the war was to restore the Union and that in all the Southern states—which might reenter the Union by January 1, 1863—the institution of slavery should remain under the control of those states and be retained or relinquished, as they might see fit. It was a clear and unmistakable offer that, if the South would renounce independence, it could retain slavery. Not a single Southern state accepted Lincoln's offer. Why? Because we were not fighting for slavery; we were fighting for our freedom! The Yankee Empire fears that if Southerners understand this the South will rise again.

38

The South and the Origins of Slavery in America

"Hurry up, Billie Jean," Uncle Seth called out to his great-granddaughter. He wanted to make sure Billie Jean did not miss Dr. M'Kim's speech. He knew it would be the high point of the Nashville United Confederate Veterans annual reunion. Each year, Uncle Seth selected one of his great-grandchildren to attend the reunion with him. He wanted them to be able to one day pass on to their children the stories about the men who wore the gray in the War for Southern Independence. It was his way to get even with all those anti-South Yankee textbooks that had become the fad throughout the Southern education establishment.

Uncle Seth and Billie Jean made their way into the meeting hall and took their seats. "Now, Billie Jean," admonished Uncle Seth, "I want you to listen to what Dr. M'Kim has to say about how slavery got started in this county. The next time your teacher tells you the war was fought over slavery, I want you to tell your classmates the truth."

Soon Dr. M'Kim was introduced and began his lecture. Billie Jean greatly enjoyed coming to reunions, but as far as she was concerned speeches like this were the price she had to pay in order for Uncle Seth to invite her. Besides, what could these speakers tell her that Uncle Seth had not already explained to her several times? But being the obedient child she was, she sat quietly as Dr. M'Kim began his speech.

"New England educators and the vulgar press," he began, "tell the world that slavery was the cause of the war and that the citizen-soldiers of the South sprang to arms in defense of slavery. I take this opportunity to remind the world that the merchants of New England seaports monopolized the immense profits of that lucrative and detestable trade. And when it came to the

Dr. M'Kim

principal of abolition, it was profits, not humanity, that motivated the New Englander. Their entire effort was to transfer slaves held by Northern slave owners to Southern markets. Profits and a desire to rid themselves of a people of color with whom they had no desire to mix were their motives. On March 26, 1788, the legislature of that grand New England State of Massachusetts passed a law ordering all free Negroes out of the state. If any failed to comply, they would be publicly flogged. Remember it is the fine New England State of Massachusetts that has the distinction of being the first American colony to legalize slavery and also the first to pass a fugitive slave act."

Dr. M'Kim paused and looked around the audience to judge the impact of his words. When he had assured himself, he continued, "I call your attention to a fact that is of capital importance in this discussion—that is the South's early view on the abolition of slavery. The desire to abolish slavery was very strong and spreading rapidly in the South early in our history. In 1826, there were 143 emancipation societies in the whole U.S.A. Of that number, 103 were established in the South. It is well-known that in 1832, one branch of the Virginia Legislature came within one vote of abolishing slavery in the state. I was assured in 1860 by Col. Thomas Jefferson Randolph, Pres. Thomas Jefferson's grandson, who was a member of that 1832 Legislature, that emancipation would have certainly been carried out in the following year had it not been for the fanatical agitation of the subject by the New England abolitionists. It is my belief that, but for passions naturally roused by the violent attacks made upon the moral character of the Southern slaveholder, in contradistinction to Northern slaveholders of the period, slavery would have been peaceably abolished in the border states before the middle of the nineteenth century."

Billie Jean looked up at Uncle Seth's face; he seemed to be drinking in every word, totally unaware of her presence. She slipped her arm through his and pressed her cheek against his arm. Uncle Seth's past was becoming a part of her future.

"Fanatics and abolitionists," continued Dr. M'Kim, "demanded immediate emancipation without compensation or consideration of any kind. England abolished slavery in the West Indies in 1833, but they compensated the slave owners, devoting $100,000,000 to that purpose. But, in the long history of New England's agitation on the subject of abolition—from 1836 to 1861—those people never made any proposition to remunerate the South for the loss of her slaves. The people of the South were expected to make a sacrifice that had never before been required of any people and that New Englanders had earlier specifically avoided. New England made a profit and cleansed her states by her simple experiment in abolition. She then turned upon the people of the South and demanded that we both bankrupt our economy and turn a slave population loose within our states—a population that had never before in history engaged in democratic government!"

By this time, Billie Jean was fast asleep. Uncle Seth eased her head down on his leg. "Oh well," he thought, "what she does not hear today I'll be sure to tell her tomorrow. That's the way it is with old soldiers of a 'lost cause.' We never quit fighting, and I hope our blood relatives in generations to come never quit fighting—at least not until the South is once again a free nation."

§ Deo Vindice §

ON THE SKIRMISH LINE WITH UNCLE SETH

When the Yankees captured the Southern privateer vessel *Savannah* early in the war, Lincoln issued a proclamation declaring all private vessels carrying arms to be pirates, which allowed the U.S. government to hang them as pirates. This was in conflict with the laws of nations and brought a condemnation from the British House of Lords. In their condemnation of Lincoln's proclamation, the House of Lords noted that privateering was not piracy. After much international controversy, Lincoln recalled his piracy proclamation. Always remember that the Yankee Pres. Abraham Lincoln recalled his piracy proclamation not because he realized the immorality of sending privateers to the gallows but because his immorality had been made public. He was no different than the man-eating lion retreating from the village of innocent humans not because it had lost his taste for human flesh but out of fear of the huntsman's rifle. When the huntsman's rifle is no longer present, the bloodthirsty beast will return.

39

The Girl Who Saved General Lee's Army

An early spring chill was in the air as Uncle Seth rocked in his chair next to the fireplace hearth. Billie Jean, his young great-granddaughter, climbed onto his lap and snuggled next to him more out of love for the old man than to break the chill.

"Billie Jean," began Uncle Seth, "you know, a young girl not much older than you helped to save General Lee's whole army during the war." Almost before Billie Jean could offer encouragement to him, the old Confederate veteran began to relate his story.

"It was in early spring of 1865, the war was almost over, we were worn down, our equipment was all but worn out, and our once invincible ranks depleted. We knew the end was coming but were determined that our Confederacy would 'die game.' I was serving around Petersburg, Virginia. Gen. A. P. Hill sent me and four others out to find out what United States general Grant intended to do. The next morning, four of us left the safety of our camp and crossed both our line and the Federal line. We cautiously made our way to the rear of Grant's army. It was our duty to get the information back to General Hill regardless of the dangers we faced. We knew the U.S. forces would most likely shoot us as spies if they caught us, even though we were in the attire of Southern soldiers. By the accepted rules of war you do not shoot as spies men caught behind your lines if they are in uniform. But Union soldiers often overlooked such niceties.

"Local civilians had warmly received us during prior scouting expeditions. We had become acquainted with a local family who lived in a small log cabin not more than a mile from the Yankee encampment. They were just like the plain folk who made up most of our country: fiercely patriotic and willing to do anything they could to defend their state and country. Their humble log cabin was always open to Southern soldiers. The log cabin was home to an elderly mother, a young boy, and two girls, the older not yet eighteen years old. The boy had often been useful in obtaining information from local Yankees. He would go into the Yankee camp selling homemade pies and come back full of vital information that we would take back to General Lee.

"We had left that cabin about mid afternoon and traveled the back roads until around midnight. Our captain heard a horse coming down the road and ordered us to prepare an ambush. As the nightrider came into our trap the captain sprung the trap, grabbed the horse's bridle, and commanded the rider to halt! In a flash, the rider pointed and fired a revolver at our captain—the bullet barely grazing him. He immediately pulled the rider to the ground only to be startled at the voice of a young girl as she struggled with him. 'Would you murder a woman?' she asked more as an insult than an inquiry. We immediately recognized the voice as that of the young girl from the log cabin.

"It seemed that shortly after we left the cabin, Yankee troops began to march past their cabin. It was easy to find out from the troops where they were going. Their plan was to get to the rear of Lee's army. If they could do it before we found out, it would force General Lee to surrender. This young girl rode from early afternoon and into the dark night, alone, on roads crawling with Yankee bummers, Jay Hawkers, and other criminal types. She had crossed several swollen streams. During one of the crossings her horse went under and plunged her into the cold, dark, and deep waters. She was almost frozen when she came upon us. We wrapped her in one of our gray blankets and gave her a shot of brandy. I took her back home while my comrades split up and headed back to our lines. When we got to her cabin I hid her in the woods while I went to make sure no Yankees were stationed in her cabin. I peered into the cabin and found her aged mother on her knees praying for her daughter's safe return. In no time at all I had her back in the warmth of her mother's humble home.

"Two of the other four scouts made it back to Confederate headquarters in time—one of the four was caught and executed by the Yankee invaders. General Hill was suspecting an attack by the Federals. He got his army on the move and sent word to General Lee. In less than five hours the army was in line of battle. Because of the patriotic courage of this young girl, General Lee was able to meet Grant at every point of attack. Even at such a late hour in our struggle for freedom, our army was still determined to prove to the world our devotion to the cause of Southern independence. We could not have lasted so many years had it not been for the support of our people, none more heroic than that young girl."

Billie Jean looked up at Uncle Seth with eyes betraying uninhibited admiration for the old man. He was unconsciously reaching back into ancient memory and projecting it far into the future. Uncle Seth was doing a great work; and because of him and many others like him, generations of Southerners yet unborn would one day remember and perhaps honor those brave men who wore the gray in the War for Southern Independence.

§ Deo Vindice §

40

CSS *Alabama* Sinks the USS *Hatteras*

Uncle Seth was up early in the morning and had already started a fire in the wood stove to brew the morning coffee. It was the first day of September 1924 and the elderly Confederate veteran was still following his usual routine of rising early, brewing his coffee, and planning his day before the rest of his extended family rolled out of bed. Billie Jean, the old man's great-granddaughter, came in as he reached up to change the calendar from August to September. The calendar, usually given away by a local business, was used much like a Southern almanac. It had the phases of the moon—important for planting and other farming chores—as well as predictions for the weather, gestation records necessary for the purpose of breeding livestock, and significant historical dates such as birthdays for Generals Lee and Stonewall Jackson and President Davis.

"Look, Billie Jean," Uncle Seth announced as he studied the new calendar page, "September 27 is Adm. Raphael Semmes' birthday."

"Who is he, Uncle Seth?" the young girl asked, knowing that she would get more than just a short answer.

"Admiral Semmes was the most successful commerce raider to ever attack the United States naval commerce fleet. None of the Kaiser's fancy U-Boats even came close to sinking as many of the United States merchant marine ships as the Confederate Admiral Semmes did in the CSS *Sumter* and the CSS *Alabama*." Uncle Seth's voice was full of pride—as if he was celebrating the distress of a detested enemy.

"Come over here and let me tell you what one of his officers told us about the fight the CSS *Alabama* had with the USS *Hatteras*. I was attending the Alabama United Confederate Veterans reunion held that year; it was back in the 1890s, in Mobile, Alabama. You know that Admiral Semmes is buried in the Old Catholic Cemetery in Mobile—he

CSS Alabama (Courtsey Charles Hayes)

died August of 1877. Well anyway, one of the *Alabama*'s officers was there to regale us about the adventures they had chasing Yankee merchantmen, burning Yankee ships, and sinking one of those hated Yankee gunboats off the shore of Texas." Uncle Seth stopped long enough to pour some steaming coffee into his tin cup—the same one he carried during the last year of the War for Southern Independence.

"The Yankee invaders were occupying New Orleans, Louisiana, and when they were not busy oppressing the citizens of that Southern city, they busied themselves with making plans to invade and destroy the Confederate state of Texas. Now you recall that Texas had seceded from Mexico and had established itself as an independent republic before it voluntarily joined the Union. The New Englanders tried to prevent Texas from joining the Union, but their efforts failed. Now, twenty-two years later, they were trying to convince the world that the poor New Englanders could not survive as a nation without Texas and her Southern sister states! Well, Yankee General Banks had taken over in New Orleans and had planned to rendezvous his fleet and army at Galveston, Texas, on the tenth of January, 1863. Poor ole Banks, he spent the entire war trying to locate an army he could defeat! You know that General Stonewall Jackson gave him quite a beating in the Shenandoah Valley up in Virginia. By the way, Billie Jean, ole Banks never did find that army!

"The *Alabama* was cruising the Gulf of Mexico at the time and Admiral Semmes wanted to pay General Banks' invasion fleet a courtesy call before returning to his primary task as a commerce raider. As they approached the cost of Galveston, they could hear the sound of naval bombardment. Now, Admiral Semmes had expected to find Banks in possession of Galveston but it appeared that the Yankee invaders were bombarding Galveston. It was later learned that the brave Texans had attacked Yankee-occupied Galveston and driven the hated invader from the soil of Texas. Now the invader was using his naval fleet to punish the people of Galveston and its defenders.

"Admiral Semmes knew that he could not single handedly attack the entire Yankee invasion fleet but decided to see if he could trick one of the ships into coming out to investigate the appearance of the *Alabama*. It was not long before a Yankee ship was dispatched to determine the identity of the warship standing off the coast. As the Yankee ship approached, Admiral Semmes would retreat, slowly pulling the Yankee ship further away from the protection of the Yankee's superior numbers, all of which were busy doing what Yankee warriors were noted for doing during the war—shelling innocent civilians.

"At last the Yankee warship was far enough away from the safety of its fleet for the *Alabama* to turn and challenge the invader. The *Alabama* was under sail but had steam up in her boilers and was ready on deck for a fight. The Yankee foe was a large steamer. When it had been drawn out twenty miles from the protection of its fleet, the drum beat to quarters was given. The two ships now approached each other very rapidly. As they came within hailing distance both warships stopped their engines. They were about one hundred yards apart. The Yankees shouted, 'What ship is that?' The *Alabama*, still not yet showing her country's flag, cunningly replied 'This is her Britannic Majesty's steamer *Petrel*' and returned the hail by demanding to know who the challenger was. All the *Alabama* could hear was 'the United States,' but the name of the Yankee warship was undecipherable. The first part was all the *Alabama* needed to know—they knew for a fact that the challenger was an enemy ship and part of the invasion fleet. An awkward pause ensued and presently the Yankee demanded the right to board in order to verify the claim to be in her Britannic Majesty's service. The *Alabama* replied that they would be glad to have the privilege of entertaining the boarding party. The *Alabama*'s crew could hear the Yankee's boatswain's mate call away a boat and the creaking of the tackles as they lowered the boarding party into the water.

"Admiral Semmes determined that it was time to begin the action, but first they were required by the rules of international war to make known their true identity. He told his first lieutenant, Kell, to announce to the Yankee invader who we were and, as soon as the announcement was clearly made, to give the Yankee our full broadside, while running up the Confederate battle flag. It was with great pride that Kell trumpeted to the Yankee, 'This is the Confederate States steamer *Alabama*!' Turning to the crew standing to their guns—the gunners with their sights on the enemy and lock-strings in hand—Kell gave the order to fire. A horrific blast, flame, and smoke immediately filled the void between the two warships. The entire ship rolled with the recoil of its guns—roll *Alabama* roll—as she sought to return to the hated enemy a mere portion of the destruction it was giving innocent Southern women and children. The moon was not out, but the stars provided sufficient light for the two antagonists to see each other—being they were no more than half a mile apart on the open ocean.

"The wind was blowing in the direction of the enemy fleet and it was not long before they understood that their comrades were in the battle for their lives. A most unwelcomed thought because Yankees do not like to fight man to man. The Yankee prefers to overwhelm an innocent man with the superiority of numbers—numbers not hindered by rules of honor and civility. The Yankee admiral immediately set out to join the fight in his flag ship, the *Brooklyn*, accompanied by two of his other steamers. Yes, indeed, four to one odds were more to the Yankees' liking. But the engagement between the *Alabama* and the *Hatteras* was taking place twenty miles out at sea, a distance that gave the *Alabama* plenty of time to finish its work before the Yankees could reach them. As soon as the first broadside was fired the Yankees returned the favor and a hot action pursued. Each ship was under steam and running parallel to the other, firing broadside after broadside. The crew of the *Alabama* handled their guns with great efficiency and, after just thirteen minutes, the Yankee ship hoisted the white flag of surrender as a cheer and Rebel Yell went up from the *Alabama's* crew. Admiral Semmes then steamed up close to the wounded Yankee ship to ask if it required aid, this being the accepted tradition of civilized nations, to which her captain replied that his ship was sinking and he needed immediate help to avoid needless loss of life. This is quite different from the way the Yankees would later respond at sinking of the *Alabama* in the English Channel by an ironclad Yankee warship. But again, the rules of civilized warfare were never an impediment to the Yankee invader as he sought to punish impendent Southerners who merely asked to be left alone to live in their own country under a government based upon the American principle of the consent of the governed.

"When the United States naval officer commanding the sinking ship came on board the *Alabama,* it was learned that the opponent ship was the USS *Hatteras*. In reporting the battle, the Yankee press attempted to downplay the significance of the man-to-man battle between the CSS *Alabama* and the USS *Hatteras* by claiming that the *Hatteras* was unfairly matched against the better armed *Alabama*. It was claimed that the *Hatteras* could use only four guns on a side. But the sailors rescued from the sinking *Hatteras* told Admiral Semmes that the *Hatteras* carried eight guns; six in broadside and two pivots, just like the *Alabama*. The only real difference was that the *Alabama's* pivot guns were heavier. The facts prove that the *Hatteras* was larger than the *Alabama* by some one hundred tons and was manned by 108 men while the *Alabama* was manned by 110 men.

"The only casualty suffered on the *Alabama* was one man wounded. The damage to the ship was only slight; there was no hull damage requiring repair and not even her ropes required splicing. But Admiral Semmes was always proud that after the surrender of the sinking Yankee warship, not a single United States naval crewman or officer drowned," Uncle Seth concluded with a note of pride.

§ **Deo Vindice** §

41

The Charge of the Confederate Light Brigade

Uncle Seth worked slowly with his ax as he carefully split the fat-lighter pine that would serve as kindling wood for the kitchen stove. The smell of pine rosin engulfed the entire wood pile. The old red oak chopping block was conveniently located to allow Uncle Seth to keep an eye out down the lane. He knew the young children would soon be home from school. The old homeplace seemed so quiet without them, although he got more work done without them being underfoot. Somehow work did not seem as important to him as it once did. Strange, thought Uncle Seth, how the oldest generation in the home served as a bridge to the youngest generation.

"Uncle Seth," cried out his great-grandchildren in unison, "guess what we learned about in school today?"

"Well, now, if you learned anything at all it will be a great improvement for your hard heads," joked Uncle Seth.

"Uncle Seth, we learned about the charge of the Light Brigade," exclaimed Joe William.

"Ah yes, the Light Brigade, half a league, half a league, volley and thunder, as I recall," replied the old man, attempting to maintain his assumed position as expert on all things related to the military sciences.

"Uncle Seth, did you all ever make such a heroic charge?" Joe William asked the old Confederate veteran—fully confident that his Uncle Seth was more than equal to anything recorded in a textbook.

"I recall one of the most daring and dangerous charges ever made during the war was made by Col. Wirt Adam's regiment back in 1862," Uncle Seth began as he looked at the sketch in Joe William's textbook depicting the Light Brigade's famous charge. "It was the first day of September, and after failing to dislodge a well-entrenched Federal force in his front, General Armstrong called upon Colonel Adam's regiment of cavalry to do the job. Up ahead was a long, narrow road—Britton's Lane, with deep gullies on both sides of the narrow road and a high stake and rider fence on each side for the enemy to hide behind. Directly across the road ahead

were two Yankee artillery pieces supported
by additional troops. In addition, there were
plenty of heavy brush and small trees for the
Yankee skirmishers to hide behind. All in
all there were around two thousand Yankee
troops plus two artillery pieces ready to resist
our charge," Uncle Seth said with a sigh.

"Were you scared, Uncle Seth?" Joe
William blurted out.

"At times like that you don't have time
to be scared. You just automatically do what
you've been trained to do," admitted the
Confederate veteran. "Now, to make matters

(Jim Whittington)

worse," Uncle Seth declared with emphasis, "that road was so narrow that
we could only form up in fours. As we emerged onto the road we could
see the death trap that awaited us, but we promptly obeyed the order
'Attention! Gallop! Charge!' As soon as we began our forward movement
the entire roadway began to spew fire and smoke toward us! We were at
point-blank range, not more than 150 yards from the muzzles of their
guns. Their cannons were vomiting double charges of grape and canister
at us as fast as they could load and fire. All the while their infantry poured
a devastating fire on us from both sides of the road. The Yankees had
an enfilade on us from their cannons. One round shot could have gone
through almost our entire regiment."

Uncle Seth paused as he collected his thoughts and caught his breath—
these many years have passed and still his heart raced as it did on that day.
"I can still hear the bugle sounding the charge and the mighty Rebel Yell
resounding above the roar of Yankee cannon and musket fire. Colonel
Adams was mounted on a beautiful cream-colored mare. He was at the
very head of our column, leading the charge. Those of us behind could
not see because of the dust and smoke. We just kept pressing our mounts
forward as the head of the column went down with each successive blast
of the Yankee cannons. Soon we were stumbling over our own dead and
wounded—both man and beast. We just kept pressing forward. Sgt.
Maj. Lee Brisco—his sister lived at Port Gibson, Mississippi, during the
war—and Lieutenant Montgomery were at Colonel Adam's side as they
rode over the Yankee cannons, and both were cut down before we could
reach them. Shortly after that, Captain Bondurant went down when his
horse was shot from beneath him. But despite the enemy's superiority
in numbers, entrenched positions, and their possession of well-placed

cannons, we nonetheless rode right over them and captured their cannons. The Yankees supporting their cannons took to their heels. You could not imagine my surprise when I saw Colonel Adams still mounted on his mare. He had his war face on, his eyes looked like

Britton's Lane Monument

panther eyes, and his pistol barrel was still smoking. His beautiful mare was blowing blood from her nostrils with each labored breath. Even though we had won the guns, we did not have enough men left to keep them if the Yankees ordered a counterattack. Lucky for us, General Armstrong sent in some dismounted troops to assist us." Uncle Seth seemed exhausted from the telling of his story.

Uncle Seth looked down at Joe William, who was watching every move the old Confederate veteran made. "Joe William," Uncle Seth said with voice so low it was almost a whisper—something between them, "you know we lost our war, and countries that lose wars don't have very many warrior poets writing about their struggle for freedom. Big empires can afford to reward poets to immortalize their conquest while slandering their conquered foe. But the impoverished South couldn't and still can't afford the luxury of rewarding poets for telling the truth about our war for independence. On September 1, 1898, the relatives and friends of those of us who made that charge erected a small monument on the spot to commemorate our brave efforts. On the top of the monument are the letters CSA. One day when we are all gone there will be no Southern warrior poets to tell our story, but the Yankee nationalists poets will still be spreading lies about the South. We depend on you and your children's children to be our warrior poets—to remember us, honor our courage, and defend the truth about why we wore the gray in the War for Southern Independence. Conquered people need their warrior poets. Warrior poets continue the battle for their people's freedom by keeping alive the memory of the past and the promise for freedom yet to come." Uncle Seth slowly closed the textbook and handed it to Joe William. Together the two walked toward the house, kindling wood in arms.

§ Deo Vindice §

ON THE SKIRMISH LINE WITH UNCLE SETH
Onward came the massed might of the Federal Empire, their well-paid

warriors neatly dressed in new blue uniforms and bearing thousands of new Springfield rifles tipped with gleaming bayonets. Their massed cannons roared death and destruction to all who would dare resist Yankee domination. But above it all could be heard the Rebel Yell as poorly supplied, hungry, and ragged Southerners shouted defiance to tyranny's might. A Federal officer said that the very sound of the Rebel Yell would often cause their ranks to break even before the Rebel charge was made. And onward the blue masses came, but the Rebel Yell had its decided effect, for it portended capture, mutilation, or death to all invaders and the promise of an early entrance into the next life for those who advanced tyranny's flag.

42

Early Southern Anti-Slavery Efforts

Uncle Seth disliked controversy and tried to live his life on a variation of the Golden Rule that Jesus taught His followers. Instead of "do unto others as you would have them do unto you," Uncle Seth believed in "live and let live" or simply "leave people alone." He still believed it was his Christian duty to help his neighbors or even strangers, but he abhorred busybodies who were constantly sticking their noses in other people's business. But occasionally he would find himself embroiled in a controversy that, while unpleasant, demanded his attention, especially when it dealt with correcting falsehoods being spread about the South.

The new minister's wife at the local Baptist Church had volunteered to teach the young people in the Sunday morning religion class. During her first class, she made the point that slavery was evil and that the war was good because, if it were not for the war, the South would have never ended slavery. Now, Uncle Seth had never owned a slave and, like the majority of pre-war Southerners, the issue of slavery was not *whether* it should be eventually ended but *how* it would be ended. The old Confederate soldier decided to write down some basic facts about Southern history that most Southern schoolchildren are never taught—being that they are educated in a Yankee-dominated educational system. The following points were listed by Uncle Seth and personally hand-delivered to the young lady:

1. Massachusetts was the first American colony to legalize slavery and was the major player in the nefarious slave trade—a commerce that formed the foundation of its commercial wealth down to this day.
2. Virginia was the first American colony to attempt to prohibit the slave trade. Its efforts, however, were nullified by the British Parliament. In the Declaration of Independence, Virginia listed this as one of the complaints against King George III. Said complaint was penned by Thomas Jefferson.
3. In 1782, the General Assembly of Virginia enacted a law whereby slaves could be set free by deed or will, and emancipating slaves at a personal cost to the slaveholder had already become so common that

when the thirteen American colonies seceded from their union with Great Britain, there were more than thirty-five thousand free people of color in the South.

4. North Carolina passed a law in 1782 that allowed slave owners to free their slaves if they agreed to support all the aged, infirmed, and children who were set free.

5. In 1790, an abolition society was formed in Virginia by the Quakers and had more than eighty members, many of whom were not Quakers. In 1791, they sent a petition against slavery to the Virginia General Assembly.

6. In 1794, Virginia and Maryland sent representatives to the first meeting of the Convention of Abolition Societies held in Philadelphia.

7. In 1801, the anti-slavery feelings in Georgia being promoted by the Methodists resulted in the suggestion that all Methodists should free their slaves.

8. Before Tennessee had been a state for even a year, an appeal for the abolition of slavery was published in the *Knoxville Gazette* and a meeting was called in Washington County to form an anti-slavery society.

9. So many Tennessee citizens of Scotch descent were freeing their slaves that in 1801 the state passed a law giving county courts authority to emancipate slaves upon petition of the owners. The law also directed the county to give the freed slaves certificates of freedom.

10. Emancipation societies were becoming so numerous in the South that one half of the delegates to the American Abolition Convention came from the South between 1794 and 1809.

11. The Quaker Charles Osborn, who was born in North Carolina, organized an anti-slavery society while residing in Tennessee in 1814. He frequently communicated with a similar North Carolina society that was organized in 1814.

12. Judge John Allison of Tennessee declared, "The honor of publishing the first periodical in America of which the one avowed purpose was opposition to slavery must be accorded to Elihu Embree, who in 1820 was publishing a monthly publication, in Jonesboro, Tennessee, *The Emancipator.*"

13. By 1824, Tennessee anti-slavery societies numbered at least twenty, had several hundred members, and had held nine conventions.

14. In 1820, the Presbyterian minister Rev. John Rankin, a native of Tennessee whose ancestors in Scotland were Covenanters, declared that it was safer to make abolition speeches in Kentucky and Tennessee than in the North.

15. According to statistics compiled by the abolitionist Benjamin Lundy, in 1827 there were 130 abolition societies in the United States, of which 106 were in the slave states of the South.

16. Membership in these Southern anti-slave societies was not restricted to only non-slave owners; among them were many earnest Christian masters seeking to solve, as best they could, an inherited problem and burden.

17. In the book *Virginia's Attitude Toward Slavery*, the author, Mr. Munford, noted, "After the years 1820-21, during which time that great struggle, which resulted in what is called the Missouri Compromise, was most active and came to its conclusion that the States of Virginia, Kentucky and Tennessee were earnestly engaged in practical movements for the gradual emancipation of their slaves . . . this movement continued until it was arrested by the aggressions of the abolitionists upon their voluntary action." Note: The acts of radicals in the North made it impossible to continue efforts toward gradual emancipation in the South.

18. Mr. Whitelaw Reid, speaking in 1911, declared, "The anti-slavery movement, which led to our Civil War, began among the Scottish and Ulster Scotch immigrants, not in New England. That is a prevalent delusion, which the brilliant writers of that region [New England] have not always discouraged. But the real anti-slavery movement began in the South and West, largely among the Scottish Covenanters of South Carolina and East Tennessee, twenty to thirty years before there was any organized opposition to slavery elsewhere, even in Massachusetts. The Covenanters, the Methodists, and the Quakers of East Tennessee had eighteen emancipation societies by 1815. A few years later there were five or six in Kentucky. By this time, there were 103 anti-slavery societies in the South, but none, so far as is known in Massachusetts." And remember, at this time—the early 1800s—the lower South was still sparsely populated.

19. In 1831, a slave rebellion was led by Nat Turner in which white women, children, and infants were brutally killed. This coupled with the stories of similar and even more brutal slave uprisings in the Caribbean caused great fear in the Southern states, where in many counties slaves outnumbered whites. To make matters worse, at this period in time the number of radical, anti-Southern abolitionists of the Garrisonian type was rising. These abolitionists differed greatly from prior anti-slavery men in both the North and South. They demanded immediate and unconditional abolition of slavery and condemned as immoral not only slavery but Southerners as well. The radical abolitionists would eventually produce men such as John Brown, who advocated murder of innocent white Southerners by encouraging and planning barbaric slave uprisings.

Uncle Seth hoped that this well-intentioned lady would be able to see from this evidence that it was not the South that stood in the way of freedom for slaves but the fanatics in the North and those crafty politicians of the Lincoln school who were more than willing to use hate-filled, radical anti-Southern propaganda to increase their personal political power. Uncle Seth was not concerned merely with historical accuracy. He knew that a far more important question needed to be asked—a question that Yankee educators fervently avoided and diligently worked, in conjunction with their political allies, to suppress. A question that would be ridiculed and cut short should a Southern student dare to raise the question. Uncle Seth wanted to ask this young Sunday school teacher this question: "Why do educators and politicians, who consistently defend the Federal Empire, insist on stigmatizing with the scarlet letter of slavery and race hatred of all who would defend the old South?

Uncle Seth knew the answer, but unfortunately "New South" Southerners were unwilling even to contemplate the question and the ramifications of the answer. He also knew that the Federal Empire's ruling elite both knew the answer and feared its ramifications. They knew that if Southerners were ever allowed to understand the truth of the invasion, conquest, and political occupation of their Southern nation, in short order a revolution would break out in the South! Prior to the Yankee invasion of the Confederate States of America, Lincoln and his supporters in the press declared, "No, no, we must not let the South go!" Today the ruling elite of the Federal Empire and their supporters in education and the press are saying, "No, no, we must not let Southerners know the truth!"

§ Deo Vindice §

ON THE SKIRMISH LINE WITH UNCLE SETH
Viewing "barbaric" Rebels held in Yankee prisoner of war camps was an exciting day trip for many Yankee civilians during the war. On one occasion in 1864, Governor Morton of Indiana and members of the state legislature and their wives and children were viewing Confederate prisoners held at Camp Morton. The Southern prisoners were ordered to fall in for a dress parade to allow the carriages to slowly pass by, affording the dignitaries and families the opportunity to view the Rebels. One carriage stopped and a well-dressed lady leaned out and asked, "Why do you Rebel soldiers dress so poorly?" To which one brave lad explained, "Gentlemen of the South have two suits—one that we wear among nice people and the other we wear when killing hogs. When we heard you all were coming we put on our hog killing suits."

43

Yankee Propaganda Proves Southerners Are a Conquered People

Billie Jean could tell that something had Uncle Seth agitated. The old Confederate veteran was clutching a newspaper as he slowly rocked back in his chair, which was pulled up next to the fireplace. Billie Jean, Uncle Seth's great-granddaughter, took it as her responsibility to look after the old man and would usually be the first one to notice if he became ill or upset. "Uncle Seth, would you like me to bring you some more coffee?" she asked. Billie Jean was not so much concerned about the old man's coffee cup as she was with finding a way to get him to relax and tell her what was bothering him.

"No, Billie Jean," the old veteran replied. "I think if I had anything else to drink it would have to be hard liquor."

"Now Uncle Seth, I have told you many times that you should not excite yourself over things that you have no control over." Billie Jean knew that the old Confederate veteran was once again fighting that unfinished war.

"I just cannot believe that our people are not up in arms over these continued Yankee slurs and insults! The Yankee Empire overpowered our small Southern nation and now they are determined to fix upon Southerners the label of international villain while wrapping themselves in finely woven robes of self-righteousness. 'We the people' of the South were invaded by the Yankee Empire, our homes were burned, our possessions looted, our women rapped, and noncombatant old men and young boys were murdered. And now the Yankee Empire uses its political power to tell the world that they are the heroes of humanity and the Southern people are the villains. It's just not right!"

"Now, Uncle Seth." Billie Jean realized that the old veteran would not calm down until he had his say on the matter. "What's got you so riled up?"

"Look here, this article in the newspaper," the old man declared as he held the paper up for her inspection—although he had clutched it so hard that it was crumpled and unreadable. Billie Jean had to hide her amusement because the newspaper in the old Confederate veteran's hand seemed more like a weapon in search of a Yankee.

"The reporter for this newspaper was making a tour of Arlington—you know, Gen. Robert E. Lee's former home that the Yankees took control of at the outbreak of the war. What do you think those Yankees have placed in General Lee's home? There, on the wall, was a framed copy of a speech by Robert G. Ingersoll—he was one of the many freethinkers and socialists who surrounded Lincoln before and during the war. This speech contains slanderous statements against the Southern people. In his speech, Ingersoll claims that the war was about slavery. He claims that we fought for slavery and the glorious North fought to end slavery. He even claims that Southerners routinely pulled babies away from their mothers, broke up families, and inflicted unspeakable cruelty on slaves. Nothing is said about the laws and customs of the South to prevent such things from happening, nor the fact that the first abolitionist societies in America were founded in the South, nor that Virginia's colonial legislature was the first to attempt to end the slave trade. And, to add insult to injury, there is not a word about the fact that the New England colonies and then states grew rich on the nefarious slave trade and were the first colonies to legalize slavery and pass fugitive slave laws.

"Ingersoll was a freethinker—someone who rejected the Holy Bible and absolute moral values. Freethinkers include atheists, agnostics, and socialists. The Roman Catholic Church defines freethinkers as those who abandon religious teachings and the morality of Christianity and base their belief on their own reasoning, unfettered by moral traditions. And yet, this is the man the Yankees decide to honor in General Lee's home!

"Anyone who wants to know why the Yankee Empire invaded, conquered, and now occupies the South needs only look at Ingersoll's own words—words that our Yankee masters decided not to mention because it might cause Southerners to rethink their unfettered acceptance of the decision at Appomattox. In a speech honoring Lincoln, Ingersoll—unintentionally, perhaps—declared the real reason Lincoln and the Yankee war governors invaded our Southern nation: 'The great stumbling block, the great obstruction in Lincoln's way, and the way of thousands, was the old doctrine of States Rights.' There you have it, an open admission from former colonel Robert G. Ingersoll of the 11th Illinois Cavalry that the war was fought to destroy

General Lee's Home, Arlington, seized by Yankee invaders (Library of Congress)

the constitutional principle of States' Rights and create an all-powerful and supreme Federal government.

"And Ingersoll was not alone. No sir. The war-time governor of Illinois, Richard Yates, who was one of those infamous war governors who supported Lincoln's unconstitutional invasion of the Confederate States of America, declared in a message to the Illinois legislature on January 2, 1865, that the war had 'tended, more than any other event in our country's history, to militate against the Jeffersonian idea that the best government is that, which governs least.' Now, this dream of a vast Federal Empire controlled by Northern political elites was not something hoped for by only three Illinois freethinkers and radical abolitionists—Ingersoll, Yates, and Lincoln. No, this was an age-old Hamiltonian dream incubated in the commercial and banking centers of the North.

"The people of the South and indeed the people of the world must never forget the words of the *New York Herald* when it declared during the war:

> With a restored Union, prosperity would once more bless the land. If any bad blood remained on either side, it would soon disappear, or be *purged by a foreign war*. With a combined veteran army of over a million men, and a fleet more powerful than that of any European power, we could order France from Mexico, England from Canada, and Spain from Cuba, and enforce our orders if they are not obeyed. The American continent would then belong to Americans. The President at Washington would govern the New World, and the glorious dreams and prophecies of our forefathers would at length be realized.

When will our Yankee masters place these words on the walls of their war trophies?

"This newspaper article is a warning to all Southerners. We must understand that the Yankee Empire will use its political power to propagandize our people. This Yankee nation will force our people to accept and swear allegiance to their perverted and slanderous version of why we wore the gray in the War for Southern Independence. You must never accept anything that a Yankee spokesperson tells you when you visit a national monument or park that is supposed to commemorate the so-called Civil War. The sole purpose of National Civil War Parks is to indoctrinate our people to the point where we become self-hating Southerners and thereby establish Southerners as obedient, second-class Yankees who willingly accept political domination in our defeated and occupied country." The old Confederate veteran lowered his arm and released his grip on the paper. The paper fell silently to the floor as Uncle

Seth stared into the flames in the fireplace. He seemed exhausted by the uneven contest, like so many battles in the war; yet he was determined to soldier on in the hope that one day his people would once again lift up the banners of the South and strike for freedom.

§ Deo Vindice §

ON THE SKIRMISH LINE WITH UNCLE SETH
John C. Calhoun's doctrine of state sovereignty, States' Rights, and nullification was fully developed long before the radical abolitionists had made slavery a major political issue. The controversy over the Tariff of Abominations had nothing to do with slavery and everything to do with Southern resistance to being exploited by the Northern majority that controlled the Federal Congress. The South had become the North's cash cow—in effect the Northern majority had turned the Southern people into their tariff slaves. And the North was determined not to let the South, their slave property, go. The people of the South were slowly beginning to realize a simple truth: if you cannot leave, then you are not free.

44

Deathbed Confession—Why the South Fought

Uncle Seth always started his day with early-morning coffee. He was sitting quietly sipping hot coffee and thinking about the article he had just read by Rev. Mark Evans, chaplain-in-chief of the United Confederate Veterans. Reverend Evans described testimonies of dying Confederate soldiers that had been recorded by those who heard the young men's words just before they passed away. Uncle Seth had personally heard such battlefield testimonies. To him, these testimonies were proof that the Southern soldiers were fighting for their country's independence. Unfortunately, the vulgar Yankee press and education establishment continued to brand the war as an effort of evil Southern slave owners to keep men in slavery. As Uncle Seth saw it, it was a war initiated by the Yankees to turn Southerners into slaves to the Yankee Empire.

Uncle Seth thought back to the day when he knelt beside a mortally wounded young Confederate soldier of Gibson's Brigade, 4th Louisiana, CSA. His words still rung in Uncle Seth's ears. "Yes, Seth, I am dying, but I am going to heaven. I have tried to do my duty. It is God's will, and I cheerfully give myself up a sacrifice on the altar of my country." These were the young boy's last words—a young man who had no interest in slavery. He only wanted to be left alone to live under a government based on the free and unfettered consent of the governed. But the Yankees had other plans for him, his people, and his soon-to-be conquered and occupied country.

The continuing insults and slander that the Yankee government, its vulgar press, and its educators heap upon the memory of those who fell wearing the gray in the War for Southern Independence were almost more than the old Confederate veteran could bear. In his nightmares he could see anew the horror of the battlefield. At every remembrance ceremony and every memorial service attended, he would be reminded that almost one third of the young boys who fought to defend their homes, families, and country never returned. So many young Southerners lie in unmarked graves, their lives freely given as a sacrifice to the cause for freedom, their blood freely spilled on their country's altar—a defeated and occupied country, but a country sanctified by the effusion of patriots' blood. Outnumbered three and four to one and without a friend in the world to offer aid, they fought on—and the Damn Yankee would have the world and even Southern schoolchildren to believe they fought against such odds in order to maintain slavery. Did the patriots of 1776 who came from colonies that allowed slavery or were actively engaged in the infamous slave trade—did those men fight for slavery?

Uncle Seth thought back to that day when Jefferson Davis took office as president of the Confederate States of America. He declared, "We feel that our cause is just and holy, we protest solemnly in the face of mankind that we desire peace at any sacrifice save that of honor and independence. We will continue to struggle for our inherent right to freedom, independence, and self-government." Words could not be any clearer. Yet with no government to promote its version of history the South has no way to defend itself from the continuing onslaught of Yankee slander.

Uncle Seth remembered the words of Confederate General "Stonewall" Jackson when he declared, "I do not wish to outlive the independence of my country." Perhaps General Jackson was right. Uncle Seth agreed with Southern warrior poet Father Ryan, who penned the words explaining that in a conquered and occupied South only the dead are free.

Uncle Seth's mind rushed back to words of the dying young man, his declaration that he was dying for his country's independence. Uncle Seth knew that a dying confession could be admitted in a court of law. Why, then, are these words ignored by modern "New South" Southerners? He could not understand it. He knew the awful results of defeat, but defeat does not require the renunciation of principle or the denial of the right to be free. At Appomattox, General Lee surrendered what was left of an army—he did not surrender the right of the Southern people to be free. Uncle Seth could not understand why his fellow countrymen were so willing to accept for themselves and their children the assigned position as second-class subjects of the Yankee Empire. Unlike Esau of the Old Testament, New South Southerners have sold their birthright for not even a bowl of soup but the Yankee promise of a bowl of Yankee soup; and history proves that Yankees seldom, if ever, keep their promises!

Post-war Richmond (Library of Congress)

Perhaps another sip of coffee and

more thinking on the matter would bring reason to light. But deep down inside the old Confederate veteran knew the battle would never be over until the South was once again a free and independent country.

§ Deo Vindice §

45

Twelve-Year-Old Confederate Soldier

Uncle Seth sat on the bench to the side of the door of the corncrib. He was amusing himself by watching the young boys as they played soldier. Every now and then one of the boys would ask Uncle Seth to settle a dispute regarding some intricate matter of military decorum. Uncle Seth would promptly resolve the issue, sending the boys back to their play as he reached into the crib to find another ear of corn to shuck and shell for the chickens waiting at his feet. As soon as the last kernel of yellow corn was removed from the red cob, the boys would hear the warning, "Yankee grenade coming over the top," as Uncle Seth sent the cob flying in the direction of the closest gathering of youngsters. The boys, for their part, knew that to win the contest they had to catch the cob before it hit the ground and in one smooth motion send it back toward Uncle Seth—"jess the way we used to do it during the war," according to the Confederate veteran.

"Uncle Seth," shouted one of the boys, "which one of us is the best soldier?" Uncle Seth shook his head and tactfully replied, "I really can't say, you all look mighty good, but none of you are as good as the twelve-year-old boy who I saw during the war." The teaser distracted the boys long enough to make them forget their rivalry and focus their attention on Uncle Seth's explanation.

"Me and Pvt. A. L. Slack from Tallulah, Louisiana, were up in Virginia in early 1861. A. L. was a member of the Second Louisiana Volunteers. One day, while we were in camp, we noticed a young boy 'bout your size strolling about camp. He appeared to be around twelve years old. We asked who he belonged to and found out that he had attached himself to a neighboring regiment. We soon found out that he was a rather cosmopolitan critter because he was at home anywhere. Several weeks later we saw him with the First South Carolina Volunteers. Well, I guess a full year went by before I saw him again," explained Uncle Seth.

"It was at the Second Battle of Manassas on the 29th of August 1862. Our brigade received orders, 'charge bayonets—forward,' and the entire battle line moved toward the Yankee enemy. We advanced and ran almost immediately into the Yankees, who, after giving us a deadly volley, fell back rapidly across a field and into the woods beyond, where a U.S. artillery battery, supported by a swarm of blue-coated U.S. troops, was posted. Nothing could check our advance. Under a withering fire of minie balls and canister shot, we pressed our attack forward. When we arrived within a hundred yards of the artillery battery, our captain ordered, 'halt!' Under this raking fire we began to 'dress right' even as our men in line dropped one by one—but we would dress right to fill the hole in our battle line left by our fallen comrade," explained Uncle Seth.

"I have often thought that it was crazy to give such a command under those circumstances, but officers don't ask private soldiers for tactical recommendations at such times. Even in spite of this, nothing could stop us. Not a single man waivered in the face of what seemed to be certain death. At last, our captain gave the order 'forward' and we charged straight for the Federal guns. Just then I felt a thud and a burning pain across my upper chest. The force of the impact twisted me around as if I were a child's Christmas top. A minie ball had struck my pocket Bible edgewise and, passing nearly through the New Testament, dug a trench across the flesh on my left side. Wounded and with blood spurting from my wound, I started toward the rear seeking medical aid. Meanwhile the boys in butternut and gray went up and over the Yankee battery and scattered the Yankee troops like chaff in the wind," Uncle Seth declared with a detectable note of pride in his voice.

"As I struggled to the rear I heard a great rumbling to my left. I turned and saw that our artillery was plunging to the front, under lash and shouts of the drivers. Their aim was to seize a small hill to the flank of the United States forces and pour deadly Confederate fire into the invaders. I can still see them tumbling, bouncing, and surging to gain that hill. What else do you suppose I saw in the midst of all that carnage and hell? So close I could have almost touched him, the little boy sitting on the limber, locked arm to arm with a stout artilleryman on each side, all holding on for dear life. The boy's eyes were aflame, his hat waving by a rawhide strap, his treble voice shouting excitedly, and his whole being lit up and aglow with the terrible magnetism of battle, cheering on the line. That was the last time I saw our little soldier," Uncle Seth said.

"Uncle Seth," inquired one of the youngsters, "do you suppose the young boy lived through the war?"

"Well as a matter of fact," replied Uncle Seth, "at the last United Confederate Veterans Reunion I attended I was told that the young boy's name is W. J. Pucket and he lives in Armstead, Mississippi. He was thirteen years old at the time of Second Manassas and he had attached himself to the Louisiana Guard Artillery toward the end of the war. He stayed with them until the end and surrendered after Appomattox.

"So boys, you all remember that while you play at being soldiers, we had youngsters not much older than you fighting for the South during our struggle for independence. The next time you go to town and see that monument at the courthouse erected by the United Daughters of the Confederacy, you all remember the many young boys who volunteered to defend your home long before you were even born." Uncle Seth discretely turned to wipe the moisture from his eyes. "Too much dust in this old crib," he mumbled to himself as he turned and walked away.

§ Deo Vindice §

On the Skirmish Line with Uncle Seth
Yankee General John McNeill captured ten men from Palmyra, Missouri, accused them of being spies, and ordered them hanged the next morning. One of the men had adopted a young orphan boy and raised him in his home. The young boy, in his late teens, eluded McNeill's roundup of pro-Southerners by hiding in nearby woods. When the boy heard his benefactor was to be hung, the boy went to the Yankees and asked to be allowed to exchange places with his adopted father. The request was granted. The next morning as the ten innocent men were marched out to their execution, the young lad was heard encouraging his fellows not to shed tears and to show the Yankees that Southern men knew how to face death at the hands of tyrants and villains.

46

Money: The Yankee's One True God and Cause of the War

Uncle Seth and the boys had hitched the team to the wagon and were headed down to the grist mill. They spent the prior day shelling two bushels of yellow corn, and today they intended to have the grist mill grind the corn into yellow cornmeal. Their usual custom was to keep half and sell the other half to Mr. George Page, the mill owner. Mr. Page also owned the local syrup mill, where every fall Uncle Seth and the boys would take their sugar cane to be processed into molasses. Together, with their hogs and beef cattle, this provided the three "m's" of their diet—meat, meal, and molasses. In rural Mississippi during the early 1900s, the family farm provided most of a family's food. Small cash crops, such as a few acres of cotton, and an occasional load of logs and later pulp wood would provide the money to purchase basic staples such as wheat flour, sugar, and salt.

"Boys," Uncle Seth broke the silence, "you all know that it is not corn we are taking to the grist mill."

"Of course it's corn," declared Joe William. "We planted corn, we raised corn, we pulled corn, we shucked corn, and yesterday we shelled corn—what else could it be but corn?"

"Well JW," Uncle Seth would often call Joe William by his initials, "you are right, except the word *corn* refers to grain. It's even in the Holy Bible and I know that Moses did not raise what we call corn! No, what we call corn is really Indian corn or maize—we got it from the Indians. The early settlers used the same grinding methods to grind Indian corn that they used in Europe to grind wheat. You boys know that there is a grist mill in Kemper County that has been in business since 1790. It's near DeKalb, Mississippi, and has been owned by the Sciple family since the 1840s." The boys were always amazed at Uncle Seth's knowledge of almost any subject. What the boys did not appreciate was that the old man was constantly reading—he was a self-educated man who had an unquenchable thirst for conversational knowledge.

"Uncle Seth, if we are not careful we may turn into rich Yankee merchants." Joe William's brain was busy calculating the money they would make from the sale of half of the cornmeal.

"Yes, but boys, before I would let that happen, I would burn all the crops and the barns to boot!" The boys and Uncle Seth all laughed loudly but all knew that Uncle Seth meant it to be more than a mere joke. "You know, boys," Uncle Seth began seriously, "money and material possessions are not the most important things in this world. People like the Yankees who live in a commercial world think it is, and they measure a man's worth not by his character and sense of honor but by how much money he has. You all remember what Adm. Raphael Semmes of the CSS *Alabama* said about the Yankee:

> The Yankee is certainly a remarkable specimen of humanity. He is at once a duck and a chicken, and takes to the water, or land with equal ease. Providence has certainly designed him for some useful purpose. He is ambitious, restless, scheming—especially scheming—energetic, and has no inconvenient moral nature to restrain him from the pursuit of his interests, be the path to these interests ever so crooked. In the development of material wealth he is unsurpassed, and perhaps this is his mission on earth. But he is like the beaver or bee; he works from instinct, and is so avid of gain, that he has no time to enjoy the wealth he produces—he does not understand the usefulness of leisure. Some malicious demon seems to be goading him on, in spite of himself, to continuous and exhausting exertion, which consigns him to the tomb or grave before his time, leaving a pile of untouched wealth behind him.

Yep, ole Bee's Wax—that's what his sailors call him because of the way he waxed his moustache. He had the Yankee pegged."

"But Uncle Seth, money is important! How else could we buy stuff we need like flour, sugar, or coal oil for our lamps?" asked Joe William.

"That's true, JW," Uncle Seth agreed, "but money must not become all-important. Remember what the Holy Bible says about money—the love of money is the root of much evil. It is the love of money, not money itself, that is the cause of so much evil in this world. The Yankee's love of money and his pursuit of increasing wealth at any cost—that was the Yankee's primary motive for refusing to allow the South to secede and become an independent nation. Money—that was the cause of the war. The South had become the Federal government's primary source of tax revenue, and the majority of that revenue was being used for the benefit of Northern commerce. You know that back in the 1820s, Sen. Thomas Benton from Missouri, who opposed slavery, declared that the Southern states provided more than seventy-five percent of the revenues required to run the Federal government. And most of those moneys were spent for internal improvements that favored the Northern states. Yep, the South had become the North's milch cow—or milk cow, as you all would say—of the Union and the Yankees were not about to let their source of wealth escape."

Sen. Thomas Benton (Courtesy State Historical Society of Missouri)

"Yes, boys, the Yankees like to hide behind their well-constructed false face, the one they use when telling the world that they were motivated to invade, conquer, and occupy the South by a desire to free the slaves. But that is just one more Damn Yankee lie. The way to prove that they are liars is to look to see what these high-minded Yankees did as soon as Southern senators and congressmen left the United States Congress. I'll tell you what they did not do—they did not pass an amendment freeing the slaves then being held in many Northern states. What they did do tells the whole story about the money-grubbing Yankees. The first thing they did was to increase the tariff to the highest level in American history! They could not do this as long as we were part of their Union, but as soon as we were gone their first thought was of money. In March of 1861, the Yankee newspaper the *New York Times* publically admitted as much when they declared in an editorial, 'The commercial bearing of the question has acted upon the North. We were divided and confused till our pockets were touched.' A newspaper in Manchester, New Hampshire, was even more direct when it declared, 'It is very clear that the South gains by this process and we lose. No, we must not let the South go.' Boys, you all need to always remember that the Yankee's love of money was the cause of the war. In reality money is the cause of most wars." The old Confederate veteran tapped the backs of the mules, gave the strict order "get-up," and away they went.

§ Deo Vindice §

47

Col. Santos Benavides—Hispanic Confederates on the Rio Grande

It was a cold February night. The supper dishes had been put away and the entire family was huddled around the fireplace. These were times when folks would talk to each other, a time when storytelling was prized and Uncle Seth was in his element. The dried red oak firewood provided just the right amount of warmth. Red oaks grew well in the swamps and low bottomlands of Mississippi. They seemed to thrive in the often wet and mostly acidic soil. Uncle Seth and the boys would help cut the trees, split the wood, and stack it to dry all summer so it would burn hot and not smoke too much when they used it during the coming winter.

During these cold nights, the fireplace seemed to draw the family together. Uncle Seth was proud of his chimney. He had supervised its construction, and his chimneys would always draw the smoke straight. He was proud of his workmanship because his chimneys never smoked the house. Suddenly a loud crack as from a child's toy pistol came from inside the fireplace as an air pocket in the wood heated up and exploded. Occasionally the popping of the wood would cause a small ember to be expelled out toward the folks sitting around the fire. Uncle Seth would always warn the boys, "Look out boys, the Yankees are shooting at us again." When things became quiet, one of the boys would ask Uncle Seth a question about the war and before long, to the delight of the boys, they would be entertained by one of Uncle Seth's war stories.

"Uncle Seth," Joe William said, breaking the silence, "who do you think was the best Confederate officer?"

"Well, Joe William," Uncle Seth began, "we had so many good officers that I would hate to pick just one. Also, there were a lot of officers who did great service for the South but who most folks have never heard about—it's a shame, too. I was reading about the Confederacy on the Rio Grande the other day and learned about a famous Texas officer of Spanish and Mexican descent who deserves our respect. His name was Col. Santos Benavides of Laredo, Texas. I think he and his brothers were the first officers in North America of Spanish and Mexican decent to lead white

American troops in battle. He and his kin, who were of Mexican blood, exercised a strong pro-Confederate influence over the area along the Rio Grande border. Colonel Benavides was known by his friends and enemies as an extremely brave man who never backed down, even when facing a much larger enemy force. His brilliant defense of the Rio Grande area around Laredo, Texas, kept the Yankees from controlling the international border between Mexico and Confederate Texas. This was important because Mexico was the only nation that the Confederacy could freely trade with, due to the Yankee blockade of our Southern ports. Colonel Benavides kept the Texas-Mexico border in Confederate hands. Confederate officers such as Gen. Hamilton Bee and John Bankhead Magruder praised Colonel Benavides for his gallant defense of the 'Confederacy on the Rio Grande.'

Col. Santos Benavides, CSA (Courtesy Webb County [Texas] Historical Society)

"One of the key elements of a good leader is his ability to command respect from his men—will they willingly follow him into battle even when the odds are seemingly impossible? Units that are commanded by incompetent officers have high rates of desertion. If the rate of desertion of his men was a test of whether or not Colonel Benavides was a good officer, then he passed with flying colors. His unit had an extremely high retention rate. He was well-known and respected in his community—known to be an honest man who treated all men fairly and who was brave in battle. He was a natural leader who believed in the cause for which he fought, and his men shared his passion for Southern freedom.

"In March of 1864, Colonel Benavides led his men in the Battle of Laredo. The city was attacked by a force of two hundred Yankee cavalry, which was the advance party of the main force of around three hundred infantry and two artillery pieces. At the time, Colonel Benavides had only sixty men in Laredo with which to repel the two hundred Yankees; but their gallant counterattack, which lasted until dark, drove the Yankees back toward their main force encamped at the Rio Grande River. Colonel Benavides said in his report that the reason the Yankees got so close to the city without being seen was that they had crossed the Rio Grande—in violation to Mexican sovereignty. But the Yankees were actively violating the sovereignty of the Southern states, so why should they respect the sovereignty of any other nation? According to Colonel Benavides, the Yankees re-crossed the Rio Grande somewhere between Eagle Pass and Laredo, Texas. Luckily for Colonel Benavides, a Mexican national saw the Yankees while they were traveling up the Mexican side of the Rio Grande. This friendly Mexican quickly crossed the Rio Grande himself and came to Laredo to warn Colonel Benavides of the advancing 'Gringos.'

"Even though he was greatly outnumbered, he sent a report to Confederate headquarters that he and his men were determined to 'do [their] utmost in defense of [their] homes.' He stated that he planned to move out and attack the enemy as soon as the rest of his command rallied in Laredo. He dispatched a courier to Colonel Giddings at Eagle Pass asking him to send reenforcements. Not only was he outnumbered, he had no artillery and only enough ammunition for a short fight. Nonetheless, he intended to attack the Yankee invaders. As he was leaving Laredo to attack the Yankees, Benavides left his half brother Capt. Cristobal Benavides and his company in charge of the city. In his own words, his orders were to burn the five thousand bales of cotton belonging to the Confederacy 'if the day goes against us.' In addition, he told Captain Benavides, 'Then you will set fire to my new house so that nothing that is mine shall pass to the enemy. Let their victory be a barren one.' Now I ask you boys, where in the entire South would you find a braver and more dedicated Southern soldier?

"Colonel Benavides continued to serve the Confederate States of America until July of 1865. He and his men were some of the very last land-based Confederates to relinquish the military struggle to obtain Southern independence. I think that if the South had managed to maintain our independence Colonel Benavides would have been appointed as the Confederate ambassador to Mexico. With the Confederate States as a friendly neighbor and a buffer between the aggressive Yankee Empire to the north, the two nations—Mexico and the Confederacy—would have become close and prosperous trading partners, and who knows what the world would have looked like. Perhaps the world would have thought of South and Central America as being everything south of the Mason-Dixon Line." Uncle Seth chuckled at the though—mere wishful dreaming, but the old Confederate veteran would never surrender his dreams.

§ Deo Vindice §

ON THE SKIRMISH LINE WITH UNCLE SETH

As told to Uncle Seth by the Hon. Charles Scott: "While visiting in Paris, France I was enjoying the music at the Grand Hotel. Sweet tones of inspiring music floated across the yard and spilled into the street. It was an international gathering and so the orchestra began playing the various national anthems from Germany, Great Britain, the United States, all of which were respectively appreciated by the throngs of people gathered. The French 'Marseillaise' was played, and it received equal treatment. But then something unusual happened—the orchestras struck up 'Dixie' and the crowd began to cheer and before long there were loud Rebel Yells coming from foreign throats! It was an involuntary homage paid by the civilized world."

The truth is that this is the greatest danger faced by the Yankee Empire. If the world ever learns the truth about why the Yankees invaded, conquered, and continue to oppress the Confederate States of America, an international support for recognition of the South's right to be a free and independent nation may emerge. No wonder Yankee propagandists work overtime spreading their lies about why the South fought the so-called Civil War!

The Origins of Dixie

Welcome to the Deep South; welcome to Dixie. The South is a land of memories. It's a land of beauty, charm, and grace, but most of all it's a land that remembers. Fathered by patriots of 1776 such as Patrick Henry, Thomas Jefferson,  and George Washington, its soil has been sanctified by the blood of her sons fighting for their kith and kin's freedom. The South was formed in the furnace of war and tested in the crucible of reconstruction. Those who know and love her call her home and still stand when they hear "Dixie" played.

Before the War for Southern Independence, when men from upriver would float their goods down to New Orleans, they would brag that they would return with their pockets full of Dixies—the ten note issued by the bank of New Orleans. Soon all the land south of the Ohio River was referred to as Dixieland or Dixie.

The Dix note is an example of market-produced money and was in use up to 1860. Unlike government-issued currency, the use of Dix notes and other bank notes could not be forced upon the people. Bank notes relied on the reputation of the bank to convince consumers that it was a safe and reliable "storage of value." If a bank issued unsound notes it would go out of business; those who ran the bank would be subject to charges of fraud and would no longer be viewed as trustworthy business people. But the government can use its printing press to issue worthless paper money to pay for government projects and pass the cost on to citizens in the form of inflation. The free market uses voluntary cooperation to create sound money while government uses force to produce unsound money, which leads to inflation and eventually tyranny.

Beauvoir, circa 1904, the last home of Jefferson Davis, Biloxi, Mississippi (Courtesy Beauvoir, Biloxi, Mississippi)

Gen. Nathan Bedford Forrest Boyhood Home, operated by the Sons of Confederate Veterans, Chapel Hill, Tennessee

Confederate Memorial Hall, Camp Street, New Orleans, Louisiana (Author's collection)

Jackson McCurtain, Lt. Col. of 1st Choctaw Battalion, Confederate States of America, future Principal Chief (Courtesy Research Division, Oklahoma Historical Society)

Confederate General Jubal Early's Home, Roanoke, Virginia (Courtesy Jubal A. Early Preservation Trust, Rocky Mount, Virginia. Photo by K.C. Furr.)

Elm Springs, National Headquarters of the Sons of Confederate Veterans, Columbia, Tennessee (Courtesy National Sons of Confederate Veterans)

Henry Brown, Black Confederate Drummer, Darlington, South Carolina, circa 1905 (Courtesy Darlington County Historical Commission)

Col. Ambrosio Jose Gonzales, CSA, Cuban revolutionary who served on Gen. P. T. G. Beauregard's staff during the war (Courtesy Charles Hayes)

Loreta Janeta Velázquez, a Cuban-born woman who masqueraded as a male Confederate soldier and later became a Confederate spy (Courtesy Charles Hayes)

Rosemont Plantation, the childhood home of Jefferson Davis (Courtesy Rosemont Plantation, Woodville, Mississippi)

Jefferson Davis Memorial Monument (Courtesy Jefferson Davis Historical Site, Fairview, Kentucky)

Cherokee Indian Confederate veterans at a New Orleans UCV Reunion, 1903 (Courtesy Mountaineer Publishing, Waynesville, North Carolina)

Judah Benjamin, second Jewish United States senator (Louisiana), Confederate States of America secretary of the treasury, first Jewish North American cabinet member (Library of Congress)

Pope Pius IX sent this crown of thorns to Jefferson Davis as an expression of sympathy for his post-war treatment at the hands of the North. (Courtesy Confederate Memorial Hall, New Orleans, Louisiana)

Lt. Gen. Leonidas Polk, CSA, Episcopal bishop known as the "Fighting Bishop" (Library of Congress)

Gen. Patrick Cleburne, Irish Confederate (Courtesy Arkansas State Archives)

Emmanuel Dupre, one of many Louisiana Creoles who served the CSA during the war (Courtesy Betty Kennedy)

Wilson Carter, Confederate veteran, Georgia

48

The Sinking of the USS *Arizona*—1863

Uncle Seth had looked forward to the 1917 reunion of the Louisiana United Confederate Veterans ever since he received a letter from his old friend John A. Drummond from Port Barre, Louisiana, informing Uncle Seth that he would be attending. Added to that was the fact that the good ole Rebels from Louisiana were always happy to treat the Mississippi Rebs to a good time down in the bayou country. Uncle Seth had been saving his "egg money" all year and carefully depositing any additional cash he had in the Merchants and Planters Bank in Hazlehurst, Mississippi. He liked the bank—even though he had a high distrust for big banks. But this bank was founded by a former Confederate, Maj. R. W. Millsaps. The major was born in Copiah County, graduated from Harvard University, and was the respected founder of the Methodist college in Jackson, Mississippi. To Uncle Seth it seemed like family, not business men, were watching over his money. After withdrawing his spending cash from the bank, Uncle Seth purchased a round-trip ticket to New Orleans on the New Orleans, Jackson, & Great Northern Railroad.

After settling in his accommodations in one of New Orleans' finest hotels, Uncle Seth set out to find his old friend. It wasn't long before he ran into his old buddy. "John, it is wonderful to see you again," he said. Uncle Seth and John embraced in the manly fashion of former warriors, comrades, and friends.

"Seth, the years just keep on rolling by, but you are still as strong as during the war," John jokingly replied. Uncle Seth was still active for his age, but at seventy-three he knew that verbal battles against the Yankee invader were about the best he could do.

Uncle Seth had gathered a group of young people and had a specific request for his old friend. "John, I want you to tell these folks about how you all sunk the USS *Arizona* during the Battle of Sabine Pass."

"Well," John paused as if to gather his thought, "you know I have told that story many times, but maybe these young folk have never heard it." John turned around looking for the most comfortable chairs for him and

Uncle Seth. After they had found the best chairs available and had given the audience time to pull chairs around them, he began his account. "It was on a mild day, September 8, 1863. The Jeff Davis Guards, numbering around forty Irish soldiers, were assigned to a sand fort at the mouth of the Sabine River—you all know that's the river that serves as the border between Louisiana and Texas. Our limited armament consisted of two 32 pounders—which had been condemned and removed from service by the United States military department prior to the war—two 32-pound brass howitzers, and two 24 pounders.

"The Yankee invaders had a sizable fleet consisting of twenty-three vessels, twelve of which were armed war vessels. The others were transports carrying more than six thousand troops and supplies for the invasion of Texas. Having no time to reinforce the fort, our commander, Captain Odlum—who was stationed several miles away—sent orders to Lt. Dick Dowling, who was commanding the fort, to spike the guns, evacuate the fort, and fall back to a better defensive position at Johnson's Bayou. By the time these orders came to us, twelve Yankee warships had entered the harbor in front of the fort. Lieutenant Dowling called us together and told us about his orders to retreat. When we heard the news a great murmuring arose from the men. 'No, No,' was heard along the line of men. Almost as one we declared, 'We will stay by the fort until she goes down; and if she goes down, we will go down with her!' Lieutenant Dowling sent a message to Captain Odlum telling him that the men refused to evacuate the fort, to which the captain replied, 'If that be the case, then hold the fort at all hazards!' Captain Dowling's new orders were read and met with great cheers from all of us. Just about that time a courier arrived on horseback carrying a Confederate flag. This was a source of great pride because up until that time we had not even been provisioned with our country's flag to fly over our fort. Lieutenant Dowling received the flag and, waving it over his head while we cheered, sprang upon the parapet and shoved the staff with all his strength into the sand bank. Bowing his head and waving his hand to heaven he shouted, 'Dick Dowling is a dead man before this flag shall come down!' The sight of our country's flag and the pride we held for what it represented—and still does—infused us with even greater determination to make the Yankee invader of our country pay the price of his evil invasion.

"The United States gunboats *Sachem* and *Arizona* came up on the Louisiana side—that would be the eastern side—and with all the other United States ships began a constant fire on us. Our old guns were too weak to answer their fire. There was always a danger that one of the old weak guns would explode, killing or injuring more Southerners than Yankees. All we could do was keep low and wait until the United States warships got within the range of our guns. The Yankee fire was so intense that at times we had to venture out into the open with shovels and remove sand that had been thrown into our gun positions so we would be ready to fire our guns when the Yankees came within our range.

"At last the United States ships were within twelve hundred yards—the range of our guns. Lieutenant Dowling then gave the command: 'Every man to his post!' And shortly after that came the order to 'commence fire.' After the second or third round from our guns, the *Sachem* was shot through her steam chest. That fixed her. A white flag was raised immediately and we withheld any further fire in her direction. We then paid our respects to the USS *Arizona*, which was following behind the *Sachem*. It took the *Arizona* very little time to appropriately respond to Confederate fire by raising the white flag also. Because the white flag of surrender was raised on the *Arizona,* we withheld our fire even though she was well within our range. After that the *Clifton*, which was the flagship for the invasion force, came forward on the Texas side of the river to receive its share of Southern hospitality. Luckily we had one man, James Corcoran, who had the foresight to remove a stake marking the point of a reef three hundred yards below the fort. Upon reaching the reef the *Clifton* went hard aground right in front of our feeble but very accurate guns. About this time one of our guns exploded, causing a slight arm wound on one of the gun crew but no other causalities. As a matter of fact, that was our only causality during the entire engagement. The *Clifton* received a murderous fire from our remaining guns. She also received a shot through her steam chest and soon the Yankee sailors were jumping from their ship. About seventy-five of these Yankee sailors landed on the beach in front of the fort and most of them were armed. Now all we had were some forty men who were vigorously engaged in exchanging cannon fire with the invading fleet. Lieutenant Dowling knew that the Yankees would be able to overrun the fort with little effort. He quickly ordered the two closest cannons to be loaded with grape and canister shot and trained it on the Yankees, who, upon realizing what was being prepared for them, immediately threw down their weapons and surrendered.

"While this was taking place, the USS *Arizona*—with her white flag of surrender flying and enjoying the privilege of safety conferred on combatants under a white flag by civilized nations—slowly drifted downriver and out of range of our feeble guns. In typical Yankee fashion, as soon as they were out of range, they lowered their white flag and raised the flag that best represents the honor of all Yankeedom. Flying the invader's banner—the Stars and Stripes—the USS *Arizona* drifted out to sea. But being loaded with more Confederate ball and shot than it could carry, it soon sank. We were told that the *Arizona* sank in the Gulf of Mexico a few miles out of our harbor, but others have reported that it sank after returning to the Port of New Orleans." John seemed pleased with his rendition of his story and sat back in his chair to gaze into the faces of his young audience.

Speaking to the young folks, Uncle Seth gave them a stern warning: "Remember Lt. Dick Dowling's vow that our country's flag—the flag of the Confederate States of America—would never come down as long as he lived. It is your responsibility to tell the truth about the South's struggle to be a free country. The day will come when our own people will forget that they are a people, a conquered and occupied nation, a people who are not allowed to be the masters in their own home. The day will come when our nation's flag—the flag of the Confederate States of America—will be unwelcomed in the Southland. On that day, freedom will be dead."

§ Deo Vindice §

49

Rape and Murder—Yankee Treatment of Southern Civilians

Uncle Seth had just settled in his room at the United Confederate Veterans reunion in Jacksonville, Florida. The May 1914 reunion was his twenty-fourth reunion, and Uncle Seth was not sure how many more he would be able to make. He had been corresponding with Walter Brian from Jacksonville and was planning to meet him during the reunion. Walter had been working on a collection of accounts detailing various war crimes committed by the Yankees against Southern women and children during their invasion of the South.

Uncle Seth felt that Walter's work was very important because by now many "modern" or "New South" Southerners did not understand why so many of the old Confederate veterans still harbored resentment against the United States government. Uncle Seth hoped that Walter's work would demonstrate to future generations of Southerners just how cruel the Yankees were during the war. But even more important, he hoped it would show Southerners that nothing had changed except for the fact that the South was now completely under the rule of the Yankee Empire. A knock on the door announced Walter's arrival.

"Walter," Uncle Seth extended his hand and invited his new friend and comrade to sit down and visit for a while. "Now tell me, have you been able to document the beastly acts of the Yankee invader?" Uncle Seth asked hoping to get Walter to share some of his valuable research.

"Yes, I have, Seth, and it is not a flattering picture of the United States military, its government, and its political commanders," Walter answered. Uncle Seth noticed that the expression on his friend's face portrayed both anger and sadness. "I have found so many cases of robbery, looting, and wanton destruction of the private property of non-combatants that I am having a problem deciding which ones to include in my collection. The one thing that is true with all of these accounts is that the invaders looked upon the Southern people as less than human, people undeserving of the common respect due to humanity. If possible, they wanted to exterminate all of us!

"Early in 1862, when Lincoln appointed Sen. Andrew Johnson to be the Yankee commander of occupied Tennessee, the senator—who later became Lincoln's vice president—declared that Southerners who did not want to live under the rule of the Yankees were 'odious traitors and should be punished and impoverished.' Yankee Brig. Gen. Grenville M. Dodge was more precise. He declared, 'I propose to eat up all the surplus, and perhaps the entire crops in the country. These people are proud, arrogant rebels; all they possess belongs to the United States Government.'

"This type of barbarism did not become less common during the war—in fact, it got worse. In 1864, in Franklin County, Tennessee, Yankee Major General Robert H. Milroy drew up a list of 'disloyal' local civilians, making notes beside each name such as 'KILL, HANG AND BURN, BURN EVERYTHING, SHOOT IF YOU CAN MAKE IT LOOK LIKE AN ACCIDENT.' On February 7, 1865—only a few months before the end of the war—this same Yankee officer drew up another list containing the names of eighteen civilians who were to have their homes burned and another thirty-four who were to be shot. This United States military officer had four civilians to whom he wanted special attention paid. His orders for the four were that they were to be 'hung from the first tree in front of their door and be allowed to hang there for an indefinite period.' These were not random acts of an out-of-control, solitary Yankee soldier. These were official acts of the United States government! These were acts that began when the Yankee invader first stepped foot on our soil and continued both during the war and Reconstruction. How can our people, who are blood relatives of these men and women who suffered such barbarism, now accept as legitimate the rule of the current Yankee Empire?" Walter asked.

Uncle Seth could see that Walter was a fellow traveler and comrade in the ongoing struggle to tell the truth about the war and to undo the lies that the Yankee press, pulpit, politicians, and educators were constantly pumping out for Southern consumption. "Walter," Uncle Seth began cautiously, "there is a question I want to ask, but it is of such a nature that decent folk should not even have to discuss it. But I think it is too important to ignore."

Walter looked at Uncle Seth as if he already knew what Seth would ask. "What's that, Seth?"

"Are you documenting any accounts of rape by the Yankee invader—against black and white Southern women?" asked Uncle Seth.

"Yes," intoned Walter sadly, almost in a whisper. "I have too many to list them all, but several remain with me and keep returning to my thoughts as if crying out for vengeance—no, justice. But justice will never be granted by the arrogant Yankee Empire. I recall a case from Aiken, South Carolina. Some Confederate cavalrymen came upon an elderly Baptist minister standing in front of his home weeping. He informed the Southern soldiers that his daughter had just been raped and murdered by a bunch of Yankee soldiers. In another instance, a Lutheran minister, Rev. Dr. John Bachman, testified that he was present when a group of United States soldiers forced a woman to publicly undress—much to their perverted enjoyment. In another case, a group of seven Yankee soldiers broke into the home where a mother and her teenage daughter were hoping to be left alone. The Yankees tied up the mother and gang raped the daughter. The poor girl died shortly after the Yankees completed their sport with her; her mother went completely insane, never to recover. In North Carolina outside of Fayetteville at the home of Duncan Murchinson, Yankee cavalrymen dismounted and broke into the Murchinson's home, where their small girl was bedridden with typhoid. When they failed to find gold or silver, the Yankee officer announced to his men, 'Go ahead, boys, do all the mischief you can.' The seventy-year-old grandmother was dragged to the swamp and raped while other vandals destroyed furniture, slashed family portraits, and poured molasses into the family's piano. The poor little girl died while the United States troops were still looting her home." Walter stop for a moment—it seemed that the retailing of such barbaric acts was about to overcome the man.

"Walter," Uncle Seth interrupted the man's brief repose, "I understand that as bad as the Yankees were to the white Southern women, they were even worse to black Southern women."

"That's right, Seth." Walter looked at Uncle Seth as if to thank him for reminding him. "During Yankee General Sherman's occupation of Columbia, South Carolina, a black woman servant of the Episcopal minister Peter Shand was raped by a gang of the invader's soldiers. After they had finished their perverted sport, they forced her face down in a ditch and held her head down until her lungs were full of ditch water. There in that ditch she died. The famous Southern warrior poet of Columbia, William Gilmore Simms, also reported that Yankee regiments, in successive relays, committed gang rape on scores of slave women while General Sherman was in Columbia.

"Even though Yankees like to tell the world that they were fighting to free their black brothers and sisters, men like General Sherman did not have much use for blacks. For instance, once when General Sherman came upon a scene where a black man was lying dead on a Columbia street, he asked his men what happened. His soldiers replied, 'the damn black rascal gave us his impudence, and we shot him.' General Sherman then declared, 'Well bury him at once! Get him out of sight!' Later, when asked about the incident, General Sherman noted his contempt for Southerners and the rules of civilized warfare by declaring, 'We have no time for courts-martial and things of that sort.' Here is a case where a high-ranking United States military officer—and hero to modern Americans—actually conspired with his troops to hide the evidence of government-sponsored murder.

"Mary Chesnut recorded the news that she received from eyewitnesses of the dead bodies of eighteen black women in the Sumter District plantation. These black women all had bayonet wounds in their chests. Obviously, the Yankee invaders were through with them! I think there were a lot more cases of rape, but because of the humiliation of the victims they were never reported. There is also another reason—rapists do not want their victims to identify them, so they typically kill them." Walker looked at Uncle Seth as if pleading for some rationale for such hideous conduct.

"You know, Seth," Walter began in almost an apologetic tone, "I don't want to give the impression that all Yankee soldiers were murders, robbers, and rapists. No, there are many instances of Yankee soldiers acting in a friendly manner to local women and children. There were kind acts of providing sick and starving individuals and families with food and medicine."

"I understand that," Uncle Seth declared, his voice was anything except apologetic. "But how many smiles from the invader's troops does it take to atone for the rape of one woman? How many acts of kindness must an invading army perform in order for that army to demonstrate repentance for the impoverishment of whole communities? How much free food must the invading nation provide to the occupied people before the Yankee nation receives absolution for the lynching of a single innocent Southern civilian?

"You see," Uncle Seth continued, "the problem with the South is that our people have been too willing to absolve the invader of his guilt. Perhaps it is an attempt to regain equality in the Union—something that the Yankee Empire will never allow. Our people refuse to recognize that the old Union—the constitutionally limited, Jeffersonian, Republic of Republics—died at Appomattox. What we have now is a Federal Empire, and who wants to be an equal partner in a cruel empire? Besides, if the invader had left us alone to live in a country of our own choosing, to be governed by a government ordered upon the consent of the governed, then none of these outrages against the Southern people would have occurred in the first place! But as we well know, the Yankee is not inclined to mind his own business—especially when his profits are at risk." Uncle Seth and Walter both sat quietly in their chairs. They felt the heavy burden they shared—almost too heavy to bear.

They knew the truth, but the most oppressive truth of all was that they lived in an occupied nation and had no way to keep this truth alive as new generations of Southerners are born. They also knew that with the passing of each generation the agents, lackeys, and cronies of the Yankee Empire were slowly convincing rising generations of Southerners that those who wore the gray in the War for Southern Independence were evil, un-American men fighting to maintain the system of slavery. Surely somewhere out there in this world there must be people who are willing to help tell the truth about the War for Southern Independence.

§ Deo Vindice §

ON THE SKIRMISH LINE WITH UNCLE SETH
Yankee Brigadier General Quincy Adams Gilmore was not having much success against the Confederate military position at Morris Island. Morris Island was part of Confederate General P.G.T. Beauregard's defensive position protecting Charleston, South Carolina. On August 21, 1863, the Yankee general sent General Beauregard an ultimatum warning him that the Yankees would begin shelling Charleston if Beauregard did not abandon his Morris Island position. When Beauregard refused, the Yankees began shelling Charleston with a Parrott rifle. The Yankee artillery piece fired thirty-five rounds of incendiary shells into the city filled with noncombatant women, children, and old men. This is but one more example of Yankee honor—with liberty and justice for all?

50

Gen. Robert E. Lee's Coffin

It was late fall in central Mississippi. Uncle Seth hitched a team of mules to his wagon and prepared to take a load of white oak planks over to his cousin's house. His cousin, Mike Guess, was preparing a coffin for the recent death of an aged uncle. In later days, it would become common to purchase "factory-made" coffins, but in the Deep South of the early 1900s, a homemade coffin would be provided by the family of the deceased. It was looked upon not so much as a duty but as a loving tribute owed to the deceased by the extended family. Cousin Mike was much younger than Uncle Seth and would need the guidance of his older cousin to properly complete the task.

In birth or death, good times or bad times, extended families and the entire community pulled together. It was the one thing that Southerners could count on to get them through the harsh times following the war and Reconstruction—a time characterized by poverty and pellagra (a disease confined mostly to the post-war South that was caused by poor nutrition). Uncle Seth was always quick to point out to anyone willing to listen that pellagra and poverty were gifts to the South from our Yankee masters. The post-war South, denuded of its wealth and political power by war and Reconstruction, languished in poverty while the Northern masters of the Federal Empire enriched themselves by expanding their colonial holdings as well as their national and international commercial dominance.

"Every time I help make one of these it reminds me of the coffin that was used to bury Gen. Robert E. Lee," Uncle Seth noted as he unloaded the broad, white oak boards from his wagon.

"What do you mean?" asked Cousin Mike.

Taking that as his invitation to give the young man a history lesson, Uncle Seth began his story. "General Lee died in Lexington, Virginia, on October 12, 1870—about five and a half years after the end of the War for Southern Independence. The area around Lexington and the upper drainage of the James River had been hit by a great storm a few days before General Lee's death, causing flooding that completely cut off Lexington from the rest of the world. Because of the flooding, there was no way to obtain a proper coffin for General Lee—although if I know anything about him, he would have been satisfied with a common wooden box similar to the ones used to bury his fellow Confederate veterans. But such was the love for General Lee that the folks wanted to lay him to rest in a coffin befitting such a great man. During this dilemma a box was found that had floated down the swollen river and was stranded on a sandbar. Upon opening the box it was discovered that it contained a beautiful, newly constructed casket. The casket was taken to Lexington and the mortal remains of the Confederate States' great general was lovingly placed in it, a God-sent gift. The South's beloved military chieftain was then placed in the chapel of the university. The acquisition of the casket was so inspiring that Miss Nellie T. Simpson of Gallatin, Tennessee, wrote a poem commemorating the occasion. I just happen to have a copy with me." Uncle Seth stopped speaking as he felt around in his pockets looking for a little scrap of folded and worn paper.

Cousin Mike had been politely listening while he worked on the coffin. He smiled to himself when Uncle Seth declared that he had just happened to have the poem in his pocket.

"Yes, here it is," Uncle Seth exclaimed as if he had won a great victory. "I will read it to you—its title is 'A Coffin Befitting General Robert E. Lee':

> Even nature assumed the emblems of woe,
> And drenched was her bosom with tears that did flow;
> On the James' swollen tide a coffin she rolled,
> A coffin the form of the hero to hold.
> But selfish we are in our love and our grief
> When we claim as ours only this Heaven-sent chief.
> Shall Syria claim as her special dower
> All the fragrance distilled from the stately queen flower?
> Can Bethlehem claim as her right by birth
> The Prince of Peace sent to teach good will to earth?
> To all who love goodness, who greatness admire;
> To all who to goodness or greatness aspire;
> To peasant and crown-head, to convict or priest,
> General Lee's life is a light like the star of the east.

Oh my goodness, Mike, do you think that could be said of very many people today?"

Although it had been a little more than fifty years since the unfortunate ending of the War for Southern Independence, the reality of the consequences of the war remained as a constant reminder to Uncle Seth that the war continues. And, as far as Uncle Seth was concerned, it would never end until the right of the people of the South to live under a government ordered upon the American principle of the consent of the governed is recognized. No, as far as Uncle Seth was concerned the fighting continued in a different form.

§ **Deo Vindice** §

51

Abraham Lincoln's High Priest and Cult Followers

Uncle Seth slowly pulled his chair up to the kitchen table as he drew in the aroma rising from his hot coffee. He loved early mornings, especially in early winter in South Mississippi before the first frost had driven the green out of the grass. The air was crisp and the sun was just beginning to warm it. He knew the boys would soon be in to get their breakfast and tell him about their plans for the school day. Carroll Ray was the first to come in and immediately began asking Uncle Seth for his advice about his history project.

"Uncle Seth, I need to write a short report about Abraham Lincoln. My teacher wanted us to write about how much Lincoln loved black people and wanted to give them freedom and equal rights," Carroll Ray explained.

"Well, boy," Uncle Seth laughingly exclaimed, "you have an almost impossible task facing you—unless you intend to write fiction."

Now Carroll Ray knew that Uncle Seth was not an admirer of Lincoln, but because he had waited so late to prepare for his school assignment, he knew that following Uncle Seth's direction might be his only chance of turning in his assignment on time. He remained quiet and waited to hear Uncle Seth's response to his request for help.

"The first thing any Southerner needs to understand about Lincoln is that in today's America Lincoln has become the center of a religion with a high priest, acolytes, and cult followers. Lincoln's high priest and acolytes receive generous rewards and honors from the Federal Empire for their efforts in maintaining the Lincoln myth—a myth that is so necessary in maintaining the legitimacy of the Federal Empire. Anyone who dares to question the god-like status assigned to Lincoln will face virulent charges of treason and heresy. If you are an educator, you will never advance in the ranks of the learned elite; or, if you are a politician, you will never be allowed to join the ranks of the political elite who control the machinery of American government." Uncle Seth stopped long enough to make sure his grandson was following the explanation.

"Now, Carroll Ray," Uncle Seth continued, "you remember what I have told you all about how, when Lincoln was a member of the Illinois legislature, he urged the state to approve money to remove free blacks from the state and deport them out of America. Well to be exact they didn't use the term 'deport'; what they called it was 'colonization of blacks.' Lincoln's cult followers now claim that Lincoln ceased to believe in deporting blacks, but there is no evidence that he ever changed his mind. But lack of evidence has never been a hindrance to the advocates of an expanding empire." Uncle Seth's tone was stern and hinted at a deep revulsion not only for Lincoln but even more so for the thought of the supreme Federal Empire that now occupied and ruled his beloved South.

"It is unfortunate that most Southerners do not know that, up to his dying day, Lincoln had been actively negotiating with Great Britain and other foreign nations to deport the soon-to-be-freed blacks to distant parts of those foreign empires." Uncle Seth's voice became soft as if tiring from the effort to fight back the endless onslaught of Yankee lies and, even worse, the unhesitating willingness of pacified Southerners to accept such lies.

"Now, Carroll Ray," Uncle Seth seemed to regain his determination to continue the fight, "you also need to include something about how Lincoln supported the 1848 Illinois constitutional amendment to prohibit free blacks from living in Illinois. And don't forget to include the fact that Lincoln also supported the Illinois Black Codes that declared black people have no legal rights that white people were bound to respect. No one can find anything written by Lincoln or any speeches he made during this time in which he took the side of free blacks or slaves." Uncle Seth had worked himself into prime fighting spirit and was determined to set the record straight once and for all—even though he knew it would be a small and insignificant victory. Uncle Seth knew that small victories were all that a conquered people could hope for as long as the oppressor held ultimate power over the occupied nation. He also knew that sometimes honor requires men to fight, even when to more practical and pacified folks the fight seemed hopeless. But just like Leonidas and the three hundred Spartans who died at Thermopylae, Uncle Seth was determined to leave future generations an example that one day might inspire them to resist the invader and reclaim their liberty.

Seeing that Carroll Ray had absorbed just about all that he could, Uncle Seth decided to bring the discussion to a close; but first, just one more point needed to be made. "Don't forget to remind everyone that Ole Abe never freed a single slave. The Lincoln cult worshipers love to refer to him as the Great Emancipator, but the truth is that he never freed any slaves. You see, the Emancipation Proclamation was a war measure similar to the efforts of the British during the Revolutionary War. Shortly after the thirteen colonies declared their independence in 1776, the British offered freedom to any slave who would revolt against their master and join the British effort to prevent the secessionist efforts of the thirteen colonies. Lincoln was hoping for a huge slave uprising with all of its brutality aimed at defenseless, white Southern women and children. He thought this danger would cause Southern men to abandon the Confederate army and rush back home to defend their women and children. Lincoln's proclamation was no more successful than the earlier attempt by the British. Remember that Lincoln's Emancipation Proclamation only applied to the states controlled by the Confederacy—it did not apply to Northern states or to Southern territories then controlled by Yankee armies. In other words, Lincoln declared slaves free in areas where he had no way to enforce his proclamation and left in slavery those blacks in Northern states and Southern territories that *were* controlled by Yankee armies. The proclamation specifically excluded by name the counties in what is now known as West Virginia and six parishes in Louisiana then occupied by Yankee armies."

Uncle Seth could see from the excited expression on Carroll Ray's face that he was looking forward to writing his paper. But Uncle Seth also knew that the young boy's report would not be enthusiastically accepted by the Yankee-educated teacher (or miseducated teacher, as Uncle Seth usually described self-hating Southern educators). It pained him to think about this young son of the South. Carroll Ray and his generation had no way of measuring the inheritance of freedom that the Yankee empire stole from them; his generation and generations to follow would be taught that a supreme, all-powerful Federal government is the legitimate government as designed by America's founding fathers and that to swear allegiance to an indivisible Federal government is the highest form of patriotism. These were Yankee lies, but lies that were necessary if they were to keep "we the people" of the South under their absolute and complete control.

"Carroll Ray," the tone of Uncle Seth's voice hinted that a warning was coming, "you need to understand that everything I have told you is the truth, but truth is a dangerous enemy to empires. Those who control and enjoy the perks and privileges of the empire will not take lightly those who dare to threaten it by contradicting their lies. They will stop at nothing to enforce the lies and myths by which they keep their conquered subjects pacified. Regardless of how good your paper might be, don't expect a good grade from your Yankee-educated teacher. She has been taught to hate the South and to adore the Yankee Empire, its lies, its myths, and its ability to promote and reward those who, like her, help maintain their federal empire."

§ Deo Vindice §

ON THE SKIRMISH LINE WITH UNCLE SETH

On June 20, 1863, Lincoln and his government violated Article IV, Section 3 of the United States Constitution by seizing a large part of Virginia's territory and railroading it into the Union as the State of West Virginia. The United States secretary of state at the time, William H. Seward, called attention to the fact that there was no law to sanction the seizure. Still, he supported the Lincoln government's utter disregard of laws of nations and the original American Constitution by stating, "We have the power and might makes right." This could well be the motto of the Federal Empire since Appomattox.

52

Civilians and the Terror of Yankee Invasion

Uncle Seth moved cautiously over the churchyard. He held his walking cane securely in his right hand and a plate of fried chicken balanced in his left. He sat on the ground in the shade of a sprawling red oak tree. The community Baptist church held its annual protracted meeting every year beginning in the fourth week of June. The meeting lasted for a week or more. A daily series of preaching, praising, praying, and singing, it was held after the farmers had "laid-by" their crops. While the crops were maturing in the field, the farm families were free to enjoy the fellowship of their neighbors and thank God for "the blessings He has bestowed upon us." This had been the custom as far back as Uncle Seth could remember. Somehow, the keeping of this tradition seemed to give him a sense of permanence—some things should stay the same.

It was not long before several of the local children had joined him. All who knew the old Confederate veteran admired him. Everyone, including his grandchildren and great-grandchildren, insisted on calling him Uncle Seth. Even those who were not related to him by blood referred to him as such. The children looked forward to listening to his endless stories about the war. Uncle Seth would look at the children and tell them a story about one of their relatives who served in the Confederate army. Uncle Seth felt a keen obligation to those brave men who struggled during the war —and especially to those who died—in a vain effort to protect their Southern homes. He felt that if he did not tell the true story about why they fought, these young folks around him would be taught by Yankee textbooks to hate their own people. Without realizing it, the community had in Uncle Seth a bridge connecting the past to the future.

Soon, one of the boys at the churchyard asked Uncle Seth to tell them who was the bravest during the war. No doubt, the boy was hoping Uncle Seth would select one of the boy's blood relatives—such bragging rights go a long way in a closely knit community.

"You all know that I just got back from a United Confederate Veteran reunion—it was held in Memphis this year. While up there I met a lady,

204

a Mrs. W. H. Sebring, who related an incident to me that makes me think perhaps the bravest of our people were not those of us in the ranks fighting the better-equipped and more-numerous Yankee invader but those civilians who had to endure the terror inflicted upon our people by those people. You all know who I'm talking about—I'm talking about the soldiers of the United States," declared Uncle Seth with a disdain in his voice that many thought would cause him to turn around and spit on the ground. The children were munching on their dinner but their attention was on the old Confederate storyteller.

Uncle Seth continued, "Mrs. Sebring had moved out into the country about three miles east of Memphis after the Federals had occupied the city. All the civilians in the area were exposed to frequent invasions of their homes by marauding bands of United States troops. She had with her at home Joe, an invalid brother; Charley, another younger brother; her sister Mary; and an Irish girl and a young black girl who worked as maids. One night the boys awoke to the sound of men breaking into the house. Joe and Charley came out armed with an old gun. They confronted three blue-coated Yankee soldiers who had broken into their home. The Federals immediately attacked Joe and, in order to save him, Charley shot the Yankee. The marauding party fled, leaving their dead comrade's body. The next morning around eight o'clock, they returned with a mob of forty or fifty United States troops. The leader from the prior night's attack pointed to the invalid Joe and cried out, 'There's the damn rebel! 'Shoot him! Shoot him!' Two of the soldiers, having forced their way into the home, leveled their guns on Joe and fired. As they did, Mrs. Sebring threw herself into the two Federals, causing their guns to fire harmlessly into the ceiling. One of the Yankees then grabbed Mrs. Sebring and, placing his gun barrel against her temple, declared with the vilest oaths that he would love to 'blow her damn rebel brains out of her skull!' Unmoved, this brave Southern woman responded to her tormentor in blue, 'All you are fit for is to frighten children.' By this time other blue devils had pulled Joe out and began to beat him with their rifle butts. Mary then rushed over and threw herself over her invalid brother in an attempt to protect him from the merciless beating being inflicted by the United States troops. Seeing that this was not producing the desired

Mrs. Sebring circa 1890

protection for little Joe, the black girl joined the fray by picking up a chair and declaring, 'You Yankee devils hit Mars Joe again and I'll break dis chair over yo head.' More than anything else, that single act enraged the Yankee brutes, who immediately began cursing and threatening the 'damn nigger.' The Yankee soldiers went into every room in Mrs. Sebring's home breaking furniture and cutting apart feather mattresses in order to scatter the feathers. After this, they poured molasses on the floor and stomped the feathers and molasses into a sticky mass. They turned the stove upside down and broke every dish they could find in the kitchen. Two or three Yankees then dragged Joe outside and threw him into a wagon in which they had placed the body of their dead comrade. The Yankees called out to the women folk in the house that Joe would not be returning.

"As they began to depart, the Irish maid seized one of the Yankee's cavalry hats, went outside, and tied it to a turkey that had been killed by the troops. As the victorious United States troops left the scene of their latest gallant conquest, she flung the dead turkey with its blue cavalry bonnet into the wagon next to the dead Yankee and shouted, 'Here, take all your dead! We want none of them.' Mrs. Sebring and her sister followed the wagon on its way back to the Yankee camp. These Yankees shouted threats to return the next day and burn the house with the women folk tied up inside of it. When they reached the Yankee military camp, a great crowd of Yankee soldiers surrounded the wagon and loudly complained to their fellow Yankees by declaring, 'Why didn't you hang the damn rebel in front of his house? They have fine trees there!' After great effort, this brave Southern lady managed to secure an audience with the camp commander, who eventually ordered Joe's release." Uncle Seth paused to gauge the reaction of his audience and then continued, "So you see, boys and girls, I think the civilians were the bravest."

"But Uncle Seth, wasn't it nice of the Yankee commander to release Joe?" asked one of the girls sitting around him.

Uncle Seth sat quietly for a long time contemplating the question and mentally constructing an answer that would fix forever in the minds of his audience the cruel reality of invasion, conquest, and occupation. "You know, if those people had minded their own business and allowed us to have a country of our own, then none of this would have ever happened. The South did the same thing that the thirteen American colonies did back in 1776 when they seceded from Great Britain. The South had and we still have a right to be left alone—to enjoy living in a country of our own based on the free and unfettered consent of the governed, to be the master in our own home. An occasional, convenient, and isolated act of kindness on the part of the invader and occupier does not absolve him from the crimes he commits when he uses bloody bayonets to deny other people their unalienable right of self-determination." The finality in his voice told the children that he had uttered his last on the subject.

Looking around at his audience, Uncle Seth noticed a serious, almost sad expression on the face of one of the young girls. "What's the matter, Peggy Sue?" asked Uncle Seth.

"Uncle Seth," Peggy Sue uttered softly, almost as if she was whispering, "my grandmother Wemire, who lives in the cabin up at the head of the creek, will not let us talk about the war in her house. Every time one of us mentions the word 'Yankee' Grandma Wemire turns around and spits on the floor and then makes us clean the floor!"

Uncle Seth couldn't help but join in the rest of the crowd as they chuckled at Peggy Sue's story. "Yes, Peggy Sue," Uncle Seth explained, "your grandma suffered the loss of all three of her brothers, a son, and her husband in the war. She was alone during the war and lived through several visits from the troops of the United States army. People who did not live through the war have a hard time understanding the depth of the loss our people suffered—it's your job, Peggy Sue, to make sure your children's children understand why we fought and why we deserve to be free." The church bell began to ring, signaling to all the beginning of the song-fest. Slowly, Uncle Seth's audience melted away as they rejoined their families in the church.

§ Deo Vindice §

ON THE SKIRMISH LINE WITH UNCLE SETH
"Tell them [future generations] how we exhausted every honorable means to avoid the terrible arbitrament of war, asking only to be let alone, and tendering alliance, friendship, free navigation—everything reasonable and magnanimous—to obtain an amicable settlement. Tell them how, when driven to draw the sword, we fought the mercenaries of all the world until, overpowered by tenfold numbers, we fell; like Leonidas and his Spartans of old, fell so heroically that our defeat was more glorious than their victory."
–Gen. R. E. Colston, CSA, circa 1868

53

Brave Yankees Make War on Arkansas Civilians

It was a beautiful May morning in Little Rock, Arkansas. Uncle Seth and hundreds of other good ole Rebels had gathered there to enjoy the 1911 annual reunion of the United Confederate Veterans. He was seated in the hotel lobby enjoying a cup of coffee and visiting with a lady close to his age who was telling him about her experience with the Yankee invaders of Arkansas in fall of 1864.

"Seth, I tell you those were the worst days of my life. We did not know if we would survive from one day to the next. Groups of Yankees were robbing and burning and killing throughout the countryside—no one was safe. It seems that Yankee General Blount—he was with that infamous Yankee General Lane's army—had put a Yankee captain named Curtis in charge of destroying all pro-Southern people in our area. Of course, that would have been most of us there.

"In a neighborhood close by, the Yankees murdered one of Confederate General Price's soldiers who was on his sick bed at home. They then went into Mr. Jim Moore's home—he was away with the Confederate army— and stripped Mrs. Moore and her daughter down to their undergarments looking for hidden jewelry. When the Yankee robbers did not find anything, they burned down the house. They also burned my aunt Naomi Buchannan's home and several other homes around Cane Hill. To make a good impression on secessionists, they hanged three men who were innocent of any crime; and you know, one of the men those Yankees hung was an ardent pro-Union man! That did not make any difference to the Yankees—Union or Confederate, he was a Southerner and, therefore, as far as those Yankees were concerned he deserved to die. My sister and I helped to cut down and remove the Yankee lynch rope from poor old Mr. Crozier. He was seventy-five years old, and his only crime was that he was a Southerner." The Arkansas lady finished her story and sat quietly looking down at the floor. The elderly woman seemed to get some relief from telling her story, but her face nonetheless displayed the effects of pain and grief carried for these many years after the active fighting had ceased.

"You know," Uncle Seth broke the silence, "the Yankee Captain Curtis met his match during that expedition. He had divided his men and sent them out to rob and terrorize the women at Cane Hill and surrounding areas. The Yankees were not concerned because they knew that all able-bodied men had left to serve in the Confederate army. In essence, the United States army was intentionally making war on innocent and defenseless women, children, and old men. But empires always feel that they have a right to do anything they desire to their victims. Captain Curtis and five men went to Cheatham place and captured an old man, Carroll Clarey, and his fourteen-year-old son. There were several other younger children in the home. Mr. Clarey's wife, the mother of his children, had passed away, leaving the old man both father and mother to his family. When the Yankees took the father and the fourteen-year-old boy from the home, they told the young children that they intended to hang their father and older brother. The fourteen-year-old managed to escape by running into a thorny blackberry patch as the Yankees were leading them to a tree to be lynched. The Yankees went ahead and lynched the father.

"At this time, there were several Confederate soldiers home on leave—actually, they had come home to get winter clothes. Upon hearing about the marauding Yankees in the area, Confederate Captain Beaty and Lieutenant Rich gathered a small group together and ambushed the Yankees. The Confederates crowded in so close that they engaged in hand-to-hand fighting; our boys were eagerly extracting revenge from the Yankees. Well, the Yankees were not accustomed to fighting man to man or with anything remotely close to even odds, so they skedaddled. But our boys were close behind them. The Yankee Captain Curtis, hearing the commotion, rushed to the aid of his cowardly band of pillagers. Captain Beaty, Lieutenant Rich, and the rest of the Confederates suddenly realized that the Yankees had received reenforcements, but they charged into the mass of Yankees anyway! Our boys killed six Yankees and secured all of their arms, ammunition, accouterments, and horses. All of this and not a single Southern man nor horse suffered a scratch.

"Oh, by the way, Yankee General Blount, who sent these men down to conquer Arkansas and make it a part of the new Federal Empire—he was born in Trenton, Maine, and moved to Ohio when he was fifteen. He was trained and educated as a physician. Now think about it: here was a man who had dedicated his life to healing the sick, relieving suffering, and bringing comfort to the dying, and now he had turned himself into a barbaric vandal, waging war on innocent civilians. He and his fellow Yankees needlessly terrorized the people of the South—a people whose only crime was wanting to be left alone. We only wanted to live in a country ordered upon the free and unfettered consent of the governed. Yet this was too much to ask of the emerging Yankee Empire. Men like Blount, Lane, Sherman, and Lincoln would stop at nothing in order to force the South into remaining the Yankee's cash cow—not citizens of our own country but subjects of the Federal Empire. The guilt of his sins must have caused great internal conflict for the Yankee general because either God, or the devil, drove the man crazy. He died at the age of fifty-five after being committed to an insane asylum," Uncle Seth concluded. He was convinced that Blount must eventually answer for his actions on this earth. He was also convinced that his fellow Southerners had a duty to pass on to their children the truth about why he and his comrades wore the gray in the War for Southern Independence. He also hoped that the day would come when his descendants would realize that the war is not over. Principles do not cease when an army is compelled to surrender; principles of liberty remain alive forever, waiting the day when the next generation will rise again!

§ Deo Vindice §

ON THE SKIRMISH LINE WITH UNCLE SETH

On entering Williamston, North Carolina, the Yankee invader made no effort to respect civilian property. Not a single house was exempt from Yankee vandalism; it mattered not whether the family was home or absent; doors were broken open and soldiers of the United States army took from noncombatant civilians whatever they liked. What they did not take they destroyed. Furniture, food, and clothing of every description were committed to the flames, and any citizen regardless of age who dared to protest was threatened with beatings or death. Justifiable punishment for a people who dared to leave the Yankee Empire, they believed. If you can't leave you are not free—and "we the people" of the South are not free!

54

Moonshine Whiskey Saves the Day

A cold February wind blew through the cracks in the wall of Uncle Seth's bedroom. It seemed to him that of late the cold wind had begun to blow through his wrinkled skin to chill his very bones. He slowly ambled to the mantle, grasped his toddy bottle, and sucked down a warming swallow of whiskey sweetened with honey. "Ahh!" he thought. "Nothing like a hot toddy to warm chilled bones."

"Uncle Seth," warned Billie Jean, his great granddaughter, "you know that stuff has quite a bite. You should take your time with it." She felt it her responsibility to keep a close watch on her ill great-grandfather.

"Now, Billie Jean, don't you worry yourself about me. I know how to handle my whiskey," he explained as he replaced the cork in the bottle. "You know, once during the war a bottle of whiskey saved me and helped to free a number of Confederates POWs," Uncle Seth began. Billie Jean stopped what she was doing, more in courtesy to the old Confederate veteran than the desire to hear his story, and quietly settled down within arm's reach of him.

"John Cunningham, who now resides in Ravenna, Texas, and I were enjoying a furlough. We were on our way to Trigg County, Kentucky. Our horses needed a rest, so we stopped at a little war-deserted village along the way. The only store open for business was a small saloon run by a discharged Southern soldier. His main stock and trade was some of his own Kentucky moonshine—or as we all called it, mountain dew. Before long, we had gathered around his red hot stove and were engaged in a friendly drink and swapping tales of fighting Yankees. All of a sudden a ruckus began outside and then someone began pounding on the door demanding entrance or else they would

(Jim Whittington)

211

burn us out! To our horror, we discovered that while we were drinking, the saloon had been surrounded by elements of Colonel Bird's East Tennessee Regiment—Yankee loyalist! We were trapped! John took the only course of action left. With bottle in hand, he flung the saloon doors open and bravely faced half a dozen Navy revolvers." Uncle Seth paused and looked down at Billie Jean.

"Oh, don't stop Uncle Seth! What did you all do?" she pleaded. Her inquiry was just what Uncle Seth was hoping to hear.

"Well, ole John wasn't about ready to surrender or die. 'Come on in, gentlemen,' John happily proclaimed as if suddenly finding a bevy of new drinking buddies. 'Drink mountain dew to your heart's content, and, I tell you, it's the best you ever put to your lips.' At the sight of the bottle and the promise of getting all they could drink, the 'good ole boys' from East Tennessee holstered their pistols and remembered their first calling— one that overcame what little semblance of military bearing they had. Before long, the contents of that bottle and several of its companions had disappeared. The Yankee loyalist promoted John to the rank of Colonel Liquor," Uncle Seth chuckled, remembering those long-ago days.

"Shortly thereafter, the rest of the Yanks had arrived and had in tow a number of local citizens who loudly asserted their loyalty to the Yankee Cause and a number of Confederate POWs taken in their raid. Several of the captured citizens had papers declaring them to be loyal to the Union Cause, but to their dismay, none of those East Tennessee boys knew how to read—not even their captain! The captain came into the saloon and began sharing my bottle. He looked around and asked if anyone could read. No one responded, so John, hoping to endear himself to the captain, volunteered to read for him. John followed the captain outside and was presented the parole papers from one of the captured citizens. Slowly, John began to read and memorize the words. Sure enough, the Yankee captain released his captive. The other citizens submitted their papers, John read them, and they, too, were released. John looked over at the Confederate POWs and gave them a wink. They got the message and began rummaging through their haversacks to come up with any excuse for paper. One by one, John read their 'papers' declaring them to be paroled soldiers on their way home! In a matter of minutes the Yankee captain watched as his entire day's work was sent home 'never again to fight against their country,' a solemn promise that they were all willing to keep. After all, the Confederate States of America was their country—and they sure as heck wasn't going to fight against it!" Uncle Seth slapped his knee and chuckled with satisfaction.

"With just a little more mountain dew, the Yankee captain listened as John read our 'parole' papers and then allowed us to continue our journey home. Yes sir, I do believe it was the best whiskey I ever tasted," Uncle Seth said as he put his arm around his great-granddaughter and wondered if her children would remember him and all his comrades who wore the gray in the War for Southern Independence.

§ Deo Vindice §

ON THE SKIRMISH LINE WITH UNCLE SETH
"The old Continental soldier fighting for American independence against the British Empire circa 1776, had friends. France, Spain and Holland helped him with fleets and armies and munitions and money, but the old Confederate had no friends; no, not one. He stood alone, but he stood undaunted, and he fell, when he did fall, like a noble lion who succumbs at last not so much to the prowess of his enemies as to his own absolute and utter exhaustion. He fought not to maintain slavery, not to erect an oligarchic form of government, not for gold or conquest or glory! No, no, no! He fought to be free, to govern himself as he himself saw fit, leaving to all others the same privilege."
—Capt. Salem Dutcher, Confederate Survivors Association,
April 26, 1898

55

Civilized Warfare—Respecting the Rights of Non-Combatants

"Uncle Seth," exclaimed the eight-year-old grandson at Uncle Seth's feet, "look at my sheriff's badge! I'm going to be a Texas Ranger."

Uncle Seth smiled at the youngster, picked him up, and placed him on his lap. "You know, Buddy," began Uncle Seth, "I rode with the Texas Rangers during the war. They were a cavalry unit from Texas known as Terry's Texas Rangers." Buddy's attention was firmly fixed on his grandfather as Uncle Seth continued his story.

"We had about one hundred men in the unit and were stationed at Bowling Green, Kentucky. We received orders to go to the village of Jimtown, which was about forty miles east of Bowling Green. The people in the county were basically ignorant and Unionist. Many of them looked upon the Texas Rangers as devils incarnate," Uncle Seth explained.

"Upon hearing of our approach, the men of that area fled, abandoning their homes, wives, and children. You see, they had already heard about how harshly the Yankees were treating Confederate civilians and they expected similar treatment from us. But we were not like the Yankee invaders—we were protecting our people, not looting them," Uncle Seth declared with an almost acidic emphasis. His mind briefly raced back to the harsh times when "his" people of the South endured the terror of Yankee invasion. Uncle Seth realized that his tone of voice was inappropriate for such a young audience, so calmed himself before continuing. "Our men were in the habit of stopping at homes along their march, asking for buttermilk and such. As a matter of fact, Terry's Rangers were often laughingly referred to as Terry's Buttermilk Rangers." Uncle Seth chuckled as he remembered those days. "The first day of the march we were able to find only two homes occupied. Now, we never entered a home, not even the home of an enemy, unless we were invited to enter. So we just kept on marching until we reached the first house where we spied human life. At this home we found a woman whose husband, like the others along the line of our march, had run away as we approached. She was braver than her husband and was determined to remain at her home and face whatever terror the 'evil Southerners' were going to visit on innocent civilians. One of our boys went up to her as she stood there, the very picture of a woman in dread of imminent terror, and asked her for some buttermilk. She soon gave the men all the buttermilk she had and would have given us anything else within her possession. You should have seen the surprised expression on her face when our men politely thanked her and reached into their pockets and paid for the buttermilk. You see, our officers had given strict orders that nothing would be taken from civilians unless we paid for it." Uncle Seth wanted to make sure the youngster understood the difference between the Confederate army, which was protecting their country from invasion, and the United States army, which was invading and, with the utmost cruelty, destroying the South and her people.

"The next house was about two miles down the road. When we reached it, we saw one young woman hiding in the cornfield clutching a young child. Another child—about your age, Buddy—was hiding behind her skirt. On the porch we saw a much older lady with a pistol on her lap and knitting in her hands. We went over to the one in the cornfield and, after much encouragement, managed to convince her and her two children to return to their home. Even still, they expected us to inflict some horrible evil upon them at any moment—after all, that was the custom of Yankee soldiers when dealing with Southern civilians. When some of our men dismounted to go up to the old woman, she put down her knitting, picked up her pistol, pointed it directly at them and announced that she would kill the first man who came on to her property. Our men were immediately halted by the surprising turn of events and were even more embarrassed by the gales of laughter behind them coming from their fellow Confederate soldiers." Uncle Seth slowly rocked back in the old rocking chair.

"Now, no doubt we could have forced the issue—we could have, that is, if we had been thieves, barbarians, or Yankees. But the rules of war require that, if at all possible, civilized soldiers respect the lives, property, and liberty of noncombatants, even those civilians who may be opposed to you. The humorous standoff was broken when a woman came rushing in from the woods behind the house, entered the back door, and came on to the front porch. As she took her place next to the old woman she exclaimed, 'Mother! Put down that thing. Treat those men right. They are perfect gentlemen; they came to my house and never hurt a thing!' And so our captor allowed us to move on, but she still remained defiant, declaring that no one would be allowed to trespass on her property. We, of course, respected her wishes," Uncle Seth explained.

The old man looked down at his eight-year-old grandson and

wondered if the boy understood what he had been talking about—not just the war stories, but the truth behind the South's failed struggle to maintain Southern independence. "Buddy," Uncle Seth announced in a commanding voice, "one day you will go off to some big college."

"What college do you think I will go to, Uncle Seth?" interrupted Buddy.

"Oh, let me see", continued Uncle Seth, "you will probably go to the rich folks' college up in Oxford, Mississippi." Uncle Seth grimaced when he told the boy that because he knew it was a bad joke. Buddy's family would not likely be able to afford the cost. In an attempt to recover the high ground after such a bad joke, Uncle Seth continued, "When you get to college—wherever you go—you will have a smart but less-than-educated history teacher who will tell you that evil men like the Yankee General Sherman were not the only ones to plunder and kill innocent civilians. That teacher will try to convince Southern children that we were even more evil than the Yankee invaders. When he tells you things like that, Buddy, I want you to remember what your old Confederate veteran grandfather taught you. I want you to defend the honor of the men who wore the gray in the War for Southern Independence." These last few words of Uncle Seth's story sounded, even to an eight-year-old boy, to be more like a prayer than a simple request—a prayer that Uncle Seth hoped would transcend generations to reach Southerners yet unborn and still waiting to live in a country of their own.

§ Deo Vindice §

ON THE SKIRMISH LINE WITH UNCLE SETH
The United States Federal government committed itself to a policy of unlimited aggression and war against civilian populations—in violation of its own Lieber code for the conduct of civilized warfare. The government of the United States of America waged a barbaric and imperialistic war against a people who only asked to be left alone.

56

A Barefoot Confederate at Gettysburg

Ole Beau, the family's Redbone hound, was barking a warning, so Uncle Seth thought he had better go see what was causing all the ruckus. He stood under the large red oak tree and peered down the lane. Curtis and Joe William, two of Uncle Seth's numerous great-grandchildren, eased up behind him to see what the problem might be. "Oh heck, Beau!" exclaimed Joe William. "It's only one of those barefoot Hamiltons headed to the creek."

"Hush," whispered Curtis. "You know how it upsets Uncle Seth when we talk about the poor Hamiltons."

The "poor" Hamiltons were a family of sharecroppers who had moved into a vacant cabin a couple of hundred yards up the lane. White sharecroppers were now common in the Deep South, but Uncle Seth remembered a time before the war when there were no such people. Poverty was also common in the South these days—a result of the Yankee invasion, referred to by the unknowing as the Civil War, and the post-war occupation, known as Reconstruction. Poverty was now the common inheritance of all Southerners. As Uncle Seth often reminded the young'uns, "we are all poor, just some of us more poor than others."

"You all shouldn't poke fun at those folks. They're just plain folk who have fallen on hard times, and Lord knows there are enough hard times to go around," admonished Uncle Seth. "You know, boys, I talked to Capt. John H. Leathers at the Louisville United Confederate Veterans reunion last year, and he told me about a young boy no older than that Hamilton lad—nineteen years old—who was part of his unit at Gettysburg. This young lad, Joe Ersom was his name, was from the mountains of Virginia. He volunteered early in 1862. He could not read or write and had never worn shoes! Yep, he came into camp barefoot. His feet were so unaccustomed to shoes that he could wear them for only a short while before the blisters would begin to form on his feet. So off would come the shoes, and he would continue drilling barefoot. As a matter of fact, the boy had only worn shoes during the harshest parts of winter. Well, you can

217

imagine how the better-off boys from the Shenandoah Valley poked fun at this poor mountain boy. But he did the menial tasks assigned to him by his social betters and continued to drill with the men of Gen. Stonewall Jackson's army." Uncle Seth turned away from the lane and sat down under the cool shade of the red oak to finish his story.

"I bet that mountain boy could shoot better than any of those fancy valley boys," insisted Curtis.

"Yes, Captain Leathers said that the barefoot boy became an excellent soldier. He was well-acquainted with camp life, shooting, and hard work. During the Battle of Kernstown, four miles above Winchester, Virginia, General Jackson ordered the captain's company into action. Well, this was the barefoot boy's baptism into the fire of battle. He behaved splendidly and at once won the admiration of the entire company of veteran soldiers. From that day forward no one mocked him. He was accepted as an equal—a man among men," explained Uncle Seth.

"Shortly after the victory at Chancellorsville—you all know that's where Gen. Stonewall Jackson was killed—General Lee began making plans to move into Pennsylvania. General Lee had obtained a limited supply of fine English boots. He ordered that they be distributed to those men in his army who needed replacements. He knew that his men would be in for a long march and wanted them equipped for the journey. Well Joe, naturally, was issued a pair of these fine, new boots. He could only wear them for a short while, but he was determined to keep them. Yep, they became his prized possession. As he said, 'first pair of Sunday go-to-meeting shoes I ever owned.' And he was determined to keep them," laughed Uncle Seth.

"It wasn't long before Joe and the rest of Captain Leathers' company was on the march headed for Gettysburg. The first two days of the battle, the Confederates pushed the Yankees before them. It was on the first day that Captain Leathers' company was ordered to assault some Yankee breastworks." Uncle Seth paused slightly to allow his audience to dwell on his words.

"Uncle Seth," broke in Joe William, "was Gen. Stonewall Jackson still in command of Joe's company?"

"No," replied Uncle Seth sadly, "by this time he had died and General Ewell was in command of Jackson's old army. Well, anyway,

Captain Leathers circa 1904

Joe and the rest of his company charged across a wheat field into the raging fire of the entrenched Yankees. Now, Joe just happened to have his new boots on at the time and they began to blister his feet. So he fell out of line of battle, sat down with minie balls whizzing around him, and took his new boots off, tied them around his left arm, and quickly rejoined his comrades in the charging line of battle. The charge covered over four hundred yards of bitter mayhem, terror, and death, but our boys carried the day! They took the breastworks and planted our beloved Confederate battle flag where formerly the Yankee Stars and Strips had flown. But alas, poor Joe was found on the very top of the Yankee breastworks, dead, his bayonet-tipped Enfield in one hand and precious boots in the other.

"So you see, boys, don't ever laugh at a man because of his lack of material substance. We had many a good man in our ranks who was poor by the world's standard, but I know them to have been heroes. Yes, and remember they fought for the independence of their country; they fought to repel a vicious invader, a tyrant who would replace our once-free Republic of Republics with an all-powerful Federal Empire. You all remember those barefoot boys—those men who wore the gray in the War for Southern Independence." Uncle Seth's voice faded as he turned to look down the lane—or was he looking back at unsung and almost forgotten heroes?

§ Deo Vindice §

ON THE SKIRMISH LINE WITH UNCLE SETH
While attending the Constitutional Convention in 1787, William Samuel Johnson, a moderate Federalist from Connecticut, declared, "The states do exist as political societies [and] must be armed with some power of self-defense." Even Federalists recognized the ultimate authority of the sovereign state in the newly created American Republic of Republics, a fact denied by Lincoln and his propagandists.

57

A Nankeen Shirt Used to Signal the Yankees' Coming

Uncle Seth was watching Billie Jean as she carefully removed the clean, sun-dried shirts from the clothesline and placed them in the white oak basket. He loved the smell of clean shirts that were dried in the clean air of south-central Mississippi. At eighty-one years old, he could not get around as well as he did when his great-grandsons—the 'boys,' as he called them—were young. He now kept busy pretending to help, mostly by keeping Billie Jean company. "Uncle Seth, I washed your new calico print shirt, and it is now dry. I'll iron it today and you can wear it to church on Sunday." Billie Jean took great pleasure in doing small things for the old Confederate veteran. He had always been a part of her life and she could tell that time was taking a toll on his physical abilities. She knew that she would not have his company much longer.

"Did I ever tell you about how we used a nankeen shirt as a secret code to warn General Taylor that the Yankee General 'Cotton Thief' Banks was marching toward Shreveport, Louisiana?" Uncle Seth asked as he admired his newly washed shirt.

"What is a nankeen shirt?" inquired Billie Jean.

"It's a shirt made from a type of cloth woven from a cotton plant that has a brown tint to it. The more you wash it, the more the cloth takes on a brown, copper tint. And, best of all, it does not fade. Nankeen cloth was developed in China, somewhere on the lower Yangtze River, many centuries ago. It was used extensively for making garments in the South, especially during the war. Just about everyone, soldier, sailor, and civilian, wore nankeen.

"In the spring of 1864, Yankee General 'Cotton Thief' Banks (he really was a cotton thief; he and his brother made a lot of money stealing it and sending it back to Massachusetts) was eager to demonstrate his military abilities in order to improve his post-war political status and give him another opportunity to plunder innocent Southerners. We used to joke that the first Yankee invader of New Orleans was a beast who stole spoons, and the second was a thief who stole cotton. What the Romans would call

Carthaginian Faith, the South could call Yankee Honor. Well, anyway, Banks had been planning another attempt to invade Texas, this time by going through Northwest Louisiana, up around Shreveport. He left Yankee-occupied New Orleans with an invasion force of 32,000 soldiers and was supported by Admiral Porter's Red River fleet consisting of 10,000 Yankee sailors. It did not look very good for us because all General Taylor had at the time was 16,000 ill-equipped—though determined—troops under his command. But to make the odds even worse, Yankee General Steel's army in Arkansas was converging on General Taylor with 13,000 more Yankee invaders. Now let's see, that must have been about 55,000 well-equipped invading Yankees against 16,000 Confederates. A reasonable or practical man would give up the fight, but we were fighting for our freedom. Yes, the practical would recommend surrender. But surrender when fighting for freedom? We must never end the struggle until we are finally free!

"General Banks came up the Mississippi River from New Orleans and entered the Red River about one hundred miles upriver from New Orleans. He then moved toward Alexandria in central Louisiana. General Taylor expected this, but once the Yankees reached Alexandria they could either continue upriver toward Shreveport or go across land toward Mansfield and then move on Shreveport. General Taylor needed some way to know which route Banks would take in order for Taylor to position his small army to meet the Yankee invaders.

"Now, logic would tell you that a large army needing constant resupplying, such as the army Banks had at his disposal, would select the river approach. But ole Cotton Thief Banks learned that there were large stores of cotton to be had on the overland, or Mansfield, approach. Like honey calling to flies, cotton was singing its sweet and alluring siren song to General Banks, just asking to be plundered. It was not just the money; Banks knew that the New England cotton mills were all but closed down due to the war. You know that the New Englanders claimed to hate slavery but loved to make huge fortunes by weaving slave-grown cotton into cheap Americana cloth. Well, Banks was planning to ship a large amount of stolen cotton back to the mills in New England and thereby secure the support of the mill owners for his future political career. So the overland route became the most alluring, politically and economically, to General Banks.

"General Taylor sent one of his staff officers to Natchitoches, which is almost halfway between Confederate Shreveport and Yankee-occupied Alexandria. The officer contacted an elderly physician in the community who was too old to serve in the army but was still eager to do his part to defeat the Yankee invader. The physician, who made his rounds in the area where the Yankees were encamped, would be able to tell which route they were taking as soon as the Yankees began their movement. But getting a message past all the Yankee patrols would be more difficult, and anyone carrying anything that would even hint at being a coded message would immediately be hung or shot by the Yankees. The doctor had a fifteen-year-old boy staying with him; the boy's father was away in the Confederate army, but the doctor did not want the boy to be involved in the enterprise. However, desperate situations demanded immediate action. The doctor took the Confederate staff officer into the boy's room and showed him two nankeen shirts. One of the shirts was decorated with a braid down the front, while the other was plain. The doctor told General Taylor's officer that when the Yankees started to move he would send the boy to Mansfield to stay with his friend Captain Youngblood. 'Now, when I send the boy to Captain Youngblood, I will see to it that the boy wears the shirt with a braid on it if the Yankees are coming upriver but the plain shirt if the Yankees are coming overland,' the doctor explained. Captain Youngblood was informed of our plan, and as soon as the boy reached Mansfield wearing the plain shirt, Captain Youngblood rushed the message to General Taylor that the Yankees were coming toward Mansfield. The boy never knew his vital role in the whole affair.

"Thanks to that plain nankeen shirt, we were able to rally our forces at Mansfield and deliver ole Cotton Thief Banks a thorough beating, which he so richly deserved. And the poor, suffering New England cotton mill owners had to suffer a little longer." Uncle Seth chuckled as if he was enjoying even years later the financial loss of the "noble" race of New England: a people who were the first to institute slavery in America, the first to enact a fugitive slave law in America, the first to gain wealth and treasure from the nefarious African slave trade, the first to grow wealthy weaving slave-grown cotton, and the first to wrap themselves in robes of self-righteousness while condemning the South.

§ Deo Vindice §

58

A Thirteen-Year-Old Drummer Boy

"Come over here, boys," Uncle Seth called out to his great-grandsons playing under the sprawling post oak tree in the front yard. "I want to show you all a picture of a Confederate soldier no older that you boys." The boys slowly complied with the old Confederate veteran's request, more out of respect for their great-grandfather than a desire to get another history lesson. It seemed that the older Uncle Seth got, the more importance he put on storytelling about the War for Southern Independence. Perhaps the old veteran knew that his journey on this earth was coming to a close and wanted to equip his descendants with the tools of truth they would need to carry on the struggle for the principles of Southern liberty.

"See here, boys, take a look at this old picture," Uncle Seth said as he extended an old, rumpled newspaper clipping toward the group of youngsters. The boys circled around the old man and pretended to be interested in the photograph.

"Uncle Seth, what kind of uniform does he have on?" asked Carroll Ray.

Uncle Seth looked back at the photo, suddenly realizing that the drummer boy's uniform had not caught his attention. "Oh,  well," Uncle Seth began slowly trying to compose an answer, "it is a musician's uniform, which was typically supplied by a family member. You know, at the beginning of the war most of us had uniforms, but not a single one of them looked the same. Most of our uniforms were homemade; they presented some military bearing but no uniformity in design. You can see that the leggings, or gators, as we called them, do not look like military issue.

"This young boy was fourteen years old when this picture was taken. His name is Charles Mosby."

"Uncle Seth!" Joe William interrupted. "Is he related to the famous Confederate Colonel Mosby?"

"Well, Joe William, I do not know. There is

no information about it, but he was from Virginia just like Colonel Mosby, so there most likely would be some family relations. It says here that Charles was thirteen when he enlisted as a drummer on May 10, 1861. He was in Capt. Louis T. Bossieux's company, Elliott Grays, Company I, Sixth Virginia Regiment of Infantry, CSA. Charles was stationed at Norfolk, Virginia, from May 10, 1861, until May 10, 1862—exactly one year. During the seven-day battle around Richmond, he was re-assigned to Henderson's Battalion Heavy Artillery and served there until the end of the war. You see, even young boys such as you were helping us man heavy artillery in our struggle to push the Yankee invaders out of our country. Look, it says here that two other drummers, John Carr and William Crawford, who were a little older than Charles, were also put into the ranks." Uncle Seth seemed a little sad thinking about these young boys facing such death and destruction. Or perhaps he was remembering that he, as a seventeen-year-old boy, had given the last four years of his youth in the service of his country's freedom.

"You boys go back and enjoy your play while you still have the time," the veteran instructed the boys—who happily complied. Uncle Seth watched his great-grandchildren as they meandered back to the post oak tree and wondered if they or their children would ever live in a free South—or if they would be forever condemned to be servants to the Federal Empire.

§ Deo Vindice §

ON THE SKIRMISH LINE WITH UNCLE SETH
Confederate secretary of war Judah P. Benjamin was interviewed by Capt. Fitzgerald Ross of the Austrian Hussars, who noted that, during his trip to the Confederate capitol at Richmond, he observed great evidence of depredation against civilian property and persons committed by the invaders. Benjamin replied, "If they had behaved differently; if they had come against us observing strict discipline, protecting women and children . . . If they had been capable of acting otherwise, they would not have been Yankees, and we should never have quarreled with them." Judah P. Benjamin was a witness to the eventual outcome of a Union with people who did not share the same belief system as the South. In 1787, Virginian Patrick Henry warned Virginia and the South about the dangers of joining a Union dominated by a people who would one day use that same Union to enrich themselves at the expense of Virginia and the South. In the late 1780s, Patrick Henry looked into the future and saw what Judah P. Benjamin and the entire South were experiencing in the 1860s—the naked and uninhibited Yankee lust for political, economic, and commercial power. This lust continues today.

59

A Typical Southern Mother—Unheralded Heroines of the South

Uncle Seth and Carroll Ray were sitting on the front porch listening to the late-afternoon April thunderstorm. The raindrops were splashing against the white oak shingles and running off the roof, creating miniature rivers of rainwater that ran across the yard. The thunder was rolling from the southwest, "where most of our weather comes from," as Uncle Seth would always tell the boys. Occasionally, a bright lightning flash would illuminate the sky behind Cousin Mike's house, about half a mile up the dirt road. "April showers bring May flowers," Uncle Seth commented as he watched the wonders of the natural world unfold in yet another spring. For a man in the winter of his life, it always felt especially good to witness spring unfold with its promise of renewed life.

"Uncle Seth," exclaimed Carroll Ray, "that thunder sounds like Yankee cannons firing on us."

"Yes, Carroll Ray." Uncle Seth rocked back in his favorite rocking chair and looked off into the distance as if trying to see something far away. "You know the folks at Crystal Springs, not more than twenty miles from here as the crow flies, could hear the rumbling of the Yankee cannons firing on Vicksburg, Mississippi, during the war. The truth is, the Yankee invader threatened everyone during the war, even those who were not directly involved in an area where a battle was raging.

"I recall an incident back in May of 1863, at Chancellorsville, Virginia, in which a mother, with her three children, showed bravery in the face of Yankee fire that was typical of our Southern women during the war. I was with A. J. Cone of Company I, 18th Georgia Regiment, Longstreet's Corps, Army of Northern Virginia. The invading Yankee army at that time was commanded by General Hooker." Uncle Seth chuckled softly and looked around to see if anyone else was near. Then he leaned in toward Carroll Ray and spoke in almost a whisper as if telling a secret: "You know, Carroll Ray, that the Yankee General Hooker's army had so many women of ill-repute in their camp that they were known as 'Hooker's Girls' and that from that day to this prostitutes are known as hookers because of that fine Yankee general. Now you don't need to tell your mother that I told you that," Uncle Seth said with a wink.

"Well, back to Chancellorsville. It seemed that General Hooker had crossed the Rappahannock River in an effort to flank General Lee. It was a Sunday morning, the second of May, and we made a forced march and had drawn up on a plank road leading into Fredericksburg—the Yankee invaders had entrenched themselves and formed up their artillery and infantry several miles in front of Fredericksburg. They had the advantage of position on the hills to our front where they could spot Lee's advance toward their center. We had formed up in the woods on their flank and surprised them when we emerged from the woods in battle order. As soon as we appeared, the Yankees trained their artillery and small-arms fire on us. It seemed as if every cannon ball and every minie ball had my name on it! We could see behind the Yankee battle line where the Chancellor house had been set on fire by the Yankees. And then, as our men were falling right and left and Yankee bombs were exploding over our heads, we were returning fire as good, if not better, than what we got. That's when we spotted the heroine of the battle calmly walking through the Yankee battle line!

"Mrs. Chancellor's husband was serving in another theater of the war and there were no males left at home to take care of her and her three children. Before we arrived, the Yankees—out of pure spite and hatred—had set her home on fire. Now, before our eyes, we could see a young Southern mother with an infant clutched to her bosom, leading another by the hand while the third held on to her dress. This was happening while the battle raged on all sides. Her face, and a beautiful face it was, was stern and determined, showing no fear. Her eyes were fixed on our battle lines. As she strode through the Yankee lines she looked neither to her right or left, as if refusing to make eye contact with the men who had invaded her country and set fire to her home. I guess the Yankees were as busy as we were trying to dodge bullets and cannon balls and decided not to waste any attention on a 'crazy secessionist woman.' But we were horrified! Several of us ran toward the plank road to encourage her to hurry to the rear of our battle line and find safety. Yankee cannon balls were tearing up the plank road and sending fragments of boards as well as fragments of cannon balls in every direction.

"I wish you could have seen the serenity and composure that brave Southern lady exhibited that day. We were begging her to hurry, but she was as cool and calm as if she and her children were taking a Sunday stroll to church. Here, before our eyes, was a perfect example of the undaunted spirit of our people even when they were faced with overwhelming opposition from the Yankee Empire. She looked at us and, with a slight smile on her beautiful face, said, 'Go on by, brave boys. The Yankees have burned my home and all I had, but I managed to save the clothes on our backs and my little darlings, you see.' She stood there with her children in the middle of the chaos while the invader's bombs exploded all around us. We had to force her to go to the rear; I think that if she had not had the responsibility of the children, she would have picked up an Enfield rifle from one of our fallen men and joined us in the charge. And Carroll Ray, this is why I still hate the Yankees: they invaded us when all we asked was to be left alone, they made war on innocent women and children as punishment for our wanting to live in a country that was not ruled by Yankees, and now in their victory they tell the world that Southerners like that woman were fighting to keep their slaves! Yankees lies, damn Yankee lies!

"Lincoln and his henchmen were determined to destroy the Southern people. You remember what the Yankee Colonel Osband said about his expedition to eradicate Southern resistance to the United States' invasion in Northeast Louisiana. After waging war against innocent women and children, he sent this noble message back to his superiors, celebrating his 'victory': 'No squad of men can live anywhere we have been. These people do not have seed, corn, bread, or the mills to grind the corn, even if they had it, as I burned them where ever found. I have taken from these people the mules with which they would raise a crop the coming year, and burned every surplus grain of corn.' Notice that he is talking about 'the people' and celebrating his efforts to eradicate the Southern people by starvation. Carroll Ray, I want you to remember Yankee invaders like Colonel Osband and what they represent. They represent the efforts of the United States of America to enslave the people of the South—to make us an occupied territory of the Federal Empire and obedient tax serfs of the ruling elite in Washington, DC. And also remember Mrs. Chancellor and what she represented. She represented defiance to Yankee tyranny; she represented our people's efforts to be free, to live in our own country under a government ordered upon the consent of the governed. Carroll Ray, every time you see the United States flag I want you to remember that it is not your country's flag but the flag of the country that tried to exterminate your people! No war in modern history has ever been fought with more hatred and cruelty than the one waged by the United States of America against 'we the people' of the Confederate States of America. That shame belongs to the North. But we, too, are earning our share of shame. The shame of the South is that our people do not understand that no honor can be had for a people who will willingly bow down and kiss their conquering master's boots. Maybe one day, when I am long gone, our people will realize that the boot of the Federal Empire is on our necks—but a tyrant cannot put his boot on the neck of a people who are standing up!"

The thunderstorm had passed, the sun was shining, and the ground gave forth the sweet smell of rich, warm soil incubating the seeds of Southern spring. Uncle Seth sat back and took it all in as he wondered how many more springs the Good Lord would allow him to enjoy and how many more springs would pass before his South would once again bloom with liberty.

§ Deo Vindice §

ON THE SKIRMISH LINE WITH UNCLE SETH
In 1870, Yankee General Sheridan was in Prussia as the guest at a banquet given by Otto von Bismarck. At the banquet, he admitted to the Prussians that he was in favor of treating the enemy's civilian population with the utmost rigor. He advised that "the people must be left nothing but their eyes to weep with."

60

Battling the "Battle Hymn of the Republic"

Uncle Seth sat on the front porch sipping cool well water from his favorite tin cup. In the distance he could hear the mechanical clanking of a Tin Lizzy (the nickname for the Ford Model T) as it maneuvered the dusty dirt and gravel road that passed through the Pearl Valley community. As the Tin Lizzy turned off the road and into the driveway, Uncle Seth recognized the driver as the community's new preacher. The church could not afford a full-time preacher, but this young man of God took the position on a part-time basis while he taught in the local school. The young preacher parked the Tin Lizzy under a large red oak tree—no doubt hoping to take advantage of the shade to keep his car cool.

"Good morning, Uncle Seth," announced the preacher as he approached the steps leading up to the porch, being careful not to disturb the three Redbone hounds eyeing him. "I was told to be sure to come by and invite you to the Wednesday night prayer meetings we are starting this week," he informed Uncle Seth. "Several of the church folks also warned me that you would not remain in your pew if I asked the congregation to sing the 'Battle Hymn of the Republic.'" The preacher betrayed his apprehension. Everyone in the community knew and respected Uncle Seth. Everyone also knew that he—the last Confederate veteran living in the community—had never asked for a pardon from the Federal government. Whenever someone would inquire about whether he had asked for a pardon, Uncle Seth would tersely reply, "Why should I ask the invaders for a pardon for simply doing my duty of defending my country? I have not pardoned them for the evil they did and continue to do to my people and country!"

"Well, young feller," Uncle Seth began. He flicked the remainder of the cool water out of his tin cup and deliberately sat the cup on the porch railing while he carefully studied the young preacher's deportment. Uncle Seth's war experience had taught him to carefully size up the opposition before developing a battle tactic. For the old Confederate veteran, such discussions as these were just another battle in the ongoing war to free his people from the invisible bonds of Yankee lies that had been fixed on Southerners since

229

the war. He could see that the preacher was being honest and was perhaps a little perplexed by Uncle Seth's seemingly unreasonable stance.

"You realize that I have seen with my own eyes the horror inflicted upon our people by the Yankee invaders?" Uncle Seth asked rhetorically, in order to set up an opportunity for instruction. "I also have personal memories of how prosperous and peaceful the South was before the war. I remember a time when the people of the South were the economic equals to the New Englander. I also remember a time when the states were the ultimate authority as to whether our agent, the Federal government, was conducting itself according to the Constitution." Uncle Seth wanted to set the stage for this young man's understanding of why small things were ultimately very important when it comes to maintaining the hope of regaining freedom, liberty, and constitutional government.

"It is unbelievable to me," Uncle Seth continued, "that Christian churches could sing a song that was sung by an invading army as it dealt out death, rape, robbery, and utter destruction on unarmed women and children. But more importantly, this is not a Christian song! That song was written by a Yankee Unitarian, Julia Ward Howe, to celebrate the destruction of the South. Now, preacher, you know that Unitarians are not Christians. They do not believe, as all Christians do, that Jesus Christ is the Son of God; they believe He was just a good teacher." The words seemed to come from deep within Uncle Seth's soul, like he was able to call them forth unconsciously. They were motivated by the anguish of pain for a people who were too willing to accept their assigned position as conquered subjects of the new Federal Empire—impoverished second-class citizens in a country that would no longer be recognized by the Southern founding fathers who were so instrumental in creating the original and legitimate United States of America.

"Now, preacher," Uncle Seth continued without allowing the young man to respond, "words of a spiritual hymn are very important. You would not want to sing a song in church just because it had a catchy tune or was popular. No, you reserve religious singing for those songs that will glorify God and help to create in the hearts of the congregation a sense of worship and reverence. Look at the words of the battle hymn! The non-Christian songwriter uses words and phrases from the Holy Bible to encourage uninhibited killing of Southerners. Her song reduces our people to sinners who deserve the judgment of the 'day of the Lord' to be delivered by the moral authority of bloody bayonets held in the hands of invading Yankees. She equates the glory of the invading Yankee armies coming into our homes to burn, rape, and kill to the glory of the 'coming of the Lord.'

This song celebrates our invasion, conquest, and destruction by equating the acts of the Yankee invader to God 'trampling out the vintage where the grapes of wrath are stored.' In her song, she is not speaking about some winepress in distant Galilee. No! She is referring to the South. She hated Southerners and was celebrating and encouraging our destruction! How can Christians sing such a vulgar song? She writes that God 'hath loosed the fateful lightning of His terrible swift sword.' Remember, she testified that she wrote these lines after observing, in Washington, DC, the marching of Yankee troops and the large stores of war materials being prepared for the invasion of our young Southern nation. She saw the coming of the Lord and the invading Yankee army as the same thing. Preacher, that is blasphemy! How can Christians sing a vulgar and blasphemous song in church? Remember that 'terrible swift sword' was used to wound and kill your kinsmen—men and women who were killed simply because they feared to remain in union with a people who hated them. You know, preacher, that some verses of this battle hymn are so evil that they are not included in most versions used by so-called Christian churches. And to top it off, the song is not historically correct. It claims that Christ was born 'in the beauty of the lilies' when in fact He was born in a stable and laid in a manger. More importantly, though, it is not theologically correct! She speaks of a glory that 'transfigured you and me.' This is pure universalism as advocated by Unitarians—not Christians. Jesus was the one who was transfigured, not you and me. The heresy continues in the next verse when she writes that Jesus's death for sinners is the same as Union soldiers dying to 'make men free.' Union soldiers did not fight to free anyone; they fought to enslave the South, to keep us in their empire and subject to their will. The "Battle Hymn of the Republic" is not a Christian hymn—it is a partisan, Yankee, political song glorifying bogus history and blasphemous theology. It is just one more piece of Yankee propaganda used to pacify Southerners and keep us subject to their federal empire." Uncle Seth sat back in his chair, crossed his arms, and waited for the preacher's response.

The preacher sat quietly with a perplexed look on his face. Uncle Seth had seen the look on other young faces so many times before. No doubt the preacher meant well, but he had no way to fathom the loss his people had suffered. Uncle Seth knew well the problem with youth—no memory of what it was like to live in a free nation, to be the master of your own home. All they know is the world they were born in, a world in which the South is a land of poverty, pellagra, and sharecroppers. Their world is a world in which economic, social, and political decisions are made in faraway Washington, DC. To the young this is normal—to them this is the way it is. Uncle Seth also knew that this is the way the Yankee conquerors of the South want it to remain. He understood that empires need to remove any memory of past freedom and prosperity from the conquered people; this makes each passing generation more willing to accept their assigned positions as subjects of the empire. But Uncle Seth wanted to leave them with the dream, the vision of a better world in which they and their children could once again be free and prosperous.

§ Deo Vindice §

ON THE SKIRMISH LINE WITH UNCLE SETH

The Southern idea of civil liberty rested upon a correct perception of moral distinctions. Robert Lewis Dabney and other Southern religious leaders taught that man's liberty is not the liberty to do whatever he wants to do. Rather, it rested upon his duty to do what was morally right to do. Therefore, membership in a civil society was premised upon the recognition of man as a fallen creature who has a natural propensity to do evil. This natural propensity to do evil must be restrained by the moral teachings of the church and the civil restraint of a limited government. Government had the *limited* duty of protecting the life and property of the innocent from violations committed by evil men.

61

But the War Is Over!

"Come on, Billie Jean, you and Joe William try to keep up with this old soldier," Uncle Seth said, teasing his young great-grandchildren. He had saved his meager Confederate pension, paid by the State of Mississippi, all year to purchase the train tickets to bring the three of them to the annual meeting of the Georgia Division of the United Confederate Veterans. He had many friends from the war who still lived in Georgia, and he always looked forward to renewing old acquaintances. But this year was special; those in charge of the meeting had arranged a tour of the Jones Plantation in Jenkins County. Uncle Seth had served in this area during the war and felt that what he personally saw at this plantation would be the best example to answer the children's often-repeated question: "Why are you still fighting the war?" This particular question especially irritated the old Southern soldier because he knew the question originated in the false history being taught to his grandchildren and great-grandchildren by self-hating Southerners using Yankee-authored and Yankee-published textbooks.

"I visited this fine plantation during the war," Uncle Seth spoke more to himself than to his young audience.

"How old is this house?" Joe William asked as he peered into the stately gardens surrounding the plantation.

"The Jones Plantation is a part of an original grant given by King George III to Francis Jones, a Welshman. The total grant was around 66,000 acres. Now this house was built in the early 1760s. It is a great study in history; look at the old, white Colonial clapboard and its Greek Revival front and the last addition over there— you see it, Billie Jean?" Uncle Seth's enthusiasm made it difficult for the youngster to keep up with her limited knowledge of antebellum architecture.

The Jones Plantation, Jenkins County, Georgia (Courtesy Betty Kennedy)

But before Billie Jean could admit this, Uncle Seth continued. "See there the Victorian side porches," he explained as he walked around the huge structure. "Yes, this plantation has seen a lot of American history and played its small role quite well. Back in Colonial times the stagecoach road from Savannah to Augusta rolled right through this plantation. In pre-Revolutionary War times, a small village sprung up not too far from here. A couple of the old clapboard buildings still remain; they served as the inn, stagecoach station, and post office. The proprietor's last name was Bird, so the small village became known as Birdsville." Uncle Seth seemed to be rambling, but Billie Jean and Joe William knew that he had something special on his mind—but what it was, well, they just were not sure. Joe William had noticed an old wrought-iron fence that gave the appearance of protecting a family grave. With each word, Uncle Seth moved the small group toward that fence.

"I was here shortly after the Yankee raiders had broken into the plantation," Uncle Seth explained, hinting that his story was beginning. "It was right here," he noted, reverently touching the wrought iron fence. "Right here it was—yes, indeed, this is the spot. Oh, my, there they are," Uncle Seth declared. He spoke each word more and more quietly than the one before, like a prayer. Joe William and Billie Jean looked around and tried to determine who Uncle Seth was talking to, but there was no one else around. It was as if the old Confederate soldier was reverently speaking to the dead.

"You see, Mrs. Jones had given birth to twin girls just a few days before the Yankee invaders arrived. Her husband, Dr. William B. Jones, was serving with the Confederate army at the time. Both girls died a few hours after they were born. There, y'all see?" Uncle Seth pointed toward two small headstones, both inscribed with the same single date—the day the twins were born and died.

"Oh, Uncle Seth," Billie Jean's voice disclosed that special kind of grief and sorrow felt by a people who love unknown friends. "How sad that Mrs. Jones never saw her girls grow up—and in the middle of such a cruel war—her husband away with the army!"

"That's not the worst of it, Billie Jean," Uncle Seth said sternly, as if he were about to strike out at an unseen but devilish force. "You see, when I first got here, the servants were all standing around afraid to touch anything. The Yankees had just left, but not before they attempted to burn the house down with poor Mrs. Jones still in her bed, incapacitated by grief and the natural infirmities of childbirth. You see, Yankees had the habit of demanding that the owners of a large house surrender all their silverware, silver servings, gold plates, and watches. If the owner refused or claimed that they no longer had such items—often they were already looted by previous visitors from the United States army—the Yankees would burn down the house and sift through the ashes for the melted silver and gold.

"Their attempt to burn down this plantation was diverted by the sight of the freshly dug graves. The Yankee looters assumed that the family had sought to hide the family fortune in those small graves. When I arrived, the graves had been dug up, the small caskets had been broken into, and the bodies of those little infant girls were thrown over there." Uncle Seth pointed to the far corner of the enclosure.

"That's just not right. What an evil thing to do to innocent civilians," Joe William declared. His tone of voice strangely mimicked Uncle Seth's—not so much in age and maturity but in intensity and passion of conviction.

"I got the servants to help me place the twins back in the ground—hopefully, their angel wings will always stir the Georgia breeze and stir our people's hearts with love and respect for our Southern home and kin." Uncle Seth now stood at the foot of two small graves, his hat in hand. "You see, children, when an enemy comes into your home and treats you worse than the British Red Coats did during the Revolutionary War, when he tells the world he is doing it for the good of humanity, when he uses his economic and political dominance of the occupying government to force his will upon the children of the occupied nation—well, when this happens, you remember this spot of Southern soil; you remember that an invaded, conquered, and occupied country must never forget!"

Uncle Seth stood silently for a while at the foot of those tiny graves. Then, without directing his comments to anyone particular, he noted: "These little ones will rise on resurrection day—I pray to God that we will not be forced to wait that long for the South to rise again!" Uncle Seth moved slowly away, carrying a terrible, heavy burden. The children stood in silence as they gazed down at the two small graves and, in their own minds, tried to decide how to handle the emotions of love and anger now burning like fire within their breasts.

§ Deo Vindice §

ON THE SKIRMISH LINE WITH UNCLE SETH

The sufferings of Southern women as a result of Yankee invasion did not lessen their dedication to the Cause. The case of a New Orleans Jewish lady is of special interest. Her husband was a Union man and moved them to Cincinnati, Ohio, where he served the Union forces. Every week, this fine Southern lady would put her young son in a stroller and take her walk across the Ohio River to her friends on the other side, in Yankee-occupied Kentucky. There she would deliver various medical supplies smuggled past the Yankee guards at the river's edge. Many a wounded Confederate soldier's life was saved and suffering eased by the brave work of this New Orleans woman.

62

Confederate Cavalry Defends Oklahoma Indians from Yankee Raiders

Uncle Seth was amusing himself by watching the boys play a game of Cowboys and Indians. The boys were having a great time with their imaginary guns as they defended themselves from each new attack. Charging forward, Barry announced that he was leading the Confederate cavalry against his opponents. This took Curtis by surprise; he stopped the boyish game entirely and declared, "The Confederate cavalry never fought against Indians in the West!"

"Yes they did, and I am leading them against your tribe!" Barry emphatically responded. Uncle Seth was immediately called upon to settle the argument.

"Well, boys," Uncle Seth laughed out loud at the boys and their endless arguments, "you know, you both are correct."

The boys stopped and looked inquisitively at the old Confederate veteran—surely there was no way both of them could be right. "Come over here and I will explain," Uncle Seth said with a wave of his hand. "You see, Curtis is correct in that we never saw action against the Indians of the plains and far West. But the 11th Texas Cavalry was called upon to defend our Indian allies in the Oklahoma Territory from attacks from the Pin Indians and Kansas Jayhawkers back in late 1861. So, Curtis, you see that Barry is also correct when he says that the Confederate cavalry fought Indians.

"I recall meeting Colonel Bill Young at the United Confederate Veterans convention—I believe it was in Fort Worth, Texas. He was the leader of the mission to protect the friendly Indians from Yankee raiders. He related the story to me. He said that he was given the job of repulsing the incursion of a force of around twelve hundred Yankee raiders—including Pin Indians who had been reenforced by members of several Western tribes and numerous Kansas Jayhawkers. These Yankee raiders had been robbing and burning local Indian villages that were sympathizing with the Confederates and murdering anyone who got in their way. The Pin Indians and the Western Indians were longtime enemies of the 'civilized tribes' who were loyal to the Confederate State of America. The Kansas Jayhawkers were whites who hated anything Southern and saw this as an opportunity to punish the Indian friends of the Confederacy and to acquire a rich load of loot as well.

"Colonel Young picked two hundred and fifty of the best mounted men in the 11th Texas Cavalry and left camp on the White River in Arkansas. They arrived at Fort Gibson around the 20 of December 1861. Young said they crossed the Grand River and then, the next day, crossed and traveled up the western side of the Verdigris River. Shortly after that, they found the Yankee raiders' trail. It was easy to find because the Yankee raiders were pushing over a thousand stolen horses, cattle, and ox carts loaded with loot stolen from our Indian allies. The Yankee raiders' trail looked like a broad road through the countryside that even a blind man could have followed. It was at least fifty yards wide, the grass was as high as their horses' heads on each side, and the grass was all bent in the same direction. In all directions, the country was desolate for miles around—the inhabitants had either been killed or had fled for their lives. You see, boys, the Yankees used the same methods against innocent civilians regardless of who the civilians were or who the invaders were. It made no difference—uniformed Yankees or pro-Yankee Indian raiders, they were all barbarians!

"So Colonel Young followed their trail. At the mouth of Bird Creek they left the river and headed up the creek to the Osage Agency. That evening, Young's command was making camp when a squad of men came in from what seemed like a patrol. But when the men saw the Confederate uniforms and flag in the camp, they wheeled around and fled. The men in camp could see the riders were Indians, and not friendly ones either. It turns out they had made camp just twelve miles away from the Yankee raiders' stronghold in the nearby mountains! At daybreak, the men of the 11th were in their saddles and ready for a fight. Colonel Young said that it was freezing, but he and his men mounted their horses and galloped about ten miles up the valley toward the Yankee raiders' stronghold.

"It was then that Colonel Greer's regiment of Texans came into the picture. They began a heavy skirmish with the Yankee raiders, who fell back against the fierce Confederate onslaught. Colonel Young told his men, 'Boys, tighten up your belts. We are in for a fight now.' Greer's men pushed the Yankee raiders on the left and Young's men made a frontal advance at the gallop. Facing such a well-organized attack, the Yankee raiders broke and began to flee for their lives, taking what loot they could carry. When the raiders reached Bird Creek (the Indians called it Oostenaula Creek) they crowded the creek bank looking for a safe crossing while Greer's men dismounted and advanced. The Yankee raiders were weighted down with all of their ill-gotten loot, yet they had the height advantage and outnumbered the Confederates at least five to one.

"Colonel Young said that at this point the Yankee raiders regained their fighting spirit and began making sport of the Confederates by calling them names and hurling insults at the Confederates. Young led his men up the mountain along a zigzag trail, keeping as low a profile as possible to avoid the rain of Yankee bullets coming from higher up the mountain. When he reached the top, where he could hear the rushing water coming down the mountain, he found Yankee raiders behind every rock and tree. The men moved forward—they were all on foot by now—and began to flank the Yankees on their right. At the same time, Greer's men pressed their left and crowded toward the Yankees' center. This type of military fighting was more than the Indians could stand—and the Indians composed most of the Yankee raiders' force! They broke and ran, thinking that they would leave their white Kansas Jayhawkers allies to fend for themselves. But those white Kansas Jayhawkers showed their Indian friends what they were made of. Yes, indeed. The Jayhawkers pushed their Indian friends aside and outran them! Young claims that the Jayhawkers were carrying more loot but still beat the Indians across Bird Creek. The remaining Indians held their ground until their arrows ran out and they, too, decided to join their white friends, leaving Confederate territory as fast as they could.

"Colonel Young's official report said that they counted more than five hundred dead Yankee raiders, eighteen dead Confederates, and just over sixty wounded Confederates. One of the Confederate captains had fought the entire engagement on horseback, which made him a perfect target. All of this captain's men wondered at his bravery and determination. But at the end of the fight, they discovered that an Indian had attacked him early on by jumping from behind a large rock. Just before the captain dropped the Indian with a well-placed shot from his Navy colt revolver, the Indian had loosed an arrow; it went through the captain's right thigh and pinned him to his new Texas saddle! His men had to break the arrow at the fletching and lift the captain off his horse. The next day, the 11th started back to their winter quarters at Camp Lubbock on the White River in Arkansas."

The old Confederate veteran knew that for this short moment he had the boys' full attention. He wanted to make sure his boys would remember why he and his comrades wore the gray in the War for Southern Independence. He wanted, in some small way, to undo the lies that the Yankee masters of the "New South" were forcefully injecting into the heads of young

Southern schoolchildren. He knew that his time on this earth was limited. He had so much to do and so little time and resources at his disposal— not much different than the South's struggle during the war. Uncle Seth looked the boys directly in the eyes, trying to permanently impress the truth in their heads. "Now, boys, the Yankees are telling the world that the Confederate States of America was an all-white society that attempted to impose slavery on other people. But you remember that the men of the South fought against an empire that was forcing its will on people who only asked to be left alone; we only asked to enjoy the right to live in a country based on the consent of the governed. The men of the 11th Texas were not a group of slave owners trying to extend their slave-holdings; they were men who risked their lives to protect their Indian friends—friends who were being oppressed by agents of the Yankee Empire."

As the sun broke from behind a large, puffy, white cloud, the old man slowly moved away from the boys and toward the shade of a large red oak tree. The boys instantly turned their interest to yet another boyhood game. As he sat down on the cool ground under the tree, Uncle Seth wondered if, a hundred years from now, anyone would remember that the struggle for Southern freedom was worth the effort. Would future generations of Southerners still think it worth the effort, or would Southerners become pacified, second-class Yankees dutifully obeying their Yankee masters?

§ **Deo Vindice** §

63

Confederate Prisoners at Camp Chase

Uncle Seth was wrapped tightly in his overcoat and stayed close to the fireplace in an effort to keep warm on this cold February day. The wind was blowing and the temperature outside was a little above freezing. In south-central Mississippi, the folks expected this to be the coldest part of the winter. Uncle Seth was glad he did not live up north where temperatures routinely dipped below freezing and stayed there for days, if not weeks.

"Come over here next to the fireplace, Billie Jean." Uncle Seth invited his great-granddaughter to join him. "You know, I was reading about Maj. Coleman Alderson's experiences as a prisoner at that horrible Yankee prison camp up in Ohio. It was called Camp Chase."

"Why would the Yankees name a prison Camp Chase? Were they hoping to chase you all if you escaped?" the young girl asked. Uncle Seth chuckled at her innocence.

"No, Billie Jean," the old Confederate veteran replied, "they named it after Federal Supreme Court Justice Chase. He was the Supreme Court justice who the Yankees' president appointed to replace Justice Taney when he died. Chase was a potential political opponent of Lincoln, so Lincoln appointed him to the Supreme Court to make sure Chase stayed out of his way.

"Major Alderson was captured on June 12, 1864, during a fight with Yankee General Duffie's army. Even though he was wounded, the Yankees forced him to march to the prison camp at Wheeling, West Virginia, and then on to Camp Chase in Ohio. He entered Camp Chase on July 3, 1864. The Yankees imprisoned not only Southern soldiers but numerous Southern civilians the Yankees

Maj. Coleman Alderson circa 1863

described as "disloyal" citizens. (Yankees were well-known for making war upon non-combatant civilians.) It has always seemed strange to me that the Yankees focused on 'disloyalty' so. If you come into a man's home and force him to accept you as his master, why *wouldn't* you think that he would be disloyal to you and your country? There is no explaining or understanding the Yankee, unless you use the logic of profit. Anything they do is right if it makes profit for them; anything you do is wrong if it denies the Yankee the opportunity to make his profits.

"Listen to what Major Alderson says about Camp Chase," Uncle Seth said as he reached behind his chair and grabbed an old newspaper. Without even a slightest hesitation, he began reading:

> There were twelve to fifteen prisoners jammed into each prison room. The prison room was 15 X 17 feet and the walls were a little over ten foot high. The sleeping cots were occupied by two or three men each and were made of rough sawed planks. The Yankees did not furnish us with any bedding or straw to sleep on. The Yankees allowed us only one blanket. The temperature often went ten to twenty degrees below zero. Many of the Southern boys became emaciated due to the intentional starvation inflicted upon us by our Yankee captors. You could actually count the bones stretched over their thin skin. Poor creatures, it was not long before their hip bones broke through their skin. This was made more likely because we had to cover ourselves with the blanket— we had nothing to cushion the rough planks. We were not permitted to have fires in our little stove in the prison rooms at night. The barracks were so poorly constructed that the wind blew through one wall and passed through the other side. Add to this the fact that we had been captured in our home country and were not accustomed to such harsh winters nor were we wearing clothing appropriate for such climates. It is a wonder that any of us survived.

"Major Alderson says that he met a Captain Bouldin while they were both prisoners at Camp Chase. Fortunately for Captain Bouldin, he was exchanged shortly before General Lee's evacuation of Petersburg. Upon his exchange, he was immediately placed in command of a regiment. He led the last charge against Sheridan's cavalry about two miles west of Appomattox Court House. His job was to open a route out for General Lee's army to retreat to safety. He was successful, but, unfortunately and unbeknown to Captain Bouldin, General Lee had already surrendered.

"Major Alderson says that during his incarceration at Camp Chase his health became compromised and he was often close to death. Several times the men in his barracks would urge him to save himself by taking the loyalty oath—you know, by pledging allegiance to the United States. But Major Alderson refused. He said that he could not swear allegiance to the same United States that had invaded his country, raped innocent women—both black and white, and burned homes of non-combatants."

"Uncle Seth, why didn't the Yankees exchange their Confederate prisoners for the Yankee prisoners that we held?" asked Billie Jean.

"Well, the Yankees knew that when a Union soldier was exchanged he went straight back home and was not inclined to reenlist. They also knew that back home the discharged Yankee soldier would spread the word about how determined their Southern opponents were to be free of Yankee domination; that would significantly chill the enthusiasm for enlisting in the Union army. On the other hand, Yankees knew that Southern soldiers, like Captain Bouldin, would immediately rejoin their units and continue the fight for Southern independence. You see, we were fighting to protect our families, our homes, and our country; the Yankees were fighting for an empire." Uncle Seth put his newspaper down and poked the fire with the iron fire poker he kept handy. He was happy sitting there in a warm house surrounded by his family and friends. "I wonder," he thought to himself, "if the rich Yankees up in Chicago know the meaning of real love of family and the importance of keeping faith with those who have gone before us."

§ Deo Vindice §

ON THE SKIRMISH LINE WITH UNCLE SETH

"We failed, but we [the South] have the satisfaction of knowing that no people on earth endured or fought more from patriotic desires. We were overcome by the hirelings of the world, who were ignorant of our people, devoid of honor and patriotic duty. As we all surrendered, it behooves us to abide by the terms imposed. Nobody cares that slavery is obliterated. It was not the loss of slavery we so much objected to, but the manner of its abolishment. The war has demonstrated that the constitution amounts to naught. After all, what matters the most is massed bayonets."

—Letter from Confederate Gen. Joe O. Shelby, August 2, 1885

64

Fighting in the Cane Fields of Louisiana

Uncle Seth was standing on the back porch watching the boys come out of the canebrake down in the bottomland near the creek. From the sounds of dogs and shotgun blasts, it seemed that they were having a successful rabbit hunt. "Guns, hunting, and the love of the outdoors make young men good soldiers," thought Uncle Seth as he watched the boys approaching, rabbits in hand.

"Uncle Seth!" shouted Larry. The tone of his voice announced that the boys were still full of the excitement of the hunt. "You should see how thick that canebrake is since we took it off the open range." Larry was referring to the fact that the canebrake had been recently enclosed by a fence, thus preventing the cattle and hogs on the open range from grazing the cane down. Uncle Seth often reminded the boys about the danger lurking in the new, "progressive" ideas of modern farming such as enclosing the South's vast areas of open range. The cattle and hogs that were raised on the open range were leaner and made for better eating than those penned in and fed fattening food. Uncle Seth would remind the boys that before the war the value of cattle and hogs roaming the South's open range was greater than the value of the annual cotton and sugarcane crops. Cotton may have been king for the plantation class; but for the country folk or plain folk, cattle and hogs were king. Yet progress in the form of modern agriculture and enclosure laws—laws requiring the owners of cattle and hogs to control their animals by fencing them in—had become the rage.

"You boys had better be careful; you might run into some Yankee soldiers down there in that thick canebrake," he chuckled as he teased the boys. "I had the fight of my life in a couple of Louisiana canebrakes during the war," he explained, hoping they would pause from the cleaning of their rabbits long enough to visit a spell with him. The boys paused long enough to indicate to Uncle Seth that they were interested in hearing the account of his Louisiana canebrake adventures.

"Private E. C. De Jarnett of Company F, 12th Texas Cavalry, and I were on picket duty down in Rapids Parish in 1864," Uncle Seth began.

"The United States troops were burning and plundering sugar houses across Bayou Rapids. De Jarnett and I crossed the bayou by swimming our horses across to see what we could find out about the enemy's strength. You know, boys, we Southerners had just given the Yankees a thorough licking at the Battles of Mansfield and Pleasant Hill. The U.S. troops were in steady retreat and we wanted to help them along a bit," mused Uncle Seth. "Of course, they always seemed to find time to stop and plunder defenseless women and children. We went about a mile up the bayou when De Jarnett, who was about fifty yards ahead of me, came upon a man on horseback dressed in civilian clothes. We could see that about one hundred yards behind him there was a group of around half a dozen U.S. troops. De Jarnett thought he recognized the civilian on horseback and was taken by surprise when the man announced that he was a Federal—a Yankee soldier in civilian clothes! The Yankee pointed a revolver at De Jarnett's head and informed De Jarnett that he was now a prisoner of the United States cavalry. Well, De Jarnett quickly informed the gentleman that we were fighting to get away from unpleasant folks like him who were in charge of the United States and that he would therefore decline the invitation to come back to the cruel embrace of their Federal union. That is to say, he did all of this simply by grabbing the Yankee's revolver by the cylinder so that he could not fire it." Uncle Seth paused as he thought about the incident still so fresh in his mind even after so many years. "The two of them immediately began a mounted hand-to-hand contest in which the Yankee returned the favor and seized De Jarnett's revolver. De Jarnett managed to get a shot off, but it only hit the hind tree of the Yankee's saddle. The ineffective shot must have startled the Yankee, who most likely thought either he or his horse had been shot. De Jarnett quickly seized the moment and clubbed the startled Yankee with his revolver, knocking the Yank off his horse. By this time I caught up to him, but the Yankees following the one in civilian clothes were also coming at full gallop. Both De Jarnett and I wheeled around and headed back to our side of the picket line—which, as you may recall, was across a seven-foot deep bayou." Uncle Seth slowed in order to catch his breath; he was fighting the battle all over again!

After pausing a moment and observing his audience to make sure he still had their full attention, he continued. "By the time we got through the canebrake and plunged into the bayou, the Yankee cavalry was peppering the water with hot lead—meant for us! Our pickets fired and the Yanks pulled up short of their goal and high-tailed it back to the safety of their camp. Halfway across the bayou, De Jarnett was startled to hear a third horse closing in on him. Thinking it to be the remounted Yankee, De Jarnett again reached for and pulled his revolver and prepared to settle the affair right there in the middle of Bayou Rapids. To his surprise and relief he saw a riderless horse leaping through the canebrake and plunging into the bayou. The horse came across and stopped next to De Jarnett. It must have been a loyal Southern horse," Uncle Seth said with a wink and a grin. "De Jarnett's prize for the adventure was not only a very beautiful and expensive horse but a fine pair of pistols and soldier's baggage.

"I think De Jarnett still lives in Texas," explained Uncle Seth. "Now, you boys need to get those fine rabbits dressed and see if your mother will fix us some dumplings to go along with them." Uncle Seth moved slowly off the back porch and toward the fireplace, seeking its warmth to ease the cold

Confederate officer

pain in his joints. The old Southern patriot felt confident he had won another skirmish in the continuing war against Yankee invasion and occupation of his Southern nation.

§ Deo Vindice §

ON THE SKIRMISH LINE WITH UNCLE SETH

A Yankee veteran and member of the Grand Army of the Republic—the post-war political arm of Union veterans—observed an annual meeting of the United Confederate Veterans and noted that, while it appeared these former Rebels were now loyal to the national government, he was distressed by something. Although there were numerous Rebel flags in parades and events associated with the meeting—he could not locate any Untied States flags! And while bands regularly played "Dixie"—accompanied by the most enthusiastic outburst of the Rebel Yell—he never heard the national anthem played. And the point was . . . ?

65

Confederate Prisoners of War Capture Yankee Boat and Escape

"Seth, what are you laughing about?" asked Sarah, Uncle Seth's twin sister. She had come over from the homeplace to visit with her brother. She had several copies of the Jackson, Mississippi, newspaper, and she knew that her brother would enjoy reading every word.

"Sarah, look here!" the old Confederate veteran exclaimed. "It is a story about how some of our men who had been captured by the Yankees managed to escape. The paper reprinted a copy of a letter one of the soldiers sent home back on June 26, 1863. Lt. Robert C. Noland wrote it to his sister to tell her about how he and his comrades had just escaped. It says here that Robert was seriously wounded in the battle of Murfreesboro. His friends were able to save his life but could not keep him hidden from the Yankees. He was found and put with ninety other prisoners and taken to Fort Delaware by boat. The Southerners hatched a plan to overpower the Yankee guards—men who had never felt the sting of battle—and compel the boat pilot to land them on the Virginia side of the river a little below the Fort Henry Lighthouse. This they accomplished, but they had many miles to cover while still in Yankee-controlled territory—about two hundred miles to be exact. The entire time they were pursued by Federal cavalry. About seventy-one of the ninety men made it back to the safety of our lines. A few days after reaching Confederate lines and rejoining their units, they found out that Lieutenant Noland had been declared a pirate by the authorities of the United States and was under condemnation to be hung as soon as the Yankees managed to recapture him. It seems that he had been the leader of the enterprise to capture the Yankee ship the *Maple Leaf*. He was so concerned that he told his sister to destroy the letter after she read it in case it fell into Yankee hands. Lucky for us she decided to hide it away in a safe place and now many years later is sharing it with us as evidence of her brother's bravery and the evil measures the invading Yankee was willing to stoop to during the war."

Sarah was now sitting next to her twin brother, devoting her full attention to him just as she had done so many times when they were children. She was always his supporter and primary source of encouragement. There was a special connection between the twins that other people never really understood. "Seth, what do you think the Yankees hoped to accomplish by branding those brave men as pirates? They were soldiers, and isn't it a soldier's duty to try to escape and return to his unit?" Without pausing, Sarah continued with an observation that so many Southern civilians had noted both during and after the war: "All we asked was to be left alone, to solve our problems in a way that would be best for all concerned, to live and let live—was that too much to ask?"

"You know, Sister, Yankees have always told untruths about the South and our people. During the war they claimed that Admiral Semmes of the CSS *Alabama* and officers of other Confederate commerce raiders were pirates and should be treated as such if they were caught. They even tried to convince British governors of foreign ports not to allow our ships to enter; the Yankees told them we were not a real nation and did not deserve the treatment accorded by the rules of international law. Lucky for us the British were not fooled by Yankee lies. The British, even though they never recognized our nation, granted us the protections afforded by international law. I remember how during the beginning of the war the Yankee General Custer threatened to hang all rebels he captured, both officers and enlisted men. But he was stopped from doing so when we sent him a message that if he did such an evil act we would hang every Yankee officer and non-commissioned officer we captured.

"This hatred for all Southern people has been and continues to be a part of the Yankee's picture of the South. When the rabid abolitionist John Brown went into Kansas in the late 1850s claiming to be on a mission to free slaves, his first victims were Southerners who did *not* own slaves. They pleaded with Brown and his men, but to no avail. Why? Because Brown did not care whether or not those innocent civilians owned slaves. All he cared about was that they were Southerners, and every good Yankee knows that Southerners are naturally evil and need to be destroyed, so he killed them. It was not long after Brown's Kansas "mission" that some of the leading men of the North—some of whom ended up in Lincoln's government—put up huge sums of money to finance Brown's raid on Harper's Ferry for the supposed purpose of freeing slaves in Virginia. And what do you know; the very first causality of Brown's raid was a free man of color. Brown and other extreme Northerners did not care about color. All they cared about was killing Southerners, black or white. As far as they were concerned, all Southerners deserved to be either killed or at least controlled by the United States government—a government completely controlled by the Yankees.

"Northern newspapers were full of examples of this hatred, especially at the beginning of the war. They often used the disparaging terms "rebel" or "rebellion" to describe the Southern people's decision to become an independent nation. Of course, this is the same thing that the British did to the American Colonies back in 1776 when we seceded from the British Empire, but this point was overlooked by the South-hating Northern press. The *New York Tribune* boastfully declared that the 'hanging of traitors is sure to begin' and that 'the nations of Europe may rest assured that Jeff Davis and Company will be swinging from the battlements at Washington before the 4th of July.' That paper even stated that they 'spit' on such people. The *New York Times* urged Lincoln and company to send twenty-five thousand men to Richmond and 'burn the rats' there. The *Philadelphia Press* described the Southern people as 'rebels' and a 'mere band of ragamuffins.' And who can forget—although I'm sure the New South Yankee educators will never teach our children this—that Colonel Billy Wilson of New York marched his regiment up to a hotel in the city and ordered, 'Attention, kneel down.' Every Yankee soldier dropped down to his knees, and the United States colonel began, 'You do solemnly swear to cut off the head of every damned Secessionist you meet during the war.' His men answered as in one voice, 'We swear.' A New York paper described this incident and noted, 'The gallant souls then returned in good order to their quarters.' This demonstrates the hatred and venom that had long before been injected into the thinking of too many Northerners regarding the people of the South. It is no surprise, then, that the United States declared escaping prisoners to be pirates and outside of the protections of the rules of civilized warfare."

Sarah reached over and touched her brother's arm. The two sat there in silence for a long moment. She knew how it pained Seth to think too much about the defeat and destruction visited upon the Southern people by the invading Yankee. She could do nothing about such matters, but she was always there to comfort her brother when he seemed so down and depressed. She knew he needed her and he knew that she would always be there for him when he needed her the most.

§ Deo Vindice §

ON THE SKIRMISH LINE WITH UNCLE SETH

Patrick Henry of Virginia warned his fellow countrymen about the dangers of a supreme federal government as would be created under the proposed constitution of 1787. He cautioned: "This Constitution is said to have beautiful features; but when I come to examine these features, sir, they appear to me horribly frightful. Among other deformities, it has an awful squinting; it squints toward monarchy . . . There will be no checks, no real balances, in this government. What can avail your specious, imaginary balances, your rope-dancing, chain-rattling, ridiculous ideal checks and balances? But now sir, the American spirit, assisted by the ropes and chains of consolidation, is about to convert this country into a powerful and mighty *empire*. If you make the citizens of this country agree to become the subjects of one great consolidated *empire* of America, your government will not have sufficient energy to keep them together [as free men]. Such a government is incompatible with the genius of Republicanism" [emphasis added]. Patrick Henry saw no danger to American liberty in the limited government under the Articles of Confederation, but he saw that gradual consolidation of power into the Federal government under the proposed constitution would result in a supreme Federal government that would destroy the sovereign states and create a power-hungry Northern ruling elite that would control the Federal Empire—with the Southern minority reduced to subjects of their empire.

66

The Battle of Sabine Pass—the Improbable Victory

The quiet of the evening was Uncle Seth's favorite time of the day. The old Confederate veteran knew that the boys would soon be through with their chores and would find a place close beside him on the front porch in anticipation of yet another of his exciting stories about the war. The boys were Uncle Seth's grandchildren, great-grandchildren, and an assortment of great-nephews and cousins.

The old soldier sat quietly, enjoying the melody of the Southern whip-poor-will. Many a night in camp, he and his fellow Southern soldiers would engage in a great debate over what the whip-poor-will was saying. Was it "Chip fell out the white oak," or was it "Chip married the widow"? "Oh, I hope the day never comes when Southerners will be so far removed from the soil that they will not understand the beauty and joy of such meaningless debates," Uncle Seth mused to himself.

Cousin Barry broke the silence with a question that was intended to get Uncle Seth's "Irish up." "Uncle Seth, my history teacher says that the South was so outnumbered that there was no way we would have been able to defeat the United States," the boy announced as he measured the reaction in Uncle Seth's eyes.

"Well, boy," countered Uncle Seth, "only a Southern fool would believe everything a Yankee history teacher says about our people." Barry's history teacher was not actually a Yankee, but according to Uncle Seth, any Southern teacher who used Yankee textbooks and taught Yankee lies was really worse than a Yankee. However, out of politeness to the children, the old man stopped short by simply calling such teachers "Yankee teachers." Uncle Seth knew that since the end of the war it had become profitable for some segments of the "educated and progressive" class to betray their Southern heritage. Like all traitors, they valued immediate satisfaction and financial gain over honor and loyalty to their oppressed people.

"You know, boys," continued Uncle Seth, "it's not the size of the dog in the fight that matters; it's the size of the fight in the dog that really counts. Let me tell you about my experience at the Battle of Sabine Pass. You boys know that Sabine Pass is on the Sabine River between Louisiana and Texas. We knew that the Yankees were planning an invasion of Texas, and we made great efforts to meet them around Galveston. Instead of invading at Galveston, they assembled a fleet at the mouth of the Sabine River on September 7, 1863. I was sent as a courier to the Davis Guards, a group of Irish soldiers who at that time were best known for their drinking and fist-fighting abilities. The Davis Guards numbered thirty-eight men, and they had five old cannons that had been condemned by the U. S. government prior to the war as too old and dangerous to use. Well, those guns *were* old and dangerous, but they were all that our Confederate government had to give for the defense of the Sabine River. Their maximum range, assuming they fired at all or did not explode in the process, was no more than half of the range of serviceable cannons.

"The United States' invading fleet, on the other hand, consisted of up to fifteen war vessels and five thousand U.S. army troops—all well-equipped, well-fed, and rested. Now, boys, how's that for odds? Barry, your Yankee teacher would tell you that defending Sabine Pass under such circumstances would be a forlorn hope, wouldn't she? Well, I asked Lieutenant Dowling if his Irishmen were ready to run, but I knew the answer before I asked. We were going to fight and if possible we would turn the invader back—but regardless of the odds or cost, we would defend our country.

"The United States forces opened fire on us before noon on the 8th and kept up their fire until 2:00 p.m. I tell you, boys, the cannon fire was so constant that I verily believe a rabbit could not have lived outside the fort or anywhere in its immediate vicinity. At 2:00 p.m. the invading fleet began its approach up the river channel. Their plan was to run past us and take us from behind or the upriver approach. You see, our guns were mounted 'en barlette' and could only be fired in one direction—downriver. If the Yanks passed us we were finished!

"The USS *Clifton* and three other ships came up the Texas, or west, channel, while the USS *Sachem* and the remaining ships came up the Louisiana, or east, channel. They all kept up an incessant and tremendous fire. We were

The Battle of Sabine Pass (Courtesy Charles Hayes)

behind the sand walls of the fort trying to avoid the exploding bombs the Yankees were throwing into the fort. Now, the U.S. forces began the fight when they were miles away. Because our old guns would only reach less than half that distance, we were forced to stay down until the Yankees got within our range. It looked like the fort would be demolished before we would be able to fire a single shot. At last the order to man our guns was given, followed quickly by the second order to load and fire at will. One of our guns recoiled after the second discharge and fell off the platform. So early on we lost one of our five guns. Boys, I tell you, the odds were not getting any better. I am sure glad your Yankee teacher was not there," Uncle Seth said looking directly into Barry's eyes. "We didn't have enough men to work even four guns to their maximum efficiency—but work them we did! The Davis Guards operated with perfect discipline and, above all, with perfect coolness, which compensated for our want of men. After the second shot from each gun, we had the invaders' range and from then on every one of our shots hit their mark. Before long the USS *Sachem* was within five or six hundred yards of passing our fort. Then Jack White's crew of gun number 1 succeeded in planting a solid shot through the *Sachem*'s side and into the center of her steam chest. The USS *Sachem* was disabled and immediately surrendered. This enabled us to concentrate our fire on the USS *Clifton*. She ran aground on an oyster reef about six hundred yards from us. The *Clifton* was the invader's flagship. You cannot imagine our excitement when we saw her haul down the United States flag in surrender. We Confederates, of course, honored her surrender and ceased firing on her. The USS *Arizona* also hauled down her flag, hoisted a white flag, and latter sank. Soon, the entire Yankee invasion fleet was in disarray, floundering and attempting to extricate itself from the vicious and deadly Confederate fire.

"The U.S. loss numbered more than four hundred killed, wounded, and captured men; three gunboats; and numerous transport ships. Our loss was nothing! Well, almost nothing. We did have one man who was grazed by a Yankee cannonball just above his wrist, but it didn't even break the skin.

"Thirty-eight brave Irish Confederate soldiers fighting with outdated equipment against overwhelming odds gained an amazing victory at Sabine Pass. Their heroic efforts helped us to keep our pledge that Texas was sacred and not to be invaded or polluted by an enemy—unless the enemy came to Texas as a prisoner of war.

"Remember, boys, the odds should never be considered when you are defending your country from invasion or insults," Uncle Seth admonished as he slipped his hand into his vest pocket trying to locate a chaw of Virginia tobacco.

§ Deo Vindice §

ON THE SKIRMISH LINE WITH UNCLE SETH

Brig. Gen. Paul J. Semmes of Columbus, Georgia, fell mortally wounded on the first day of the Battle of Gettysburg. He was taken to Virginia, where he suffered in silence. On the day of his death he was interviewed by a foreign correspondent. General Semmes told the correspondent, "I consider it a privilege to die for my country." Yankee propagandists seeking to justify their criminal acts carried out to establish their supreme federal empire will have Southerners and the world believe that General Semmes and those like him died in order to keep their slaves.

67

CSS *Tennessee*'s Six Guns Against Two Hundred Yankee Guns

Uncle Seth and the boys had traveled to Natchez, Mississippi, to see the antebellum homes there; Uncle Seth also particularly wanted the boys to see the mighty Mississippi River. The boys were more impressed with the wide river than the antebellum architecture. The largest river they had ever seen was the Pearl River, which bordered Copiah and Simpson counties back home. The rivers back home were no longer served by riverboats; the railroad and improved roadways had put a stop to river traffic on such small rivers. The boys were amazed at the large amount of river traffic on the Mississippi.

"Uncle Seth, did the Yankees have this many ships on the river when you were at Vicksburg during the war?" asked Carroll Ray.

"Yes, Carroll Ray, the Yankees always had a lot of ships and guns firing at us during the war. Empires can always marshal huge amounts of material against the most determined local defenses. Eventually the empire will wear down any conventional resistance to the empire's aggression." Uncle Seth found a bench and sat down to rest awhile.

"Is that what happened to us during the war?" Carroll Ray inquired of the old Confederate veteran. It always made Uncle Seth feel good to hear his boys refer to the Confederacy as "us," because he knew the importance of keeping alive the belief that "we the people" of the South are a special folk who deserve to be remembered as a nation—even if only as an occupied nation.

"Yes, we wore ourselves out whipping Yankees." The old man chuckled at his own joke, although he knew that many a truth is said in jest. "Let me tell you about how the CSS *Tennessee,* with only six naval cannons, fought an entire United States naval fleet with more than two hundred Yankee naval cannons firing on it.

"Lewis Cole now lives in Paris, Texas, but he lived in Tennessee in 1861. He joined Company A of the 55th Tennessee Regiment under Colonel A. J. Brown. He fought in many battles and in January of 1864, his unit was ordered to Mobile, Alabama, which was, at that time, being attacked by a large Yankee fleet. In Mobile he was transferred from the infantry to the Confederate navy. The CSS *Tennessee* was built in Selma, Alabama, and was towed to Mobile in order to be fitted out for war. She would soon be called upon and put into action against the Yankee fleet attacking Mobile. Confederate admiral Buchanan called for volunteers to man the *Tennessee,* and Lewis was one of those brave men who volunteered."

CSS Tennessee (Courtesy Charles Hayes)

"The *Tennessee* would be facing a Yankee fleet of seventeen ships, two of which were ironclad double-turreted monitors. The battle began as the Yankee fleet attempted to run into Mobile Bay. Admiral Buchanan knew that the forts protecting the bay and the city could not be held if the Yankee fleet got into the bay and began firing on the unprotected side of the forts. In a courageous attempt to hold the forts, Admiral Buchanan moved the *Tennessee* away from the protection of the fort's guns and advanced on the enemy's fleet. The Yankee Admiral Farragut had ordered his ships to stay well away from the fort's guns as they moved into Mobile Bay. Despite the overwhelming odds, the *Tennessee* charged forward. It was an uneven battle from the beginning, but the *Tennessee* and her crew did their duty. Great damage was done to the Yankee ships; one of the Yankee ironclads sunk when it hit a Confederate torpedo. (Today we would call them mines.) The result of the fight was foregone: the Yankees had seventeen ships that could bring more than two hundred guns to bear on one Confederate ship. The Confederates' action was brave but futile. Like so many of our battles during the war, the CSS *Tennessee* exhausted herself in the struggle to keep her country free—outmatched in material and numbers but not in fighting spirit.

"You know boys, if we had had just two ships like the *Tennessee* that could work together against the greater numbers of Yankee warships, I believe we would have won the day. But empires can afford the material and can hire enough troops to overcome a small country. Even the bravest must eventually fall to the overwhelming might of massed men and material. Those who volunteered to man the *Tennessee* were fighting against impossible odds, and they knew it. They knew that their chance of surviving was slim; and they knew that at this late stage in the war the South's hope of maintaining its freedom and independence was fading. Yet despite all of this these brave men fought on. They fought to protect your right to be free of meddling Yankees, your right to simply be left alone. Yet the victorious Yankee would have the world believe that those men were fighting to keep their slaves! Damnable Yankee lies! And the world believes these lies because, as a conquered and occupied country, the South has no one to defend its honor; so Yankee slander goes unanswered and eventually will become accepted history. If 'we the people' of the South allow that to happen, then we deserve to become second-class Yankees, the servants to those who invaded, raped, burned, and pillaged our free Southern nation. We will deserve to be the slaves of the Yankee Empire." The old man turned to look at the river flowing toward the Gulf of Mexico and to listen to the sound of steam whistles.

§ Deo Vindice §

On the Skirmish Line with Uncle Seth
Gen. Robert E. Lee described the sufferings of the Southern soldier in a letter to his wife: "I received a report from one division the other day in which it is stated that over four hundred are barefooted and over a thousand without blankets. I fear they suffer, but still they are cheerful and uncomplaining." Ill-equipped, outnumbered, and facing an aggressive and powerful industrial empire, these men soldiered on for four long years. The majority of them did not own slaves—yet Yankee propagandists would have Southern schoolchildren and the world to believe these men fought for slavery. And why would Yankee propagandists continue their vilification of all things Southern so long after the ending of the "Civil War" and so long after their glorious victory? Is there an unconscious understanding among those who support the Federal Empire that, should the people of the South ever learn the truth about the Yankee's motive for invading and conquering the Confederate States of America, those who enjoy the benefits of empire would perhaps awake one day to the rousing sounds of Rebel Yells coming from deep within Dixie? Perhaps they understand that the task of keeping a conquered people pacified and submissive is never-ending. But it is a task made easier by numerous self-hating Southern educators, media personalities, and politicians.

68

Heroic Death of a Nineteen-Year-Old Southern Soldier

The excited screams coming from the backyard alerted Uncle Seth to an altercation between Carroll Ray and Barry. Barry was known for having a fiery Irish temper and would begin a fist fight at the drop of a hat with little provocation. After the scuffle, though, he would be equally as fast to resume normal play—no hard feelings. "All right, boys!" shouted Uncle Seth, "settle down or else I will knock a wart on both of your heads." The two junior pugilists quickly snapped to attention at the sound of Uncle Seth's command. "Now, boys," the old Confederate veteran began lecturing the cousins, "how many times have I told you that there are better ways to settle a disagreement than by fighting. You should save your combat strength for times when you really need it.

"I was just reading an account of a nineteen-year-old Confederate soldier whose heroic act cost his life but saved many of his comrades." The two boys were rather crestfallen and embarrassed by the scuffle and were agreeable to hearing the rest of Uncle Seth's story. "The young lad's name was Richard Somers Edwards. One of his direct ancestors was Capt. Richard Somers, who was in the United States navy and who in Tripoli in 1804 sacrificed his life when he threw a lighted torch into more than one hundred barrels of gunpower to prevent them from falling into enemy hands. Such was the blood that flowed through our young Southern patriot's veins.

"Young Richard and his mother were living in Macon, Georgia. He was barely seventeen years old when the war began in 1861. His health had never been good and as a result he was frail and looked more like a young child than a boy of seventeen. His father had recently died and he was left to take care of his mother. He begged his mother to allow him to join the Confederate Cause, but she could not bear the thought of sending such a frail boy off to war. 'Wait until our country really needs you; there are so many volunteers going just now,' she told her young son with tears in her eyes. By 1863, though, it was a different story. The country needed all her sons to meet the overwhelming numbers of Yankee invaders. It was then that the heroic mother—ready to defend her country as mothers had before her—placed her son's cap on his head with trembling hands and mutely kissed him goodbye, tears held back and silent prayers racing toward heaven.

Richard Somers Edwards circa 1863

"The family were friends of Edward Pollard, the editor of the *Richmond Examiner*, and decided to send young Edward to Richmond with a request for Pollard's assistance in gaining Richard an assignment in a unit in the city. Richard was assigned to an artillery unit at Drury's Bluff in 1863. Shortly after that he was reassigned to a Georgia artillery unit, the Macon Light Artillery. He was proud to be a part of his home unit. He served in numerous engagements and was sent home in 1865 on his first furlough. He had been wounded, his arm and face were black, and he had numerous open wounds. He recovered quickly while at home under his mother's tender care. By the time his furlough was almost expired, the Yankees had occupied most of the territory between Macon, Georgia, and Richmond, Virginia. In order to return to his unit Richard would have to travel the back roads and on foot. If the Yankees caught him, they would surely hang him as a spy. His mother, neighbors, and local attorneys all suggested that he stay in Macon. But he refused, declaring, 'I'll risk everything to get back to my unit and make sure that no one ever slanders my family's name by calling me a deserter.' After a perilous journey Richard made it back to Richmond.

"This was shortly before the fall of Richmond. The Confederate lines had been broken on both sides of Richard's unit's emplacement. The Macon unit lost so many men that they were having trouble servicing all of their guns and their battery was rapidly being surrounded by Yankees. The command was given for the men to retire and save themselves. It seemed as if every Yankee in the Army of the Potomac was coming toward Richard's position. As everyone was hurrying to the rear, Richard noticed that the man holding the lanyard cord of their unit's cannon had been killed by a mass of Yankee bullets. Someone yelled out that the cannon was charged with canister shot! Richard knew that if the Yankees overran the cannon and turned it around and fired it, the discharge would kill all of his comrades. Without thinking of his own safety—just like his ancestor in 1804—he ran back to the cannon, seized the lanyard cord, and with Yankee bullets stinging his flesh he pulled the lanyard cord with his last ounce of energy. The cannon report produced vast devastation for the approaching Yankees but our nineteen-year-old Confederate hero fell— another Southerner sacrificed on freedom's altar."

"Because young Richard did not originally join a Georgia unit, his name was not listed on the Georgia roster of Confederate soldiers, nor can it be found listed on the Virginia roster. The young boy, a Southern hero, lies in an unmarked grave, his mortal remains embraced by the soil of the country he died defending."

Uncle Seth looked at the young boys standing there next to him. They were so young; would they remember? Would their children and grandchildren remember? He thought of these things often, but he had no answer. Those who come after the old Confederate veteran will have the responsibility to answer such questions.

§ Deo Vindice §

ON THE SKIRMISH LINE WITH UNCLE SETH

America's founders designed the Constitution as a procedural document detailing how to govern the federal government, *not* as a means to govern the people of the various sovereign states. At least 20 percent of the Constitution details what the federal government *cannot* do. The founders' primary aim was to create a reasonably effective but limited federal government—a government that would essentially leave the people alone. The Constitution of the Confederate States of America followed this principle.

By 1860, the Constitution of the United States of America, as interpreted by those who desired to create an American economic and commercial empire, had morphed into a thing of clay to be molded into any form that best served the desires of the ruling elite who controlled the federal government. The prophetic warnings of Virginians such as Patrick Henry and Thomas Jefferson had, by 1860, at last materialized. The South had reached the point of desperation predicted by John Randolph, "when the little upon which we now barely subsist will be taken from us." Limited constitutional government with *real* States' Rights would live or die with the Confederate States of America.

69

Did the South Intentionally Mistreat Yankee Prisoners of War?

Uncle Seth was a young lad of seventeen back in 1861 when he joined the Confederate army. Many years have passed, but the old man, even at eighty-four, was still active around the community. He was one of the last living Confederate veterans and as such was treated with special kindness and respect. Every Remembrance Day—or Memorial Day, as it was now known—the ladies of the United Daughters of the Confederacy or the Sons of Confederate Veterans in Hazlehurst or another south-central Mississippi town would invite the old veteran to say a few words about the Cause for which so many had struggled and died. Uncle Seth was excited because today was one of those special days. The Brookhaven Sons of Confederate Veterans had sent a 1926 Dodge sedan to pick him up and take him to their annual Lee-Jackson barbeque. And of course, they expected him to say a few words about the war.

The Dodge sedan made good time traveling over the gravel roads between Pearl Valley community and the big city of Brookhaven. In the old days it would have taken several days to make the trip, but the sedan was clipping along at thirty-five to forty-five miles per hour and within two hours they had arrived. Uncle Seth decided to speak briefly about the often-repeated Yankee allegation that the South intentionally mistreated U.S. soldiers who were held as prisoners in the POW camp at Andersonville, Georgia. The old soldier knew that his remaining days on this earth were few, and he wanted to make sure the next generation of young men—the Sons—would understand the importance of constantly and aggressively defending the principles and honor of their fathers who wore the gray in the War for Southern Independence.

The Brookhaven SCV (as the

Uncle Seth's ride to a Brookhaven, Mississippi, SCV meeting, 1926 (Courtesy Betty Kennedy)

Sons of Confederate Veterans was generally referred to) camp commander introduced Uncle Seth—although he needed no introduction. The crowd gave the old soldier a loud and enthusiastic reception. He stood at the podium and listened to the applause and shouts—he knew that they were not applauding him so much as their kin who had already crossed over from this life to the next and were resting in the shade of the trees. The crowd settled down and Uncle Seth began. "I want to make sure you all have a correct understanding of why so many men, Northern and Southern men, needlessly suffered and died in prison camps during the war. The Northern-controlled education system uses its control of education to misinform our children about the war. They constantly slander the Cause for which we fought, and they use their control of education as a means to constantly slander that Cause. The Northern-controlled newspapers continue their slander of all things Southern, and the Northern-controlled Federal Empire continues to use the force of its government to compel acceptance of their version of the war—a version based on lies and unmitigated Yankee arrogance.

"Let me first say a few words about the cruel and unjust treatment of Confederate Major Wirz, who was the last commander at Andersonville prison camp. One of the charges against Major Wirz was that he had personally killed numerous prisoners. The Yankee court that tried and sentenced him had the entire resources of the Federal Empire at its command but still could not name a single individual who Major Wirz had killed. Oh, they had names, but none of their names matched the name of a prisoner who had been held at Andersonville. All of the Yankee charges against Major Wirz were imaginary charges, supported by well-paid witnesses who testified in a court that had already convicted Wirz before the so-called trial began—typical Yankee justice when dealing with the South or things Southern. One of the Yankee prisoners at Andersonville was so shocked by the treatment of Major Wirz that he wrote a book defending his former enemy! Lt. James E. Page of Company A, 6th Michigan Cavalry, wrote that the Federal government was responsible because it rejected the Confederate government's repeated offers to exchange prisoners. And here is the crux of the matter: the Federal government, under instructions from Lincoln, knew that if they exchanged prisoners the Northern soldier would go home and not re-enlist in the Yankee army; but the Southern soldier *would* go back to the Confederate army in order to defend his home! For Lincoln, refusing to exchange prisoners had nothing to do with humanity. It was a war policy. It was just like his so-called Emancipation Proclamation—a means to secure victory over the people of the South who merely asked to be left alone. But Lincoln and his commercial and banking supporters knew that if the

South was able to maintain its freedom, the Yankee political, commercial, and banking interests would no longer be able to loot Southern resources for their political and commercial advantage.

"The exchange of prisoners was not equally advantageous. Lincoln and his generals knew that prisoner exchange would free more Southern soldiers than Northern. Even with the greater numerical advantage the Yankees already enjoyed, they were having a difficult time conquering the Confederate States of America. The leadership of the Yankee Empire did not relish the thought of releasing Southern men who would continue the fight against the Yankee invader—an invader who was actively raping, burning, murdering, and pillaging innocent Southern civilians. But there was an advantage for the Yankee Empire in forcing the South to keep Northern prisoners of war. Lincoln and his generals knew that the expense of holding Northern prisoners put added stress on the Confederate government. In other words, allowing their men to starve in Southern prison camps when Lincoln and his generals knew the South was not able to properly supply these camps was merely another war measure as far as the leadership of the Yankee Empire was concerned.

"Early in the war an exchange system had been established by the commanders in the field. The South carried out its obligations under these agreements— known as cartels—but the North broke nearly every one and eventually denied the validity of a cartel itself. The North vacillated in the exchange of prisoners, whereas the South stood always ready to exchange on whatever terms the North would adopt. General Grant sent directives to General Butler in August of 1864, ordering him not to exchange prisoners with the South. The Yankee General Grant wrote in his memoirs that the freeing by exchange of one Southern soldier 'was equal on the defensive to three Union soldiers.' The Yankee Secretary of War Stanton declared, 'We do not propose to re-enforce the Rebel Army by exchanging prisoners.' Yankee General Butler testified to the Federal congress that his effort to exchange prisoners was defeated by the intercession of Secretary of War Stanton and General Grant.

"Knowing the dire situation of the Yankee prisoners being held by the South, our President, Jefferson Davis, ordered Gen. Robert E. Lee to go under a flag of truce to General Grant and ask in the name of humanity to allow for the exchange of prisoners. President Davis specifically instructed General Lee to explain to the Yankees that it had become impossible for the South to adequately provide for the Yankee prisoners. But General Grant would not accept the offer to discuss the issue with General Lee.

"The Confederate government made another effort to relieve the suffering of Northern prisoners in January of 1864. A dispatch was sent to the Federal agent of exchange, General Hitchcock, suggesting that each side allow the other to send physicians, medicine, and other supplies to the camps wherein their prisoners were being held. The Yankees never even made a reply to this humanitarian offer.

"The Confederate government was well aware of the conditions at Andersonville but was not able to supply the desperately needed resources. In August of 1864, the Confederate government sent an agent under a flag of truce down the James River to communicate with Yankee General Mulford about the terrible and desperate conditions at Andersonville. The Confederate government requested that the North send food and medicine; the South would then assure safe conduct. The message was sent to Washington. After the passage of two or three weeks the United States government sent a message back rejecting the offer.

"There is so much that I could tell you." Uncle Seth wanted to say so much more, but just like the Confederate Army in 1865 he was exhausted. "I will have to save it for another day. The one thing I want you, the Sons and Daughters of Dixie, to remember is that we fought for you—for your right to live in a country of your own, a country ordered upon the American principle of the 'consent of the governed.' You must not forget that today 'we the people' of the South are in fact a conquered people—a people ruled by outsiders. Our economic, social, and political interests— not to mention our desire to be left alone—will never be respected by an arrogant and supreme Federal government that holds in its hands the bloody bayonets with which it conquered your people, your true nation. They lie and slander our Cause because they know that if our people ever understand the truth the South shall rise again!"

§ Deo Vindice §

On the Skirmish Line with Uncle Seth
After two years of suffering from Yankee invasion, many of Georgia's civilian population had been made homeless and left with no means to feed themselves. In an effort to alleviate its people's suffering, the State of Georgia in the winter of 1863 appropriated funds and supplies for 45,718 children, 22,637 kinswomen of soldiers in the field, 8,492 orphans, 4,000 widows of deceased soldiers, and 550 disabled soldiers.

No doubt Lincoln and his fellow Yankees felt that the suffering thus inflicted upon these innocent civilians by the United States of America was just punishment for a people who desired to live in a country of their own. Arrogant Yankees viewed such desires as a threat to the Yankee Empire—and they still do.

70

Our Reunited Country?

Ever since childhood, Uncle Seth hated controversy. Live and let live, mind your own business, and leave well enough alone—those were his social guides. Yet some things were just too aggravating to leave be! The old Confederate was known throughout the community as a partisan defender of the old South—an unreconstructed Southerner.

The local schoolhouse was full of parents, students, and local schoolboard officials. As Uncle Seth strolled in, the crowd hushed and every eye turned to gaze upon the old Confederate veteran. You could tell by the reaction of the crowd that the community held him in high esteem. But some of the younger teachers were determined to move progressively into a new South where the past would be recast and retold in a manner more fitting with the national myth as expressed in the Northern textbooks used in local Southern schools. This was more than the old man could tolerate. But the straw that broke the camel's back was the announcement that the school would put on a program saluting "our reunited country."

Rising to address the gathering on the issue, Uncle Seth began, "Now, folks, I thank you for allowing me to talk to you all tonight. I'll hurry 'cause it's well past my bed time," he said to the amusement of the crowd. "This country," he began again, "is 'ours' only in a historical sense. It is not ours by choice—that is, ours by the free and unfettered consent of the governed, which at one time was the hallmark of this once-free Republic of Republics. The unity of the original United States of America was based upon mutual respect and willingness to compromise on differences in order to maintain that unity. It is reunited today not by mutual respect but by the moral suasion of bloody bayonets! Now I know that there is nothing new in these words of mine; y'all have heard me say them time and time again. But what I would like to give you tonight as evidence to support my words are the words of Mississippi's senator L. Q. C. Lamar. He gave an address to the U.S. Senate on March 1, 1879, defending Jefferson Davis's right to receive his Mexican War pension from the government of our 'reunited country.'" Uncle Seth paused to gauge the temper of his audience. Seeing that they were following him, he continued.

"Senator Hoar from Massachusetts introduced an amendment that would exclude Jefferson Davis from the benefits of a bill that allowed the payment of pensions to all Mexican War veterans regardless of which side they subsequently fought on during the war of 1861-65. Not being satisfied with stealing the pension from a wounded veteran of the Mexican War, the Northern senator further insulted President Davis by declaring him to be a traitor on the same level as Aaron Burr and Benedict Arnold. This affront was more that Senator Lamar was willing to tolerate. Rising, he addressed the Senate:

> I must confess my surprise and regret that the Senator from Massachusetts should have wantonly, without provocation, flung this insult. [At this point the president of the Senate ruled Senator Lamar out of order. The Senator objected and the question was put to the entire Senate. The Senate voted in favor of Senator Lamar and he continued his reply to the Yankee Senator's insulting remarks.] The only difference between myself and Jefferson Davis is that his exalted character, his preeminent talents, his well established reputation as a statesman, as a patriot, and as a soldier enabled him to take the lead in the cause to which I consecrated myself and to which every fiber of my heart responded. There was no distinction between insult to him and the Southern people except that he was their chosen leader and they his enthusiastic followers, and there has been no difference since. The Senator from Massachusetts, it pains me to say, not only introduced this amendment, but he coupled that honored name with treason; for, sir, he is honored among the Southern people. He did only what they sought to do; he was simply chosen to lead them in a course which we all cherished; and his name will continue to be honored for his participation in that great movement. The people of the South drank their inspiration from the fountain of devotion to liberty and to constitutional government. Senator Hoar for Massachusetts affixed upon this aged man, this man broken in fortune, suffering from bereavement, an epithet of odium, an imputation of moral turpitude.
>
> Sir, it required no courage to do that; it required no magnanimity to do it; it required no courtesy. It only required hate, bitter, malignant, sectional feeling, and a sense of personal impunity. The gentleman might have learned a better lesson even from the pages of mythology. When Prometheus was bound to the rock it was not an eagle, it was a vulture that buried his beak in the tortured vitals of the victim."

Uncle Seth paused and slowly looked around at the audience. For him, the vulture was an appropriate symbol of the Yankee nation that conquered and still occupies the South. The eagle was the symbol of the old union, the original and legitimate United States of America that was destroyed by the Yankee Empire. Uncle Seth lowered his voice and asked, "Where is 'our' country if our warriors must be the victims of insult and discrimination? How can we claim to be reunited on any principle other than force and abject subjugation? We are pinned together by the overwhelming force of bloody bayonets. Teach our children the truth; teach them that a republic is held together by mutual respect of each other and mutual adherence to the organic constitution that served as the contract of union. Do not do the bidding of those who destroyed our liberty and continue to oppress us by teaching falsehoods hatched in the corrupt bowels of Yankeedom; do not deny our children their birthright of liberty—a birthright that will be denied if we do not teach them about the freedom that came naturally to my generation but that has been so wrongly denied them."

The room remained silent as the old veteran slowly left the building. Some were glad to see him leave and looked forward to the time when his kind no longer served as a hindrance to national progress. But others felt more than they were able to say. For those people, Uncle Seth's words burned within them. They ached for a way to echo Uncle Seth and express the emotion the old veteran stirred within them. Somehow Uncle Seth made them see themselves as a people—a special people. Yes, they had a past; but they also had a future. Somehow, that future could perhaps come with the freedom to once again live as a people with a country of their own.

§ Deo Vindice §

ON THE SKIRMISH LINE WITH UNCLE SETH

America's founders, especially the moderate Federalists and anti-Federalists, were inclined to treat with suspicion lofty platitudes of high sounding principles, such as equality and mass democracy, because such high-sounding declarations are often used by unprincipled individuals to promote self-serving interests.

John Stuart Mill said, "One of the greatest dangers of democracy lies in the sinister interest of the holders of power; it is the danger of class legislation . . . intended for the immediate benefit of the dominant class, to the lasting detriment of the whole."

71

Yankee Gunboats and Runaway Masters

Uncle Seth stood at the riverbank peering downriver as if trying to see around the river's bend. From where he stood, he could plainly see the old wooden pilings that had formerly served as the landing and hitching-post for the riverboats that once plied the Pearl River. "Uncle Seth," inquired his great-grandson Curtis, "do you remember when all the stores at Rockport were here on the riverbank?"

"Yes, I do. That was before the GM&O Railroad came through. When that happened, all the stores were put on wooden rails and moved to the railroad depot about a mile from this old riverboat landing," replied Uncle Seth.

"I bet it took a lot of logging mules to haul those stores up the road," Curtis mused.

"Well, for the most part they used logging oxen," corrected Uncle Seth.

"Uncle Seth, did any Yankee gunboats ever come up the Pearl River to Rockport?" From the tone of Curtis's voice Uncle Seth new the boy's wandering thoughts had taken him into an unrelated area of boyish curiosity.

"I don't know about here, but when I was at Vicksburg with your cousin John Wesley Kennedy I saw more of those Yankee mechanical monsters than I really cared to see," Uncle Seth replied as he leaned against the large white oak next to the river's edge. Curtis knew that Uncle Seth was about to give him a lesson on fighting Yankee gunboats, so he made himself comfortable.

Uncle Seth stared down the river for a long while without really looking at anything, as if trying to find lost memories. Then he slowly began: "It was the summer of 1862 and we were encamped at Vicksburg on the bank of the mighty Mississippi. We had just been given orders to move our artillery unit miles downriver from Vicksburg close to Warrenton, Mississippi. Our mission was to conceal ourselves in the driftwood along the banks of the Mississippi River and harass any Yankee boats moving on the river. We spent a pleasant five days eating what little rations we had brought, sleeping any place we could find a dry spot, and fighting mosquitoes the size of hummingbirds." Uncle Seth let out a low, soft chuckle, finding humor in his own wit. "On the fifth day, one of our pickets reported that a small craft was coming across the river from the west bank—you know, the Louisiana side of the river. The moment the small boat touched our side of the river, we all jumped them with leveled rifles. It turned out to be a boatload of slaves trying to get away from the Yankees who were raiding the plantations over on the Louisiana side. We sort of put the scare in them and felt really bad about it. We spent some time trying to make amends for our mistake and convincing them that we meant them no harm. It seemed that their master, fearing the Yankees more than the loss of his slaves, had run away, leaving the slaves to fend for themselves. These slaves had no higher opinion of the Yankees than their master and were trying to get to a plantation on the Mississippi side where some of their relatives lived. No sooner had we calmed these folks and sent them on their way than we spotted a Yankee steamboat coming around the bend. We put several solid shots through her but she managed to escape our ambush. After that we decided to move to another location; we knew what was coming. The next morning, a large Yankee gunboat proudly flying the Stars and Stripes—the Yankee invader's banner—rounded the bend and poured several broadsides into the drift where we had been hiding the day before. Having no particular desire to engage such a monster single-handedly, we held our peace."

"Why didn't y'all try to sink that Yankee gunboat?" inquired Curtis with youthful enthusiasm.

"Well you know, we were a lot like those slaves; we were not running away but we had done our job and it was now time to find a safer place, preferably among friends," responded Uncle Seth as he eased his slouch hat over his eyes and settled back against the cool shade of the oak tree. Seeing this, Curtis knew that Uncle Seth intended to rest his eyes a spell, his story concluded.

§ Deo Vindice §

ON THE SKIRMISH LINE WITH UNCLE SETH

As his farewell to his troops, Confederate Maj. Gen. Joe Wheeler said: "You have fought your fight; your task is done. During a four years' struggle for freedom you have exhibited courage, fortitude, and devotion. You are the sole victors of more than two hundred sternly contested fields. . . . In bidding you adieu I desire to tender my thanks for your gallantry in battle, your fortitude under suffering, your devotion at all time to the holy cause you have done so much to maintain. . . . Brothers in the cause of freedom, comrades in arms, I bid you farewell."

"In the cause of freedom"—this is not exactly what modern Yankee history textbooks and self-hating Southern history teachers claim was the cause of the war!

72

Lincoln Invades Florida Hoping to Gain Three Electoral Votes

Uncle Seth watched the boys as they paid the fruit peddler for a small sack of oranges. The boys always looked forward to purchasing fresh fruit from the peddler. He would have some of his fruit shipped up by rail from the Florida Parishes of Louisiana, but the prized oranges always came directly from Florida. "Boys, bring me one of those Florida oranges," Uncle Seth asked. "One day I'm going to take you all to Olustee, Florida, where we beat back ole Abe Lincoln's effort to capture Florida for his reelection effort," the old Confederate teased the boys, hoping they would settle down and listen to his story.

"Did they have orange groves with delicious oranges like these when you were there?" asked Curtis as he held up his prize orange, already half peeled.

"No; when we were there it was the 20th of February, 1864, and the orange groves had not even set blooms yet. It was early in the election year and Lincoln was concerned because the war was dragging on, causing a great outpouring of Yankee blood and no small amount of discontent among many Northerners. Lincoln found out that it would take considerably longer to destroy the Confederate States of America than ninety days— the length of time he had boasted. Lincoln thought that a quick victory in Florida before the November presidential election would improve Yankee morale. And, as a bonus, it would allow him to bring Florida back into the Union to vote in the election. Of course Lincoln knew that since his military would manage the vote, Florida's electoral votes would go to him. However, 'we the people' of the South had already demonstrated that we no longer wanted to play politics with Yankees, so we had a Confederate reception planned for them when they got to Florida.

"This was the fourth invasion of Florida; we beat them back each time. Each time we had close to the same number of troops as the Yankees. It just goes to show that when Confederate troops were evenly or almost evenly matched we could deliver the enemy the justice an invader of free people deserves. This fourth invasion of Florida was designed by the Lincoln administration with the specific purpose of bringing the state into

270

the Union under the leadership of Lincoln's private secretary, who was sent to Florida to manage the political part of their invasion scheme. Poor fellow, he had to leave the state of Florida in great haste before he could become Florida's first Lincolnite governor.

"We had around five thousand troops and the invading Yankees had around six thousand troops plus eighteen transport ships. The Confederate state of Florida was under the protection of General P.G.T. Beauregard. Beauregard knew about the enemy's movement toward Florida and anticipated the exact place where the main thrust would be made. He sent reenforcements and, by the time we met the invaders at Olustee, we were only slightly smaller in numbers. We were led by General Finnegan and the Yankees were led by General Seymour. Our battle lines met around 2:00 p.m. on the 20th. A furious fire was exchanged between the two armies. The Yankee general thought he was being resisted by local militia and was overconfident of the ultimate outcome. He sent his men into battle piecemeal whereas our general committed his entire force. We exchanged rifle and cannon fire for some two hours. We maintained pressure on the invader and gradually he began to yield ground. In the first two hours we managed to push the enemy back and capture five pieces of artillery. By this time, the invader was down to his last reserve of troops. But our firing had been so heavy that we were now out of ammunition and firing from our battle line became decidedly less. The Yankee invader realized this and doubled his firing on us. We refused to yield our ground, even though we were hardly able to reply. We were prepared to defend our homeland with nothing but the cold steel of our bayonets.

"Our bravery and determination paid off—our commander managed to resupply us with ammunition and suddenly well-aimed Southern lead was once again answering the Yankee invaders. When the battle line was resupplied, the order to charge was given. With a rousing Rebel Yell, we swept forward toward our adversary. The 27th Georgia, commanded by Colonel Zachry, made a furious attack on the Yankee center, and this gallant attack was echoed by a brilliantly executed flanking attack on the Yankee's right by the 6th Georgia led by Colonel Lofton. It was at this point that these Yankees demonstrated their rendition of the world-famous Yankee Manassas Quick Step. As they broke and ran, we continued to press them until dark. The invaders did not stop until they got the St. Mary's River between them and us. We had repulsed their invasion, captured five pieces of artillery, two stands of colors, two thousand small arms, and five hundred prisoners. The invading Yankees left 350 dead on the battlefield and abandoned a great number of their severely wounded. On our side we had 80 killed and 650 wounded.

"A lady along the route of the Yankees' retreat from Olustee saw General Seymour, who looked haggard and pale and told her he had lost over half of his troops. If he had been successful at Olustee and Ocean Pond, where most of the action took place, he would have been able to control the railroads and the state capital of Tallahassee would have been forced to surrender. The Yankee invaders would have then been able to put their puppet governor in control of Florida much as they had already done in Maryland, Kentucky, Missouri, and their newly created West Virginia. You see, boys, political leaders of aggressive empires know how to assure their political

Dedication of the monument of the Battle of Olustee, Florida, 1912 (Courtesy State Archives of Florida)

victories much better than their military victories. But with the vast resources of their empire and with no concern or care about spilling their soldiers' blood they know that eventually their military victories will be as successful as their political victories—all equally stained with immorality!

"Lincoln's political adversaries jumped on this Yankee defeat as a means to question Lincoln's ability to lead their nation. An investigation was ordered in the Yankee Congress to determine why the invasion failed and what its particular military purpose was. The *New York Herald* denounced the affair as something that grew out of political jugglery in anticipation of the upcoming U.S. presidential election. The *Herald* branded the whole affair as a scheme by Lincoln to seize Florida's electoral votes and condemned the fact that 'a thousand lives were lost in the attempt to get three electoral votes.' You see, boys, the blood of innocent civilians and common soldiers is of little value or concern to the ruling elite of the Federal Empire. It wasn't back then and it isn't today." Uncle Seth held the large, plump orange to his nose and slowly drew in the sweet fragrance.

§ Deo Vindice §

On the Skirmish Line with Uncle Seth

"General Hamilton, one of the principle writers of the *Federalist Papers*, was undoubtedly at heart a monarchist. On more than one occasion he plainly avowed himself such. In the [Constitutional Convention of 1787], which framed the Constitution he exerted his commanding influence to impart centralized, consolidated or monarchical powers to the Federal Union. But, signally failing in this, in his subsequent interpretations of the Constitution, he did what he could to bend the instrument to suit his views. Judge Story and Chief Justice Kent, and earlier, Chief Justice Jay, belonged to the same political party as General Hamilton. They were Federalists, and so odious did this [political] party become to the American people, that it was driven out of power at the expiration of old John Adams' single presidential term in 1800.

"[John Adams'] book on the American Constitution had made known his political bias. He was taken up by the monarchical Federalists and was made by them to believe that the general disposition of our citizens was favorable to monarchy.

"Even to ridicule the President [Adams] was pronounced by the corrupt partisan [Federal] judges a violation of the law. Men were beaten almost to death for neglecting to pull off their hats when the President was passing . . ."

—Charles Chauncey Burr, a Northerner (Maine), circa 1868

73

Patrick Henry and the Dangers of Forming a Union with Yankees

Uncle Seth was listening to Carroll Ray practice the speech he would present in his history class the next day. The teacher had given each student the opportunity to select an American colonial hero to research and then present the findings to the entire class. Tomorrow, Carroll Ray would tell the class about Patrick Henry.

"Uncle Seth, my history teacher said that Patrick Henry fought against the Constitution, that he was opposed to it and did not want Virginia to ratify it," Carroll Ray said, expressing his confusion because he knew that Uncle Seth often quoted Patrick Henry and was a great admirer of the man.

"Well, as usual, Carroll Ray, your Yankee history teacher is part right and completely wrong," Uncle Seth responded. Carroll Ray snickered in amusement at Uncle Seth's comment. His history teacher was not a Yankee; as a matter of fact, she was born and raised in a neighboring community and was educated in one of the best colleges in the state. But Uncle Seth always referred to such teachers as Yankee teachers because they tended to teach the Yankee version of the war. They spouted the Northern-scripted reasons why the South seceded from the United States of America back in 1861 and especially the reasons why the United States invaded the Confederate States of America. According to Uncle Seth, such teachers were not educated; they were miseducated and had become self-hating Southerners dutifully seated upon the stool of everlasting repentance while parroting anti-South, Yankee propaganda.

"Patrick Henry was governor of Virginia during the American Revolution—you know, the war the British waged against the thirteen American colonies after we seceded from our union with Great Britain," Uncle Seth continued. "As governor, he had to deal with the members of the Continental Congress and, in so doing, he became very familiar with the representatives from the New England states as well as those from Pennsylvania and New York. Today we would refer to those states as the North and their people as Yankees. Patrick Henry knew that the people in those colonies—well, by that time they were no longer colonies but had become independent and sovereign states—had a very different view of the world than the people of Virginia and the South.

"Not only were we different economically—their economy being that of commerce and shipping and ours being primarily agricultural—but we were also different culturally. The people of New England were more English and tended to place the value of a man on his material possessions, whereas the people of the South, being mostly Scotch-Irish, judged a man not by his material possessions but by the code of honor and chivalry. In the South, a gentleman was expected to speak the truth and his word was his bond. No written document was needed once a gentleman gave his word; the only formality was that the word would be sealed with a handshake, although even the handshake was not a requirement. The merchant classes of the North were fond of quoting Ben Franklin as saying that 'honesty is the best policy.' But Southerners would reply that honesty is not a policy. It is a principle. A merchant sets business policies to maximize profits, and if profits are hampered by a business policy, then the policy is adjusted or replaced with another policy that will produce better profits for the merchant. Southerners view honesty and truthfulness as a principle that therefore never changes, regardless of its possible negative economic impact.

"A gentleman's word, truthfulness, and personal honor were his measure in the agricultural South, not his material possessions. The plain folk of the old South who lived in the upland hills and mountains and lived leisurely off the bounty of land followed this code with the same intensity as the economically well-off plantation aristocrat. Falsehood, like an act of cowardice, would cause a man to lose his standing in society, and the community would rigorously enforce this by shunning a man who was known to be a coward or whose word was not trustworthy. If a man's word was questioned, he would immediately demand an explanation. If the matter could not be settled, then he proved his dedication to the truth of his word by putting his life on the line in a duel. In a phrase, truth and honor were more important than life. The acceptance of this code of honor by the general public in the South encouraged people to speak softly and slowly so as not to inadvertently give an offense, because every man was armed and quick to rise to the defense when his honor was questioned or offended.

"Patrick Henry was wise enough to understand that two people who had such different views of basic principles would not be able to agree on how to word the Constitution: a constitution that created a central government that would be controlled by the Northern majority and therefore would become an instrument the Yankees would one day use to enforce their policies on the South and eventually the entire world. He warned the people of Virginia and the South about the inherent dangers of the Federal government that would be created by the proposed constitution. Henry told them, 'I am sure that the dangers of this system are real, when those who have no similar interests with the people of this country [Virginia] are to legislate for us—when our dearest interests are to be left in the hands of those whose advantage it will be to infringe them.' He could see the day when the North would use the Federal government's taxing powers to protect their commerce by enacting high tariffs that would be paid not by the North but by the South. Recall what Sen. Thomas Benton of Missouri said in 1828, just thirty-nine years after the adoption of the Constitution; he complained in Congress that the Federal government was forcing the South to pay three-fourths of the revenues that flow into the Federal coffers.

"Patrick Henry is famous for his speech in Virginia's House of Burgesses in which he declared 'Give me liberty or give me death,' but our Yankee masters do not want Southern children or the world to remember his statement 'The first thing I have at heart is American liberty, the second thing is American Union.' You see, to Patrick Henry a Union that did not protect the liberty and individual rights of the people of the sovereign states was worse than no Union at all. It would be an active danger and predator upon the people's rights, liberty, and property. The reason Patrick Henry opposed the adoption of the Constitution was that he knew it to be a contract between sovereign states by which they created an agent, the federal government, to do certain and specific things for the principles— the sovereign states. But just like any business contract, it would be subject to conflicts of interpretation of the language of the written agreement. And he knew that when this conflict was eventually exposed in the Federal system created by the Constitution, the majority—the North—would use its political power to adjust constitutional policies to maximize Northern profits. You see, Carroll Ray, Patrick Henry was not so much unsure about the effectiveness of the wording in the constitution as he was concerned about the morality of the characters with whom we were forming a Union," Uncle Seth said with finality.

The old Confederate veteran hoped that Carroll Ray would remember some of the things he told him and one day pass them on to his own children and grandchildren. He feared that the negative and destructive effects of the Yankee-imposed education and political systems on his beloved South would be worse than the effects of Yankee invasion. He could see that slowly the Yankee masters of the defeated South were turning

Southerners into self-hating, second-class Yankees—an impoverished people who, perhaps because of the poverty foisted upon them, were now more concerned about materialism or mere economic survival than principles such as honor, truth, and liberty.

§ Deo Vindice §

ON THE SKIRMISH LINE WITH UNCLE SETH
"If centralism is ultimately to prevail; if our entire system of free Institutions as established by our common ancestors is to be subverted, and an *Empire* [emphasis added] is to be established in their stead; if that is to be the last scene of the great tragic drama now being enacted: then, be assured, that we of the South will be acquitted, not only in our own consciences, but in the judgment of mankind, of all responsibility for so terrible a catastrophe, and from all guilt of so great a crime against humanity."
—Alexander H. Stephens, 1868 (Vice President,
Confederate States of America, 1861-1865)

74

The Federal Government Taxes Southerners to Pay for War

"Cotton is king," shouted Barry as he jumped from the wagon's side planks into the load of recently picked cotton. Uncle Seth enjoyed watching his great-grandchildren. They always found time, even when helping with chores, to play and enjoy life.

"Barry, you are not exactly correct," the old man admonished the young lad. "Cotton was never king as far as the plain folk of the old South were concerned." Barry and the other boys emerged from the cotton and peered over the wagon's side planks as if asking Uncle Seth to explain.

"You see," Uncle Seth began, "cotton was very important to the large cotton plantation owners, most of whom were members of the Whig Party. But plain folk like us were Democrats; even Jefferson Davis, who owned a large plantation, was a Democrat. Democrats back before the war believed in low taxes and free trade. The Whigs, Federalists, and Republicans believed in high protective tariffs and wanted to use the tax money to support Northern commercial interests. You remember how I have told you that, because of the high protective tariffs, the Southern people were forced to pay for more than 75 percent of the cost of running the Federal government. The people of the North were getting a free ride at our expense. That's why the Yankees did not want us to leave their Union—we were their cash-cow!

"Before the war the assessed value of our cattle and hogs exceeded the value of the cotton, tobacco, and hemp crops, but somehow everyone thinks of cotton as being the Southern people's only source of money. The great thing, as far as the Scotch-Irish plain folk were concerned, was the fact that our hogs and cattle needed very little human attention. We just turned them out on the open range and let them do their thing. Each fall we would round up our cattle and hogs, clip the ears of the new arrivals (instead of branding them), send a few to market to gain a little spending cash, slaughter what we needed to replenish the smokehouse, and turn the rest loose again on the open range. That lifestyle was destroyed by the war.

"I recall those dark days after the war when the Federal Empire passed a tax on cotton as a way to replenish Federal dollars spent on the invasion, conquest, and occupation of the South. Well, you know who produces cotton—the South! Now the South had been devastated by four years of war—most of our railroads, bridges, and state and local government buildings were destroyed. And, as a war policy, the Yankees did all they could to starve the Southern population by destroying private farming implements, stealing or killing plow animals, and breeding stocks of hogs and cattle. Many of the men capable of farming had been killed or crippled in the struggle to maintain our independence. Yet, at a time like this, the Yankee government in Washington, DC, decided to tax the people of the South. It was a grievous tax burden on our occupied people. Added to this was the fact that the Yankee blockade during the war had forced the cotton mills in England to find another source of cotton. This new supply of cotton depressed prices. The new tariffs and taxes made it even less likely that the English mills would buy Southern cotton. Of course this worked to the great advantage of the Yankee cotton mill owners in the North. We were forced to sell our cotton to them at a radically reduced price—Yankee windfall profits and Southern poverty were the results!

"During the years from 1866 to 1868, more than $68,072,388 of Southern money was extorted from the devastated people of the South—and we had no way to defend ourselves. We were—and still are—a conquered people and the Federal Empire was making sure we understood our place in their 'one nation indivisible.' This tax was imposed without constitutional authority, but the constitution has no meaning or power over those who control the Federal Empire! What do they care about the written limitations imposed by the original constitution? The South was their conquered province and it was our duty to pay tribute to our Federal masters. These and the years to follow were economic boom time for the North, but we of the South did not share in the boom. As one Southern writer of the time declared, 'All of living now is simply the struggle not to die.' You know, it is amazing how fast cities like New York and Chicago can grow when they are nourished by the resources extorted from their Empire's conquered provinces." The old Confederate veteran realized that he had forgotten his audience—these young boys did not understand such matters. "Unfortunately," thought the old man, "I'm afraid their descendants will not understand either."

§ Deo Vindice §

ON THE SKIRMISH LINE WITH UNCLE SETH
In an issue of *De Bow's Review* in November of 1866, a complaint was

registered about how Southern railroads, factories, and debt had been acquired by Northern interests as if they were spoils of war. Southern aristocrats who had lived as neighbors with the people of the South had been crushed and replaced by Northern, commercial, absentee aristocrats. The world had never seen an aristocracy half as corrupt, half as greedy, nor half as dishonorable as the new rulers of the prostrate Southern economy.

75

The Real Reason John Wilkes Booth Shot Abraham Lincoln

The country store at Rockport, Mississippi, was unusually busy for a weekday morning. Uncle Seth and several of the locals were busy discussing the topics of the day and debating various points of politics, both past and present. One of the men asked Uncle Seth if he thought Lincoln's death was part of a conspiracy by Southerners who were upset about the outcome of the war. Uncle Seth remained silent for a good while—some of the men asked him if he had heard the question. But Uncle Seth was thinking about the question because it had been reported many times in the Yankee press that Jefferson Davis and other Southern officials were involved in a conspiracy to kill Lincoln.

"I can tell you this," Uncle Seth began slowly. "Back in the late 1860s— it was 1866 or 1868 or maybe even a little later; time flies and I just don't really remember, but shortly after the war—a report was published in the Wilmington, North Carolina, *Messenger* claiming to be the true story about why Booth was so angry with Lincoln. The story did not confirm the Yankee notion of an evil, bloodthirsty South and a saintly Lincoln, so it was not reported much up North and almost not at all down South. You see, during Reconstruction the South didn't have the time or the luxury to engage in such speculation. Not only that, but if the Yankees got wind that Southerners were questioning the North's accepted history of the 'Civil War,' they just might use it as an excuse to put even more troops into our occupied Southern nation and inflict even harsher methods on our people. You have to remember that our states had been dissolved and we were then living in Yankee-established military districts.

"As I recall, this particular account of Booth's motive for shooting Lincoln centered on the imprisonment of a young Confederate captain by the name of John Yates Beall. Captain Beall was born in Virginia in 1835 and was hung by the Yankees as a spy on the 24th of February 1865. Now let me see—that would have made the young man about thirty years old when he was hung. Before his death, Captain Beall was held at Fort Columbus, New York, in a prison cell next to Dr. George A. Foote of Warrenton, Virginia. Dr. Foote was a surgeon in the Confederate army but had been captured the prior year. Dr. Foote described the efforts to save Captain Beall's life; even Governor Andrew of Massachusetts had interceded on behalf of the Confederate captain. It seems that many persons of high social and political standing were convinced that Captain Beall was being persecuted out of pure hatred for all things Southern.

"Before the war, Captain Beall was a classmate and shared a dorm room with another Virginian by the name of John Wilkes Booth. The two were dear friends and Booth had been active in trying to prevent his friend's execution especially on such trumped up charges. During the war we all knew that any Confederate so unfortunately caught behind Yankee lines—even in uniform, which was the case with Captain Beall— or traveling alone in contested territory stood a good chance of being hung or shot as a spy or bushwhacker. I think this must be what happened to Captain Beall.

"Booth was an actor who lived in Washington, DC and was familiar with many government officials in the city. He managed to get a meeting with Lincoln and Secretary Seward. Now stop and think about it—if Booth was a Southern extremist, do you think he would have gotten an interview with the president? If he wanted to kill Lincoln, why didn't he do it then? No, instead he begged Lincoln and Seward on bended knees to release his friend or at least commute the death sentence to life in prison—knowing that the war would very likely soon be over and his friend would hopefully get another, better hearing when tempers cooled after the end of the war. Lincoln promised to do exactly that and Booth left elated, thinking that he had managed to save his dear friend's life. But after Booth left and before the night was over, Lincoln sent orders to hang Captain Beall the next day. When the disappointed and enraged Booth found out what Lincoln and Seward had done, he swore revenge against both Northerners for what he called the 'perfidy of President Lincoln toward himself [Booth] and his friend Captain Beall.'

"So, as you can see from this account, it appears that the loss of the war was not the motivation for Booth's acts at Ford Theater that fateful night. Rather it was the loss of a friend and Lincoln's typically dishonorable character that caused the whole affair. Rather ironic that Lincoln, who had spent his entire political career bending the truth to his own advantage and giving half answers to direct questions, would become the final victim of his own sophistry."

§ Deo Vindice §

ON THE SKIRMISH LINE WITH UNCLE SETH

The January 7, 1863, edition of the *New York World* reported: "The President [Lincoln] has purposely made the [Emancipation] proclamation inoperative in all places where we have gained a military footing. . . . He has proclaimed emancipation only where he has notoriously no power to execute it. [Rendering] the proclamation not merely futile, but ridiculous."

Yet another example of Lincoln's sophistry in action—say anything if it profits Lincoln.

76

Union Officer Gives Sword as Gift to Confederate Officer

It was a cool fall morning and Uncle Seth was enjoying watching the boys playing in the corn field. The corn had already been harvested and safely stored away in the corn crib. The corn fodder had been collected and all that remained were row upon row of dried cornstalks. The boys, who imagined these rows of stalks to be ranks of enemy soldiers, would attack them with their wooden swords. Uncle Seth smiled as he watched the boys playing just like he did when he was their age. As one of the boys came close to the old Confederate veteran, Uncle Seth grabbed the boy by his collar and demanded, "Hand over your sword, I'm the commander of the cornstalk army and you are my prisoner."

The boys roared with laughter and one immediately asked the old soldier, "Uncle Seth, did any Yankee officer ever surrender his sword to you during the war?"

"No, officers generally did not surrender their swords to rank and file soldiers. They would hand them over to another officer in the other army. But I did witness something that most likely had never happened in an American army before—I saw a United States army officer call a truce and give a new sword to an officer in the opposing army. Of course, boys, that opposing army was the Confederate States army." Uncle Seth looked around at his young audience to make sure they seemed interested in his story. Seeing that he had their attention, Uncle Seth leaned back against a sturdy oak fence post and began his story.

"It was sometime around September 30, 1864. I was sent as a courier to tell Lane's North Carolina Brigade and McGowan's South Carolina Brigade that our commanding general wanted about two hundred sharpshooters to attack a well-emplaced Yankee force at the Pegram House nearby. We were about four miles from Petersburg, Virginia, near the crossing of Boynton Plank Road and Church Road. Our general felt that the attack would be so costly to us that he promised the survivors a thirty day pass it we routed the Yankee invaders from their defensive position. I fell in with Capt. Ingraham Hasell's unit—he was commanding Company

A, Battalion of Sharpshooters of McGowan's South Carolina Brigade, Wilcox's Division, A. P. Hill's Corps, Army Northern Virginia.

"Well, boys, at the command to form up and charge, we gave as if with one voice the famous Rebel Yell and rushed upon the invaders. Our charge was so ferocious that the enemy could not resist us. We quickly overran the Yankee position and captured over two hundred United States soldiers and a large store of supplies. Our loss was so small that the general decided not to give us the thirty day pass! We thought about inviting the Yankees back to give them a second chance to defend the place—you know, so we could get our passes," the old Confederate soldier chuckled at his own joke.

"Now during the fight, Captain Hasell captured a young Yankee lieutenant who upon surrendering gave up his sword. Captain Hasell had a crudely made Confederate sword and was very impressed with the quality and workmanship of the surrendered Yankee weapon. The Yankee lieutenant complained that it was against the rules of war for a prisoner to be kept under fire. You see, we were so busy capturing Yankees and firing back at those who had not surrendered that Captain Hasell could not afford to send a detail back with the prisoners. Shortly afterward, the captain was able to send the lieutenant and other prisoners to our rear under guard—all according to the rules of civilized warfare, something the Yankees were quick to demand of us but slow to follow themselves.

"That night, Captain Hasell gave his old sword to another Confederate officer who did not have one and proudly fastened his new prize to his military belt. The following morning we had a truce to allow the Yankees to collect and bury their dead. I went with Captain Hasell to the no-man's-land between the two armies, where we met a Yankee officer. We noticed that he was carefully scrutinizing Captain Hasell's newly acquired sword. At length, the Yankee captain approached and asked Captain Hasell how he had managed to obtain the sword. Captain Hasell replied that it was a prize of war captured from a young Yankee lieutenant during the previous day's battle. The Yankee officer responded in the most respectful manner, declaring, 'Pardon me, I did not mean to offend you; but that sword belonged to an officer killed in the front at Petersburg, and I had it in my keeping to return to his widow. I loaned it to a young lieutenant who had not yet been issued a sword. I would give anything to recover it.' Upon hearing the Yankee's story, Captain Hasell unclasped the sword and handed it to the Yankee captain. Hasell told him: 'I present it to the deceased officer's wife in the hope that this token of her husband's bravery will in some small way comfort her in her hour of grief.' Captain Hasell returned without a sword, and he refused to ask for the return of the crude

Confederate sword he had given to another officer. Captain Hasell was an honorable man—he did the honorable thing even though it did not materially profit him to do so.

"The next morning the two armies were facing each other expecting the battle to resume at any moment. All of a sudden we noticed a white flag being waved from the top of a small hill where the Yankees had placed several cannons. Captain Hasell asked me to find a white handkerchief and tie it to my rifle's ramrod. Well, it took some time for us to come up with anything that remotely looked white—such dainties were not usually found in a Confederate soldier's haversack. After some searching we found something that would hopefully pass as a white flag. I tied it to my ramrod and followed Captain Hasell as he walked out to meet the Yankee officer. There he met the Yankee officer to whom he had returned the captured sword the prior day. This fellow then presented Captain Hasell a handsome sword made in Newark, New Jersey."

"That was real nice of the Yankee officer wasn't it, Uncle Seth?" said one of the boys.

"You know," Uncle Seth began as he looked off into the distance, "most of those boys in blue were doing their duty as commanded by the politicians who controlled their country. But whether or not they knew it, they were carrying out the orders of an empire—an empire determined to extinguish forever the lamp of freedom in Dixie. Those who controlled the Yankee Empire were determined not to let us go in peace. Many a time I recall having Yankee prisoners ask me why I was fighting, because they could tell that a poor man like me—and poor men made up the vast majority of the Confederate soldiers—did not own any slaves. I would always reply that I was fighting because they were down here in my home trying to force me and my people to surrender our God-given right to be left alone and live in a country based upon the free and unfettered consent of the governed.

"Boys, it does not matter how many good deeds an invader may do while conquering a people—he is an invader nonetheless! He has the blood of innocents on his hands as he treads heavily upon the inherent rights of his newly acquired subjects. Perhaps one day the people of the South will understand what has happened to their country—what the Yankee invaders did to the very concept of a free republic. How the invader converted a constitutional Republic of Republics into the Federal Empire in which the Federal government is the supreme authority and 'we the people' of the once sovereign states are mere subjects who now approach the Federal government not as free citizens but as suppliants, begging for mercy."

Uncle Seth had been holding one of the boys' toy swords. He swung it at the cornstalk close to him. The cornstalk flew apart with a loud crack. The boys cheered and for a short time the old Confederate soldier felt young again—young and ready to 'charge 'm boys' one more time.

§ Deo Vindice §

ON THE SKIRMISH LINE WITH UNCLE SETH
"The great defect of Northern civilization is in its materiality. It is of the earth, earthy, and ignores the spirituality of our nature. Its grand motive and object is the accumulation of money, and its prime boast is of the things money can buy—'the lust of the eye, the lust of the flesh, and the pride of life.' Mammon is its god, and nowhere has he more devout or abject worshippers, or has he set up a more polluted civilization than in the North. The whole spirit of Christianity is opposed to this sort of civilization."

—Albert Taylor Bledsoe, 1869

77

Yankee Torch Applied to Southern Homes

Uncle Seth was glad to be home after a visit to his homeplace. Now that Uncle Seth was up in years, he did not get to travel as much as he once did. But every now and then he would climb into his grandson's Model A Ford and take a quick trip to look at the old homeplace where he and his twin sister, Sarah, were born and raised. The old log house with its two chimneys was still standing. Memories of his youth would come rushing back to Uncle Seth with each visit. It had been an enjoyable trip, but he was glad to get back and find a place to rest. Uncle Seth gently settled down in his favorite rocking chair on the front porch and began a conversation with his great-grandson.

"Joe William," Uncle Seth began, talking more to himself than to the youth, "I just can't believe that the old house and those two chimneys are still standing. Why they must be at least ninety years old. Boy, my daddy and the neighbors sure did a good job building our home."

"Uncle Seth, my Mississippi history book says that Jackson, Mississippi, was once referred to as Chimneyville. Was that because they had so many houses with two chimneys?" asked the young boy.

"No, Joe William," Uncle Seth rocked back as if to signal to the youth that he was about to give him a history lesson. "The state capital of Mississippi was called Chimneyville after the Yankee General Sherman came through and burned just about all the private homes in the city. All that was left were the chimneys where once-proud homes had stood." Uncle Seth's words and tone hinted at the cruelty that such needless acts of barbarism caused throughout the South during the War for Southern Independence.

"But Uncle Seth, what happened

Typical plain folk home (From *The Foxfire Book,* courtesy Foxfire Museum and Heritage Center, Mountain City, Georgia)

to the people whose homes were burned by the Yankees?" Joe William asked innocently.

"The Yankees' plan was to create a large homeless population of civilians that would put a great strain on the Confederate government as it tried to protect and house its noncombatant citizens. Remember that Lincoln did something similar when he issued the Emancipation Proclamation, declaring slaves to be free if they were in territory controlled by the Confederates but not in territories occupied by the Yankees. By doing this, Lincoln hoped that the threat of a slave insurrection would cause Southern soldiers to desert the Confederate army and rush home to defend their wives, mothers, and children. It did not work, but as you can see the Yankees were not opposed to making war on innocent women and children.

"Here, Joe William, I have a copy of a letter that was sent to one of Lincoln's officers by Mrs. Edmund I. Lee of Virginia." Uncle Seth rummaged through a pile of newspapers and books he always seemed to have at hand. "Ah, yes, here it is," he announced triumphantly. "It is dated July 20, 1864, and postmarked from Shepherdstown, Virginia. She is writing to the Yankee General Hunter who had recently burned down her home. Now, you need to understand that this Yankee General Hunter's parents and ancestors were from Virginia. But he was born in New Jersey, went to West Point, and while at West Point was court-martialed for challenging his commanding officer to a duel. He was well-known at West Point for his propensity to resort to dueling. As a result, he was dismissed from service, but the Federalist John Quincy Adams later revoked the penalty while Adams was president of the United States. Hunter accompanied Lincoln to Washington, DC, for Lincoln's first inauguration as president of the United States. In April 1862 Hunter was given command of the Department of the South, which included occupied Savannah, Georgia. Hunter issued a proclamation declaring all slaves in territory that he controlled to be free. It is interesting to note that Lincoln countermanded Hunter's proclamation and issued his own, declaring the government had no knowledge or part in Hunter's proclamation, which was therefore void. Lincoln also asserted that neither Hunter nor any other military commander had been authorized to free the slaves in any state. Hunter had several other conflicts with higher authority but he always seemed to have someone in high places looking out for him. In May 1864, Yankee General Hunter announced that he would burn to the ground any town or village within the vicinity of an attack on Federal wagon trains. Yankee troops carrying out General Hunter's orders were responsible for burning Mrs. Edmund Lee's home.

"Listen to just parts of her letter to Lincoln's henchman:

General Hunter: Yesterday your underling, Captain Martindale of the 1st New York Cavalry, executed your infamous order and burned my house. You have had the satisfaction of receiving from him the information that your orders were fulfilled to the letter—the dwelling and every outbuilding, seven in number, with their contents, being burned. I, therefore, a helpless woman whom you have cruelly wronged, address you, a major general of the United States Army, and demand why this was done? What was my offense?

My husband was absent, an exile. He has never been a politician, or in any way engaged in the struggle now going on, his age preventing. The house was built by my father, a 1776 Revolutionary War soldier, who served the whole seven years for your independence. There I was born, there the sacred dead repose; it was my house and my home, and there your niece, who has lived among us through all this horrid war up to the present moment, met with all kindness and hospitality at my hands.

Was it for this that you turned me, my young daughter and little son out upon the world without a shelter? Or was it because my husband is the grandson of the revolutionary patriot and rebel Richard Henry Lee, and the near kinsman of the noblest of Christian warriors, the greatest of generals, Robert E. Lee? You and your government have failed to conquer, subdue, or match him; and disappointed rage and malice find vent upon the helpless and inoffensive. Your name will stand on history's page as the hunter of weak women and innocent children; the hunter to destroy defenseless villages and refined and beautiful homes; to torture afresh the agonized hearts of suffering widows; the hunter of Africa's poor sons and daughters to lure them on to ruin and death of soul and body; the hunter with the relentless heart of a wild beast, the face of a fiend, and the form—of a man.

Can I say, God forgive you? No prayer can be offered for you. Were it possible for human lips to raise your name heavenward, angels would thrust the foul thing back again and demons claim their own. The curses of thousands, and the scorn of the manly and upright, and the hatred of the true and honorable will follow you and yours through all time and brand your name, Infamy! Infamy!

"You see, Joe William, this is just one letter from just one Southern civilian who needlessly suffered from the Yankee invader's torch. The post-war South was populated with many Chimneyvilles—the price we paid for daring to ask the Yankee to leave us alone, to allow us to live under a government based upon the free and unfettered consent of the governed, and to be free of Yankee domination. As far as the Yankee was concerned that was too much to ask! You must understand that to them the South and her people are Yankee property to do with as they please." Uncle Seth's voice was unusually harsh and stern.

§ Deo Vindice §

ON THE SKIRMISH LINE WITH UNCLE SETH

It was May 12, 1863. The Battle of Raymond, Mississippi, was over, the Yankees outnumbered us greatly, and thus we had to withdraw; but we killed more of them than they killed of us. As the army of Yankee invaders marched past the home of Confederate General Freeman, his daughter stepped out onto the balcony with a Confederate flag in her hand and began singing the "Bonnie Blue Flag." The Yankee invaders immediately set fire to her home. The United States army won another battle against unarmed women and children. Shall we forget? Hell no! We must not forget!

78

Young Southerner Refuses to Polish Yankee Officer's Boots

Uncle Seth was busily applying saddle soap on his boots to make sure they would "turn water" and to keep the leather pliable. Taking care of what you had was a part of living in the poverty-stricken South. The general motto was to take care of your possessions, reuse everything you could, and never buy new what you could make or reuse.

Carroll Ray was watching the old Confederate veteran working the polish into his leather boots and began explaining to Uncle Seth, "I read about how, when Gen. Andrew Jackson was a young boy during the Revolutionary War, a British officer beat him with the back of his sword when Andy refused to polish the officer's boots." Uncle Seth paused for a moment and looked at the young boy, who seemed to be confused. "Why would a grown man do that to a young boy?" Carroll Ray asked.

"Carroll Ray," Uncle Seth began, "you have to remember that the British army officer was part of an invading army; an army sent there to protect the British Empire's territory; to keep the land and the people under the control of the central government in London. When an invading army comes into a country, the people in that army feel that the enemy population is less than they are, inferior people who must be conquered and subdued by whatever means it takes. Anyone who resists the Empire is automatically wrong; anyone who fights for the Empire is automatically right—regardless of what he does to those lesser people who dare to resist the Empire. That British officer had servants back home who did his bidding. He looked upon Colonial Americans as his servants because he represented the interest of the British Empire. If a servant back home refused his orders, he would discharge the servant; if a Colonist refused to obey the Empire, then he, as the representative of the British Empire, would punish the Colonial rebel.

Gen. Andrew Jackson (Library of Congress)

"Carroll Ray, you know that the British called the American Patriots rebels. All we were doing was attempting to maintain the rights that were due all Englishmen, but to the British we were rebelling against the legitimate authority of the central government in London—as far as they were concerned all American Patriots were rebels. The British used this term in an effort to stigmatize American Patriots—they wanted to make us appear to the rest of the world as criminals who did not deserve the respect of civilized mankind and should not be extended the protection afforded to combatants and non-combatants in war. You know that they also promised all slaves in the American Colonies freedom if they would leave their masters and join the British—they hoped to start a slave revolt that would weaken the patriots' zeal for the war. And you know that all of the American colonies at that time had slaves. What was so ironic was the fact that the American colony of Virginia had previously attempted to end the slave trade by an act of her colonial legislature, but the central government in London nullified Virginia's effort. London was looking out for its financial interest in the lucrative slave trade. empires always look out for the interest of profits for the empire and profits for those with close connections to the empire's ruling elite. This is what empires do—they have no respect for the rights of the invaded people and will do anything they think will help them defeat the invaded people and add the defeated country to the empire's domain."

The old man stopped and looked around. As he put his polished boot on the floor, he motioned for Carroll Ray to take a seat next to him there on the back porch. "Have I ever told you about the young Southern boy-soldier who refused to polish a Yankee officer's boots?" the old man asked. Carroll Ray looked up at Uncle Seth and shook his head.

"The young Confederate soldier's name was Roger Morris. He was fifteen years old when the incident occurred. He was from Grenada, Mississippi, and had joined Blount Craig's company in the 29th Mississippi Regiment. Roger was captured during the Battle of Missionary Ridge and sent to Rock Island Prison. The prison was opened in December of 1863, when the temperature was 32 degrees below zero. Now stop and think about it: here you have a group of Southerners from Mississippi who lived in a country where it was rare for the temperature to fall below freezing. These men's clothing was not designed for such climate; and now the enemy put them in a prison camp on an island in the middle of the Mississippi River with poorly constructed buildings and only one wool blanket to fend off the cold wind blowing across the icy waters of the river. In their weakened condition, it was not long before an epidemic of smallpox broke out in which over six hundred Confederate soldiers died. Fifteen-year-old Roger was one of the victims of smallpox, and it seemed that he too would die.

"One day a Yankee officer was making an inspection of the prison barracks and spied young Roger. He had compassion for the boy and had him moved to a storage building next to the place where the officers stayed during the day. He promised to make sure the young boy got better food; and the Yankee kept his word. The officer warned Roger to be careful around the other Yankee officers because most of them had never seen battle before and had no respect for real soldiers. It was not long before Roger had regained his strength and was walking around his new quarters when he was approached by a Yankee officer who demanded to know what the prisoner was doing. Roger explained and the officer left, grunting curses about 'rebel trash.' The Yankee officer returned with a pair of his boots and demanded that Roger polish them. The young Southerner, just fifteen years old and still recovering from smallpox, immediately refused, just like Andrew Jackson. All manner of threats and curses poured forth from the Yankee's mouth with the promise that if the 'rebel trash' did not do as he was told, he would be returned to the barracks with the rest of the 'trash' and would have to cross the deadline to get back! If any prisoner got too close to the deadline, the guards had orders to shoot them without warning. Even in the face of certain death, Roger refused to polish the Yankee's boots. He was soon returned to the barracks with his fellow Southerners, having safely navigated the trip across the deadline, and joined his countrymen as they starved in the Yankee prisoner of war camp at Rock Island.

"Roger survived the war and returned to Mississippi, but with all the destruction at his home, he decided to move to Texas and start anew. He established himself in Liberty County and was soon elected county sheriff. He held that position until he died around 1910." Uncle Seth ended his story, picked up his other boot, and began working the saddle soap into the boot leather.

Carroll Ray sat there next to the old Confederate veteran and wondered what he would have done if he had been faced with such an order. Would he have been as brave as Andy Jackson or Roger Morris? Uncle Seth had other thoughts, similar but distinctly different. Uncle Seth wondered if Carroll Ray's children and grandchildren would have the courage to challenge the all-powerful Federal Empire. Often the old Confederate veteran would wonder about the soil of Dixie on which so many Southern patriots fell—did it drink not only our blood but the courage of future generations as well?

§ Deo Vindice §

ON THE SKIRMISH LINE WITH UNCLE SETH
During the Constitutional Convention (1787) the High Federalists proposed to give the Federal government the power to call forth the forces of the Union against any member of the Union failing to fulfill its duty under the proposed constitution. Mr. Madison—who at the time was a Federalist—objected to the proposed coercion clause, declaring that "a union of the States containing such an ingredient seemed to provide for its own destruction. The use of force against a State would look more like a declaration of war and would probably be considered by the party attacked as a dissolution of all previous compacts by which it might be bound." He moved that the proposed clause be postponed; it was and was never again taken up.

"The alternative to secession is coercion."

—Pres. Jefferson Davis, CSA

79

Uncle Seth's Reply to a Self-Hating Southern Newspaper Editor

Whenever he had the opportunity, Uncle Seth liked to try to set the record straight about the War for Southern Independence. Many of the folks in his community held fast to the Yankee post-Reconstruction "history" of the war. As he was reading his morning paper one day, Uncle Seth read a comment by a newspaper editor about Gen. Nathan Bedford Forrest and Fort Pillow: "General Forrest's massacre of black Union soldiers at Fort Pillow is a black mark upon Southern history," the man claimed.

Uncle Seth wasted no time in penning a response to the editor. He wrote: "In a recent editorial celebrating Memorial Day and the decorating of the graves of Confederate soldiers, you thought it necessary to publically apologize for what you termed the massacre of black Union soldiers by General Forrest at the Battle of Fort Pillow. This is a false charge that Yankee propagandists have leveled against General Forrest ever since his destruction of the Yankee Fort. The charges were promoted by hysterical newspaper accounts; said accounts were developed not from eyewitnesses but from second-hand accounts of virulent anti-Southern Yankee partisans. These distorted 'facts' were repeated over and over in various Yankee newspapers until the big lie became accepted Yankee fact. But during a Congressional hearing on the matter, and in an attempt to charge General Forrest with 'war crimes,' Yankee facts became the substance of mist and fog. During the hearing, numerous leading questions were offered by the members of the inquisition panel; but even before an obviously biased hearing panel, the 'testimony' of ignorant 'eyewitnesses' could not produce enough proof to support a charge against General Forrest. Fortunately for the general and the South, there were enough honest men from both sides who attested to Forrest's innocence. In the end the United States had to take General Forrest off their list of war criminals. This is all part of the public record as documented in the *Reports of Committee of the Senate of the United States.*

"The entire mythical charge of General Forrest orchestrating a massacre of black Union soldiers at Fort Pillow was based on the allegation that he allowed the 'slaughter' of black Union soldiers 'after the Fort had surrendered.'

Yankee newspaper accounts describe how General Forrest both encouraged his troops to slaughter Yankee prisoners and then turned a blind eye while the killings were taking place. Testimony of both General Forrest and members of his command verified the fact that the general was over four hundred yards to the rear during the twenty-minute assault and surrender of the fort. Most people would have expected the general to be at the forefront, actually leading the assault—which was, after all, his custom. But at the time of the assault of Fort Pillow, Forrest was still recovering from a fall from his horse and was therefore not able to lead it. The fact that he was not physically present during the assault did not deter Yankees from finding 'eyewitnesses' who would swear under oath that they personally saw Forrest during the attack. Let me give you an example of the testimony of just one of the so-called witnesses, and you then judge the credibility of his testimony against General Forrest. This is taken from the record—it is the testimony of Jacob Thompson:

> **Committee:** Did you see any rebel officers about there when this [the supposed massacre] was going on?
> **Jacob Thompson:** Yes sir, old Forrest was one.
> **Committee:** Did you know Forrest?
> **Jacob Thompson:** Yes sir; he was a little bit of a man. I had seen him before at Jackson.
> **Committee:** Are you sure he was there when this was going on?
> **Jacob Thompson:** Yes sir.

"I am sure the committee members got a good laugh out of this 'eyewitness' who claimed to have recognized General Forrest and described him as a 'little bit of a man.' General Forrest was over six feet tall and weighed over two hundred pounds. He had killed men with his bare hands and in knife fights. During the war he removed a Yankee officer's head with one swift blow of a cavalry saber. General Forrest may have been a lot of things to many different people, but no one who had ever actually seen him would have described him as a 'little bit of a man.'

"What then, was the reason for the high loss of Union life at Fort Pillow? For one thing it could not be described as a massacre because over 60 percent of the Union forces were made prisoners. A 40 percent death rate is high, but many of our Confederate units suffered even worse death rates during the war. If our self-hating new-South editor had taken the time to review the historical record, he would have found out that there were three main reasons for the high Yankee death rate at Fort Pillow. First, the Yankee commander's refusal to surrender his command when presented the opportunity under a flag of truce, coupled with his refusal to surrender when the Yankee fort was overrun. Second, the unmilitary deportment of

Yankee troops caused by the consumption of alcoholic beverage prior to the assault. Many of the black Union soldiers were drunk, and our troops found open kegs of alcoholic beverages in the fort after the conclusion of the fighting. And third, the unfulfilled promise of the Yankee gunboat captains to remain close to the fort and provide support to the Union troops if they were forced to evacuate the fort. This last reason was a major cause for the continued fighting even after the fort had been overrun because the Union troops refused to surrender in hopes of reaching the 'promised' safety of their gunboats.

"This is what General Forrest said in his official report:

> As our troops mounted and poured into the fortification the enemy retreated toward the river, arms in hand and firing back, and their colors flying, no doubt expecting the gun-boat to shell us away from the bluff and protect them until they could be taken off or re-enforced. As they descended the bank an enfilading and deadly fire was poured into them by the troops under Captain Anderson, on the left, and Barteau's detachment on the right. Until this fire was opened upon them, at a distance varying from 30 to 100 yards, they [the Yankees] were evidently ignorant of any force having gained their rear. The regiments which had stormed and carried the fort also poured a destructive fire into the rear of the retreating and now panic-stricken and almost decimated garrison.

"Now during this entire time the United States flag was still flying over the fort—an obvious signal that no surrender had taken place. It was fortunate for the Yankee defenders that after they had fled the fort, leaving their hated flag still flying over Southern territory, one of the Confederate soldiers cut the halyards, causing the United States flag to fall to the ground. Upon seeing the lowering of the U.S. flag, troops on both sides ceased firing. Many of the panic-stricken troops, including the fort's commander, attempted to hide from the Confederates by entering the river, causing many who could not swim to drown. The Yankee commander was caught as he waded out into the river—the water being up to his chin.

"The Yankee gunboats either ran out of ammunition or were forced to move out of range by the accurate Confederate cannon fire now coming from the fort above. The major point is that the promise made by the captains of the Yankee gunboats to support their fellow Union troops never materialized. Not only did the Yankee gunboats not drive the 'rebels' away from the fort, they did not remain in place to evacuate those Union soldiers who refused to surrender and continued the fight as they moved back toward the river and the supposed safety of the Yankee gunboats. The Union soldiers who evacuated the fort ran into a murderous Confederate crossfire at almost point-blank range. As General Forrest noted in his report, the Union soldiers were not aware that Confederate forces had moved behind the fort. The horrific Confederate crossfire plus the accurate fire coming from the Confederates behind and above them caused the Union soldiers to panic and rush into the river.

"A review of the historical record demonstrates that the primary reason for the high causality rate was poor leadership and lack of coordination between the United States navy and the United States army. After the fighting was over, General Forrest directed Captain Anderson to take a captured Yankee, Captain Young, with a flag of truce and signal Captain Marshall, the Yankee gunboat captain, to see if he would come to the aid of his wounded comrades. Despite their best efforts to convince the last Yankee gunboat to at least send a vessel to discuss the issue, the Yankee gunboat ignored the effort and steamed upriver, completely abandoning the Yankee wounded and prisoners to their fate.

"General Forrest reported that Confederate losses during the engagement totaled twenty killed and sixty wounded. He noted that they buried two hundred and twenty-eight Yankees on the evening of the battle and quite a few more the next day. Forrest captured six pieces of artillery, two 10-pounder Parrott guns, two 12-pounder howitzers, and two 6-pound guns plus 350 stands of small arms. Most of the arms picked up from the battlefield were found at the river's edge; only a few were taken from the fort. This is evidence that no surrender was contemplated by the Union forces as they left the fort with weapons in hand seeking the security of their gunboats.

"So much was made of the disastrous defeat dealt to the Yankees at Fort Pillow by the Yankee propagandist newspapers at the time—trying to confuse the issue of Yankee military incompetence by slandering the general who had for so long been troublesome to the Yankee invaders—that General Forrest wrote a letter to Gen. S. D. Lee on May 16, 1864, making a request for an official inquiry. General Forrest asked that Judge Scruggs be sent to question Yankee Captain Young and other Federal officers who were present during the battle regarding the truthfulness of the allegations being bantered around in the vicious Yankee press. How would our modern day, self-hating, new-South editor explain the fact that General Forrest solicited an investigation to include the testimony of his former adversaries? A guilty man would do all he could to avoid such an investigation. General Forrest knew that the charges brought against him in the hate-filled Yankee press were mere fabrications of that same press—a fabrication kept alive by our anti-Southern Yankee masters in conjunction with their self-hating Southern stooges.

§ **Deo Vindice** §

80

Andersonville Prisoner of War Camp and the Lynching of Major Wirz

The country store at Rockport, Mississippi, was buzzing with excitement and Uncle Seth was enjoying the festive air. It was December of 1918. The Great War in Europe was over and many of the young men who were part of the American Expeditionary Force were returning home. Some of the local soldiers who had been prisoners of war (POWs) were arriving today. "Uncle Seth," called out Theodore Kennedy, one of Uncle Seth's neighbors, "were you ever held as a POW during the war?"

"No, boy!" exclaimed Uncle Seth jokingly. "The Yankees never had a chance to capture me. They were always too busy running away from me." The men at the store all joined in the joke with laughter and comments about Uncle Seth's fighting skills—more as a communal acknowledgement of his age and the respect he had earned as a former warrior for a common cause. The lull in the conversation was broken by another question from Theodore.

"Uncle Seth, is it true that the South mistreated Yankee POWs at the prison camp in Andersonville, Georgia?" he asked.

"You know, Theodore, the Yankees have always been experts in the great lie. Even the most outlandish falsehood, if repeated often enough by enough people, will eventually become accepted as the truth. Of course, for the great lie to work you have to be in a position of authority and power so you can suppress any view that opposes that lie. This is what the Yankees have done in so many instances. They have their own "truths" about why the South elected to remove itself from the Yankee Empire; why the United States of America elected to invade, destroy, and occupy a sovereign nation, the Confederate States of America; and how they conducted their war against the Confederate States of America. One of the North's many big lies is that the South purposefully starved, mistreated, and murdered Yankee POWs at Andersonville and that the camp commander, Major Wirz, was guilty of war crimes—for which they hung the poor man.

"Major Wirz was a foreigner by birth—a Swiss—and this alone made him a target of the nativists: Americans who disliked foreigners. They were very powerful in the North and actually were the leaders in the New York draft riots during the war. Well, being a foreigner and an officer in the Confederate States army made Wirz a perfect scapegoat to the still-enraged Yankee public. The poor man never had a chance. But neither has anyone else who appeals to truth, honesty, and honor when facing the Yankee Empire. Here is the truth:

Gallows used by the United States to lynch Maj. Henry Wirz, CSA (Library of Congress)

1. More Southerners died while being held in Yankee prisoner camps than Yankees who were being held in Southern camps. Northern camps had plenty of supplies, warm clothing, food, and medicine available, but they refused to provide those necessities to Southern prisoners.
2. The Confederate government was under great stress trying to defend itself against the overwhelming numbers of an aggressive invader; our supply channels were being destroyed and bringing supplies to prison camps was no less difficult than the army's task of defending our homes.
3. In the South, the same quantity and quality of rations were given to prisoners and guards.
4. The Confederates arranged for the exchange of prisoners by a special cartel, but this cartel was deliberately disregarded by the Yankees.
5. Southern leaders offered to permit Yankee surgeons to bring medical supplies to the prisoners, but the offer was never accepted by the Yankees.
6. As the needs of Northern prisoners increased, Southern leaders offered to buy supplies for the prisoners; this offer was also ignored.
7. The United States government treated medicine as contraband of war, making it unavailable to not only prisoners but innocent Southern civilians—women and children.
8. One final effort to exchange prisoners was made by sending a delegation of Yankee POWs from Andersonville to Washington to meet with Lincoln and plead for the adoption of an exchange program. President Lincoln refused to meet with this delegation of his own soldiers.

9. Prior to the period of time that saw the greatest death among the prisoners at Andersonville, Confederate authorities offered to release thousands of prisoners—without requiring an exchange of Southern prisoners—if the United States government would provide transportation for them. This offer was needlessly delayed by the United States government until it was too late. Thousands died while waiting on the Federal response.

"These facts are supported by records and testimony of those who had personal knowledge of the whole affair; yet even at this late date the spiteful Yankee press still promotes the great lie that the South purposefully mistreated POWs. An editorial in *Collier's Weekly* about two years ago—it was February 17, 1917—promoted the Yankee lie. They have the power to promote anti-Southern lies, and the South has no means to respond. The North will therefore continue to lie until even Southerners believe that their Confederate ancestors were evil people and that the gallant Yankee saved the world from such evil folks. This is the way an empire keeps the rising generations in their conquered territories pacified and submissive.

"Many of the first arrivals at Andersonville were foreign by birth. These men had a very difficult time adapting to the food that was offered to them because they had not grown up eating a diet based on cornmeal. The bread that we could provide came from local sources and was mainly cornbread, but these men's digestive systems were used to a wheat-based diet. This caused many to become weak and susceptible to disease. I thought about this early this year when I read an account from the United States Food Administration encouraging Americans to eat corn instead of wheat because the wheat was needed to feed the Europeans. I just happen to have a copy of the message. It says: 'When we use more corn, the Allies, our associates in the war, can use more wheat. They cannot use cornmeal instead of wheat in their daily diet, as we do, because neither their cooks nor their appetites are adapted to it.' The course cornbread, and the pork grease used to make the bread, most likely contributed to the Yankee prisoners' weakness and susceptibility to dysentery. This, added to the crowded conditions and the South's inability to obtain medicines, caused many avoidable deaths.

"But why would the Yankees allow their soldiers to needlessly die in POW camps? This is easy to answer if you understand that the South was fighting an evil empire. A soldier of the empire is merely an expendable and replaceable unit. The South was more like an extended family fighting to protect its own family and home. But the North had become an empire controlled by powerful elites whose primary purpose was to do whatever it took to maintain the empire's territorial control. If they exchanged prisoners, most of the exchanged Yankees would go home and not reenlist; plus they would warn their friends about how cruel war actually is and how determined Southerners were to defend their homes. Southern prisoners, on the other hand, would return to their units and continue the fight to maintain their nation's independence. Federal leaders, both civilian and military, acknowledged this fact. For example, General Grant declared his opposition to exchanging prisoners: 'It is hard on our men in Southern prisons not to exchange them, but it is humanity to those left in the ranks to fight our battles,' he said. The thing I always wondered is why no one ever asks why so many of our men died in Yankee prison camps. After all, the Yankees had an abundance of food and supplies. So why were our men treated so badly? Perhaps it is because, since the South is an occupied nation, we have no one who will ask these pointed questions.

"The Yankees did offer Major Wirz an opportunity save himself. The proposal was overheard by Major Wirz's priest, Fr. F. E. Boyle, and another prisoner in an adjoining cell, Captain C. B. Winder. Both individuals set out the whole affair in letters. Major Wirz was told that he would be spared the death sentence scheduled for the following morning if he would implicate Jefferson Davis in the deaths of POWs in Andersonville. It is reported that Wirz indignantly spurned these propositions and assured his captors that, never having been acquainted with Mr. Davis either officially, personally, or socially, it was utterly impossible that he should know anything against him; and that the offer of his life, dear as the boon might be, could not drive him to treason and treachery to the South. Yankee cunning met its match in the person of Major Wirz. Here is a man whose name is slandered by Yankee lies to this day. Just like the South that he adopted and loved, there is no one to defend this man of honor and truth. This is yet one more of the great disasters that resulted from our defeat and surrender at Appomattox." Uncle Seth's spontaneous lecture was interrupted by the sounds of shouts of joy as uniformed men began to enter the general store looking for their folks.

§ Deo Vindice §

ON THE SKIRMISH LINE WITH UNCLE SETH
"Her [the South's] conservatism, her love of the Constitution; her attachment to the old usages of society, her devotion to principles, her faith in Bible truth—all these involved her in a long and bloody war with that Radicalism which seeks to overthrow all that is venerable, respectable, and of good repute."

—Gen. D. H. Hill, 1868

81

Confederate Raiders Capture
St. Albans, Vermont

Uncle Seth sat in his rocking chair, pulled close to the coal oil lamp, reading a newspaper and occasionally chuckling out loud. "Uncle Seth, what are you reading so late at night? Why it's almost eight o'clock," asked his grandson Lloyd.

"I'm reading about how a group of escaped Confederate prisoners managed to capture the Yankee city of St. Albans, Vermont, during the war. St. Albans is almost up at the Canadian border," explained Uncle Seth as he looked at the paper closer and held it to the lamp, inviting more light.

"How did we get troops up that far into New England?" asked Lloyd.

This was just the invitation Uncle Seth wanted. "Well," the old Confederate veteran began, "when our Southern boys escaped from a Yankee prisoner of war camp located in a Northern state, some of the escapees headed north. The Yankees thought, of course, that the escapees would head south trying to get back home. So some of the boys figured it would be easier to avoid Yankee patrols by going north. If you travel long enough in that direction, eventually you will cross the Canadian border. The story I'm reading was written by Prof. J. L. Driscol of Nashville, Tennessee. It seems that there were many escaped Confederate soldiers in Canada. Driscol himself was one of them when St. Albans was captured. But Professor Driscol says here that they had plenty of company in Canada because there were also many Yankee soldiers there—if you could call them soldiers. They were bounty jumpers, Yankees who would take the money given to them by the government for enlisting and then slip away to Canada. They would enjoy spending the money and then return to another part of Yankee-land, enlist again, and 'jump' again.

Prof. J. L. Driscol of Nashville, Tennessee

"Well, the local Canadian newspapers were full of reports about the terrible crimes being committed against Southern civilians by Yankees, and our boys decided to do something to even the score a little. There were discussions about using Greek fire to burn Northern towns, but this was ruled out. Still the men wanted to do something to show the Yankees what it was like to have their home invaded and innocent civilians put under the guns of an invader's army. When news reached the men that the North had burned Atlanta, they were determined to act.

"Earlier, a Confederate non-commissioned officer, Bennett H. Young, had been captured during Morgan's raid into Ohio. He escaped from the Yankee prisoner of war camp and made his way to Canada, where he met many other Southern escapees. Being an experienced raider, he could see the possibility of striking a blow at the Yankee Empire by using the men who were in Canada. But he did not want to sully the Cause by having it appear that robbery was the motive. He left Canada, returned to the South, and presented his proposal to the Confederate secretary of war. Bennett Young's plan was accepted; he was commissioned as a lieutenant and returned to Canada to organize the raid. They selected St. Albans, Vermont, as their target.

"St. Albans had a population of nearly four thousand and a male population of military age of around eight hundred. Now, boy, you need to think about this—here is a town in the Yankee Empire that had eight hundred able-bodied men of military age who were going about their lives as if nothing unusual was happening in the world. At the very same time down South, you would have been lucky to find eighty such men in a town of similar size! The Federal Empire was busy making war and expanding the territorial domain of its empire; in the meantime these civilians were going about their lives normally while 'we the people' of the South were fighting for our very survival as a nation and a people.

"St. Albans is located about fifteen miles south of the Canadian border, in the heart of the most populated area of the state. It is honeycombed with good roads, railroads, and telegraph lines. Our men were making a raid hundreds of miles away from their home base with no secure station to retreat to after the raid. I think they wanted to make a statement about their loyalty to the South even if it would go unnoticed by the world. They were loyal to the South and to their own sense of duty and honor.

"Young checked in at the hotel in St. Albans in the afternoon of October 10, 1864. He claimed to be there for a hunting expedition. Every day or two thereafter, one or two men would check in at a local hotel. By October 19, all of the Confederate forces had arrived. The Confederate force numbered twenty-one. At around 3:00 p.m. the Confederate raiders appeared in uniform and announced that the town was under the control of Confederate States forces and demanded immediate surrender. Each Confederate was armed with two revolvers. Before the telegraph lines could be cut, the word was flashed to the world that St. Albans, Vermont, had been captured by a 'Rebel horde.' The mayor and city council met and agreed to surrender the city. So the population was rounded up and held under guard in the town square. Raiders were detailed to go to each bank and confiscate all the money and other negotiable paper held in the banks. A Yankee bank teller—a brave soul but no match for his Southern adversary—leveled a rifle at a Confederate sergeant. However, his aim with a rifle was not as good as the sergeant's pistol shot. This Yankee was the only person killed in the entire affair. The causality list for the raid was one Yankee killed and two wounded and no injuries for the Confederates. Some people claim that the raiders left town with more than $5,000,000 in Yankee greenbacks and bonds, but a more likely estimate is around $200,000. And while some of the raiders wanted to burn the entire town, only one building was put to the torch.

"According to Professor Driscol, the Confederate raiders made it safely across the Canadian border, where the real battle began. After all, the Canadians were not willing to allow their nation to become a raiding camp for the Confederacy. Yankee howls reached the Canadian authorities, and every Southern man was arrested on criminal charges including murder and robbery. The Yankees, of course, claimed the entire affair was but a pretext for criminal activity and demanded the Southerners be returned for swift Yankee justice. The Confederate raiders were arraigned before a Canadian judge in Toronto, where each man pleaded that he was a belligerent. (You recall that England had recognized the Confederate States of America as a belligerent and extended us belligerent status in her ports.) The best attorney in the area was obtained for the Confederates and paid for by money raised from their fellow Confederates and Canadian friends. Their attorney asked for and was granted a twenty-day delay to prepare the defense.

"The Confederate raiders knew that if Canada decided to send them back to the United States the price for their patriotism would be paid with their lives. Lieutenant Young did not dare carry any official papers back from Richmond. This put the defense in a very precarious position. The Canadian court had to look at the facts, and the facts were that a group of strangers crossed the border, robbed several banks—killing one person in the process—and then fled with the money back across the Canadian border. The Confederates then devised another daring plan, this one to prove their status as belligerents. They selected three of the shrewdest and bravest among them to escape across the border, travel through the North, cross into Confederate territory, and make their way to Richmond to obtain official papers. Then these men would return to Toronto—all within twenty days! They selected three because they felt that perhaps at least one would make it there and back in time.

"Well, the twenty days expired and the trial was ready to begin, but no one had made it back from Richmond. The Yankee observers in the court were no doubt already sending instructions to get their gallows ready. The attorney for the Confederates was attempting to convince the judge to grant his motion for another twenty-day delay when a great commotion occurred at the back of the courtroom. A wiry little man elbowed his way to the front of the courtroom where the attorney was standing and whispered something in the attorney's ear. The attorney immediately asked the court for a five-minute recess, which was granted, and the two alone with several of the raiders went to a back room. In the back room, the man removed his overcoat and began using his pocket knife to separate the coat's lining from the outer coat. He then reached in and pulled out an envelope containing certified papers verifying Lieutenant Young's commission, the enlistment of the other raiders in the Confederate army, and the authorization for the raid. The papers were signed by the secretary of war, Confederate States of America.

"The trial reconvened and continued until all evidence was presented by the parties. The court held that the Confederate raiders were in fact belligerents within the meaning of the law and were therefore released. The Yankee secretary of state, William Seward, used various measures to bring pressure upon the Canadian provincial government, but to no avail. However, the Canadian provincial government did pass an alien law requiring all non-citizens from south of the border to leave within forty-eight hours. This most likely caused more interference with the Yankee bounty jumpers than it did for the Confederates. Professor Driscol took passage on a steamer to England with the intention of traveling to Cuba and running the blockade, but General Lee was forced to surrender before he could make it back to Dixie. The other Confederates had similar plans but were likewise soon disappointed by the news of the surrender."

Uncle Seth thought on the matter for a while. "You know, Lloyd," the old Confederate veteran began in a quiet, reverent voice, "here were men who had escaped from the horrible conditions in Yankee prison camps, and yet they were willing—no, determined—to continue the struggle against the evil Yankee invader. Even in the darkest hours of the war, they were still willing to risk all in the defense of their invaded nation. This is true honor, true patriotism; these were men worthy of the title of Confederate soldiers. Yet the Yankee propagandists would have Southern children and the entire world to believe that these men were fighting to keep their slaves while the noble Yankee was fighting to free his beloved black brother from that cruel bondage. They do this because they have the power. They do it because 'we the people' of the South are a conquered nation who must endure without question the lies and slander Yankees and scallywag Southerners heap upon our occupied nation. They will continue to do it until we decide to act like a people who deserve to be free—to live under a government of our own choosing."

§ Deo Vindice §

On the Skirmish Line with Uncle Seth
"In McGavock Cemetery, near the Harpeth River, rest our comrades who fell in the Battle of Franklin. We were right and we make no apologies for the past. But, comrades, we should firmly insist that history should be fairly and correctly written and that our motives should be fully expressed. Fifty years is a long time to love, cherish, and honor a government departed, but we are justified in our devotion to the Southern Confederacy—the only government that ever rose, reigned, and fell without the guilt of a single crime."

—Remarks made by a Confederate veteran at a
Remembrance Day gathering, 1915

82

Southern Lady Warns Confederates of Approaching Yankees

Uncle Seth was sitting under the giant red oak in the front yard watching the boys playing war. His youngest great-granddaughter, Dorcas Fay, was complaining to Uncle Seth because she had no one to play with. "I wish I had been born a boy," the young girl declared. "Then I could play army and one day be a famous soldier like you, Uncle Seth."

The old Confederate soldier looked down at the girl and smiled as he reached out to touch the top of her head. He was amused that she though he was a famous soldier; but then again he was the most famous Confederate soldier she knew in her little world. "Now don't you worry yourself, Dorcas Fay, you know Mildred will be finished with her chores before long and you all will be able to play together. And anyway, don't you know that during the war there were almost as many heroines as heroes?" Uncle Seth tried to make an effort to assure the young girl of her important place in the family and community. Often he had told the young girls, in front of the boys, that the rise and maintenance of civilization depends on females. Women, he would tell them, tend to take a long-term view of things whereas men tend to react to the present. A country's defense may fall primarily to the male population, but the development of civility and those things that separate us from the animal world requires the influence of the female population. Uncle Seth remembered firsthand the suffering and courage of Southern women during the war.

"Dorcas Fay, you sit down here next to me and I will tell you about one of the brave Southern ladies who so often came to our aid during the war. It was around June 10, 1861, and up in Virginia the Yankees wanted to strike a decisive blow against the Rebels in order to demoralize the South and encourage enlistments in the Yankee Empire's army of invaders. Yankee General Ebenezer Peirce, who had around 3,500 troops at his disposal, decided to attack the Confederates who were under the command of Gen. John B. Magruder. Magruder only had around 1,400 troops, so the Yankee thought it would be an easy victory. Peirce planned a surprise attack against the Confederates. He thought that he would have the element of surprise on his side, plus a three to one superiority in number of troops; he was confident that the United States army would make short work of the Confederates. But the arrogant Yankee did not consider the fact that a brave Southern lady would undo his carefully designed plan.

"The Yankees began their secret movement against the Confederates early on the morning of June 5. Their plan was to surprise the Confederates at Big Bethel. Mrs. Hannah Tunnel, a local lady from Hampton, Virginia, had left her home out of fear of the invader's torch and was seeking safety with friends near Big Bethel. Unbeknown to Mrs. Tunnel, she was fleeing not away from but directly towards the oncoming Yankee invaders. Early that morning she ran directly into the advance elements of a New York unit that was moving almost at the double quick toward Big Bethel. She at once determined their intentions and calculated the danger they posed to her new country. You know, it was easy to get information from Yankee soldiers. They were all bragging about how they were going to destroy a nest of rebel traitors.

"Mrs. Tunnel's carriage was blocked from moving forward and the Yankees were standing guard to make sure she did not leave; she feared that perhaps they had designs on her horse and carriage or—heaven forbid—even more hideous designs on her person. At first opportunity, she leaped from the carriage and began a desperate run through the undergrowth, briars, and saplings. With little or no concern about tearing her dress and skin on the briars and thornbush, she ran onward. She knew that if her Yankee pursuers caught her she would most likely be hung as a spy, but she was willing to take that chance. Determined to get back to Confederate lines before the Yankees could make their surprise attack, she continued her cross-country trek. After about an hour of hacking her way through the undergrowth, she came to a road and there met a small unit of Confederate cavalry. The Confederates were reconnoitering the area. She gave them her valuable information—and what do you know, one of the men was none other than General Magruder himself. The Confederates were ready to meet the invading Yankees when they attacked and dealt the invading United States army a decisive defeat. So remember, Dorcas Fay, the successful defense of our country at the Battle of Bethel Church was made possible by a Southern lady and patriot who risked her life to aid in the defense of the Confederate States of America.

"But you know, similarly to the end of the war, there is a sad ending to this story. Mrs. Tunnel's home was in Hampton, Virginia. It was standing during the Revolutionary War and had been occupied by the British General Cornwallis. Her home was confiscated by the Yankees and she never again saw it. Her sister went back to Yorktown, Virginia, in 1881 and was charged fifty cents to tour Mrs. Tunnel's home—the home that was stolen from her by the Yankee invaders. That's the way it is with evil invaders; they take what they want, they destroy what they don't want, and they answer to no one for their crimes against innocent civilians. The Yankees took our homes, our country, and used bloody bayonets to deny our right to live under a government based upon the consent of the governed. They ignored our plea to be left alone. 'We the people' of the South must never forget the heroes and heroines of Dixie. We must remember that Southerners still have the right to be left alone, to live under a government ordered upon the free and unfettered consent of the governed." Uncle Seth looked down at the young girl who had no way to understand his last words. Still, she intuitively knew that Uncle Seth spoke with deep passion and wisdom.

§ Deo Vindice §

ON THE SKIRMISH LINE WITH UNCLE SETH
"Will any candid, well informed, man assert that, at any time between 1776 and 1790, a proposition to surrender the sovereignty of the States and merge them into a central government would have had the least possible chance of adoption? Can any historical fact be more demonstrable than that the States did, both in the [Articles of] Confederation and in the Union [under the Constitution] retain their sovereignty and independence as distinct communities, voluntarily consenting to federation, but never becoming the fractional parts of a nation? In all free governments the constitution is supreme over the government [not the people] and in our Federal Union this was most distinctly marked by limitations and prohibitions against all which was beyond the expressed grants of power to the General Government. Those who resisted violations of the compact [the Constitution] were the true friends and those who maintained the usurpation of un-delegated powers [Federal supremacy] were the real enemies of the constitutional Union."
—Pres. Jefferson Davis, Confederate States of America

83

Yankee Invaders Hang Seventeen-Year-Old Arkansas Boy

"What are you reading, Uncle Seth?" Billie Jean asked her great-grandfather as she swept the floor around the old Confederate soldier's feet. She knew that he would spend every minute of the day reading the latest magazine he received if it had anything of interest to him.

"I'm reading about the dedication of a monument to a seventeen-year-old Arkansas boy who was hung by the Yankees during the war," the old man answered without looking up from the magazine.

"Why would anyone do such a thing to a young boy?" Billie Jean asked.

"It seems that the boy's father wanted to gain a supply of tobacco to sell in his store. But his store was in Confederate-held Arkansas and the tobacco supply was in Little Rock, which was in Yankee-controlled Arkansas. So the man obtained a pass from the Confederates to allow his son, David O. Dodd, to cross the Confederate lines. He hoped that David, as a youth, would be allowed through by the Yankees with that pass and a copy of his birth certificate. All went well up to a point. Being a young person, David did not appreciate the danger around him and decided to use his knowledge of Morse code to document information about the number of Yankee soldiers he saw in Little Rock. Much of the information was obtained from a Yankee soldier who was either disloyal to the Yankee cause or just wanted to impress the boy with his great knowledge of Yankee military strength. In either case, it was dangerous information for a civilian to have in an occupied country. When the boy left Little Rock and was crossing the Yankee line to get back home, the pickets found his paper containing dots and dashes. When it was decoded—which was not too hard because at that time many people knew Morse code—he was arrested as a spy.

"At David's trial, the Yankees offered to spare him the death penalty if he would tell them who the disloyal Yankee was. But he refused to betray the man. As a result, he was found guilty of spying and was sentenced to death by hanging. Now there is something called "short rope hanging" that is a cruel form of torture, a way to extract extreme punishment from the victim before he dies. This is exactly what the United States government officials did to this seventeen-year-old boy! In a civilized execution by hanging, the victim is placed high on a gallows and the weight of the body and the distance of the fall causes the victim's neck to be instantly broken; death is almost immediate. But in a short rope hanging, the victim is strangled to death, which can take between five to ten minutes. All the while, the victim's body squirms and struggles in ghastly agony. It was reported that many of the Yankees who viewed the boy's execution became physically sick. In the end, several of the Yankees grabbed the boy's legs and pulled down to add weight to the boy's small frame—thereby choking him.

"Just prior to the boy's funeral, a Yankee commander, General Steele, issued an order that none of the boy's relatives living in Confederate Arkansas would be allowed to attend the funeral and no songs or elegies would be allowed. No doubt the Yankees hoped that the world would soon forget this as well as many other hideous crimes committed by the United States forces during their war of aggression against the Confederate States of America. But there are still a few of us who remember and who will never relent in our honor of Southern courage and the defense of our right to be free from Yankee domination.

"See, here is a picture of the monument the UDC paid to have erected at the state capitol of Arkansas in Little Rock." Uncle Seth held the magazine up for Billie Jean's inspection. "Look, you can see the inscriptions on the monument:

David O. Dodd
Born November 10, 1846
Executed January 8, 1864

Aye, such was the love of the boy for his Southland
Such his endurance, his courage, his pride
That, ere he'd betray his own beloved land
He sacrificed all and gallantly died

Dark was his doom as the darkness of ages
Hard was his fate as the fellest of crime
A blot on the enemy's blackest of pages
To murder a boy in his proud boyish prime
But never a word of the source of his secret
Never a word for the sake of e'en life
True to the core for the hearts that had trusted
A martyr to man beneath the standard of strife

"You know, Billie Jean, this is just one of many cases in which the invader used his overwhelming power to persecute and murder our people. This monument is testimony to the world that 'we the people' of the South fought for a noble Cause against a criminal enemy who would do whatever was deemed necessary to maintain the Empire's domain. My fear is that one day the people of the South will no longer remember and will accept without question the Yankee's excuses for his invasion and conquest of the Confederate States of America. Of course, they will drape their propaganda in the mantle of history—Yankee history—while true Southern history will become unknown at best or, more likely, forbidden. When that day comes, 'we the people' of the South will have become second-class Yankees. Our Federal masters will see to it that all Southerners will be assigned the duty of remaining meekly seated upon the stools of eternal repentance, endlessly apologizing for slavery, treason against the Federal government, and for being the source of race hatred." Tired, the old man let the magazine fall to the floor and stared off into distant space.

§ Deo Vindice §

ON THE SKIRMISH LINE WITH UNCLE SETH
"Let no one ask, then, except a dead soul, why [we still] argue the question of secession? For, it is precisely as this question is decided, that the Jacksons, Lees, and Davises of the South will be pronounced traitors or heroes and martyrs, the South itself will be disgraced or honored by mankind."
—Dr. Albert Taylor Bledsoe, 1866

84

Honor Better Than Riches—A Letter by Adm. Raphael Semmes

The following are extracts from a letter written by Admiral Semmes to his brother a few months after the end of the War for Southern Independence. Yankee propagandists claim that men such as Semmes were fighting for slavery and that it was years later that they tried to hide their crime of treason against the United States of America by claiming to have been motivated by high principles of constitutional government. Uncle Seth kept this letter in his stack of reading material as ammunition to use against such Yankee slander.

Adm. Raphael Semmes, CSN
(Library of Congress)

Mobile, Alabama
August 12, 1865

My Dear Brother,

The cessation of the war leaves me at liberty to renew my correspondence with you without subjecting you to suspicion and annoyance. You have been frequently in my thoughts in our unfortunate struggle, and I have often felt much solicitude on your account, lest a part of the odium and ill will which a zealous performance of my duty has called down upon my head from a 'mad nation' [the United States] should attach to you and your family. Indeed, I have no doubt but that the prejudice against me was the secret of the barbarous and malignant persecution of your son. As for myself, I have nothing to regret, *save only the loss of our independence* [emphasis added]. My conscience, which is the only earthly tribunal of which a good man should be afraid, bears me witness of the uprightness of my intention in choosing my course, when, with many regrets, I severed my connection with the old government and hastened to the defense of my home and section; and now, upon reviewing the whole of my subsequent career, I can see no act with which I have to reproach myself as unbecoming a man of honor and a gentleman. I approved the secession movement of the Southern States, though I had no agency in it. I thought that the separation of these two sections of our republic, which had been engaged in a deadly mortal conflict for thirty years, would ultimately result to the great advantage of them both. The world was wide enough for them to live apart, and peace, I thought, would be the fruit of their mutual independence of each other. Although I cared very little about the institution of slavery, I believed that the doctrine of State Rights was the only doctrine which would save our republic from the fate of all other republics that had gone before us in the history of the world. I believed that this doctrine had been violated and that it would never be sufficiently respected by the controlling masses of the Northern section to prevent them from defacing with sacrilegious hands our national bond of Union where-so-ever its letter was meant to guard the peculiar rights of the South. Believing this, there was but one course for a faithful Southern man to pursue and maintain his self-respect. I pursued that course. . . . I rendered this service without ever having treated a prisoner otherwise than humanely, and, I may say, often kindly, and without ever having committed an act of war, at any time or in any manner, which was not sanctioned by the laws of war; yet my name will probably go down to posterity in the untruthful histories which will be written by bigoted and venal historians as a sort of 'Bluebeard' or 'Captain Kidd.' But I am content, my brother. My conscience is clear, my self-respect has been preserved, and my sense of manhood remains unimpaired. I think too, the South will be content, notwithstanding her immense losses and sacrifices. If she had yielded to the intolerant extreme action of Northern selfishness and fanaticism without appealing to the arbitrament of war, she would have played a craven and unworthy part.

It is better to have lost everything than lose our honor and manhood. I know you will believe me, my brother, when I tell you that I should feel greatly humbled in my own opinion were I this day entitled to wear an admiral's flag in the old [U.S.] Navy and in possession of all the means and appliances of wealth if I thought my honors and rewards had been gained by a sacrifice of creed. The preservation of my own self-respect is infinitely preferable to all such gains. I have come out of the war poor, but, God willing, I shall make a support for my family. The [U.S.] President treats me as an outlaw, unworthy of amnesty. I have nothing to say. If I am deemed unworthy to be a citizen, I can remain in my native land as an alien. A magnanimous people would have passed an act of general amnesty, it being absurd and ridiculous to talk about rebels and traitors in connection with such a revolution as has swept over the length and breadth of this land in which States, not individuals merely, were the actors. But enough of this subject.

Remember me kindly to your family, my dear brother, and let me hear from you. We have become old men. We have both had our troubles, but the chain of affection which binds me to you remains unaffected by the cares of the world and is as bright now as when we were young.

R. Semmes

§ Deo Vindice §

ON THE SKIRMISH LINE WITH UNCLE SETH

The Legislature of Massachusetts in 1844 passed the following resolution: "Resolve, That the project of the annexation of Texas, unless arrested on the threshold, may drive these States [New England States] into a dissolution of the Union."

And again, the following year, the same Yankee legislature passed the following resolution: "Resolve . . . the powers of the Legislation granted in the Constitution of the United States to Congress, do not embrace the case of the admission of a foreign State, or foreign territory . . . such an act of admission would have no binding force whatever on the people of Massachusetts."

These resolves demonstrate the fact that the political body and people of Massachusetts accepted, endorsed, and threatened to use the state's right of both nullification (the later resolve) and secession (the former resolve). Yet nowhere can it be found where the unrestrained Yankee press slandered these "high-minded" Yankees as traitors, charging them with illegally conspiring to deny the faithful execution of the laws of the Union. You will not find calls for volunteers to join the United States army and head "on to Boston" to rape, pillage, and murder citizens of Massachusetts for daring to express the will of the people of that Commonwealth. But remember the actions of these same Yankees in 1861.

85

Fighting in Georgia with
Gen. Joe Wheeler's Cavalry

Uncle Seth was excited to hear that Posey Hamilton had arrived from Pleasant Hill, Alabama, to visit with his relatives, the local Hamilton clan that lived near Rockport, Mississippi. Posey had written an account of his experience with Joe Wheeler's cavalry and Uncle Seth had invited him over to visit and share his adventures with the boys. Looking down the lane road, Uncle Seth could see a Model T Ford making its way up the dusty road toward his home. Before long the two old Confederate veterans were enjoying each other's company and exchanging stories of their youth.

"Posey, will you to tell the boys about your adventure with Gen. Joe Wheeler in Georgia?"

"Ok, boys, you all settle down over here and I'll tell you about what happened one hot July day in 1864." Posey paused while the small audience of young boys seated themselves on the porch steps; the two youngest attempted to balance themselves on the banister. "As I recall, this all happened between July 2 and 5—we didn't have time to celebrate the holiday on the 4th," he said as he chuckled at his own joke. "I was a young soldier back then. I suppose Seth and I were about the same age when we volunteered to defend our country. Well, I was with the 10th Confederate Cavalry under Gen. Joe Wheeler. We had moved to the north side of the Chattahoochee River in North Georgia. Our regiment was in constant motion, but for no obvious purpose. At least that's what it seemed like to those of us in the ranks. On July 2, we came to a halt on a road next to a large field that had grown up with young pine saplings. In war, you spend many a day in dull routine and then, occasionally, it is interrupted by the exciting call to form up for battle. Well, we thought this was another one of those dull days. Then, all of a sudden, from behind the field of pine saplings the Yankees opened up on us with a load of canister. Their cannons flattened the pine saplings and tore into our mounted cavalry. It was a complete surprise and we were caught in utter confusion. Our division commander, Gen. John H. Kelley, was close by and quickly restored order. You boys should have seen him; he sat on his horse right in front of our company while the Yankees were pouring shot and shell into us at a fearful rate. But if a unit is to be saved at a time like this, a leader must restore order and make command decisions. Otherwise the unit dissolves and is overrun, killed, or captured. We all rallied around our general, and as order was restored we began to answer the Yankee cannon with our small-arms fire. I think this did more good for us, because we felt we were doing something to save ourselves. But small arms against hidden cannons were not much of a threat to the enemy.

"As this was happening—it seemed like an eternity but it was probably not more than two to three minutes—Gen. Joe Wheeler himself rode to the front. In the midst of all the carnage he had a conference with General Kelley. It was as if nothing unusual was happening around them. I tell you, boys, it embarrassed me because frankly I was terrified inside, even though I did my best not to let it show on the outside. General Wheeler was as cool as a cucumber floating in spring water. He showed absolutely no excitement whatsoever even though both he and General Kelley could have been killed in an instant. I tell you, I had seen him in some dangerous places, but I never saw him show the least excitement at any time. I don't think the world has ever produced a better field commander than ole Joe Wheeler." Posey's deep respect and love for his former commander was evident; it was the type of respect that inspires men to charge the gates of Hell when they're told to.

"Well, after what seemed like an eternity, General Wheeler galloped back toward the rear, and before long he had ten pieces of Confederate artillery answering those Yankee boys. By then we had dismounted and by fours sent our horses to a safer place. You boys know what 'by fours' means, don't you?" Posey continued before even allowing the boys to acknowledge his question. "That means that when a mounted unit dismounts to do battle on foot, one man in four will take his horse and the horses of three other men to a safe area while the dismounted men fight. Now, we were ordered to hold our fire because we could not see the enemy. We stayed as low as we could while the Yankee artillerymen tried to find us with canister and solid shot. In the meantime, our boys were sending hot Confederate shot and shell over towards the Yankees. We all had as much iron around us as those Yankee sailors in their ironclads. It was a real artillery duel for over an hour. We were ordered to carefully move forward and take cover at a place closer to the Yankee artillery position. The plan was to get to a position where we could gain cover and begin to pick off individual Yankee artillerymen.

"Those Yankees did not think much of us wanting to get close to them, and as soon as they spotted us in our new position they turned their attention to us with grapeshot, canister shot, and solid shot. Now, this was even worse than the first blast that they gave us. I think they knew that they were fighting for their lives because the Yankees knew what good shots Southern soldiers were. All we could do was to continue to try to get as close to our native soil as we could or else we would be buried in that soil before the day was over. It looked as if every last one of us would be taken out by Yankee shot or shell. And what made it so bad was that we could barely get a shot off at our hated adversary. But for every shot they did allow us to get off, one Yankee would pay the price of invasion with his life. I recall seeing a shot hit Ruff Robert's gun while he was holding it. It destroyed the gun and put a hole in Ruff's hat. We thought for sure he was dead, but he didn't even get a scratch! We never did find the parts of his gun. All he had left was the gun's stock, which he was holding when the gun was struck by the Yankee cannonball. But believe it or not, it was not Yankee cannonballs that were the most dangerous; it was the tree limbs that were being hit by those cannonballs. When one of the limbs fell from ten to twenty feet above, it could kill a man before he could get out of the way.

"Well, either our artillery fire or pure exhaustion on the part of the Yankee artillerymen—one or the other—caused them to cease firing and pull out. I tell you boys we were all glad to get back on our horses. I think General Forrest was right when he would tell his men that it was safer to charge Yankee cannons than to lay cringing under their fire.

"On the 5th, General Wheeler's force fought a hard engagement with Yankee infantry. Gen. Joseph E. Johnston had taken our army across the Chattahoochee River, leaving General Wheeler on the north side to hold the Yankees in check until all of our supply and baggage wagons were safely across. This would have been an almost impossible assignment for most, but General Wheeler executed his orders with the efficiency that made him famous on both sides during the war. General Wheeler managed to keep the Yankees away from the river long enough for all of our army and supply wagons to get across. All that was left was one pontoon bridge. But the Yankees were closing in as fast as they could—they thought that they at last had a chance to capture or destroy General Wheeler's cavalry. Wheeler had to hold off a force vastly superior in numbers while sending his units across the last pontoon bridge.

"Oh, boys," Posey stopped his story as if he had suddenly remembered something important, "do you know how a pontoon bridge is made? You pull a large, heavy rope across the river and tie it to a tree on each bank. You then place boats side by side with their bows facing the river flow and connect them to the strong rope that you anchored to the trees. Now, flat-bottom boats work best, but you use whatever is available. Then you run planking lengthwise across the boats, and after that place another layer of planks crosswise on the first layer of planks. If it is done right you can march men eight abreast across it or horses in fours. But it is very unstable—it rocks and rolls in the water and both man and beast will tend to panic if they are not accustomed to it.

"Well, here we were on July 5 with overwhelming numbers of Yankees at our front, and more were closing in on our flanks; to our rear was the Chattahoochee River with only one pontoon bridge. We had to cross the river and hold off the Yankees at the same time—impossible for most, but not for General Wheeler. He took about fifty of his best men and kept charging the Yankees, pulling back and charging at another place. He was moving and attacking so fast that the Yankees must have thought that we were making a stand on the river bank. This confused their leaders and caused them to delay their final assault. In the meantime we had our number fours swim our horses across at various spots and form up on the opposite bank next to the pontoon bridge. The dismounted troops marched across the bridge as if we were on dress parade. Eight men abreast and at close order—when the man's foot in front of you stepped forward your foot immediately took the spot his foot just vacated. If one man had misstepped, the entire rank would have fallen into the river. But we were well-trained soldiers and we all made it across and regained our horses. At the very last moment General Wheeler led his fifty men across the pontoon bridge and we cut the rope as soon as the last horse cleared it." Posey stopped and sat back with a large grin on his face.

Uncle Seth enjoyed the company of men who, like himself, had volunteered to defend their country in the War for Southern Independence. He made special efforts to pass on this rich Southern heritage to his kith and kin. Each year more and more of the South's soldiers in gray were answering the last roll call. Uncle Seth knew that time was running out and before long there would be no one to honor the memory or defend the Cause of Southern Independence, unless the new generations of Southerners could be told the truth—a truth that the ruling elite of the Federal Empire were determined to crush.

§ Deo Vindice §

On the Skirmish Line with Uncle Seth
"The political hostilities of a generation were now face to face with weapons instead of words . . . The actual fact on the battlefield in the face of cannon and musket was that the Federal troops came as invaders, and the Southern troops stood as defenders of their homes, and further than this we need not go."

—Gen. G.P.T. Beauregard, CSA

86

Adm. Raphael Semmes, CSN—Confederate Hero of the High Seas

August 30, 1907, seemed like a good day to be in Mobile, Alabama. Uncle Seth had taken a trip to the Confederate Soldiers Home at Beauvoir in Biloxi on the Mississippi Gulf Coast and had extended his trip to include a short visit to Mobile. He had always enjoyed reading and rereading *Memoirs of Service Afloat* by Admiral Semmes, Confederate States Navy, and today marked the thirtieth year since the death of Admiral Semmes. So Uncle Seth decided to go to the Old Catholic Cemetery in Mobile where the admiral was buried and pay his respects. Upon reaching the cemetery, he was not sure where to go. Seeing several men his age standing with their hats in hand, he moved toward them to ask if they knew where Semmes was buried. To his surprise, they were three of the surviving members of the CSS *Alabama*'s crew; they were also there to pay respects to their former admiral.

"Tell me," Uncle Seth asked politely to the nearest man, "about how it felt to be under the direct command of such a fine man as Admiral Semmes."

"Well, it was exciting and as a young seaman I thought of it as a grand adventure. You know youth have no concept of danger. And I have to admit that there were times of excitement and actual fun. I recall the time right after we sunk the Yankee ship *Hatteras*. We had her captain and around a hundred of her crew on board—rescued them from drowning, you know. Well, we made it into Port Royal, which was still under British control. There were three British warships anchored in port. One of them, the *Greyhound*, had a band on board and every evening the band would treat us to a naval serenade. At the end of the serenade they would play the national anthem of each ship anchored in the harbor. Port Royal had fallen on hard times and there were usually only a few ships in harbor, so it did not take long to play all the anthems. It was a great joy to hear them play "Dixie" in honor of our country, the Confederate States of America.

"The Yankee captain of the sunken *Hatteras* had recently been paroled and was ashore waiting for passage back to the United States. Well, for some reason he took offense at the mere sound of the South's unofficial national anthem—can you imagine that? The Yankee captain took it as an insult to all of Yankeedom and lodged a formal protest with the British governor of Port Royal. The governor must have enjoyed this tempest in a tea cup—there's not too much to do in such a remote assignment. According to the captain of the *Hatteras,* this had all the workings of an international incident. Why, war between Great Britain and the United States may be just over the horizon should the situation be mishandled. The British governor, whose sense of humor was as sharp as his perception of the Yankee's ill will, knew how to save the world from yet another war. He ordered the band on the *Greyhound* to play something for the offended Yank after playing "Dixie"—and I tell you it was the best performance they had done all evening. I think they really wanted to make us feel good. Well, as soon as the last note of "Dixie" gently floated out to sea, the *Greyhound*'s band struck up the most obnoxious rendition of "Yankee Doodle." We all had a great laugh and the Yankee captain could make no complaint because it was, after all, his nation's song," the old salt said with a chuckle and grin.

The second man then jumped in with a story of his own. "Let me tell you what I remember the best. Maybe it is because of the way the history of the war is being written by the Yankees, but I can't help but think that the way we accepted and respected Dave, our black seaman, is the most important part of the *Alabama*'s story. I remember when he became a part of our crew. It was after we had taken three Yankee ships. As a result of burning so many Yankee ships, we were laden with prisoners. After burning the first two we decided to put the prisoners on the smallest ship, the *Tonawanda*, and send them on their way. But on board the *Tonawanda* was a slave belonging to one of the passengers from Delaware. You recall that the state of Delaware was under Yankee control. The slave's name was Dave. He was seventeen years old and was to remain as a slave until he reached the age of twenty-one. That was the system that the sovereign state of Delaware had elected to use to end slavery. Admiral Semmes decided that as property of a citizen of the United States of America the slave should be considered contraband of war, so the admiral elected to keep him on board the *Alabama.* Now at first Dave was very unsure about what would become of a black youth in the hands of heathen Southerners. He was not aware that Pres. Jefferson Davis had already vetoed a bill passed in the Confederate Congress that would have allowed slaves captured and belonging to Northerners to be sold in the South. President Davis vetoed the bill because the Confederate Constitution—unlike the United States

Constitution—had a section that specifically prohibited the slave trade. Admiral Semmes was proud that during the war he had captured many slaves held by the enemy and subsequently had freed them. He would often say that he actually emancipated slaves, whereas ole Abe Lincoln only talked about it as a war measure! Before long Dave was very happy with his new conditions. The ship's physician, Dr. Galt, who was from Virginia, took Dave as his servant and before long the two were constant companions. Each respected the other in a way that Northerners could not understand.

"Admiral Semmes entered Dave's name into the ship's books as one of the crew and allowed him the pay of his grade. Really there was no difference in pay or assignments between Dave and the white waiters. Dave served us during the entire cruise. He was at liberty in port to go ashore just like the rest of the ship's crew. If he had any desire to gain his 'freedom,' all he had to do was not go back on board. But Dave was always the last to go ashore and the first to come back to the *Alabama*. And don't forget that at every port of call the Yankee consuls and general bevy of Yankee old maids and social workers would do everything they could to try to entice this 'poor abused slave' to seize the glittering prize of Yankee freedom. But you know, Dave had a sharp intellect that allowed him to distinguish between false friends and true ones. He was a good sailor and a proud member of the *Alabama*'s crew." The second sailor seemed especially proud of his story because it flew in the face of so much Yankee propaganda.

"Well, Seth, I think my best memory of serving with Admiral Semmes—no, I should actually say it is my saddest memory—is similar to the tale about Dave. Unfortunately, my story has a much sadder ending. It exemplifies, in a nutshell, the detestable depth of Yankee hypocrisy and cursed materialism. It all began with the commission of the *Sumter*, and the whole affair took place on board it—Admiral Semmes' first Confederate ship.

"When Admiral Semmes was outfitting the *Sumter* in New Orleans, Louisiana, one of his friends in that city gave him one of his best house servants to serve as the admiral's on-board steward. The servant's name was Ned. Just

On board the CSS Alabama (Courtesy Collection of Rear Admiral Ammen C. Farenholt, USN, Naval History and Heritage Command)

like Dave, Ned was treated like the rest of the crew. He enjoyed the life at sea and became close to his fellow seamen. But trouble was afoot when the *Sumter* anchored at Dutch-controlled Paramaribo, which is the capital city of Suriname, just north of Brazil. The Yankee consul there was a devious man from Connecticut who no doubt had spent many a day in New England denouncing the evil slaveholders down South while extolling Yankee virtue. He had married a mulatto after coming to Paramaribo and through her became a slaveholder! We always said the lady could have done so much better than marrying a Yankee.

"As Yankee consul this man felt it was his duty to prevent the *Sumter* from obtaining coal, thereby preventing us from continuing the destruction of the Yankee merchant fleet. He sent official protest to the Dutch governor, but the governor replied that Holland had followed the other European powers and had recognized the Confederate States of America as belligerents. Therefore, it had extended the Confederacy and its ships the protection afforded a belligerent power under international law. The Yankee then tried to threaten anyone who might allow us to purchase coal, but to no avail. He even tried to bribe the harbor pilot, offering to pay him to refuse to take the *Sumter* out of the harbor. That bribe was summarily rejected by the pilot; and to show his utter disdain for the Yankee, the harbor pilot provided us with some valuable charts of the local waters. So, failing at all his efforts to uphold the interests of the Yankee Empire, and with the typical Yankee ability to see profit in even the worst of circumstances, he decided to try one more thing that would at least provide him with a little profit.

"While Ned was ashore, the Yankee, like the serpent in the Garden of Eden, whispered the glittering promise of Yankee freedom in Ned's ear. Ned took the bait and never returned to the *Sumter*. Now this Yankee took Ned to his wife's plantation and put him to work with the rest of the slaves! You know, poor Ned was not very experienced dealing with Yankees, but it did not take him long to find out the difference between money-grubbing Yankees and Southern gentlemen. Months passed, and Ned was reduced to wearing rags and eating sweet potato soup. Ned grew up in New Orleans, had served in some of the finest homes, and was dressed and clothed by members of high society. His current condition was too much to bear; so, like the Prodigal Son, one night he slipped away and began his quest for the *Sumter*. He took passage on a ship as it was leaving Paramaribo. He ended up in Europe but no one knew the whereabouts of the *Sumter*. The next we heard of him he was in England at the Port of Southampton. Ned located the Confederate steamer *Nashville*.

Once onboard, he gave a full account of his trials and tribulations. He eventually found his way back to the United States, where he died in poverty in Washington, DC. It is a sad tale. Few know it and even fewer care about this poor slave who was happy and secure with his Southern friends but betrayed and destroyed by his deceitful Yankee 'pal.'" With these sad words, the old soldier and three sailors shook hands and parted ways.

§ Deo Vindice §

On the Skirmish Line with Uncle Seth

"It is the fashion of many writers of the day to class all who opposed the Consolidationists [Northern political leaders seeking to eliminate *real* States' Rights and establish a supreme federal government] with what they style the Pro-Slavery Party. No greater injustice could be done any public men, and no greater violence be done to the truth of History, than such a classification. Their opposition to [centralized federal tyranny] sprung from no attachment to slavery; but, as Jefferson's, Pinkney's, and Clay's, it came from their strong convictions that the Federal Government had no rightful or Constitutional control or jurisdiction over such questions; and that no such action, as that proposed by them [the consolidationists and radical abolitionists], could be taken by Congress without destroying the elementary and vital principles upon which the Government was founded. Some of the strongest anti-slavery men who ever lived were on the side of those who opposed the Centralizing principles which led to the War. Mr. Jefferson was a striking illustration of this, and a prominent example of a very large class of both sections of the country, who were, most unfortunately, brought into hostile array against each other."

—Alexander H. Stephens, vice president, Confederate States of America

87

Horse Furlough, Winter of 1865

Uncle Seth and Joe William walked out into the pasture to check on the boys' riding mare. The horse was old and had been retired from doing any major chores—put out to pasture, as Uncle Seth would say—but the boys still enjoyed bareback riding on the gentle mare. "Joe William, pick up the mare's front hoof and see if the cut is healing," the old Confederate veteran instructed his young great-grandson.

"Yes, it really looks good, Uncle Seth. I think she will be okay for riding in a couple of weeks." Joe William tried to impress Uncle Seth with his skills of animal husbandry.

"Well that is great, for a while there I was afraid you boys would have to take a horse furlough," Uncle Seth said teasingly—hoping Joe William would ask for an explanation.

"What's a horse furlough, Uncle Seth?" the youth asked, willingly falling into Uncle Seth's trap.

"Well, I had a friend during the war who was forced to take a horse furlough during the winter of 1865. His name is D. C. Gallaher; sometimes as a joke we would call him Washington, DC. He now lives in Charleston, the state capital of West Virginia. You see, unlike the Yankee cavalrymen, many of our men had to provide their own horses. So if your horse went lame, you would be given a short furlough to return home in order to acquire another horse. We called this a horse furlough.

"D. C.'s horse had gone lame and was hardly able to put any pressure on its front-right leg. His cavalry unit was camped near Orange Court House on the Rapidan River. He was given a horse furlough and, despite the icy cold weather, left camp and headed to his home in the Shenandoah Valley. He was not able to ride his horse, so he was forced to walk the entire way, leading the lame horse. On the first night he reached Charlottesville, which is about thirty miles from camp. Not bad marching, especially while leading a lame horse! D. C. knew that his furlough would soon be over so he got an early start the next morning, hoping to make it to his home at Waynesboro before dark that day. He told me that the road was frozen and covered with ice—not snow, but slippery ice. You can imagine the difficulty the lame horse was having. And neither D. C. nor his horse had had anything to eat since leaving camp. So hunger and the attending weakness added to the many obstacles that impeded his progress.

"Toward evening he had reached the foot of the Blue Ridge Mountains at Afton station, where he met a Mr. Goodloe. He recognized D. C. and insisted that he stay the night with him because it was too dangerous to attempt a night passage through the frozen mountain pass. But D. C. had a plan, and if it worked out he would be at his home before midnight. Instead of taking the longer pass he would lead his horse down the railroad track and through the tunnel. It was shorter but also dangerous. The tunnel was rather long and narrow; if he timed it wrong and a train came through the tunnel both he and his horse would be killed.

"Mr. Goodloe begged him to stay but could not sway the determined D. C. Poor old Mr. Goodloe gravely bid him goodbye. Upon reaching the tunnel, D. C. put his ear next to the iron rail to try to determine if a train was coming. He had to be careful because if his ear touched the ice cold iron rail it might become a part of the railroad track. At last, he decided to enter the tunnel. His horse was even slower than usual; most likely the railroad bed was beginning to hurt the horse's good hooves. D. C. said that eventually he had to pull the horse because he wouldn't walk at all. Just as he was about to exit the tunnel, he heard the sound of a train rounding the bend, getting ready to enter the tunnel at the very spot where he and his horse were coming out! He made a dash for the exit and somehow the horse found the energy to follow as the train came rumbling by and into the tunnel.

"By midnight, he was at his mother's window calling her name. She later told him that it frightened her fearfully. She thought he had been killed in battle and was calling her from beyond the regions of the living. It was not long before D. C. was warming at the family hearth and eating a hot supper made by a loving mother. D. C. got another horse and returned before his furlough expired."

Uncle Seth stood silently contemplating the dedication of the Southern soldier: men who were willing to stay and fight against impossible odds, men like D. C. who owned no slaves but were willing to die if necessary to defend their people's right to be free from Yankee domination. The Confederate army and navy were full of men who only asked to be left alone—but that was more than the Yankee Empire was willing to allow.

§ Deo Vindice §

ON THE SKIRMISH LINE WITH UNCLE SETH
"[To] the Union, next to our liberties, most dear."
                                        —John C. Calhoun, April 13, 1830

88

Uncle Seth Replies to a
Miseducated Southerner

"Everyone knows that Gen. Robert E. Lee was a reluctant Southern nationalist," declared a befuddled Southerner. "He was loyal to the United States of America but did not want to fight against his kin in Virginia. He was more of a Virginian than a Southerner."

"Strange that 'everyone knows' that. Somehow I missed that part of my education," retorted Uncle Seth. "Perhaps it was because instead of reading what some Yankee educator wrote, I was there and know firsthand the love General Lee had for the South.

Gen. Robert E. Lee (Library of Congress)

But instead of engaging in needless arguments, look to Lee's own testimony if you really want to know the truth. See what the general had to say about why he was willing to be a leader in his country's struggle for freedom.

"In a letter written by General Lee to Lord Acton in December of 1865, well after the war, Lee clearly points out his feelings about the South and the current dangers facing America and the world as a result of the expanding post-war Federal Empire. I will read a few selected quotes from his letter:

As a citizen of the South, I feel deeply indebted to you for the sympathy you have evinced in its cause . . . Amid the conflicting statements and sentiments in both countries, it will be no easy task to discover the truth or to relieve it from the mass of prejudice and passion with which it has been covered by party spirit. . . . I can only say that while I have considered the preservation of the constitutional power of the general government to be the foundation of our peace and safety at home and abroad, I yet believe that the maintenance of the rights and authority reserved to the States and to the people not only essential to the adjustment and balance of the general system, but the safeguard to the continuance of a free government . . . whereas the consolidation of the States into one vast republic sure to be aggressive abroad and despotic at home, will be the certain precursor of that ruin which has overwhelmed all those that have preceded it. I need not refer one so well acquainted as you are with American history to the state papers of Washington and Jefferson, the representatives of the federal and democratic parties, denouncing consolidation and centralization of power as tending to the subversion of State governments and to despotism.

The New England States, whose citizens are the fiercest opponents of the Southern States, did not always avow the opinions they now advocate. Upon the purchase of Louisiana by Jefferson, they virtually asserted the right of secession through their prominent men; and in the convention which assembled at Hartford in 1814, they threatened the disruption of the Union unless the war should be discontinued. The assertion of this has been repeatedly made by the politicians when their party was weak, and Massachusetts, the leading State in hostility to the South, declares in the preamble of her constitution that the people of that commonwealth 'have the sole and exclusive right of government themselves as a free, sovereign, and independent State, and do, and forever hereafter shall, exercise and enjoy every power, jurisdiction, and right which is not or may hereafter be by them expressly delegated to the United States of America in congress assembled.'

Judge Chase, the present Chief Justice of the United States, as late as 1850, is reported to have stated in the Senate, of which he was a member, that he 'knew of no remedy in case of the refusal of a State to perform its stipulations,' thereby acknowledging the sovereignty and independence of State action.

The South has contended only for the supremacy of the Constitution and the just administration of the laws made in pursuance of it. Virginia to the last made great efforts to save the Union and urged harmony and compromise. Senator Douglas of Illinois, in his remarks upon the compromise bill recommended by the committee of thirteen in 1861, stated that every member for the South, including Messrs. Toombs and Davis, expressed their willingness to accept the proposition of Senator Crittenden, of Kentucky, as a final settlement of the controversy if sustained by the Republican party, and that the only difficulty in the way of an amicable adjustment was with the Republican party. Who, then, is responsible for war?

"From these words lifted directly from the text of his much larger letter to Lord Acton, we can see General Lee's attitude toward the South and the United States subsequent to its victory over the Confederate States of America. General Lee specifically refers to himself as a "citizen of the South." He accepts the authority of the United States over himself and the South just as any slave would accept the authority of his master over the slave—the mere fact that the authority is accepted under the circumstances does not imply that the slave accepts the authority as being legitimate.

"General Lee also takes note of the potential of a federal government that is not controlled by sovereign states to consolidate its power and become 'despotic at home and aggressive abroad.' He also clearly points out the hypocrisy of the North when it comes to the constitutional right of secession. He shows how the North eagerly appealed to this right when it was profitable for them to do so but just as easily denounced that same right when it was no longer profitable to the Yankee.

"General Lee also demonstrated that the South was—and always has been—willing to compromise in an effort to preserve the *constitutional* Union. But it was the Republican Party—under the direction of Lincoln—the Northern war governors, crony capitalists, and radical abolitionists who refused to compromise or negotiate with the new Southern government and schemed to plunge both nations into a bloody war. Anyone who reads General Lee's own words cannot come away thinking that he was reluctant to take up the Cause of Southern Independence. That is—unless they are imbued with the same party spirit that caused the North to initiate the war in the first place. If that is the case then no amount of evidence will ever cause them to acknowledge the South's right to be free of Yankee domination and simply to be left alone."

§ Deo Vindice §

ON THE SKIRMISH LINE WITH UNCLE SETH
"The parties that threaten the Union rely not on principles, but on material interests. In so vast a land these interests make the provinces [states] into rival nations rather than parties. Thus, recently we have seen the North contending for tariffs and the South taking up arms for free trade, simply because the North is industrial and the South agricultural, so that restrictions [tariffs] would profit the North and harm the South."

—Alexis de Tocqueville, circa 1840

89

Yankee Materialism: The Root Cause of the War

"The love of money is the root of evil—that's what the Holy Bible says," announced Uncle Seth to anyone within hearing distance. Sarah, his twin sister, was in the kitchen getting dinner ready. It was almost noon and the menfolk would soon be coming in from the field hungry after a full morning of plowing.

"Seth, go ring the dinner bell so the field hands can start getting things together for dinner," she said without looking up. She knew that before the menfolk could come in they would need to plow to the end of the turn row, unhook the trace chains from the singletree, and take the mules to the pond for watering and then to the barn for their noon meal of corn and hay. In the meantime, Sarah would visit a little with her brother. She could hear her dinner bell as Seth slowly tugged on the rope. She always liked to be the first in the community to announce that dinner was ready. Soon she could hear the bells of surrounding families as they, too, called their menfolk in for dinner.

"Now, what were you talking about? I saw you were reading last week's edition of the county newspaper," Sarah asked Seth.

"Oh, it was just an article by Capt. S. A. Ashe from Raleigh, North Carolina. He published an article in his local paper and our paper picked it up. Captain Ashe looked at the report of the United States Committee on Commerce and Navigation for the year ending June 30, 1859. It demonstrated how dependent the Yankees were on Southern agriculture for import/ export duties and tariffs. The Yanks were getting rich off of Southern economic activity. In 1859, exports from the South totaled $193,000,000 while exports from the North totaled only a little more than $45,000,000. Left to their own devices and unable to use their majority of votes in Congress to continue their exploitation of the South, the North would have sunk into economic insignificance—and they knew it! That is why the Yankee war governors went to see Lincoln early after his election to urge him not to let the South go.

"It didn't take long for the Yankee press to catch on to the dire economic risk faced by the North if it no longer had the South to plunder. The March 30, 1861, issue of the *New York Times* stated the fact plainly: 'With us it is no longer an abstract question, one of constitutional construction, or reserved or delegated powers of the states to the Federal government, but of material existence and moral position both at home and abroad.' The *Times* was a close supporter of Lincoln; you can be sure that he read the article. But people in the South read it as well. Southerners at last could see plain and open admissions from radical, money-grubbing Yankees who were willingly proclaiming their intentions of making economic vassals out of Southerners!

"The Manchester, New Hampshire, *Union Democrat* was even more to the point. They declared, 'The Southern Confederacy will not employ our ships or buy our goods. What is our shipping without it? Literally nothing. The transportation of cotton and its fabrics employs more ships than all other trades. It is very clear that the South gains by this process, and we lose. No—we must not let the South go!'

"It is such a shame that so many young men, both North and South, had to die in order to maintain Northern commercial interests. They were willing to corrupt the Constitution and murder innocent men, women, and children in the South just to maintain their economic system. Without regard to the Constitution and American principles, such as the consent of the governed, the North declared itself to be the master of the Southern people. The North assumed the right to decide what type of government 'we the people' of Dixie would be allowed to live under. The North assumed, as if by divine authority, the right to reject the plea of the South to be left alone. Lincoln, the Radical Republicans, the war governors and those commercial interests with close ties to the ruling elite in Washington, DC, took it upon themselves to decide just how many Southerners would be murdered in order to maintain the Yankee's standard of living." Uncle Seth was interrupted by the slamming of the back door as the menfolk came in from the fields and new conversations began.

§ Deo Vindice §

ON THE SKIRMISH LINE WITH UNCLE SETH
"If the whole community had the same interests, so that the interest of each and every portion would be so affected by the action of the government, that the laws which oppressed or impoverishes one portion, would necessarily oppress and impoverish all others, or the reverse, then the right of [majority vote] would be sufficient to counteract the tendency

of the government to oppression and abuse of its powers. . . . But such is not the case . . . and nothing is more easy than to pervert [governmental] powers into instruments to aggrandize and enrich one or more interests by oppression and impoverishing the others; and this too, under the operation of laws, couched in general terms; and which on their face, appear fair and equal. Nor is this the case in some particular communities only. It is so in all; the small and the great, the poor and the rich . . ."

—John C. Calhoun, *A Disquisition on Government,* 1840

90

Yankee Hypocrisy—Germans in Belgium vs. Yankees in Georgia

Uncle Seth was seventy-four years old and still able to make the annual reunion of the United Confederate Veterans. This year's reunion promised to be a special one for Uncle Seth because he wanted to hear Dr. Henry E. Shepherd from Baltimore, Maryland, who would be speaking about one of Uncle Seth's favorite subjects—Yankee Hypocrisy. The year was 1918, and the Great War in Europe was finally over. Uncle Seth found it intriguing that during the Great War the United States' Northern press was outspoken in their complaints about the atrocities committed by the Germans when they occupied Belgium and parts of France. This was the same press that wrote glowing accounts of Sherman's and Sheridan's campaign against non-combatant civilians—women, children, and old men—in the South during the War for Southern Independence.

Uncle Seth slowly made his way toward the front of the auditorium. He took a chair close to the speaker's podium. The crowd grew silent as Dr. Shepherd stepped up and began to speak. "I thought a long while about what to call my address today and finally settled on the title 'Historic Ironies—Sherman and German.' As I approached the topic and reviewed the history, both the recent history of the Great War in Europe and the earlier history of our War for Southern Independence, I began to realize that this entire topic touched upon the morbid. Yes, the morbid, because it once again demonstrates, to those with eyes willing to see and ears willing to hear, that Satan is ever eager to display himself in his favorite role as an angel of light. The Northern press and politicians raise to heaven agonies of lamentation as they contemplate the proclaimed atrocities of the German armies in France and Belgium, yet these same Yankees rear lofty monuments, graved by art and man's devices and paid for out of the public treasury, to perpetuate the memory and idealize the infamy of Sherman and Sheridan." Dr. Shepherd stopped and gazed upon his audience to get a feel for their reaction. Uncle Seth, intrigued, leaned forward as if trying to be the first to hear the next words from the podium.

"Only an unmeasurably arrogant people wrapped in their comforting robes of self-righteousness could raise monuments to men whose armies were responsible for the death, destruction, and pillaging of countless numbers of their own former countrymen. These Yankee generals and their armies were composed of soldiers whose most notable campaigns were waged against age and infancy, against the cradle and the death chamber, and against the womb and the sepulcher. Listen, if you dare, to the winds from the South as they bring thousands of mystic voices from unmarked Southern graves—graves filled with the remains not of uniformed soldiers who died defending their country but the unmarked graves filled with the earthly remains of old men, young children, and women who died from Yankee bullets, Yankee lynch ropes, or Yankee-induced starvation and disease. Surely these voices have a right to be heard, a right to protest the deification of Satan disguised as an angel of Yankee enlightenment!

"The haranguing lavished upon our 'reunited country' by nationalists and the South's endless proclamations of its loyalty to the 'flag' must have fallen strangely upon the ears of the dead, if God in his wisdom has not withheld from them the sense of hearing. It is this loss—the loss of America's original, constitutionally limited Republic of Republics—that makes the irony of Yankee protest against Germans in Europe so difficult for this speaker to endure. And I will not endure it in silence. This pretended outrage, so often complained of by the Yankee press, is minor compared to the outrages they committed upon the people of the South—a people who committed no crime. For those who were not there, I will recall just a few examples drawn from personal knowledge, historical records, and from conversations with those who endured the Yankee's terrible, swift sword.

"On December 18, 1864, Maj. Gen. Halleck wrote to General Sherman: 'Should you capture Charleston, I hope that by some accident the place may be destroyed; and if a little salt should be sown on its site, it might prevent the growth of future crops of nullification and treason.' General Sherman replied that he would zealously carry out the suggestion, declaring, 'I will bear in mind your hint as to Charleston, and do not think "salt" will be necessary.' Sherman's letters and reports are without a touch of shame or realization of his own infamy. His own words are the most convincing and inexorable witness against himself. His efforts to destroy the South were heralded throughout the North by an eager press and a population anxious to read of the continuing devastation being heaped upon 'ignorant, worthless, treasonous, rebels down South.'

"We are told by the Yankee press that the U.S. was right to engage in the most stupendous struggle in world history, to avenge the wrongs inflicted upon France and Belgium, while at the same time the carnival of desolation that swept over Columbia and Fayetteville is glorified by abiding memorials and monuments, preserving in undiminished vigor the infamy of the Yankee perpetrators. For those with eyes to see and ears to hear, these are strange and irreconcilable ironies—and perhaps that is why those people who rule 'our' reunited country labor so hard to prevent the truth of our history from being taught to our children or told to the world.

"The Yankee Generals Sherman and Sheridan are ideal heroes of a people who are compassing sea and land to expand the empire of Germany; the shades of their Southern victims, delicate women and infants, haunt us, unavenged. In the retrospect of its own story, in the view of its own irrevocable past, the attitude assumed by our own Yankee-controlled country becomes not merely untenable but falls to the ground under the weight of its own logical absurdity. How can Satan cast out Satan? With what pretense of reason or consistency can the nation that has assigned Sherman a foremost rank in its pantheon of military divinities raise its hands in protest against the German's most atrocious crimes?

"A notable feature of Sherman's march through the Carolinas was his careful attention to the detail of destruction of public and private property regardless of whether or not it had any military value. His efforts were more in the nature of destroying the South than in winning a war. The war was an excuse to carry out the longed-for dream of Northern radicals—the complete extermination of 'we the people' of the South, our culture, our civilization and most of all our love for limited government enforced by real States' Rights. His army's acts of pillaging, raping, and murdering were not acts of random violence of renegade or drunken soldiers. It was allowed and even encouraged by officialdom. These acts against innocent non-combatants were not outbursts of frenzy, a paroxysm of insane rage that sometimes sweeps over even disciplined armies. This fact is attested to by the systematic method in which Columbia was destroyed. The sacking of this fair and beautiful city may justly rank with the crowning atrocities of the Thirty Years' War. When the United States army entered Columbia, the civilized world regressed two hundred years. The legions of the Kaiser in their wildest frenzies of vandalism will not surpass the infamies forever linked with the memory of the Yankee commanders Sherman and Sheridan. Yet the bands of American military units now in London regale their English allies with the strains of 'Marching Through Georgia' and the 'Battle Hymn of the Republic.' And 'we the people' of the South accept the implied indignity as meekly as a well-trained and docile slave.

"Considerations of sex, age, and infirmity stayed not for a moment the hand of the Yankee invader, nor in the slightest measure tempered the violence of his hireling soldiery. It was a crusade—minutely devised and remorselessly executed—against old men who were hardly able to move on crutch and cane, against infants at their mother's breast, and against innocent children beholding their world being ravaged in flames of Yankee hatred. Through this lens, many of the crimes attributed by our national press to the armies of the Kaiser in Belgium or France seem small by comparison. So complete was the destruction throughout the region of Sherman's march that families reared in affluence were reduced to utter destitution and subsisted for a season upon corn gathered from the ground at former Yankee cavalry camps. Let me be clear—it was corn that had fallen from the mouths of Yankee cavalry horses! Upon this discarded food of animals, our people maintained life until relief came from beyond the zone of Federal occupation. Specific or individual illustrations of atrocity, such as the Germans might aspire to emulate, may be cited without limitation; their name is legion. And today, our tax dollars are paying Yankee military bands in England to amuse our allies by playing 'Marching Through Georgia' while the South keeps time with spoons and sticks on the sideline of world history.

"In regard to numbers of these accounts, I bear personal testimony, as they occurred within the vicinity of Fayetteville; and in more than one instance, they were inflicted upon those linked to me by ties of blood and association—my kith and kin—high-bred women in remote plantation homes, isolated and absolutely devoid of protection or defense, their sons or husbands with Lee at the forefront during the expiring agonies of our dissolving Confederacy. A relative living in the circumstances I have described was attacked by a Union soldier who thrust a revolver into her face, threatening her with instant death if she did not surrender her husband's watch, silver, gold, and other valuables. The ruffian imagined those valuables to be there for the taking—booty for the conquering armies of the United States of America. This typical Southern lady folded her arms and calmly replied: 'Shoot.' The Northern vandal satisfied his violent urge by wrenching her rings from her fingers before slinking away, declaring he would return and burn her home to the ground.

"The invading Yankee did not even spare the dying. One would think that a normal human being would consider the death bed of a dying child to be sacred, but 'we the people' of the South were not dealing with normal human beings as our cultural and religious values would define the word. A young girl in the last stages of disease was lifted from her bed by Yankee invaders as they searched her home looking for booty to send back to their families up north. An aged woman of the plain folk class was choked into insensibility for refusing to make known the hiding place of a watch, a precious heirloom entrusted to her keeping. Any grave or tomb less than three years of age was open to be robbed by Yankee invaders. Their thinking was that Southerners, knowing Yankees were coming, would have hidden the family gold and silver in these new graves. Many Southern families would have the unspeakable duty of reburying their dead loved ones after the Yankees had pillaged and burned their homes and out buildings—leaving them nothing but their bare hands to move the grave soil in order to cover the face of the dead. Well put by General Sheridan was his proclamation to the Germans that it was his policy to leave the enemy's civilian population with 'nothing but their eyes to cry with.'

"Cherished portraits were cut from their frames or punctured with the point of the bayonet—many of these were portraits of ancestors who had fought in the Revolutionary War back in 1776. Musical instruments were saturated with molasses, and even infants in arms were robbed of their scanty raiment. Often fine homes would be broken into; molasses poured on the floors of bedrooms; and feather mattresses pulled from the bed, cut open, and the feathers scattered on the floor. To quote Shakespeare's character Ariel, 'Hell is empty, and all the devils are here.' These were blue-coated devils who were acting in accordance to the wishes, desires, and orders of those who had seized the reins of government in Washington, DC. Indeed, the entire Yankee nation celebrated each report of atrocity committed upon their former countrymen of the South.

"It now falls upon us, the conquered and occupied people of the South, to point out the irony—no, the arrogance—of our Northern political masters as they complain of the brutal treatment of faraway people on another continent with whom they have never had any political connections. The Yankee is well-known for his ability to pick and choose when he will express moral outrage—it occurs only when his profits are touched. His is a morality of personal and national material, economic and political aggrandizement. To him, morality is a thing of clay to be molded to the form that best suits his interests—and mammon is his god." The room was deathly silent as Dr. Shepherd slowly walked away from the podium.

Uncle Seth stood and began clapping. He was soon joined by twenty or thirty others, while the remainder of the audience stayed seated and politely clapped. This was more instructive to the old Confederate veteran than anything the speaker had said. The South desperately wanted to be an equal part of the "reunited" country, but the price of admittance was to be a loyal servant of the Federal Empire. Unquestioned support of the empire's wars and economic policies were the dues. Many a man in the audience had sons who proudly wore the uniform of the reunited country, and to question the empire's policy would be seen as being unsupportive of the men who were in uniform. Nationalism had replaced patriotism in the reunited country. Questioning the nation was unpatriotic. The South was desperately seeking to convince the North that it was loyal to the old flag—if for no other reason to avoid the re-imposition of Reconstruction. And the South's glorious politicians were anxious to partake in the spoils of political power available to those who controlled the Empire.

As the old man left the room, he could not help but think that the greatest disaster of the entire war was that the South took the surrender at Appomattox too literally. General Lee was forced to surrender an exhausted and depleted army. He did not surrender the principle of self-government or the right of "we the people" of the South to live under a government ordered upon the American principle of the consent of the governed. While the Army of the Confederate States of America was forced to surrender, the government of the Confederate States of America never surrendered and lives on in the hearts of those true Southerners who love liberty and simply want government to leave them alone. And this is the key to the Yankee's continuing efforts to destroy the Southern people; they know that their empire will never be completely secure as long as even one true Southerner remains. They then devote great efforts to propagandize each generation of Southerners and turn them into second-class Yankees who will dutifully seat themselves upon the stool of eternal repentance. This, after all, is the roll required of Southerners in the Federal Empire.

§ Deo Vindice §

ON THE SKIRMISH LINE WITH UNCLE SETH
"But old things have passed away, and new things have come to take their place. A violent, revolutionary faction had seized the United States government and as in the case of all revolution, coarse and vulgar men had risen to the surface."

—Admiral Semmes

91

Uncle Seth Replies: The South Started the War at Fort Sumter

"The South was the aggressor in the Civil War," wrote a Yankee journalist. "It fired the first shot at Fort Sumter, which left Lincoln no choice but to use military force to preserve the Union."

Uncle Seth could already feel his blood boiling after reading just this first sentences of the article. Anxious to be able to respond to this journalist in turn, he sat down to begin crafting a reply. "First let us deal with the last point made by the Yankee journalist/ propagandist when he proudly defends the tyrant Lincoln for preserving the Union," Uncle Seth began. "The Constitution requires the president of the United States to take an oath of office in which he swears to uphold and preserve the Constitution. There is nothing in the Constitution or the traditions of the United States prior to 1861 that would indicate that the president has authority to wage aggressive war to prevent a sovereign state from withdrawing from the Union. But, with reference to the idea of preserving the Union, this too, is a fallacy. The Union still existed even after the secession of the Southern states. Its geographic domain was reduced by the number of sovereign states that no longer desired to remain in compact with the Yankee-controlled Union, but the Union remained. The Union—also referred to as the Federal government or United States of America—was not threatened by invasion or violent disruption from outside forces. There is not a single word in the Constitution implying that the president, Congress, or the Federal Supreme Court has the authority to wage war on sovereign states that freely elected to withdraw from the Union. Lincoln, just like all tyrants, merely assumed this right and dressed his actions in convoluted, unfounded, unprecedented, tortuous reasoning and sophisms. Preserving the Union is not a constitutional rationale to wage aggressive war against sovereign states that freely elect to withdraw from a compact that they, as sovereign states, had previously voluntarily entered into.

"The Federal Empire's propagandists have often claimed that the South was the aggressor because we fired the 'first' shot at Fort Sumter. Therefore, the Federal government was forced to respond with force. In other words:

because the South expelled from Southern territory an armed force of foreign (Yankee) troops holding a threatening position near civilian and commercial centers, the South deserved the horrors of Yankee invasion, pillaging, raping, and occupation that resulted from the war we initiated. But such assertions avoid the most relevant question: Did the Southern states have the right to remove themselves from the Union?

"Americans today, due to the impact of years of Yankee propaganda, actually believe that secession is an un-American, illegal, and hostile act. But the truth is that in 1860 secession was a generally accepted right of all sovereign states. The radical abolitionist William Lloyd Garrison once suggested that the non-slaveholding states of the North should secede from the Union. The American Anti-Slavery Society passed a resolution declaring it the duty of abolitionists to support the effort to secede from the U.S. government and to dissolve the American Union. The *New York Tribune,* a leading organ of the Republican Party, declared in 1860:

> We hold, with Jefferson, to the inalienable right of communities to alter or abolish forms of governments that have become oppressive or injurious; if the cotton States shall decide that they can do better out of the Union than in it, we insist on letting them go in peace . . . we shall resist all coercive measures designed to keep her in. We hope to never live in a republic whereof one section is pinned to the residue by bayonets.

This is not the only Northern publication that held this view; the *New York Herald* likewise boldly proclaimed:

> Each State is organized as a complete government . . . possessing the right to break the tie of the confederation as a nation might break a treaty and to repel coercion as a nation might repel invasion. Coercion, if it were possible, is out of the question.

"Mr. James S. Thayer made a speech in New York on January 31, 1861, in which he declared, 'We can at least, in a practical manner, arrive at the basis of a peaceable separation.' This declaration was met with cheers from the crowd. He continued by warning that Lincoln's incoming administration was attempting to carry out a plan to 'construct a scaffolding for coercion. . . . What is the duty of the State of New York? That the Union must be preserved? But if that cannot be, what then? Peaceable separation . . . in friendly relations with another Confederacy.' This declaration was also met with cheers from the gathered crowd. Another Northern newspaper, the *Union* of Bangor, Maine, added its voice in favor of the right of secession by declaring, 'From one end of the State to the other let the cry of the Democracy be, COMPROMISE OR PEACEABLE SEPARATION!'

"From the above cited historical accounts—as opposed to the propagandist ramblings of Yankee-educated journalists—it can be seen that the concept of secession was well-known and accepted in America in 1860. But notice that Mr. Thayer made note that Lincoln's incoming administration was already devising means to coerce the sovereign states of the South and force the South to accept a government based not on the free and unfettered consent of the people of the South but on coercive power of massed Yankee bayonets. This then brings forth the question: Of the two opposing nations, the United States of America and the Confederate States of America, which nation pursued efforts directed to maintain peace and which nation pursued efforts directed toward initiating war?

"Judge Crawford was the first member of the Confederate Peace Commission to arrive in Washington, DC. He arrived February 27, 1861, several days before Lincoln's inauguration as president of the United States. An official communication from the Confederates States of America declared in part that the Confederate States were 'animated by an earnest desire to unite and bind together our respective countries by friendly ties.' This was presented to President Buchanan in the last few days of his administration because the South had received notice that President Buchannan would be willing to send any message received to the United States Senate. But, by the time the message was received, President Buchannan was in dread of his life due to the agitated condition then consuming many radicals who were coming into power in the United States as a result of Lincoln's election. Out of fear for his personal safety, the outgoing president refused to send any message to the Senate or engage in any other official business. Judge Crawford noted the 'feverish and emotional condition of affairs' in Washington at the time. On March 4, 1861, Lincoln was sworn in as president of the United States.

"The Confederate Commissioners sent copies of their papers to William Seward, the United States secretary of state, on March 12, informing him of their presence and declaring the peaceful and friendly purpose of their mission and requesting an appointment to discuss these matters as soon as possible. There was still hope for peace in many sections of the North. On March 15, Sen. Stephen A. Douglas from Illinois introduced a resolution in the U.S. Senate to withdraw all U.S. forces from the forts in the seceded states. The Confederate Commissioners hoped that their efforts to extend the olive branch of peace to the Lincoln administration would be accepted and war adverted.

"Now, what was the response by Lincoln's government to the expressed desire of peace by the Confederate States of America to the administrations of both Presidents Buchannan and Lincoln? No written answer was given to the Confederate Commissioners until twenty-seven days *after* the Confederate message had been delivered to the United States government. The Confederate Commissioners were kept waiting by continual oral assurances that the new administration desired to settle the matters concerning Forts Sumter and Pickens and other issues. The official Confederate delegation was kept waiting for a devious purpose—to give Lincoln time to organize an invasion that would force the South to 'fire the first shot.'

"When Mr. Seward finally did reply in writing, his paper was dated March 15; but the document did not have an address or signature! It had nothing that could signify that it was anything official. But more importantly, it was not delivered to the Confederate Commissioners until April 8! As I will demonstrate, this date was important because in the ensuing time the Lincoln administration had been busy secretly planning at least two separate sneak attacks on the Confederate States of America— the original date set for such an attack was April 9, but due to storms at sea the naval force was delayed, giving the South time to discover the impending invasion of Charleston and react appropriately to defend itself.

"From the time of South Carolina's and Florida's secessions, there had been an armistice in place first between the United States, South Carolina, and Florida and then, after its formation, the Confederate States of America. This armistice was an arrangement by all parties in which they agreed to maintain their current positions and engage in no movements or activities until a peaceful resolution could be worked out by the governments of the United States and the Confederate States. It was established in South Carolina on December 6, 1860, and in Pensacola, Florida, on January 29, 1861. Both documents are on file in the United States War and Navy Departments. South Carolina agreed not to attack Major Anderson, who was at that time holding Fort Moultrie at Charleston. At the same time, Florida officials agreed not to attack Fort Pickens at Pensacola. International law recognizes the principle that to violate an armistice is in fact an act of war. This includes preparing an action against the area or location concerned in the armistice as well as visiting that area with the intention of advising on or undertaking enhancements to the area's defenses. Lincoln's administration—within eight days of his inauguration of president—committed such acts of war, all the while assuring the Confederate Peace Commission of the United States' peaceful intentions. Deceit to hide an invasion is also an act of war.

"United States Captain Vogdes was sent to reinforce Fort Pickens in

January of 1861, before Lincoln became president, but he was prevented from doing so by the terms of the armistice that had been agreed upon between the contending parties. A Captain Barron (U.S.) made a report to Washington that good faith was being observed by both parties according to the status quo agreement then in force at Fort Pickens. When Lincoln became president and learned that Captain Vogdes had not reinforced Fort Pickens, he issued instructions to complete the mission anyway. The order was given on March 12, 1861, by General Scott. Captain Vogdes, then aboard the USS *Brooklyn* outside of Pensacola Harbor, subsequently issued an order to Captain Adams, Commanding Naval Forces, who was off the coast of Pensacola, to land Captain Vogdes' troops and supplies on Fort Pickens, thereby reinforcing Yankee forces holding the fort. Captain Adams refused this order. He said:

> It would be considered not only a declaration but an act of war; and would be resisted [by the South] to the utmost. Both sides are faithfully observing the agreement entered into by the United States government and Mr. Mallory and Colonel Chase, which binds us not to reinforce Fort Pickens.

"Gideon Wells, Lincoln-appointed United States secretary of navy, rebuked Captain Adams and sent orders declaring 'it being the wish and the intention of the Navy Department to cooperate with the War Department, in that object.' During the night of April 11, 1861, the USS *Brooklyn* landed troops and marines to reinforce Fort Pickens—an act of war. The next day, the South was compelled to fire on Fort Sumter to prevent a similar reinforcement from an invasion fleet then lying off its cost.

"At the same time, the government in Washington was busy conspiring to reinforce Fort Sumter in Charleston Harbor. On December 20, 1860, Major Anderson (U.S.) occupied Fort Moultrie and remained there as per the armistice entered into between the United States and the government of South Carolina. The agreement established that neither side would take *any* hostile actions but would maintain the status quo while waiting for the contending governments to work out a peaceful resolution. Major Anderson, in open violation of the agreement, destroyed Fort Moultrie's military equipment and evacuated Fort Moultrie and moved his troops to Fort Sumter. Fort Sumter was unoccupied and had not been occupied by South Carolina in accordance with the status quo agreement. Major Anderson's action was a breach of the arrangement. Moreover, it was an act of war ordered by Washington. The United States government sent the *Star of the West* to secretly reinforce Fort Sumter but was prevented from entering Charleston Harbor by the watchful efforts of local defenders. This occurred on January 9, 1861. Following this first unsuccessful effort, another plan was devised. On February 6, 1861, Lieutenant Fox (U.S.) met with Lieutenant Hall (U.S.), who had been sent from Fort Sumter by Major Anderson to discuss efforts to reinforce Fort Sumter. Again note that these were acts of war in violation of the status quo agreement then in place and being honored by the South Carolina officials.

"On March 15, 1861, Secretary of State Seward sent a message to the Confederate Peace Commission declaring, 'Sumter will be evacuated in ten days . . . there is no intent to reinforce Fort Sumter.' Yet by March 19 Lieutenant Fox was dispatched from Washington under the pretense of peace and thereby gained permission from Southern authorities to enter Fort Sumter. Once safely in the fort, he urged Major Anderson to hold out until April 15. Fox then returned to Washington. On March 20, Seward repeated that Lincoln's government had no intention of reinforcing Fort Sumter. These messages were communicated to the Confederate Peace Commissioners through Judge Campbell, who had been selected by Seward. Later Judge Campbell verified that these communications did in fact occur.

"On March 30 Lincoln sent Lieutenant Fox to New York to prepare three warships capable of transporting two hundred troops to Fort Sumter. He was to have them ready to depart by April 6. Lincoln's orders were marked "private." On the same day, March 30, Judge Campbell asked Seward about rumors that had reached the Confederate authorities concerning a pending, secretly planned U.S. attack on Fort Sumter. On April 1, Seward once again declared to Judge Campbell, 'There is no design to reinforce Fort Sumter.'

"The rumors that Lincoln's government was planning to initiate a war were so widespread that Virginian John Baldwin, a pro-Union man, met with Lincoln on April 4 and urged him to issue a 'peaceful union proclamation.' Lincoln's reply was, 'I fear you are too late.' As John Baldwin was leaving Lincoln's office, he met and spoke with several Northern war governors who were waiting to meet with Lincoln. They came to encourage the president to do whatever was necessary to prevent the Southern states from leaving the Union. On April 5, Lincoln's secretary of the Navy, Gideon Wells, issued a 'confidential' order detailing four U.S. steamers comprising 'a naval force . . . to be sent to the vicinity of Charleston, South Carolina.' By April 12, a Yankee invasion fleet with troops on board was lying offshore Charleston Harbor. The weather prevented it from attempting entry. However, with an invasion fleet offshore, the South had no choice but to reduce a foreign military position that had been secretly established within its borders. International law recognizes the fact that it is he who makes the first shot necessary who is responsible for causing the war—not the one who is forced to defend himself by firing on an approaching invader.

"When determining who started the war, it is important to determine who had more to gain from war. When wars do occur, they are usually begun in self-defense or by a desire for gain—typically material gain such as land and resources to be exploited by the aggressor. Because the South's economy was primarily based on agriculture, it had little to gain from a war with an emerging industrial empire. As a new nation with a smaller population and no formal international connections, its interests would be promoted by pursuing a policy of peace. The early dispatching of the Confederate Peace Commissioners is evidence of the South's desire to avoid conflict. The South did not threaten its larger and more powerful neighbor to the North. It did not call for the raising of large armies to invade and occupy the territory of the North. It did not seek to establish threatening fortifications within the territory of any sovereign state in the North. It did not seek to change fortifications originally established to protect local citizens into hostile military encampments designed to intimidate citizens into accepting the rule of a foreign power. But most of all, it did not promise peace while secretly conspiring to initiate aggressive war. These were the acts of the United States of America. They were motivated by the love of money and material riches that belonged to the people of the South, a people whose wealth the North had coveted for so long. The driving factors were Northern political and commercial interests in maintaining the stream of money coming into the Federal treasury from the South and to be able to maintain a protective tariff that allowed Northern industry to avoid direct competition from abroad. As the Manchester, New Hampshire, *Union Democrat* declared, 'The Southern Confederacy will not employ our ships or buy our goods . . . It is very clear that the South gains by this process, and we lose. No—we MUST NOT let the South go.' The *New York Times* was even more direct when it declared, 'We were divided and confused till our pockets were touched.' So now, who had more to gain from initiating a war—the North or the South?

"U.S. Senator Lane from Oregon noted the crafty efforts of the Lincoln administration to initiate war with the Confederate States of America by using the excuse that the South had seized Federal properties. On March 2, 1861, he declared:

> Sir, if there is, as I contend, the right of secession, then, whenever a State exercise that right, this Government has no laws in that State to execute,

nor has it any property in any such State . . . No, sir; the policy [of the Lincoln administration] is to inveigle [trick] the people of the North into civil war, by masking the design in smooth and ambiguous terms.

"Lincoln, the Northern war governors, and Northern commercial/ banking interests wanted to keep the riches of the South under their domain to be exploited at their leisure. They knew that the people of the North would not support an aggressive war to enrich a few; but the people of the North could be induced to support a war if the South could be made to look like the aggressor. This was Lincoln's plan from the day he was elected up to April 12, 1861, when that plan was finally realized. In closing, the following timeline documents Lincoln's secret plan to initiate war. Let historical facts, not emotions and Yankee propaganda, decide the truth as to who initiated the War of 1861-65. You will see that during the time the Southern peace delegates were intentionally kept waiting, the Lincoln administration was putting their plan for an invasion in place."

Date	Event
November 6, 1860	Lincoln wins the presidential election.
December 6, 1860	Armistice between the U.S. and South Carolina, an agreement to maintain the status quo until peaceful negotiations can take place, is put into effect.
December 20, 1860	South Carolina secedes.
December 26, 1860	South Carolina's peace commissioner arrives in Washington and is met with indifference from the U.S. president and other officials.
	Maj. Anderson (U.S.) violates the armistice agreement and occupies Fort Sumter.
January 9, 1861	U.S. sends *Star of the West* to reinforce Fort Sumter.
	Sen. Jefferson Davis visits President Buchanan, asking him to avoid steps toward war.
January 10, 1861	Florida secedes.
January 21, 1861	Sen. Jefferson Davis delivers his Farewell Address to the Senate, stating he hopes for peaceful relations with the U.S.
January 29, 1861	Armistice between the U.S. and Florida as it relates to Fort Pickens is put into effect, agreeing to maintain the status quo.

February 2, 1861	Captain Barron (U.S.) reports that good faith is being observed by both parties at Fort Pickens.
February 6, 1861	Lieutenant Fox (U.S.) meets with Lieutenant Hall (U.S.), who had been sent from Fort Sumter to discuss reinforcing the fort.
February 18, 1861	Jefferson Davis becomes president of the Confederate States.
March 1-28, 1861	The U.S. Senate is in executive session but receives no information regarding Lincoln's secret plan to initiate war. They adjourn March 28 without discussing the matter. (Only Congress has constitutional authority to declare war.)
March 4, 1861	Lincoln becomes president of the United States.
March 12, 1861	The Confederate States' peace commissioners present their request for peaceful relations with the U.S. and are ready to negotiate peace with the U.S. The U.S. government refuses to deal directly with the Confederate peace commissioners and appoints Judge Campbell as a go-between. The U.S. government orders Captain Vogdes of the USS *Brooklyn* to reinforce Fort Pickens. M. Blair of Lincoln's cabinet telegraphs Lieutenant Fox to prepare for the reinforcement of Fort Sumter.
March 15, 1861	Seward assures Confederate peace commissioners via Judge Campbell, "Sumter will be evacuated in ten days . . . there is no intent to reinforce Ft. Sumter." Senator Douglas (D-Illinois) introduces a resolution calling for the withdrawal of all U.S. forces in the seceded states.
March 19, 1861	Lieutenant Fox is sent from Washington, under pretext of a peaceful mission, to Fort Sumter and once there urges Major Anderson to hold out until April 15. He then returns to Washington to report.
March 20, 1861	Seward repeats his false assurances regarding reinforcing Fort Sumter.
March 29, 1861	Lincoln delivers a secret order to his secretary of

the navy: "I desire expedition . . . 6th of April . . . cooperate with the Sec. of War."

March 30, 1861   Lincoln sends Lieutenant Fox to New York to prepare three warships to transport two hundred troops to Ft. Sumter. The orders, marked "private," instruct Fox to be ready to leave by April 6.

Judge Campbell asks Seward about rumors that had reached C.S.A. authorities regarding a pending U.S. attack on Fort Sumter. Seward denies the rumors.

March 31, 1861   Captain Vogdes of the USS *Brooklyn* receives orders to reinforce Fort Pickens.

April 1861   Lincoln issues orders to "all officers of the Army & Navy . . . to aid Col. Brown . . . resupply Ft. Pickens."

April 1, 1861   Captain Adams (U.S.) refuses to reinforce Fort Pickens, stating that "both sides are faithfully observing the agreement entered into by the U.S."

Seward tells Judge Campbell that Campbell would receive notice of any change to "the existing status of Fort Pickens" and that there was "no design to reinforce Ft. Sumter."

U.S. Army HQ issues orders to reinforce Fort Pickens, noting, "The object and destination of this expedition will be communicated to no one."

Lincoln orders Lieutenant D. D. Porter to "go to New York without delay, assume command of any steamer available and proceed to Pensacola Harbor. . . . This order would be communicated to no person."

Lincoln sends order to commandant of the navy yard in Brooklyn, New York, to "fit out the *Powhatan* without delay . . . [for] Lt. Porter. . . . She [*Powhatan*] is bound on secret service; you will under no circumstances communicate to the Navy Department."

April 2, 1861   Colonel Brown of the U.S. army receives orders from Army HQ to reinforce Fort Pickens.

April 4, 1861   Lincoln replies to John Baldwin's peace request by telling him, "I fear you are too late."

As Baldwin leaves his meeting with Lincoln, he meets

and speaks with several Northern war governors. They were there to urge Lincoln to do whatever was necessary to keep the Southern states under Union control.

April 5, 1861	Lincoln's secretary of the navy issues a confidential order for four U.S. steamers that would compose "a naval force . . . to be sent to the vicinity of Charleston, South Carolina."
April 6, 1861	The U.S. secretary of the navy rebukes Captain Adams for refusing to occupy Fort Pickens. The secretary makes it clear that it is "the wish and intention of the Navy Department to cooperate with the War Department in that objective."
April 11, 1861	Lt. J. L. Worden (U.S.) is sent on a secret mission to Fort Pickens and tells C.S.A. General Bragg he was there to deliver a peaceful message to Captain Adams (U.S.). In reality, Worden brings orders from Washington to cooperate with efforts to reinforce Fort Pickens.
	The USS *Brooklyn*, in violation of the armistice agreed to by both parties, lands troops and supplies at Fort Pickens. This order was originally issued a month previously, on March 12, 1861.
April 12, 1861	With a Yankee invasion fleet off its coast, the C.S.A. is forced to fire on Fort Sumter as an act of self-defense.
April 13, 1861	Justice Campbell of the U.S. Supreme Court sends a letter to Seward declaring, "What is going on at Ft. Sumter . . . Lincoln . . . proximate cause." In other words, a judge appointed by the Lincoln administration puts the blame for the war on the North.

§ Deo Vindice §

ON THE SKIRMISH LINE WITH UNCLE SETH
"When the passions of the day shall have subsided and all the evidence shall have been collected . . . the answer by History [why the North invaded the South]: The lust of *empire* impelled them to wage against their weaker neighbors a war of subjugation" (emphasis added).
 —Jefferson Davis, president, Confederate States of America

92

Virginia Military Institute Cadets at New Market

The boys were having a great time drilling and pretending to be Confederate soldiers. They would often ask Uncle Seth to drill them just like the real soldiers did during the War for Southern Independence. The old Confederate veteran loved to use times like this as an opportunity to pass on to the next generation of young Southerners small stories that were part of their Southern heritage.

"Come over here, boys, and I will tell you about the charge of the Virginia Military Institute cadets at the Battle of New Market. Look. I have a copy of a photograph recently published in the Jackson newspaper showing one of the cadets when he was at VMI and then years later as a grown man after the war," Uncle Seth said as he held up the newspaper. The boys came over to the old Confederate veteran more out of love and respect for the old man than any desire to stop their playing and learn something.

"You see, this is Francis Lee Smith. He was one of the fourteen- to eighteen-year-old cadets who charged a heavily defended Yankee position, overwhelmed the defenders, and captured the Yankee position and its artillery battery. As I recall, there were around 250 cadets and several artillery pieces that came from VMI to answer the call to help defend the Shenandoah Valley from Yankee invasion. It says here that Cadet Smith was wounded as the heroes charged across the wheat field toward the Yankee lines. He was shot in the chin, the bullet passing through his neck and barely missing his carotid artery. As he fell from that wound, he received another Yankee bullet in the shoulder, which broke his collar bone. A total of forty-seven cadets were wounded in the battle and ten were killed. Seven of the ten VMI cadets who were killed belonged to the freshman class.

Pre- and post-war photographs of VMI Cadet F. L. Smith

"You all remember that I have told you about how most of the cadets were wearing dress shoes because as students they did not have boots. Well, as they charged across the freshly plowed wheat field, the soft soil actually pulled the shoes off many of the boys' feet. So they completed the charge barefooted. They were brave young boys who had to become men in the heat of battle in order to defend their homes and country from a vicious invader. Even the Yankees were impressed with the VMI cadets. One of the Yankee officers wrote:

> During that time those boys marked time, dressed their ranks, and when again aligned on the left came forward in the most admirable form. The whole thing was done with as much precision and steadiness as if on parade and this while all the time subjected to a destructive fire. No one who saw it will ever forget it. In after times around our camp fire the gallant conduct of those little fellows was spoken of among ourselves and always in terms of the highest commendation.

That is a rather high complement coming from the men who were trying to kill those little fellows during the battle.

"It says here that one of the Confederate officers at New Market was Col. George S. Patton, VMI class of 1852. His son also graduated from VMI, class of 1877, and his grandson George Patton attended one year at VMI before transferring to West Point. The last Patton with links to VMI just completed a tour of duty with the American Expeditionary Force during the Great War in Europe.

"You know those fellows deserve to be remembered. But, because they have no country to erect monuments to honor their sacrifice, it falls to us to remember them. Their deeds of valor are equal to the heroic charge of the British Light Brigade, but they have no warrior poets to remember them. Their gallantry should be as cherished as Spain cherishes the memory of the Battle of Roncesvalles Pass, when all her gallant men led by Roland died, but no songs are sung to their memory. Their fortitude should be memorialized like Jackson at the Battle of New Orleans, where the English invaders were dealt a terrible defeat, but they have no nation to honor them with towns and monuments. And, what is even worse, the victor uses his ill-gotten power and usurped authority to slander the Cause for which those young fellows fought and died." The old man exhaled, trying to check his feeling of utter contempt for those people who invaded, conquered, and now occupy his Southern nation. The boys knew this was a sign to leave the old Confederate soldier alone with his memories, with his dreams.

§ Deo Vindice §

93

Uncle Howard Divinity, Black Confederate and Hometown Character

It was a beautiful, warm morning, April 26, 1917. Uncle Seth had come to Hazlehurst with his grandson Lloyd to give the young man a chance to see the annual parade of Hazlehurst school children as they marched to the Confederate cemetery to honor the men who wore the gray in the War for Southern Independence. Mississippi had selected April 26 as the day when the living would pay homage to the dead soldiers of the Confederate States of America. Mississippians would always claim that their ladies were the first Southern ladies to begin the tradition of Decoration Day, which would later be known as Memorial Day. Uncle Seth and Lloyd followed the children as they moved toward the cemetery, each child carrying a collection of Paul's Scarlet roses in their small hands. It was part of the tradition for the children to stop at Mrs. S. C. Caldwell's home. Once there they would cut roses from a rose trellis in her yard to decorate the graves. As Uncle Seth and Lloyd followed the children into the cemetery, they both took off their hats as a sign of respect to the fallen.

"Uncle Seth, look over there," Lloyd whispered, "what are those two tombstones doing outside of the chain border marking the resting place of the other soldiers?"

"That's where unknown Yankee soldiers are buried. We did not want to have Yankees lying beside the men they were trying to kill, so we buried them outside the Confederate grave site," responded Uncle Seth. "When the children have placed their red roses on all of our graves, they will also take flowers over to those two graves and decorate them because they were soldiers, too."

Each grave was decorated with red roses and red and white ribbons—the colors of the Confederate Stars and Bars—and a Confederate battle flag was proudly posted at the cemetery's entrance. The children sang "Dixie" and a local pastor gave the benediction. This scene would be repeated all across the South; although in the more northern regions of Dixie it would usually occur on June 6, Pres. Jefferson Davis' birthday, because the flowers bloomed much later up there than down in the deep South.

After the benediction, as folks were leaving, several of the children came over and asked Uncle Seth if he was "one of our soldiers." Uncle Seth replied that he was, but he was not nearly as famous as Copiah County's famous black Confederate Uncle Howard Divinity.

"Come here and I will tell you about this unique man who made life so much more bearable for those of us who were lucky enough to be in his unit," Uncle Seth encouraged.

"Uncle Howard Divinity—you all know that we refer to elderly black men as 'Uncle' out of respect—well he was one of the last of the 'tree talkers' from deep within Bayou Pierre swamp. He was certainly the last one living here in Copiah County. He claimed to be 108 years old the year he died. According to folklore, a tree talker is a conjurer with great magical powers. Uncle Howard Divinity claimed he got his powers from his mother, who was a witch—perhaps a voodoo queen from down in New Orleans. It always seemed strange to us that a man who claimed to be the son of a witch and possess magical powers would have 'Divinity' as a last name. Well, he used his 'powers' to help scavenge many a chicken for his mess mates during the war. He was there with us during the entire war. After the war ended, he always attended annual reunions and was an honored part of our local camp of the United Confederate Veterans. I recall that one year just before his death he wanted to attend the annual reunion but did not have the financial ability. When the ex-service men from Copiah County heard about Uncle Howard Divinity's dilemma, they took up a collection—a love offering, as it was called—and paid the cost of his trip. Shortly after his last reunion the old man died. He had no family other than his Confederate comrades and no one to pay for his funeral. The Charles E. Hooker chapter of the United Daughters of the Confederacy paid for the funeral of Copiah County's black Confederate. One of the ladies from Copiah County, Ruth Bass, wrote about Uncle Howard in *Scribner's Magazine*. Now that his story has been published in a famous magazine, Uncle Howard Divinity will be remembered long after we have taken our resting place over there." Uncle Seth pointed over to the Confederate section of the cemetery.

§ Deo Vindice §

On the Skirmish Line with Uncle Seth

"In that part of the Union where the Negroes are no longer slaves, have they come closer to the whites? Everyone will have noticed just the opposite. Race prejudice seems stronger in those states that have abolished slavery than in those where it still exists and nowhere is it more intolerant than in those states where slavery never existed. In the South less trouble is taken to keep the Negro apart."

—Alexis de Tocqueville, circa 1840

94

Two Confederate Cannons Defeat
Yankee Army

Joe William was excited about a history lesson he had at school and was eager to tell Uncle Seth about the heroic three hundred Greeks who held off tens of thousands of Persian invaders at Thermopylae. "Yes, those were brave men whose sacrifice encouraged the rest of the Greek states and gave them enough time to organize for final victory," commented Uncle Seth, trying not to be outmatched by the young boy's newfound knowledge of military history.

"Did we ever have a battle like that during the war?" asked Joe William.

Uncle Seth was pleased with the way the young boy phrased his question. Joe William unconsciously identified himself with the Confederacy—"did *we*," he had asked. Uncle Seth understood—and knew the Yankee government understood—that the Federal Empire would not be secure as long as succeeding generations of Southerners identified themselves as Confederates. "Well, we had many a battle against overwhelming odds, but at the 1927 annual reunion of the United Confederate Veterans, J. W. Owens, from Annapolis, Maryland, gave an account of a battle in which his artillery unit and one other held off an entire Yankee army. He said that by the time they were reenforced all but one or two of their men were killed or wounded," Uncle Seth explained.

"What happened, Uncle Seth?" Joe William's interest in ancient history was suddenly sidetracked by his natural interest in the history of his people.

"As I recall, J. W. said the fight took place June 15, 1863, during the defense of a bridge near Stephenson's Depot, Virginia. Col. Richard Snowden Andrews had two artillery pieces and was given instructions to prevent the invading Yankees from passing over the bridge. The Yankee army—Milroy's army, I believe—was attempting to flank General Lee's army. The invader's plan was to capture and destroy Harper's Ferry, Virginia. Colonel Andrews was given orders to take a detachment from his battalion and hurry toward Winchester to occupy the Martinsburg road and block the invader's movement. Colonel Andrews placed two guns of Dement's Battery at the bridge. These guns were under the command of Lt. C. S. Contee. The lieutenant was given orders to hold the bridge as long as he had a man left to work a gun. Now the Yankee invaders had several thousand men, and these poor boys had only enough to work two guns: fifteen men in all. J. W. gave an exciting description of the Yankees' repeated attempts to force their way across the bridge.

"He said that it all started in early dawn. He could hear the crack of gunfire across the bridge and knew that our pickets had engaged the advanced portion of the Yankee army. Before long our pickets were pushed back across the bridge and moved to the rear, leaving the bridge to be held by two Confederate artillery pieces. Our artillerymen were exhausted from the forced march during the previous two nights; they had had very little rest and almost no food for the past several days. The men were so exhausted that some of them were sleeping as they leaned against their cannons! All of a sudden the order rang out: 'Attention, battalion! Drivers, mount! Cannoneers, to your post! Trot out! March!' While our artillerymen were preparing their pieces for action, they could see the well-dressed column of blue-clad invaders advancing on them at the double quick. The Yankee's plan was to rush across the bridge before our boys could bring their two pieces into action. The order to 'load and fire' was given, but it was not necessary because every man there knew his duty and was already well into it. That is the way a well-trained army conducts itself. The two pieces fired canister shot simultaneously into the advancing Yankee column. J. W. said that it was dreadful to see so many young men cut down like wheat being harvested by a mechanical sickle of death. But it was war; they were the invaders of our homes and we were determined to defend our people. The first blast slowed their advance. They wavered momentarily but then pressed forward. The defenders fired again and this time the enemy broke to the rear. Their officers rallied their men and pushed them forward again and again. Each time they came forward our pieces would mow them down like wheat. By now the Yankees had positioned their sharpshooters and artillery pieces and were pouring deadly fire into the two Confederate cannons. Our brave artillerymen would kill scores and scores of the Yankees, and the Yanks would kill or wound a couple of our men. If the invader was willing to sacrifice his men, it would not be long before they would be tripping over our boys' dead bodies. The Yankees charged the bridge four times and were driven back repeatedly, but each time they would get a little closer to our side of the bridge. You see, as our men were killed or wounded it would take longer and longer for the remaining men to work their artillery piece. By the time of the fourth charge our men were out of canister and had begun to use exploding shot—bombs as we called them," Uncle Seth clarified to make sure Joe William understood.

"According to J. W., by the time of the last charge they were cutting the exploding shot's fuse to go off at a quarter of a second! He didn't know for sure, but it seemed to him that those bombs must have been exploding around fifty to seventy yards in front of the Confederate artillery positions. J. W. said that the exploding shots halted the Yankee's charge even before it was halfway across the bridge. But our boys were out of ammunition and the Yanks knew it! By this time, Colonel Andrews had made it back to Lieutenant Contee to check the status of the resistance at the bridge—he had been occupied in preventing a crossing below the bridge. The colonel was badly wounded but refused to leave his men and neglect his duties. Lieutenant Contee was shot through both legs but raised himself up on his elbows. He reported that thirteen of the fifteen artillerymen were either killed or wounded but proudly confirmed that the enemy had been denied the bridge and was at that time retreating.

"About that time General Walker came up with infantry to support the defense of the bridge. He said that he had never heard anything as sweet as the rousing Rebel Yell given by our boys as they moved forward across the bridge to attack the invaders—who were at that time doing the 'Yankee First Manassas Quick-Step' away from our boys. Before long General Walker had turned the Yankee right flank and the day was won. When Gen. Robert E. Lee heard about the defense at Stephenson's Depot, he said that the heroic sacrifice of those brave men there made it a second Thermopylae.

"J. W. was proud of his unit, the 1st Maryland, because every one of the men who volunteered to fight for Maryland's right to be free had to first escape from Yankee-occupied Maryland. Colonel Andrews was one of the first Marylanders to support the cause of Southern Independence, and he and his fellow Marylanders formed the 1st Maryland. On July 13, 1861, it was mustered into the Confederate army. During the war, Maryland sent more than twenty-two thousand men to serve the cause of Southern liberty.

"So you see, Joe William, we had many battles and actions during the war that were just as daring as those of the ancients at Thermopylae. The only difference is that we did not win our fight against an evil invader—not yet anyway. And as I have told you so often before, those who win the war get to write the history of that war. When they do, it is always their version of history. It will always be a history that favorably portrays their own actions while deliberately distorting the motivations of the losing side and making the invaded people appear to be evil folks. They do that in order to justify or conceal their own evil deeds. But what is even worse is that they then use their bloody bayonets to enforce their version of history and to prevent the defeated nation from telling their side of the story. This is the way empires conqueror and rule their enemies." Uncle Seth suddenly became tired of this story-telling—perhaps he was just tired of fighting against such overwhelming odds.

§ Deo Vindice §

ON THE SKIRMISH LINE WITH UNCLE SETH
"The judiciary of the United States is the subtle corps of sappers and miners constantly working underground to undermine the foundations of our confederated fabric. They are construing our constitution from a coordination of a general and special government to a general and supreme one above. This will lay all things at their feet."
—Thomas Jefferson, December 25, 1820

A supreme Federal government that is the ultimate arbitrator of its own powers under the constitution is the essence of the Federal Empire and absolutely indispensable for the continued political and economic enslavement of the Southern people.

95

The Orleans Cadets

"Well look here," Uncle Seth exclaimed to no one in particular, "my old friend J. Waston Gaine of Amite, Louisiana, has his photograph in the newspaper." Uncle Seth was busy catching up on his reading when he ran across a story published in a local newspaper. Even though it was 1921, the local papers still published articles about the last remaining Confederate veterans.

"Who is Mr. Gaine?" asked Billie Jean as she swept the floor around Uncle Seth's rocking chair.

"He is a veteran I met during the Louisiana annual reunion back in 1903. Do you know where Amite is? It's about twenty miles south of the Louisiana-Mississippi border down around McComb, Mississippi. It is close to Camp Moore, where some Louisiana troops and men from southwest Mississippi were trained during the war.

"The Orleans Cadets were among the first volunteers who left their state at the outbreak of the war. They numbered around one hundred and were commanded by Capt. Charles D. Dreux from New Orleans. Around April 15, 1861, they began their march from New Orleans to Pensacola, Florida. The Yankees occupied Santa Rosa Island several miles off the shore from the naval yard at Pensacola. In early June of 1861, the Orleans Cadets were put together with five other companies to form a battalion, of which Dreux was elected lieutenant colonel. The other companies that composed the new battalion were the Crescent Rifles, Louisiana Guards, Shreveport Grays, and Grivot Guards—this last company was from Terrebonne Parish, deep down in French-speaking Cajun Louisiana. The new Louisiana battalion was rushed to Richmond, Virginia. The recent Battle of Bethel (it occurred June 8) was the reason for the rush. Everyone expected a Yankee attempt to seize the Confederate capitol at Richmond. But the Yankees had second thoughts about whipping the South in ninety days. They pulled back to their lines to a point near Newport News, Virginia.

"Toward the last days of June the Confederates decided to advance toward the Yankee invaders near Newport News to see if they would come out and fight. Well, the Yankees decided to stay behind their defensive lines; after all they only outnumbered us by two to one." Uncle Seth chuckled more in derision of the enemy than humor of his comment.

"Lt. Colonel Dreux was killed in a small action around Newport News while attempting to prevent the Yankees from looting the homes of local civilians. The command of the battalion fell to N. H. Rightor. The newspaper has a photograph of the last six survivors of the gallant Orleans Cadets." The old Confederate veteran held the photograph up for Billie Jean's inspection.

Surviving members of the Orleans Cadets circa 1931

The young girl looked at it with appropriate pretended interest. She loved Uncle Seth—not because of his service to the Cause of Southern liberty but because he was family. She could not comprehend the major changes that had occurred in the South as a result of the loss of the war. All she knew was that all of her kin and neighbors were working hard just to make ends meet. Her South was a South of poverty and sharecroppers. She had heard Uncle Seth tell about the days before the war when Mississippi had more rich men per capita than any state in the United States, but today it was the poorest state in the Union and had no real hope of improving its economic standing. Uncle Seth always claimed that this was because the South is an occupied nation being exploited by the Federal Empire—such things were more than Billie Jean could understand. She would leave such matters to others who hopefully would know what to do.

§ Deo Vindice §

ON THE SKIRMISH LINE WITH UNCLE SETH

The Confederate army "will deservedly rank as the best on this continent. Suffering privations unknown to its opponents, it fought well from the early days to the surrender. Without a doubt it was composed of the best men of the South, rushing to what they considered a defense of their country against a bitter invader; and they took the places assigned them, officer or private, and fought until beaten by superiority of numbers. The North sent no such army to the field, and its patriotism was of easier character. As a matter of comparison we have lately read that from William and Mary College, Virginia, thirty-two out of thirty-five professors and instructors abandoned the college work and joined the army in the field. Harvard College sent one professor from its large corps of [Yankee] professors and instructors."

—Yankee General Charles A. Whittier

96

Reconstruction—Southerners Become
Slaves of the Federal Empire

"Uncle Seth, why is it that you never talk about Reconstruction?" asked Joe William. The young boy was busy trying to complete his homework, which included a history lesson about the South after the surrender at Appomattox. His history teacher had told the class that Reconstruction was a time of progressive change in the South and gave the class a reading assignment from their textbook that covered the ten years of post-war Reconstruction. Uncle Seth always referred to the years of 1866-1876 as the South's "lost decade." It was the time after the war when the Southern people should have spent their scarce resources rebuilding their homes, communities, and states but had to spend it fighting to regain even a small semblance of local self-government. Somehow the young boy felt that what he was reading in his textbook was not the whole story; it seemed too positive about the "good" work of Northern politicians and social workers and very negative about anything concerning the efforts of former Confederates to regain control of their states.

"Joe William," Uncle Seth said with a sigh that indicated great frustration, "look at where your textbook was published. It was published up North and written by self-hating Southerners or self-loving Northerners. You should never accept anything from such people at face value because they have a vested interest in defending the actions of the Federal Empire. They are in fact nothing more than the empire's propagandists who are handsomely rewarded for propagating Yankee lies about the South! Let me tell you about what those people did to our people after they destroyed our country." Joe William knew that when the old veteran used the term "our country" he meant the Confederate States of America, not the United States. The old man rumbled around in the stack of reading material he always kept close to his rocking chair until he found what he was looking for.

"I really do not like talking about Reconstruction because it was such a painful time for the entire South. White and black Southerners suffered greatly during those years, and the evil done to us by the Yankee Empire lives on today to haunt race relations. You have to remember that Reconstruction was not a time of rebuilding but a time in which the ruling elite in Washington, DC set up a system of government that would ensure the death of America's original constitutionally limited Republic of Republics and the ascendancy of a supreme Federal Empire. You cannot understand Yankee-imposed Reconstruction if you do not understand the conditions that we found when we returned from the war.

"In 1866, the year before the Yankee-imposed carpetbagger and scalawag rule was foisted on the State of Mississippi, our legislature voted to spend 20 percent of the state's budget on the purchase of artificial arms and legs! We were returning to our devastated communities and many of the menfolk were crippled and wounded as a result of their honorable service to their country. A huge capital investment in slaves had disappeared. In Louisiana alone more than $170,000,000[1] worth of investments had been swept away. Now, I am not complaining about the abolishment of slavery. But remember that when the Yankees abolished slavery in their states they did it very slowly over many years or merely cashed in their investments by selling their slaves to the South and then re-investing their capital in other commercial enterprises. What was good for the Yankee was not allowed for the South. The poverty caused by this loss of capital would hit all Southerners hard, but it would fall the hardest upon the newly freed slaves. So when we returned home we found nothing but desolation: roads in disrepair, bridges either burned or washed away, railroads and public buildings burned, livestock killed or stolen by the invaders, and agricultural tools destroyed in an effort to force starvation upon the people of the South. But worst of all was the fact that we had no money or capital to begin the arduous task of rebuilding our homes and communities.

"In December of 1865, there were approximately 500,000 white people in Mississippi, Georgia, and Alabama who were without the necessities of life, and many starved to death from lack of food. Robert Somers, an English traveler through Virginia in 1870, described the conditions he found in Virginia five years after the military struggle had ceased: 'It consists for the most part of plantations in a state of semi or complete ruin . . . The trail of war is visible throughout the valley in burnt-up gin-houses, ruined bridges, mills, and factories . . . roads . . . impassable.' Another observer, General Boynton (U.S.), noted the desolation of a once-affluent people: 'A complete set of crockery is never seen, and in very few families is there enough to set a table . . . A set of forks with whole tines is a curiosity.

---

1. To convert 1866 dollars to 2013 dollars (the most-recent data available), multiply it by 14.71.

Clocks and watches have nearly all stopped . . . Hair brushes and tooth brushes have all worn out; combs are broken . . . Pins, needles and thread and a thousand such articles, which seem indispensable to housekeeping are very scarce.'

"Across the South about two thirds of the railroads were hopelessly bankrupt and were eagerly acquired by the United States War Department. 'Loyal' boards were then appointed. But this was just the beginning of our desperate struggle for survival under Yankee-imposed rule.

"Most people nowadays think that after the war the North was magnanimous in its victory and eagerly accepted the South back into their Union. But that is not what happened. A Federal official in Florida described the typical sentiment of the victorious Yankee toward the defeated people of the South when he declared, 'I would pin them down at the point of the bayonet so close that they would not have room to wiggle, and allow intelligent colored people to go up and vote in preference to [white Southerners].' This unbounded Yankee hatred of Southerners, a hatred that had been nurtured by Yankee propagandists for generations prior to the war, was also shown by Yankee General Halleck's order that no weddings would be allowed until the bride, groom, and officiating clergyman took an ironclad oath of allegiance to the 'one nation indivisible,' the Union. He said that he issued the order because he wanted to prevent 'the propagation of legitimate rebels.' This anti-South hatred was evident throughout the Federal government. The president of the United States— Andrew Johnson, a self-hating Southerner—demonstrated his hatred for Southerners by declaring that the Southern people were 'traitors' [and] should take a back seat in the work of restoration. . . . My judgment is that he [a Southern Rebel] should be subjected to a severe ordeal before he is restored to citizenship. Treason should be made odious, and traitors must be punished and *impoverished*.' According to our enemies, 'we the people' of the South were traitors because we dared to ask to live in a country ordered upon the American principle of the consent of the governed. We were evil because we dared to ask to be free of the domination of a Yankee nation that hated us and wanted to exterminate us.

"Rep. Thaddeus Stevens from Pennsylvania declared that 'Congress should punish the rebels' and advocated a post-war doctrine essentially adopted by the United States government by which the United States would treat the South 'as a conquered province and settle them [the South] with new men and exterminate or drive out the present rebels as exiles.' Gerrit Smith, a radical Yankee abolitionist, advocated that the victorious North should 'let the only other condition be that the rebel masses shall not, for say, a dozen years, be allowed access to the ballot-box, or be eligible to [hold] office; and that the like restrictions be for life on their political and military leaders.' This was the general thinking and intention of the United States government; this was the reality 'we the people' of the South faced as a defeated and occupied nation.

"You must remember that the sole purpose of imposing Reconstruction upon the defeated South was to establish a Federal Empire—a nation that would henceforth be controlled by the ruling elite in Washington, DC, and that would never again have its powers limited by the original constitution and the once sovereign states. Their first goal was to change the Constitution by forcing amendments that would make the Federal government the supreme and ultimate judge of its own powers. Thaddeus Stevens led the effort to change the Constitution and planned to use the politically enslaved South to help him and his Radical Republican co-conspirators pervert the Constitution. He advocated that the Southern states should not be allowed to reenter the Union 'until the Constitution shall have been so amended as to make it what the makers intended, and so as to secure perpetual ascendency to the party of the Union.' The Fourteenth and Fifteenth Amendments were pinned to the Constitution with bloody bayonets during Reconstruction, thus accomplishing the desires of those who, since the days of Alexander Hamilton, had dreamed of a supreme federal empire. Remember that those amendments were enacted against the expressed will of 'we the people' of the South. As a matter of fact they were never legitimately ratified!

"As early as 1862, Thaddeus Stevens declared in Congress that the purpose of the war was to hang the leaders of the South, arm the newly freed blacks, and confiscate the land and property of white Southerners. He boasted: 'Our generals have a sword in one hand and shackles in the other.' In 1863, this same Yankee Congressman declared, 'The South must be punished under the rules of war, its land confiscated. . . . These offending States . . . [shall be] dealt with by the laws of war and conquest.' He often stated that he planned to treat the Southern states after the war as conquered territory. He even boasted that they planned to 'turn Mississippi into a frog pond.' Remember, only empires have 'conquered' territories. The United States of America that emerged from the war was not the Jeffersonian Republic of Republics that our Colonial forefathers designed—it had become a cruel and evil empire. The *London Telegraph* explained plainly what had happened to the people of the South by writing that the United States 'may remain a republic in name, but some eight million of the people [Southerners] are subjects, not citizens.' Recall how often I have reminded you that 'we the people' of the South may pretend that we are an equal part of this 're-united country' but are not, in reality, citizens. We are subjects of our political masters in Washington, DC, and our economic masters in New York.

"Even President Johnson saw the efforts of the Radical Republicans in Congress as nothing less than an attempt to enslave the white South. In one of his veto messages, he acknowledged: 'Such a power has not been wielded by any monarch in England for more than five hundred years. In all that time, no people who speak the English language have borne such servitude.' During Reconstruction, the United States of America forced the people of the Confederate States of America to become political and economic slaves to the Federal Empire. This fact was recognized by some in the North. The *New York Herald* observed, 'But it is not right to make slaves of white men even though they may have been former masters of blacks. This is but a change in a system of bondage that is rendered the more odious and intolerable because it has been inaugurated in an enlightened instead of a dark and uncivilized age.' What a despicable history the United States has written—a history of conquest and occupation written with bayonets dipped in Southern blood! But despite the loss of civilized government, the loss of liberty, the enforced impoverishment of an entire people both black and white—despite all of this and more, the greatest loss for the South was in the realm of race relations. Yankee-imposed Reconstruction intentionally set at variance a population that had more in common with each other than either had with the ruling elites in Washington, DC, or the crony capitalists and bankers on Wall Street. The Yankees did it because it benefited their plans for total political control of their Federal Empire.

"The key to Northern political control of the South was the alienation of white and black races. Their continuing plan is to divide the people of the South and turn us into warring camps while Northern politicians would then control the voting of black Southerners. Public corruption and criminal aggression against private persons and property during Yankee-imposed Reconstruction replaced mutual sympathies between white and black Southerners with mutual distrust. During Yankee-imposed Reconstruction, crime became an ever-pressing problem. But most of the crime was committed by the newly freed slaves. Even under a government that they controlled, the crime rate for blacks in the South was almost ten times higher than the crime rate of white Southerners. Most of the criminal activity was against white Southerners. This high rate of criminality caused an ever widening gulf of distrust and fear between white and black Southerners— folks who had stood together during the war.

"Fear was the general feeling of white Southerners during Reconstruction—

fear even when white people were in their own homes. A former Confederate general, Garnett Andrews, noted this even though he had served during the entire war:

> I have never suffered such an amount of anguish and alarm in all my life . . . [as] the fear and alarm and sense of danger which I felt that time. And it was a universal feeling among the population, among the white people . . . It showed on the countenance of the people . . . Men looked haggard and pale . . . I have felt when I laid down that neither myself, nor my wife and children were in safety. I expected, and honestly anticipated, and thought it highly probable, that I might be assassinated and my house set on fire at any time.

"A young Alabama schoolteacher during Reconstruction, Sidney Lanier, responded to a friend who did not live in the South and who had asked how things were 'down South' after the war. Sidney wrote back and told his friend, 'Perhaps you know that with us of the young generation in the South, since the war, pretty much the whole of life has been merely not dying.' When we returned from the war, we found that conditions on the home front were not much better than what we faced on the battlefront; but now, to make matters even worse, we were unarmed, unable to defend ourselves, and we had no friendly government to protect our interest or plead our case to the world.

"Immediately after the war, the United States government decided to make the South pay for the expenses that the invader had incurred during their invasion and conquest of the Confederate States of America. The United States Treasury Department was authorized to seize 'Confederate' cotton. To this end, they sent Yankee agents to the South who were keenly interested in confiscating cotton 'belonging' to the Confederate government. These agents were never negligent in their efforts to acquire personal profits at the expense of the defeated and occupied Southern people. The fraud perpetrated by these United States agents was acknowledged by United States Treasury Department Secretary McCulloch when he noted:

> I am sure I sent some honest cotton agents South; but it sometimes seems doubtful whether any of them remained honest very long . . . Contractors, anxious for gain, were sometimes guilty of bad faith and frequently took possession of cotton and delivered it under contracts as captured or abandoned, when in fact it was not such, and they had no right to touch it. . . . Agents . . . frequently received or collected property, and sent it forward which the law did not authorize. . . . Lawless men, singly and in organized bands, engaged in general plunder; every species of intrigue and peculation and theft were resorted to.

"These agents stole as much as they could for themselves and then turned over to the United States Treasury Department approximately $34,000,000 worth of Southern-grown cotton. This was cotton that should have been used to help restart the Southern economy. But our Yankee masters were not interested in rebuilding their defeated enemy; they were interested in plundering their conquered territory even if it meant the death by starvation of more Southerners. Corruption, fraud, and theft were part of big business in Washington, DC, and this behavior was mirrored by the Yankees' underlings who now, with the aid of bloody bayonets, controlled the South.

"As a result of Yankee-imposed Reconstruction the conquered South was divided into military districts commanded by Yankee generals with tyrannical powers. They often removed high state officers, state governors, and state supreme judges, while our people were left with no legal recourse or means of judicial appeal. Under Yankee rule, enforced by Yankee bayonets, public corruption became an art form. Legislatures of the time issued worthless bonds backed by primarily white state taxpayers. These scallywag legislatures were aided in their efforts by financial agents in New York. The impact of federally sponsored public corruption was evidenced by the rapid decrease in property value across the occupied South. Property values on which real estate taxes are based fell in Alabama by 65 percent; in Florida they fell by 45 percent and in Louisiana dropped between 50 and 75 percent. Many large cities such as Mobile and Memphis were forced to surrender their charter and were ruled directly from the state capitol. And, of course, private property values suffered as well. For example, in 1871 railroad property in Alabama was valued at $26,000,000, but by 1874 it had fallen to a mere $9,500,000.

"Reconstruction Governors Warmoth and Kellogg of Louisiana, who only served one term each, both retired with large fortunes. Warmoth noted, 'Corruption is the fashion. I do not pretend to be honest, but only as honest as anybody in politics.' In another act of legislative excess, the federally controlled legislature of South Carolina purchased a worthless swamp valued at $26,000 for the exorbitant price of $125,000—which, of course, was a cost to state taxpayers. Similarly, the federally controlled legislature of Arkansas provided a grant of $175,000 for the construction of the White River Valley and Texas Railroad, which was never even begun. Such fraud and corruption was happening all across the South during Yankee-imposed Reconstruction. The corruption of government was demonstrated by the ever-increasing tax levies and public debt. The expense of running state governments increased dramatically under federally enforced rule. Alabama and Florida saw a 200 percent increase in the cost of running their state governments; Louisiana saw a 500 percent increase, while Arkansas experienced an astronomical 1,500 percent increase! The total cost of public printing in South Carolina between 1790 and 1868 was $609,000, but for the Reconstruction years of 1868-76 it was $1,326,589.

"Taxes on the impoverished citizens were raised at rates never before seen in North America. Alabama saw a 400 percent increase, Louisiana an 800 percent increase, and Mississippi a 1,400 percent increase! Very few landowners could afford to pay their taxes, so their land was sold at tax auctions. In Mississippi, this was the case with more than six million acres of land—a land mass larger than the Yankee states of Massachusetts and Rhode Island combined. In Louisiana, travelers reported local newspapers in which three-fourths of the newsprint consisted of notices of tax sales. All private property that was offered for sale was subject to a 25 percent sales tax, a shipping fee, and a revenue tax. This form of government confiscation of private property earned the United States Treasury Department approximately $68,000,000. Such confiscatory taxation created a major impediment to the resumption of commerce. Indeed, the destruction wrought by the Federal government during Yankee imposed Reconstruction was merely a continuation of their war against all things Southern, which they continue even today.

"The increased tax burden placed upon the defeated people of the South by the federally controlled state legislatures did not provide enough revenue to satisfy the greed of the newly elected Reconstruction politicians. As a result of political greed, graft, and overall corruption, state debt increased radically in all Southern states under Federal control. For example: in only two years under Federally sponsored Reconstruction, Governor Holden in North Carolina had increased that state's debt from $16,000,000 to $32,000,000; South Carolina's debt rose from $7,000,000 to $29,000,000 by 1873 and more was to come; by 1874 Alabama's debt climbed from $7,000,000 to $32,000,000, and in Louisiana state debt rose from $14,000,000 to $48,000,000. And this was only state debt. Radical increases were also common in cities under Federal control. Debt of the city of Vicksburg, Mississippi, for instance, increased a thousandfold! Many folks noted that it cost us less to defend the city from the Yankee invaders than it did to pay for Yankee administration of the city.

"The Federal government was responsible for the radical increase in the tax levies enacted by Reconstruction legislatures. Each Southern state's legislature had a uniformed Yankee military officer watching over its deliberations. The vast majority of white Southerners were not allowed to vote—forbidden either directly or via intimidation. At the same time, newly freed slaves, most of whom could not read or write, were given the right to vote but, of course, told how to vote by their new Yankee friends. This lead to the election of many state legislators who could not read or write. The barbaric spectacle of a Reconstruction legislature was gleefully described by a Radical Republican journalist, James S. Pike:

> It is barbarism overwhelming civilization by physical force. . . . This dense negro crowd . . . do the debating, the squabbling, the lawmaking, and create all the clamor and disorder of the body. . . . No one is allowed to talk five minutes without interruption, and one interruption is a signal for another and another. . . . Their struggles to get the floor, their bellowing and physical contortions, baffle description.

"These were the defeated South's 'law givers' during the Reconstruction years. The political pillaging of a defeated people became a profession practiced both in Washington, DC, and the various state capitals of the defeated, occupied, and politically enslaved Confederacy. In Mississippi, the state's constitutional convention organized and managed by agents of the Federal government cost over a quarter of a million dollars; four minor Republican newspapers were paid $28,519 for publishing the proceedings.

"The October 14, 1867, edition of the *New York Herald* described how Federal agents managed the black vote in the occupied South: 'The [black] voter got his ticket from the captain, the captain had it from the colonel, and he from the general, and the general of course had it from the owners and managers in Washington of the grand scheme to secure political supremacy.' At first, white Southerners were willing to share power with qualified blacks. However, their initial efforts were abandoned because of the interference of Federal agents sent down South to prevent the rebuilding of a politically effective South. General Beauregard declared in 1866 that 'if the suffrage of the Negro is properly handled and directed we shall defeat our adversaries with their own weapons. The Negro is Southern born. With education and property qualifications he can be made to take an interest in the affairs of the South and in its prosperity.' General Beauregard was not the only one to express a desire to work with the newly freed men of the South. In 1875, while speaking to a gathering of black leaders in Memphis, Tennessee, Gen. Nathan Bedford Forrest declared:

> I do not propose to say anything about politics, but I want you to do as I do—go to the polls and select the best men to vote for. I feel that you are free men, I am a free man, and we can do as we please. . . . Although

we differ in color, we should not differ in sentiment. . . . Do your duty as citizens, and if any are oppressed, I will be your friend.

But as I have already mentioned, the Yankees knew this was a possibility and made every effort to drive the wedge of race hatred between white and black Southerners; the Yankee would then use the black vote to extend their control of the Federal Empire.

"Don't let the Yankees fool you—they wanted nothing to do with blacks. In 1867, only six Northern states allowed blacks to vote, and in those states the number of blacks relative to the white population was so small that their votes had little impact on elections. The Yankee states of Ohio, Michigan, Minnesota, and Kansas had all rejected by popular vote the cause of black suffrage. Even in the Federal capital, a bill to allow black suffrage in Washington, DC, could not pass through a Yankee-controlled Congress.

"So why don't I talk about Reconstruction, Joe William? It is because it was a time in which 'we the people' of the South were punished by the Federal government for merely asking to be left alone and allowed to live in our own country—the Confederate States of America. The ruling elite of the Federal Empire showed no mercy on our people but instead destroyed or stole the few resources we had left. They perverted the original constitutional Republic of Republics and turned it into a supreme Federal government. They planted seeds of race-related bitterness among the Southern people that time may never be able to weed out. But most of all, they turned the once free and self-sufficient people of the South into political and economic slaves of the Federal Empire. All of this was done by those who hate us, and they teach Southern children that it was really a time of progressive social growth—Yankee lies used to maintain their Empire."

The old Confederate veteran seemed unusually tired and distressed. Joe William decided to leave him alone. Usually Uncle Seth was passionate when telling his stories about the war, but this was different. The young boy did not understand. Uncle Seth wondered if the new South would ever understand; would they ever have the courage to reclaim their lost inheritance of liberty?

§ Deo Vindice §

ON THE SKIRMISH LINE WITH UNCLE SETH
"On carefully examining the plan of government [proposed constitution] . . . It appears to be . . . but the first important step, and to aim strongly to one consolidated government of the United States. . . . This consolidation

of the states has been the objective of several men in this country for some time past. Whether such a change can ever be effected in any manner; whether it can be effected without convulsions and civil wars; whether such a change will not totally destroy the liberties of this country—time only can determine.

"[H]ad the idea of a total change been started [openly stated], probably no state would have appointed members to the [Constitutional] convention. The idea of destroying, ultimately, the state government, and forming one consolidated system, could not have been admitted—a convention, therefore, merely for vesting in congress power to regulate trade was proposed."

—*The Federal Farmer,* 1787

97

The Tragic Consequence of America's Empire and One Man's Revenge

It was a beautiful late-spring Mississippi evening, and Uncle Seth and his family were enjoying the cool evening air as they sat on the front porch. Off in the distance, whip-poor-wills were calling and the smell of honeysuckle bathed the humid air. They had all enjoyed supper as a family; it was a time in which each would give an account of their daily activities on the farm. Eating together as a family was an important way to bind the family together and create a sense of duty—a duty to protect each member of the family and the family's honorable reputation within the community. The responsibility to family and community was strong among the Scotch-Irish plain folk of the Old South. It was a tradition that Uncle Seth hoped to pass on to the "modern" generation of Southerners.

Out on the porch the boys were continuing to exchange tales about their day's work and play. Earlier that day they had harnessed up the family's gray mule, Ole Jeff, and took him down to help their neighbor Jessie plow out the remainder of his corn crop. Jessie had been down with the flu and stood to lose his crop to the spring rains. Being good neighbors required folks to help each other out in hard times, and the plain folk of the Old South were, by custom, always ready to help kith and kin. Even though Jessie was not blood related, his father had been a slave on the Page farm before the war. Nevertheless, he and his family had often lent a hand when a member of the community fell on hard times. This work-sharing in response to a neighbor's adversity was the only form of insurance the plain folk of the Old South needed.

"It is hard to believe that if the war had not happened, Jessie would be a slave," Curtis mused.

"Well, the Yankees would sure like for you to believe that," Uncle Seth replied for all to hear. "But you should consider that before the radical abolitionists took political control in the North, there were more abolitionist societies in the South than in the North. As a matter of fact, before the war, even Pres. Jefferson Davis advocated training slaves for the day in which they would be able to govern themselves as part of our society. The war was not fought over slavery—it was fought to create an ever-increasing, power-hungry Federal Empire," Uncle Seth announced emphatically.

"Do you think Mr. Page would have freed Jessie's father if we had won the war?" Curtis asked as he watched Uncle Seth rocking back and forth in his favorite rocking chair.

"Well, Mr. Page's farm was not part of the large plantation system where scores of slaves worked. He and his slaves worked his farm together. They enjoyed the fruits of the farm together; they hunted the woods and fished the streams together; they were more like an extended family. Unfortunately the Yankee-initiated war and Yankee-imposed Reconstruction drove a wedge of hostility between the races in the South that some feel will never be closed. But I know that other nations managed to abolish slavery civilly, and if the Yankees had left us alone we too could have solved the problem in a civil manner. But empires cannot leave "lesser" people alone. They must conquer, rule, and exploit.

"Let me tell you all about what happened to a plain folk farmer in Tennessee who owned several slaves but was pro-Union. His name was Jack Hinson, and the ruthlessness of the Federal Empire turned him from a friend of the United States into a one-man army fighting for the Confederate States of America—and his slaves remained loyal to him during the entire war." Uncle Seth paused to look over his audience to make sure they understood the importance of what he was about to say.

"Jack was like many Southerners before the war. He loved the original concept of the United States, a constitutionally limited federal government, and was willing to put up with almost any insult and political trickery in order to maintain that Union. Even though he owned a few slaves, he felt that the safety of his property and his family's security would best be served by remaining loyal to the Union. When the war began, he even worked with General Grant during the Yankee invasion of Tennessee. Shortly after that, the Yankees occupied the portion of Tennessee where Jack's home was located. One morning, two of his younger sons decided to go squirrel hunting. The young men were twenty-two and seventeen years old. Hunting, as you know, is a major part of life in the South, but the Yankee invaders did not understand this fact. A Yankee patrol captured the boys as they were coming in from the woods, determined that they were bushwhackers, and decided to execute them as an example of what happens to people who dare to resist the power of the supreme Federal government. The boys tried to explain that they were armed with small caliber squirrel guns and were merely hunting in their own woods.

They explained that their father was a Unionist and had personally assisted General Grant. But the Yankee invaders would not accept the explanation and, without allowing for any further discussion, shot the boys on the spot! And they did not stop there. No, the invader wanted to make sure word got around about what happens to Confederate bushwhackers, so they cut the head off of each boy and took the severed heads to Jack's home. In front of Jack, his wife, his children, and his slaves, the United States soldiers mounted the severed heads of Jack's youngest sons on the gate post leading to the front door of their home. All of this was done by uniformed United States officers and troops with Old Glory, the Stars and Stripes, arrogantly flapping in conquered Southern air. Suddenly it became apparent to Jack that the love he held for the U.S.A. was a one-way street! His Scotch-Irish blood boiled with rage, and from that day until the end of the war he determined to conduct a blood feud with the agents of Yankee tyranny." Uncle Seth sat back in his chair to observe his audience and take a moment to catch his breath.

"Jack began planning his revenge even before those Yankees left his home. He had a special rifle made to serve as his sniper weapon that, in his expert hands, was accurate at ranges over one half mile. He knew just the right location to attack the invader—a cliff high above the Tennessee River where the river meets Hurricane Creek. Yankee gunboats were forced by the river's current to slow down, and there he would begin his war of revenge against the heartless Northern invader. Over the next several years, his expert marksmanship would take the lives of more than one hundred Yankee officers. And Jack was careful to shoot Yankee officers only. Well, except when he located the soldiers who had brought the bloody heads of his young sons to his house. He felt that it was the Yankee leaders who had brought this tragic war to his home, his family, and his South, so he was determined to make as many of them pay the supreme price as possible." Uncle Seth's voice was stern, unconsciously validating Jack's actions.

Even cooperating with invading Yankees did not spare Southerners from Yankee atrocities (Courtesy Charles Hayes)

"Jack kept a record of each Yankee kill on the barrel of his rifle. By the end of the war, the Yankee invaders committed two cavalry regiments and seven infantry regiments to the task of ending Jack's hostility toward the Yankee invaders. But they never managed to capture him. Now, boys," Uncle Seth wanted to stress the next part of his story so the boys would remember and pass it on to the next generation of occupied Southerners, "your Yankee-educated history teacher would tell you that what Jack did was wrong and that he should not have been fighting 'our' country. But I tell you what he did was not only right, it would have been dishonorable for him to have done otherwise. Remember what the Yankee General Sherman said back in December of 1863 about Southerners who dared to resist Yankee invasion and occupation: 'For every bullet shot at a steamboat, I would shoot a thousand 30-pounder Parrots shell into even helpless towns.' This, boys, is the mentality of an evil, invading, empire—anyone who dares to resist their self-proclaimed authority will meet a similar fate. And listen, boys, this attitude was not something shared by only Sherman. No, sir. It was shared by virtually all Yankee leaders, their press, and unfortunately most of their civilian population. The people of the North felt—and they still feel—that they had a right to do anything they wanted to do to us in order to keep us under their control. In June of 1864, the Yankee General Frisk sent a telegram to one of his officers telling him to 'exterminate every bushwhacker you can find.' A few weeks later he sent another message encouraging his men to 'kill every bushwhacker [they] can put their hands on, and make the feeders, aiders, and abettors of the villains sorry for what they have done to help.' In another message he declared, 'I trust the work will begin at once and continue until the last imp [loyal Southerner] expires. . . . Hesitate not to burn down every house.' Boys, this is what the United States of America has become—a cruel and evil empire that eagerly sinks to the lowest level of barbarism in order to assure the triumph and continued supremacy of the Federal Empire.

"Poor old Jack Hinson, he tried to remain loyal to the United States. He wanted to be a good American who would demonstrate his loyalty to his country by helping the invading Yankee army. But empires do not care about principles such as honor or loyalty. The Federal Empire will use foolish Southerners when it serves to promote their empire and cruelly dispose of them when they are no longer of service. It is sad to see, but this continues even today. Our political leaders play up to those in power in Washington, DC—all the time hoping to be able to get their share of power, perks, and privileges offered to those who serve the empire. But serving the empire comes at a terrible price, one that is paid every day by impoverished and politically enslaved Southerners." Uncle Seth closed his eyes as if trying to shut out the reality of his occupied Southern nation.

§ Deo Vindice §

ON THE SKIRMISH LINE WITH UNCLE SETH

"When the Yankees come, what they do? They did things they ought not have done and they left undone things they ought to have done. [They] seemed more concerned 'bout stealin', than they was 'bout the Holy War for the liberation of the poor African slave people. They took off all the horses, sheep, cows, chickens, and geese; they took the seine and the fishes they caught, corn in crib, meat in the smoke-house, and everything. Marse General Sherman said war was hell. It sho' was. Maybe it was hell for some of them Yankees when they come to die and give account of their deeds."

—Testimony given in the 1930s by eighty-seven-year-old former slave Henry D. Jenkins

98

Just Like Ireland—The South Shall Rise Again!

Young men from Pearl Valley, Stronghope, and Providence communities brought their best hunting rifles to Quincy Guess's place for the annual fall turkey shoot to see who would win the honor of being the best shot. It was early fall 1924. Uncle Seth was now eighty years old and no longer participated in the event he had often won in years past. His grandsons and even the older great-grandsons were doing their part to maintain the family's honor in the local shooting contest. Guns, hunting, and outdoor life had been a part of Southern culture ever since the Scotch-Irish people had come to America. Uncle Seth often though about his Scotch-Irish great-grandfather who had fled Northern Ireland to get away from an English landlord who was trying to throw him in debtor's prison because of an inability to pay his rent.

"Look, Uncle Seth," called out Carroll Ray, "Curtis won the young boys' top prize!"

"Now that's what I was expecting!" exclaimed Uncle Seth as he threw his arm around Curtis's shoulder and gave the boy a well-deserved hug. It was evident that Uncle Seth was very proud that the family's tradition of being experts with firearms was being maintained.

"Uncle Seth," replied Curtis, who was overcome with the enthusiasm of the moment, "we should get all the boys together and attack the Yankees. I know we could out-shoot them—this time we could win!"

Uncle Seth chuckled at the boy's fervor. He had felt it himself when he was about Curtis's age. But even though Uncle Seth still believed that the people of the South have a legal and moral right to be free, he knew that another war and the ensuing violence would end with the same result— victory for the Federal Empire.

"You know, Curtis, you are correct that 'we the people' of the South should be fighting for our rights—the right to live under a government ordered upon the consent of the governed and the right to be left alone. But war and violence are not the way to win the struggle for Southern Independence." Uncle Seth's words seemed especially sincere, and those around him turned to hear what he was about to say. Before the old Confederate veteran could utter another word, Curtis challenged his comment about not fighting the Yankee-controlled Federal government.

"If we don't fight them, how can we ever be rid of Yankee rule?" asked Curtis. His blood was now beginning to boil with determination to defend his people just like Uncle Seth did during the war. Uncle Seth, wanting to teach the young Southerner a valuable lesson about the best way to fight overwhelming imperial power, relied slowly and with measured words.

"I was reading an article about a leader in the Irish Home Rule movement. You all recall that Ireland is ruled by the English, but the majority of the Irish people would rather have a government of their own. Empires, just like the Federal Empire, will not allow their subjects to live in peace under a government of their own choosing. The Irish have been resisting English rule for hundreds of years—they have never given up on their dream of Irish independence. One day they will win their freedom. They almost did back in the late 1880s when a young man named Charles Stewart Parnell took the leadership of the Irish Home Rule movement. He was truly a unique individual. He was a Protestant political leader in a primarily Catholic country, but religion made no difference because he loved Ireland. I saw a picture of a beautiful monument the Irish raised to Parnell; it had his likeness, an Irish harp (just like the one I wore on my kepi during the war), and a quote from Parnell that read, 'No man has the right to fix the boundary

to the march of a nation.' To that I would add not only 'no man' but also 'no Empire has such a right.'" Uncle Seth had settled down on an old white oak block to comfortably lecture. An audience of boys and young men were all intently listening to the old Confederate veteran while standing at an almost perfect "parade rest," holding their rifles safely. The momentary silence was broken by Curtis's newest inquiry.

"Was Parnell a famous Irish army officer like General Lee?" the young boy asked, still full of youthful enthusiasm for martial valor.

"No, Parnell was a man of shrewd political thinking. He knew that the

Charles Stewart Parnell (Courtesy Charles Hayes)

English Imperialists could be beaten by a well-organized political effort organized around the principle of Irish Home Rule. He was elected to Parliament as a representative of the Irish people in his district and began to carefully organize other Irish representatives in Parliament. Of course, these other representatives would have never supported Irish Home Rule if Parnell had not already organized the Irish people, who demanded that their representatives support Irish Home Rule. Parnell organized boycotts against English landlords in Ireland. He also organized the Irish representatives in Parliament as well as their English supporters in Parliament into an effective blocking force; nothing could be done in Parliament because Parnell would take the floor and speak for hours on end about the 'Irish' question. When he became tired, another Irish representative would take over. It did not matter what was being discussed—it could have been the procurement of sanitary paper for the Queen's privy—but it would be stopped by demands to address the 'Irish' question." Uncle Seth could not help but smile as he listened to those around him laughing at his explanation.

Uncle Seth then continued, "Parnell's English enemies tried to frame him by producing fake documents implicating Parnell in violent acts. This was proven to be a false charge and the newspaper that had published the documents was forced to pay a large sum of money to Parnell in retribution. Still the Irish Home Rule movement was crushed—not by the English, but by Parnell's indiscretion in becoming involved in a love affair with a married woman. But for this sin of the flesh, Ireland would be free today.

Remember, the Irish will never give up on their right to be free and never should 'we the people' of the South," Uncle Seth declared emphatically.

"But, Uncle Seth," called out a voice from the back of the small crowd, "our politicians are more concerned with cozying up to the powers that be in Washington, DC. They have no desire to work for reestablishing Southern freedom."

"Yes, you are correct. And I'm sure that Parnell faced similar scalawag sentiment in the elected Irish leadership. But he overcame it by taking his message to the Irish people first and then

Parnell promoting Irish Home Rule
(Courtesy Charles Hayes)

encouraging them to force their representatives to support the Irish Home Rule movement or replace them in the next election," Uncle Seth declared harshly, denoting his total dislike for contemporary, self-serving elected Southern political leaders.

"Uncle Seth," someone else in the crowd interjected, "how would a Southern Home Rule movement work?"

Without the slightest hesitation, the old Confederate veteran began to explain to the next generation of Southerners how they could regain their constitutional right to be the masters in their own home. "Well, the first thing is to realize that just as Vice Pres. Alexander Stephens said after the defeat of the South in 1865, 'The Cause of the South is now the Cause of all.' What he meant was that eventually the oppressive nature of Lincoln's newly created Federal Empire would be realized by all Americans. When that happens, when that day comes, it will be up to us, the South, to point the way to a restoration of America's original constitutionally limited Republic of Republics. In 1865, the farmers and small business owners in the north, west, and northwest thought they were on the winning side of the 'Civil War,' but in reality the only winners were those who controlled the Federal government and those with close connections to those who controlled the Federal government. The rest of America exists to pay tribute, in the form of ever-increasing taxes, to that government and to dutifully comply with its laws, which of course favor the Federal government's ruling elite and those who support them. But the day will come when the Federal government will claim such absurdities as water rights to the dry lands in the west and prevent the local owners from using water without first getting Federal permission! The day will come when it will become apparent to the average American that the ruling elite and their allies never suffer from economic crashes; but 'we the people' of the once-sovereign states always suffer and eventually are forced to pay the taxes to prevent or alleviate the financial sufferings of the political elites and their allies on Wall Street. This was Federalist Alexander Hamilton's dream from the beginning: a nightmare, truly, that was soundly rejected by the founding fathers but finally realized by Lincoln. Yes, I know a lot of you are thinking, 'That cannot happen here! This is America; we have States' Rights to prevent such unconstitutional acts of the Federal government.' Well, I'm here, as a soldier of the Confederate States of America, to tell you that such thoughts are completely foolish and historically proven to be completely unfounded. 'We the people' of the once-sovereign states no longer enjoy States' Rights; we have states' privileges that the Federal government allows our states to exercise only as long as they suit the purpose of the Federal Empire." Uncle Seth paused; his audience, though young, seemed to be in agreement. The truth is sometimes hard to accept.

"But even when that day comes, how can we force the Federal government to recognize the limitations imposed on it by the Ninth and Tenth Amendments?" asked one of the older men standing next to Uncle Seth. "After all, our politicians are more concerned with gaining and maintaining elected office than they are for the restoration of *real* States' Rights!"

"You are correct. That is why we must first insist that every new generation of Southerners learn the truth about the War for Southern Independence. The Federal Empire's ruling elite and privileged associates of those elite know that the only way to keep their empire together is to make sure that future generations of Southerners accept the Yankee myth that the war was fought by virtuous Yankees against evil, hate-filled, slave-holding Southerners who were trying to destroy America. If they can turn future Southerners against their own people then the South will never rise again. The English tried to do this to the Irish; they enlisted young Irishmen into the British Empire's army, placed the Empire's flag above all other flags, and taught everyone to pledge allegiance to the very nation that invaded, conquered, and still occupies Ireland. But it will not work! It will not work because the Irish are keeping their customs and traditions alive and continue to honor their historical struggle to be a free people. And so it is with the South—we must not allow the Yankees and their lackeys and scallywag teachers to indoctrinate our youth with Yankee lies.

"Eventually we will have our own Parnell—a Southerner dedicated to the people of the South and the cause of constitutional liberty and *real* States' Rights. Our task today is to keep the memory of Southern freedom alive—to pass it on to each new generation. When the pinch of the Federal Empire's tax collectors, rules and regulations, and court orders begins to be felt in Northern states, then it will be our time to strike! We will begin not a violent revolution but an enlightened one in which the people of Dixie share our vision of a renewed, constitutionally limited Republic of Republics that honors Home Rule and guards it by *real* States' Rights. Our people must then demand that our elected representatives renounce their servitude to the Empire and begin to again serve the interests of the once-sovereign states. If they will not, then we must replace them. We must demand the ratification of an amendment to the Constitution that *acknowledges* the right of the sovereign state to nullify any Federal law, rule, regulation, or court order that 'we the people' of that sovereign state feel is oppressive of our rights. The amendment must also *acknowledge* the right of 'we the people' of the sovereign state to withdraw from the Federal government if 'we the people' of the sovereign state feel that the Federal government no longer serves the purpose for which it was originally organized and has become destructive of our rights. This is the only way to restore *real* States' Rights.[1] It removes ultimate authority from the ruling elite in Washington, DC, and returns it to its proper place— 'we the people' of the sovereign state. When that happens we will have replaced imperial rule with Home Rule." Uncle Seth paused to catch his breath—it was as if he was once again in a pitched battle with blue-coated Yankee invaders.

Regaining his strength, he issued a final warning: "And remember, boys, it will not be guns and violence that gain us the final victory over Lincoln's Federal Empire. It will be courage and the use of non-violent force. Very similar to the way the young Indian lawyer Gandhi forced the British to recognize the rights of East Indians living in South Africa not long ago. Empires that claim to be democracies find it very difficult to deny over a long term the rights of a people who continually call for their freedom. We must encourage our people to remember the Cause of Southern freedom and to constantly engage the Federal government and its lackeys in the debate over the question of Home Rule and 'Southern Independence.' At every political discussion, debate, or gathering we must remind ourselves and the world: 'If you can't leave, then you are not free.' 'We the people' of the South were not allowed to leave the Federal Empire, and therefore we are not free. A gilded cage is a cage nonetheless."

§ Deo Vindice §

1. Such a proposed amendment can be found in *Reclaiming Liberty*, by James Ronald Kennedy (Pelican, 2005, 74-79).

99

Northern Prosperity and Southern Poverty—It Wasn't God Who Made Us Poor

It was early May of 1931, and Uncle Seth was watching the dust cloud on the road as the Ford truck rumbled along, bouncing over ruts created by a combination of spring rain followed by hot spring sun. The old Confederate veteran expected that Joe William would be arriving home soon from his first year at college. He was impressed with JW's desire to study law and hoped that the young man would be able to make a good crop again this year to finance his continuing education. The truck began to slow down as it approached the driveway and then turned in, stopping close to the front porch. Joe William jumped off the back of the truck, thanked the driver for the lift, and with luggage in hand turned to greet Uncle Seth.

"Boy," Uncle Seth teased, "did they manage to pour any education into your hard head this past year?"

"I think they did," Joe William said as he threw his arms around the old man.

Joe William went in to greet the other family members and after getting something to eat returned to the front porch to visit a spell with Uncle Seth. "Uncle Seth," he began seriously, "there is one fellow at college whose father is from Indiana and runs the railroad running near the campus. This fellow is always teasing us about how poor Southerners are and how much better off the people in the North are. He says that his father claims that it is because Southerners are basically lazy."

"Well," Uncle Seth began, "the South was once a very wealthy part of the United States—that was before the War of Yankee Aggression. But even before the war, Yankees came down here and, after taking a quick look around, decided that most non-plantation-owning white Southerners were poor and lazy. Now, you must remember that most white Southerners did not live on plantations. The plain folk lived on small farms in the upland hills and mountains of the South. But as far as most Northerners were concerned—then as well as now—the South consisted of rich white plantation owners, slaves, and poor whites. This description of us fits well into their propaganda scheme, a scheme that was designed to depict us as unworthy of self-government and in desperate need of Yankee salvation imposed at the point of bloody bayonets. You must always remember that it was not God who made the South poor. No, it was Yankee invasion, conquest, occupation, and continuing political domination.

"Before the war, the people of the South were far more interested in an easy-going, almost leisurely lifestyle as opposed to the work-driven, industrious Yankee. I recently read a study that was done on the hours of work performed each year by slaves on the James Mallory plantation in Talladega County, Alabama. According to the study, a slave on this plantation worked around 1,800 hours per year while the average Northern farmhand worked 3,100 hours per year. Even slaves on Southern plantations worked fewer hours per year than white Northern farmers. To the average Northerner, this was indicative of just how lazy Southerners were—both white and black. But what is missing in this estimation of worth is the means of measuring value. In the North, value or worth was and still is measured by the almighty dollar whereas in the South it was measured in the social value of leisure, the joy of living, and the ease by which the necessities of life could be obtained—leaving more time for joyful pleasures.

"When Yankee Fredrick Law Olmsted visited the South before the war, he described a non-slave-holding white Southerner with whom he spent the night as being mired in utter poverty. But in reality this man owned several thousand acres of land—albeit none of which were cultivated—and more hogs than he could count! This 'poor' Southerner elected not to engage in laborious agricultural activities because his cattle roamed the open range and provided all the cash and meat that he and his family required. With the exception of tending a small garden and annually rounding up his cattle, this man spent most of his time hunting, fishing, socializing, and pursuing other pastimes as he pleased. This type of worth or value cannot be gauged by the supreme Yankee measuring rod of the almighty dollar—a term first used by Yankee Washington Irving to describe what he viewed as the retched conditions of the Louisiana Creoles:

> In a word, the almighty dollar, that great object of universal devotion throughout our land, seems to have no genuine devotees in these peculiar villages; and unless some of its [Yankee] missionaries penetrate there, and erect banking houses and other pious shrines, there is no knowing how long the inhabitants may remain in their present state of contented poverty.

Whether it be Olmsted or Irving—Yankees use the measuring rod of their god, 'the almighty dollar,' to determine Southern worth and thereby justify their estimation of Southerners as being poor. But their values were not our values.

"Early in our history it was noted by foreign observers that Southerners loved their leisure; often those hostile to us would describe us as being lazy. In 1759, a Northern visitor described us thusly: 'They seldom show any spirit of enterprise, or expose themselves willingly to fatigue.' Another observer in the late 1700s, one Charles Woodmason, described Southern hill folk as 'very poor, owing to their extreme indolence. . . . They delight in their present low, lazy, sluttish, heathenish, hellish life, and seem not desirous of changing it.' In 1810, Charles Ingersoll attributed Southern laziness to the evils of slavery, but as you all know most of the plain folk were not engaged in the plantation economy. A Yankee, Charles F. Hoffman, attempted to convince a Southerner of the superiority of the industrious Yankee work ethic, to which the Southerner replied: 'If the people did not live up to other people's ideas, they lived as well as they wanted to. They didn't want to make slaves of themselves; they were contented with living as their fathers lived before them.' Perhaps Olmsted said it best when he observed that 'the Southerner . . . enjoys life itself. He is content with being. Here is the grand distinction between him and the Northerner.' Indeed, there is a great distinction between the North and the South—a cultural divide that in and of itself justified the South's desire to be free of Yankee domination.

"Both foreign and Yankee observers of Southern plain folk life assumed that we were lazy and preferred to suffer poverty rather than engage in constructive labor. But the plain folk of the South had all they needed to be happy! The woods and fields of the South were a virtual Garden of Eden that supplied us with the means to acquire all our necessities of life—and it did so with very little labor required. I read a study of four non-slave-holding plain folk families selected at random in Alabama that measured the number of weeks they were required to work to supply their needs. One of these families owned more than five hundred acres and one owned no land at all; all owned livestock that roamed the open range. According to the data, these families worked around eleven forty-hour weeks per year to provide all the requirements for their families. This means that they had leisure time in abundance; but outsiders who did not understand our cultural heritage would mislabel these Southern plain folk as poor and lazy.

"Our people were not satisfied with mere subsistence. No, we drove huge herds of cattle, sheep, and hogs to market every fall. The cash value of plain folk livestock in 1860 exceeded the total value of that year's cotton, rice, sugar cane, and tobacco crops combined! Why, in 1850, a federal agency estimated that the piney woods of southern Mississippi, eastern Louisiana, and western Alabama sent close to a million cows to market each year. And remember, due to our mild climate, this livestock did not require barns to shelter them through a harsh winter and did not need humans to provide feed to keep them alive during the winter. They grew and reproduced on their own out on the open range; all we had to do was to round them up once a year, mark the newborns, and collect what we wanted for food or to send to market. We then turned them loose back on the open range. Why would anyone choose to endure a life of hard labor when he could live off the bounty of the land?

"Remember, boy, this was a way of life that our ancestors had developed in Ireland, Scotland, and Wales long before our Scotch-Irish ancestors came to America. I recall reading that as early as 1185 a fellow by the name of Gerald of Wales described the Irish way of life as 'the pastoral way of life.' He said rightly that 'the tending of herds did not require the same physical toil involved in arable farming, and therefore the Irish were thought to be indolent.' He later visited Wales and noted a similar lifestyle there. He was shocked to find out that they were not even remotely interested in commerce or industry. Records from 1378 show that in that year there were 45,000 hides exported from Scotland, which proves that these kinsmen of ours had an economy based on the keeping of livestock—not that much different for our pre-war economy. As late as 1769, about the time my great-great-grandfather migrated from Northern Ireland to the South, an Englishman described the Scots as 'indolent to a high degree, unless roused to war, or to any animating amusement.' The same was said of our people here in the South, but that was before the war. We were self-sufficient and prosperous by our own measurement, but then the invading Yankees came and with their invasion, conquest, and occupation transformed our prosperity to poverty—glory, glory, hallelujah.

"After the war, everything changed for the plain folk and everyone in the South. Remember the stories you've heard about the conditions we returned to, how everything had been destroyed or was worn-out and in a state of disrepair. Many of our best men had been killed or crippled while resisting the Yankee invader, and to make matters worse there was no money or capital to invest in rebuilding the Southern economy. And, of course, we must not forget the plundering of the remaining resources by the Yankee-designed Reconstruction government that took control of the occupied South. These basically illiterate and untutored political rulers of the South began to pass enclosure laws that resulted in the closing of the South's open range. That, in turn, led to the death of the plain folk's herding lifestyle. In addition, the national government allowed the railroads to charge less to ship fattened, feedlot-raised hogs into the

South and charge more to ship Southern freight to the North. Local stores that were heavily indebted to Yankee-controlled banks began to purchase cheaper cattle and hogs from Northern feedlots and thereafter relied less on locally raised meat. This forced the plain folk to begin working their land to raise cash crops such as cotton or tobacco. But to do this they had to first borrow money from the same Yankee banks and hope that they got a fair price for their cash crop at harvest time in order to repay their debt. When the cash crop economy faltered and they could not repay the banks, the banks foreclosed and the once self-sufficient Southern herdsman and his family became homeless. Of course, the unfair rates of railroad transport and the massive increase in the plain folk's debt to the banks resulted in a financial boom for captains of Yankee industry and finance. For these railroads and banks had local offices throughout the South but their home offices were up North, so that's where the profits ended up. Oh yes, don't forget that by setting up a post-war Southern economy that relied on Northern feedlot hogs the average Southerner's diet changed. Instead of lean, range-raised meat, all we had access to was meat high in fat and much lower in protein. Our conquering Northern masters destroyed not only our economy but our health as well.

"Very shortly after the war it became evident that more and more of the white South as well as most of the former slave population were becoming dependent on sharecropping as a livelihood. This required the farmer to take an advance or loan from a large landholder, work the landlord's farm, and repay the landholder when the cash crop was harvested and taken to market. It was a system of virtual peonage, not that much different from the conditions of European peasants during the Dark Ages. It has been estimated that even today, in 1931, not one in a hundred Southern farmers produces a crop without going into debt to get the supplies necessary to farm his land or to sharecrop the landlord's plantation. This ever-increasing reliance on debt—something unheard of before the war—fixed the poor farmer to the land owned by the landlord or heavily mortgaged to the bank. Look around you, boy, and you will see everywhere poor farmers barely able to scratch a living from the soil. But these poor folks did not suddenly fall from the sky! They were made poor as a result of the Federal Empire's invasion, conquest, and occupation and our enslavement.

Impoverished Southern sharecropper circa 1935 (Library of Congress)

"In 1910, the number of landlords who had more than five sharecropper families working their plantation—that would be around twenty people working the plantation—was almost exactly the same as the number of slave-holding plantations with twenty or more slaves in 1860! In other words, the Federal Empire had exchanged the system of chattel slavery for a system of peonage in which the plantation owner now had no responsibility to the white and black folks who worked his plantation—not that dissimilar from the total lack of responsibility the Yankee industrialist had for his hired hands; all he owes them is their wages and after that they must make out as best they can.

"Conditions across the South became desperate as a result of the destruction of the plain folk's way of life. Money was hard to obtain, and for the first time finances were of central concern. But when people are ruled by an evil empire that is trying to squeeze every drop of tribute out of them that it can, society's well-being is destroyed. You can see evidence of this by looking at the analysis of the productivity of six Mississippi counties before the war as compared to their productivity in 1930. All of these counties were self-sufficient, growing or producing all the major food supplies they needed.

"That changed after the glorious victory of our new Yankee masters in 1865, when the productivity of each one of these counties began to decline. For example: before the war, hog ownership was 2.1 hogs per person; but by 1930 hog ownership per person had dramatically declined to 0.4 per person! Similarly, before the war, 48.5 bushels of corn were raised per person, but by 1930 that had fallen to 22.8 bushels per person. These counties went from being exporters of food before the war to net importers of food following the defeat of the Confederate States of America. By 1930, 71 percent of the farms in these counties were operated by sharecroppers. You see, boy, no people are better off when they are governed by outsiders—by an evil empire.

"Joe William, don't ever let Yankee-educated professors convince you that Southern poverty is part of the legacy of slavery. Poverty inflicted on both whites and blacks in the South is part of the legacy of Yankee invasion and continuing political and economic domination of our country, the Confederate States of America. Always remember what the Yankees said after they forced us to surrender; how they gloated over the victory of their superior numbers and material; how their newspapers boldly declared that it was now their purpose to colonize the defeated South with Northerners and to Yankee-fy the South to 'turn the slothful, shiftless Southern world upside down.' That is exactly what they did; they changed the South from a land of prosperity to a land of poverty, and the Yankee victors made a handsome profit in the exchange.

"Yes, Joe William, your Yankee school mate is right in one respect—today's South is a land of poverty compared to the booming economy of the modern-day North. But this poverty is not poverty of our own making! As long as the people of the South are willing to accept continued political and economic enslavement to the Federal Empire, we will remain impoverished. As long as our society is controlled by the ruling elites in Washington, DC, and their cronies on Wall Street we will never be able to build a sustainable and expanding economic system. As long as 'we the people' of Dixie are willing to allow the financiers on Wall Street to control our economy then we will remain poor. This will not change until 'we the people' of the South recognize that we have been forced to become the political and economic vassals of the Federal Empire, that our sole purpose is to provide tribute to that empire and to those with close political connections to that empire—which, by the way, includes our present-day Scalawag politicians. We must recognize that 'we the people' of the South are not free in the sense that the founding fathers intended. We are not masters in our own homes. We are controlled by those whose interests are radically different from our own. 'We the people' of the once-sovereign states of Dixie are prisoners in our own country! We are living in a cage—yes, here I am speaking metaphorically—a gilded cage. But the question your generation and the generations to follow must answer is this: Do you really want to live in a cage? That is indeed a harsh question, but by not answering it we actually are answering it! Our silence endorses the legitimacy of the ruling elite's government and gives consent to our political and economic enslavement." Uncle Seth sat back in his chair and closed his eyes, trying to shut out this harsh reality. Joe William knew that the old Confederate veteran would not be with them much longer. Somehow it seemed to him that what he had learned from Uncle Seth over the years was more practical than anything his professors were teaching him.

Jefferson Davis, president, Confederate States of America (Author's collection)

§ Deo Vindice §

ON THE SKIRMISH LINE WITH UNCLE SETH
"The States, as sovereign parties to the compact of Union, had the reserved power to secede from it whenever it should be found not to answer the ends for which it was established. . . . [I]t follows that the war was, on the part of the United States Government, one of aggression and usurpation, and, on the part of the South, was for the defense of an inherent, unalienable right. . . . In asserting the right of secession . . . I recognize the fact that the war showed it to be impracticable, but this did not prove it to be wrong."
—Jefferson Davis, 1881

100

Slavery and the Plain Folk of the Old South

Uncle Seth had brought Mildred, one of his many great-granddaughters, with him to the annual reunion of the Louisiana United Confederate Veterans meeting in New Orleans. By the turn of the century, most of the work of arranging these meeting was done by the United Daughters of the Confederacy and the Sons of Confederate Veterans. Uncle Seth wanted Mildred to hear the talk that would be given by James W. Nicholson about slavery among the hill people of the old South. Last fall, Mildred asked Uncle Seth if it was true that Southern slaveholders were mean and harsh to their slaves; her schoolteacher had assigned *Uncle Tom's Cabin* as class reading. Uncle Seth told Mildred that *Uncle Tom's Cabin* was not an accurate description of the way slavery was practiced in the South. Harriet Beecher Stowe, the book's author, did "research" by reading ads placed in Southern newspapers by slave owners seeking information about runaway slaves and by reading the typical Yankee propaganda published prior to the war. He explained that the author had no personal knowledge about slavery in the old South but wrote about the "evil" Southern slave masters anyway. It would be like someone who had never lived in New York City writing a story about the living conditions and the people of New York and basing his description on newspaper stories about the crime, fraud, and political corruption in the city, he told her. But he wanted Mildred to hear from someone who had an extensive firsthand experience with slavery in the old South—especially slavery among the plain folk.

Uncle Seth and Mildred found their chairs in the large gathering room. The crowd became silent as James W. Nicholson was introduced. "Mr. Nicholson is well-known here in Louisiana," the master of ceremonies began, "but for those who may not know 'Nick,' I will tell you that as a very young man—actually a boy—he entered the service of our Confederate nation at the beginning of the war and was honorably discharged at the end of active hostilities as a sergeant in Company D, 12th Louisiana Volunteer Infantry. Nick is currently chancellor of Louisiana State University and has had an extensive career as a professor of mathematics. Tulane University here in New

Orleans and A and M College of Alabama both conferred honorary doctorates upon him. Ladies and gentlemen, I give you James W. Nicholson."

As the applause died away, Nick began his address: "I have been given the difficult task of explaining the institution of slavery as practiced by the hill folk of the old South—the non-plantation farmers and herdsmen who made up the larger portion of the white population prior to the war. I will not attempt, in this short time, to address the subject as an academic or scholarly exercise but will address it from my own personal experience as a child born into a slave-holding society. As a child, the white and black children would run and play together, each knowing that one day as adults they would be working together. It was not unusual for these close relationships to last for a lifetime. I recall in 1845 when my father moved us from Alabama to North Louisiana we came by boat and landed in New Orleans. A house servant, Aunt Kitty, who had grown up with my mother, came with the rest of the family. She was well up in years and was almost blind, but we took care of her just like we would any other member of the family. Now by 'family,' I do not mean to imply that there were blood relations between us. But we were family nonetheless. One day we were walking around New Orleans gazing at the sites and, as we turned a corner, Aunt Kitty ran into a wooden Indian placed outside a tobacco store. Aunt Kitty thought she had run into a person and excused herself. For a moment, she just gazed at the strangely-dressed figure in front of her who refused to move or acknowledge her apology. As we continued down the street, we all got a good laugh when we heard Aunt Kitty commenting to herself, 'They sure enough have some strange white trash in this place.'" The audience interrupted with boisterous laughter.

As the crowd settled down, Nick began anew. "Now this simple story tells a lot about slavery as practiced in the old South. I have already pointed out the close, almost familial relations between many masters and slaves; but also note that Aunt Kitty felt perfectly free to describe what she thought was a coarse, uncivil white man as being 'white trash.' And note, too, that, even though Aunt Kitty was a slave who was almost blind and unable to do any productive work, she was well cared for and remained an integral part of our family. My father could never understand why he was looked down on by radical Yankee abolitionists who were supported by the loom masters of Northern industry. These loom masters—owners of large textile mills—would work Irish immigrants from can to can't while paying them starvation wages. And then when the workers became old, ill, or disabled, the loom master would turn them out to get by as best they could! Census data from the mid-1800s shows that the living quarters of plantation slaves were in most cases better than that of Northern mill workers!

"In the early 1850s, North Louisiana had transitioned from a frontier area to a modern rural area. One of the tasks we had was to maintain the roads that connected the various communities. The parish police jury—that's what other states call their county board of supervisors—would designate a certain day to work the roads and appoint an overseer to supervise the work. All able-bodied adult males—both black and white—were expected to turn out to do their part. There was no distinction between black or white, free or slave. We all worked together to keep our roads open and ensure the continued growth of our communities. The interesting thing is how folks actually looked forward to these work days because they gave us time to enjoy each other's company. My father would always say that there is no worse loss than a day without laughter. These work days were full of work and laughter—most of the time more laughter than work!

"When war was forced upon the South it was not unusual for young black servants to accompany their young masters to war. Their loyalty to their 'families' was as strong as that of their masters' love for them. Many a story has been told about our black Confederate soldiers who shared the dangers and harsh conditions in camp, on the march, or, at times, in battle. Levy Carnine was one such black Confederate from North Louisiana. His story is not unique; many other black Confederates like him went to war. He was with the 2nd Louisiana Volunteer Infantry from DeSoto Parish. Late in the war he was asked to take money and letters back to relatives in Louisiana. To do this, he had to cross the enemy line and tell the Yankees he was a runaway slave—and of course the Yankees believed him, because as pious, well-educated, and morally superior Yankees they knew that all slaves were just waiting for the opportunity to run away from evil Southern slave masters. After being received by the self-righteous Yankees, he then had to make his way back on foot several hundred miles to his home in DeSoto Parish. Word of his arrival got out, and Carnine became a local hero in DeSoto Parish; folks came from miles around to hear tales about the boys fighting way up in Virginia. He joined another Confederate unit, the last to be raised in the area, and served until the end of the war. His last request was to be laid with the rest of the Confederate soldiers after his death, so he is buried in the Confederate Cemetery in Mansfield, Louisiana.

"So how can we at this late time in our history explain the relationship between white and black Southerners of the old South?" Nick paused for a long time as he looked down at his notes. No doubt his thoughts were far away at another time and another place. "When we were discharged after the war, several of us from North Louisiana walked back from Greensboro, North Carolina, to Mobile, Alabama, where we obtained passage on a steamer headed to New Orleans. Our accommodations consisted of whatever space we could find in the cargo hole. A small storm came up and the paying passengers vacated the open deck. The storm gave us a chance to go up top and get some fresh air—as well as a much-needed saltwater bath as the water sprayed over the deck. Henry, a black waiter, came up to the deck to watch the soldiers having fun playing in the spray. He felt perfectly at home with us and soon was joking and laughing with the group. He had romped and played with white boys like us in his youth and saw no reason to distrust us—even though the Yankee propagandists claimed we had been fighting to keep him in slavery. Henry checked on us during our passage and would always bring us fresh water to make sure 'the boys' were not thirsty.

"When I finally made it back home, the entire family was waiting to greet me. There in the gathering were all the black members of our family! Now think about it: the war was over, we all knew that slavery was over, but that made no difference to our black family members. I will never forget the words of Uncle Nathan, the oldest black man on the farm, as he pushed everyone aside, hugged me tight, and declared, 'Bless de Lord for all his mercies; de boy came back a man.' Aunt Callie, who raised me from infant to young man, then put her arm around my neck and while sobbing with joy declared, 'My dear baby boy! Why you stay gone so long? Yo Aunt Callie ben waiting, watching, and praying for you all these years. My! What a big man my baby has become.' And with tears of joy flowing down my face and a heart full of love for home and family, I held to Aunt Callie's hand for the very comfort that can only be had from contact with another human.

"These are some of the stories of slavery among the hill folks of the old South. For those of us who grew up in Dixie before the war, these stories are easy to understand. But I'm afraid that those who did not share our experience will never really understand. Those who hate the South, well they will continue to enforce their version of our history, and if necessary they will enforce it with the tip of the bloody bayonet." Professor Nicholson closed his notes as he looked down at the children of the Confederacy seated on the front row of chairs.

§ Deo Vindice §

ON THE SKIRMISH LINE WITH UNCLE SETH
"Having grown-up in the old South I can testify that never did I see an exception to Henry W. Grady's observation that 'the one character utterly condemned and ostracized was the man who was mean to his slaves. For the cruel master, there was no toleration.'"

—James W. Nicholson, circa 1917

101

American Indians—Confederate Allies in the West

Uncle Seth moved cautiously down the rows of chairs in the meeting hall and found a comfortable chair within easy hearing range of the speaker's podium. The Hazlehurst and Crystal Springs camps of the Sons of Confederate Veterans were hosting a special joint meeting. They had invited a speaker from Louisiana to talk about the Indians of the West and the valuable aid they provided to the Confederacy. The speaker was Thomas F. Anderson from Dennis Mills, Louisiana. He had been attached to General Watie's Division. Stand Watie was one of the first American Indians to hold such high office in America. This was of special interest to Uncle Seth because as a boy in Copiah County he had often picked up arrowheads from plowed fields and felt a special kinship to the Choctaws who had once roamed the same hills as he did in his youth. The room became silent as the speaker was being introduced.

"Thank you for this special invitation," Mr. Anderson began. "I am always excited and honored to give a personal account of the brave acts of the South's Indian allies in our War for Southern Independence.
While much has been written about the war east of the Mississippi River, much less has been recorded about the war west of the Mississippi River; and of that, very little has been recorded about the struggle in the Oklahoma, Kansas, and Missouri theaters during the war. The Cherokees, Choctaws, and Seminoles bore a major part in the battles and actions in this theater. In 1860, Stand Watie had organized an effort to encourage the American Indian nations in the Oklahoma territory to support the Southern Cause. A local bully named Foreman, who claimed to support the North and who belonged to an organization

Gen. Stand Watie, CSA (Courtesy Research Division, Oklahoma Historical Society)

called the Pins, attempted to assassinate Stand Watie but was killed by Watie instead. I am well aware of the Pins because we confiscated their documents, papers, and records during the war. They were responsible for the burning of my home and the destruction of all my earthly possessions as well as those of many of my kinsmen during the war.

"In May of 1861, Gen. Albert Pike came to us as a commissioner from the Confederate States of America seeking to make a treaty of alliance between the Confederacy and our Indian nations. Under leadership of men such as Stand Watie, we gladly joined the effort to create a new nation. Prior to that, Gen. Ben McCulloch, CSA, had authorized Capt. John Miller and me to raise an independent unit to operate for ninety days. We called ourselves the Dixie Rangers and our task was to occupy the neutral land in part of the Oklahoma Territory and part of Kansas. About that time, the 3rd Louisiana Regiment came up to assist us. We were with them at Springfield and Pea Ridge and could testify to their fighting skill and bravery. After the Battle of Pea Ridge, the 3rd Louisiana was detached from us and sent to fight east of the Mississippi River. I can tell you that the Indians who knew them were greatly distressed to lose such brave fellows and continued to lament their loss through the end of the war.

"After the expiration of the ninety day life of the Dixie Rangers, nearly all of us joined Company K, 1st Cherokee Regiment. Our captain was Thompson Mayes, who was the brother of Chief Joel B. Mayes. Company K was Gen. Stand Watie's favorite fighting unit. The 1st Cherokee Regiment was composed of and led by Indians. In the other companies, whites and Indians were mixed together, which worked smoothly. It was probably the first time in American history that white men took orders from Indian officers. But at the time, no one thought anything of it.

"Let me tell you a little about the Battle of Springfield, a battle in which many of Gen. Stand Watie's regiment took part. We went there not as a unit but as individuals; of course, we had the general's permission to go there and lend a hand. We met a number of other 'volunteers' who came in from Missouri to help turn back the Yankee invaders. The Missourians came there with an odd assortment of weapons: shotguns, hunting rifles, pistols, and even Bowie knives. During the battle, I stood next to an elderly Baptist minister who was armed with an old flintlock rifle that could have been used by his grandfather during the Revolutionary War of 1776. Before he would pull the trigger, the preacher would load his rifle, kneel down on one knee, and offer the following prayer: 'Lord God Almighty have mercy on that poor critter's soul.' The rifle's hammer would fall;

the flint would strike the frizzen, creating sparks that would fall into the pan and ignite the power in the pan. This created a hiss followed by the exploding main charge. I would follow the invisible track of the preacher's bullet and watch as his target fell to the ground. The preacher would repeat this process more times than I could count. Now, years later, when I think of this small incident in that great war it makes me angry. Why, you ask? Well, today Northern pulpits, press, and universities would have the world to believe that this old man was fighting to keep his slaves! The poor fellow could not even afford a modern firearm. He could hardly afford the powder and lead he was expertly using against the Yankee invaders, so he surely could not have afforded the price of a slave. Why, then, were he and the rest of us fighting? It was very simple to us, but Yankee propaganda has managed to hide the truth from the world: we were fighting to protect our homes and our families, and to secure for ourselves the right simply to live under a government that would leave us alone—a novel idea even today!

"At the Battle of Pea Ridge, our Cherokees distinguished themselves by capturing a Yankee artillery battery. A Yankee artilleryman was lying face down between two of the captured cannons. One of our full-blood Cherokees walked over to the Yankee, took off the Yankee's cap, and grabbed the Yankee's hair. With a native war cry, he used his knife and began removing the Yankee's scalp! The scalping, war cry, or both resurrected the Yankee, who jumped up and began running like a frightened jackrabbit back toward his retreating lines. The Cherokees did not shoot at the Yankee, but they did amuse themselves by calling after him to come back and get his lock of hair. Well, this must have gotten back to the Yankee officers because, after the battle, a great deal of official communication ensued between the respective commanding officers of the United States and Confederate States. The result was that our commander issued an order for all Indians to keep their hands off white men's hair!

"In the spring of 1863, the Yankee military authorities hit upon the idea of returning to Oklahoma all Indian refugees who had gone over to the Yankees and sought safety in Kansas. The Yanks wanted them to return in time for them to plant and raise a crop. Of course, we did not want a large group of turncoats living within our territory. The Yankees had furnished the traitorous Indians with all the supplies they needed, including horses, mules, seed, agricultural implements, and food to last till crops were made. They were escorted by Yankee General Blount, who commanded Kansas troops, and General Phillips, who commanded our old Indian adversaries the Pins. Well, Gen. Stand Watie did not intend to allow these Yankees and their allies to remain within our territory. We attacked them and routed them from all of their settlements. They all ended up retreating and taking refuge in Fort Gibson, where we left them while we enjoyed the fine provisions they had left behind for our enjoyment.

"In early 1865, we arranged for a Council of War with the Indian tribes in the far West and Northwest— today known mostly as the Plains Indians. Our plan was to unite in an attack on Kansas, they from the north and we from the south, and put an end to the Yankee control of that area. The council met at Walnut Springs with the intention of making peace between the tribes and then to move on Kansas. Tribes from Idaho, Dakota, and Montana were present. It was one of the largest Indian councils that ever met, but before the conference got underway word had arrived of General Lee's surrender.

"It is interesting to note that in February of 1865 a group of Plains Indians attacked a Pony Express station at Mud Springs, Nebraska. I know of no direct connections between that attack and our council, but for whatever reason the Yankee authorities decided to record this attack in the Official Record of the War of the Rebellion.

"Well, this is the best account I can give from personal experience and discussions with those men who participated in these events. The Indian allies of the Confederacy provide invaluable service to the Cause of Southern Independence and should be remembered and honored for that service. I was honored to be personally acquainted with brave warrior leaders such as the Cherokee Gen. Stand Watie. We must all do our duty to always remember their brave deeds and defend their honor, especially when that attack comes from the propagandists who today dutifully serve their Yankee masters." Mr. Anderson concluded his remarks and the crowd rose to give him a standing ovation.

§ Deo Vindice §

ON THE SKIRMISH LINE WITH UNCLE SETH
"I do think she [the sovereign state of Mississippi] has justifiable cause and I approve of her act . . . Nullification and secession, often confounded, are indeed antagonistic principles. [Senator] Calhoun advocated nullification because it preserved the Union. Secession belongs to a different class of remedies and is justified upon the basis that the States are sovereign. You may make war on a foreign State, but there are no laws of the United States to be executed within the limits of a seceded State . . . [In closing] I am sure I feel no hostility toward you, Senators from the North, and *I hope for peaceable relations* with you though we must part."
—From Sen. Jefferson Davis's Farewell Address to the
U.S. Senate, January 21, 1861 (emphasis added)

102

Uncle Seth Replies: The States' Rights Theory Was Developed to Protect Slavery

The Federal Empire's ruling elite will proclaim that the "un-American" idea of States' Rights was developed by racist Southerners in an effort to protect the institution of slavery and the South's oppression of blacks.

To those individuals, Uncle Seth replies: "In America's original system of government, the sovereign state was the ultimate bulwark against centralized (federal) tyranny. In this system, sometimes referred to as a Republic of Republics, the concept of sovereignty is radically different from the concept widely held in Europe in the 1700s. In Europe, sovereignty came from God but was given to the king or monarch, representing an all-powerful central government. Indeed, the king was often referred to as 'the sovereign.' In America's founding document, the Declaration of Independence, the founding fathers set forth the radical idea that sovereign authority comes from God and is given to individuals. In that sense all men are created equal, equal before God and equal before the law of man. Under this system man creates government by delegating—not surrendering—a portion of his sovereign authority to a group of men selected by society to form the government of the state. This state is the corporate representative of the sovereign community. These states then *delegated* a portion of their sovereign authority to the federal government that they (the states) created to perform certain specific and limited functions for the mutual benefit of all states in the Union.

"Under America's original system of constitutionally limited Federalism and *real* States' Rights, the individual citizen of a state had nothing to fear from the federal government. If the federal government overstepped its authority and abused its powers to the detriment of citizens, the sovereign state could nullify such federal acts and thereby protect the individual liberties of its citizens. Pres. Thomas Jefferson acknowledged this authority of the sovereign state in his first inaugural address when he identified 'the support of state governments in all their rights as the most competent administrations for our domestic concerns and the surest bulwarks against anti-republican tendencies.' He was merely reflecting the common assumption of all states when they ratified the Constitution.

Indeed, states such as Virginia, New York, and Rhode Island even included verbiage in their ratification of the original constitution that declared 'the powers granted under the Constitution, being derived from the people of the United States, may be resumed by them, whensoever the same shall be perverted to their injury or oppression.' But those who support the supreme Federal government—the ruling elite and those crony capitalists, big bankers, and lobbyists who have close connections with the ruling elite—now deny that *real* States' Rights are a part of America's political history. What does the truth of history tell us?

"When the states were debating whether or not to ratify the proposed constitution of 1787, the Federalists assured the anti-Federalists that no sovereign state would ever be called before the Federal Supreme Court—because the states were sovereign and a sovereign cannot be called to answer before a court that he (the sovereign) created. However, in 1793 the Federal Supreme Court issued an order attempting to compel the sovereign state of Georgia to submit to the Federal Court's authority. Georgia responded by issuing a joint resolution warning that any federal agent attempting to enforce the Federal Supreme Court's order 'shall be . . . guilty of a felony, and shall suffer death, without the benefit of clergy, by being hanged.' A constitutional majority of the other sovereign states demonstrated their support for Georgia by immediately ratifying the Eleventh Amendment, which precludes such actions of the Federal court against a sovereign state.

"In 1798, the sovereign states of Kentucky and Virginia passed the Resolves of 1798, in which they nullified the Sedition Act passed by the Federalist-dominated United States Congress, signed into law by Federalist Pres. John Adams, and vigorously enforced by the Federal Supreme Court. This law was a blatantly open violation of the First Amendment rights of free speech and free press. These states were able to protect their citizens from this oppressive federal law by interposing its sovereign authority between its citizens and an abusive federal government. The words of the Virginia Resolves of 1798—penned by James Madison—are an everlasting guide to the power of the sovereign state when it opposes the abusive acts of the central or federal government:

> [T]his Assembly doth explicitly and peremptorily declare, that it views the powers of the Federal Government, as resulting from the compact, to which the States are parties, as limited by the plain sense and intention of the instrument constituting that compact; as no further valid than they are authorized by the grants enumerated in that compact; and that in case of a deliberate, palpable, and dangerous exercise of other powers, not granted by the said compact, the States who are parties thereto, have the right, and

are in duty bound, to interpose for arresting the progress of the evil, and for maintaining, within their respective limits, the authorities, rights and liberties appertaining to them.

The words of the Kentucky Resolves of 1798, penned by Thomas Jefferson, reflect the same thinking:

> That the Government created by this compact was not made the exclusive or final judge of the extent of the powers delegated to itself, since that would have made its discretion, and not the Constitution, the measure of its powers; but that as in all other cases of compact among parties having no common judge, each party has an equal right to judge for itself, as well of infractions as of the mode and measures of redress.

"These resolves were not met with cries of treason and false allegations that Madison and Jefferson were trying to destroy the Union. Instead, the majority of states voted in the next election to reject the Federalist Party and elected Thomas Jefferson president as the replacement for President John Adams.

"During the controversy surrounding the 1809 case *Olmstead v. the Executives of the Late David Rittenhouse*, Pennsylvania rejected unconstitutional federal acts but declared that the state accepted legitimate federal authority:

> [W]hen exercised within Constitutional limits, they trust they will not be considered as acting hostile to the General Government [the Union or federal government], when, as guardians of the State rights, they cannot permit an infringement of those rights by an unconstitutional exercise of power in the United States courts. [This Yankee state then went on to declare] *Resolved*, that the independence of the States, as secured by the Constitution, be destroyed, the liberties of the people in so extensive country cannot long survive. To suffer the United States' courts to decide on State Rights will, from a bias *in favor of power*, necessarily destroy the Federal part of our Government: And whenever the government of the United States becomes consolidated, we may learn from the history of nations what will be the event.

In the debate surrounding the Federal Embargo Act in 1809, Massachusetts, the most Yankee of all states, declared the act to be 'unjust, oppressive, and unconstitutional.' It then took a strong States' Rights position by declaring, 'While this State maintains its sovereignty and independence, all the citizens can find protection against outrage and injustice in the strong arm of the State government. . . . [The Federal Embargo Act] . . . is not legally binding on the citizens of this State.' Here we see a plain and open act of nullification on the part of this Yankee state. Nullification and secession are the key elements of *real* states' rights.

"Another Yankee state, Connecticut, in 1812, was engaged in a controversy with the federal government regarding the federal use of the Connecticut militia. During this dispute the sovereign state of Connecticut declared, 'But it should not be forgotten, that the State of Connecticut is a FREE SOVEREIGN AND INDEPENDENT STATE; that the United States are a confederacy of States; that we are a confederated and not a consolidated Republic.'

"In 1821, the sovereign state of Ohio was engaged in a controversy with the federal government regarding the Bank of the United States. The State of Ohio declared its belief in States' rights when its elected legislature declared 'that this General Assembly do protest against the doctrine that the political rights of the separate States that compose the American Union, and their powers as sovereign States, may be settled and determined in the Supreme Court of the United States.' Here we see a Yankee state agreeing with the Kentucky and Virginia Resolves of 1798 that the federal government is not the final arbiter of its own powers but that the right resides with the sovereign state to decide for itself.

"In all of the preceding examples of States' Rights in action, the sovereign state was interposing its sovereign authority between its citizens and an abusive Federal Court, president, and/or Congress. In each case the sovereign state in essence nullified a federal law, federal court order, or presidential edict. But the most striking example of States' Rights in action is when Northern states such as Wisconsin nullified part of the federal Constitution—a constitution that these states had pledged to uphold when they entered the Union! This occurred in 1859 when Wisconsin enacted its version of the Personal Liberty Laws, which nullified Article IV, section 2 of the United States Constitution. Article IV, section 2 is better known as the 'fugitive slave section,' in which states agreed to aid in the return of runaway slaves. This section of the federal Constitution was modeled after a section in Massachusetts's original state constitution!

"Wisconsin and other non-slave states found it morally repugnant to aid in the capture and return of individuals fleeing slavery even though they had agreed to do so when they joined the Union. They had three choices: (1) obey the federal Constitution and in so doing violate their moral principles, (2) secede from the Union, or (3) nullify that part of the federal Constitution that they now found to be a violation of their moral principles. They elected to exercise their right of nullification and thereby maintain their state's standing within the Union while protecting their newfound moral principles.

"All of these examples are notable for the complete absence of any effort to protect slavery. Indeed, the last example is demonstrative of a way that States' Rights could have been used to speed the final abolition of slavery in America. If time had been allowed for more and more states to pass personal liberty laws, it would eventually have become impossible to force an entire population to remain in a condition of servitude that they found reprehensible. But States' Rights presented a far greater threat to those who desired to create and maintain a vast commercial and economic empire.

"Patrick Henry warned Virginia not to accede to the proposed federal Union under the constitution of 1787 because it would result in the Southern agricultural states being dominated and exploited by the commercial states of the North. He knew that Northerners such as Alexander Hamilton wanted a vigorous federal government to help create a vast commercial empire—a commercial empire that would be controlled from Wall Street and other Northern commercial centers. Patrick Henry, on the other hand, wanted to establish a government that would protect the national borders while presenting limited dangers to the liberties of the citizens of the various states. As Patrick Henry stated, 'The first thing I have at heart is American liberty, the second thing is American union.' He warned his countrymen, 'I am sure that the dangers of this system are real, when those who have no similar interests with the people of this country [Virginia and the South] are to legislate for us—when our dearest interests are to be left in the hands of those whose advantage it will be to infringe them.' He foresaw the inherent schism between the people of the South who desired a limited government and the people of the North who wanted a vigorous central government that would provide for their public and personal enrichment—a vast commercial empire they would control.

"So why has the political doctrine of States' Rights been demonized by modern historians and politicians? It is very simple once you understand the reality of the Federal Empire: the Federal Empire could not come about as long as the doctrine of *real* States' Rights was an accepted political fact in America, and it could not be maintained if *real* States' Rights existed in America today. Therefore those who desired to create a vast commercial and economic empire had to destroy this American constitutional principle. *Real* States' Rights blocked the development of their desired empire. This fact was acknowledged by Yankee Col. Robert G. Ingersoll when he declared, 'The great stumbling block, the great obstruction in Lincoln's way *and in the way of thousands* was the old doctrine of State's Rights.' Ingersoll knew that *real* States' Rights of nullification and secession acted as a barrier to the development of a strong, all-powerful, supreme federal government.

"Lincoln knew this as well and indirectly admitted it in 1861, while conspiring with Northern war governors to prevent the South from withdrawing from the Northern-controlled Federal government. The newspapers of the North knew it and admitted as much when they declared, "We were divided and confused until our pockets were touched. No, we must not let the South go." Notice how both Lincoln and his sycophants in the Yankee press all viewed the Southern states: not as sovereign states with the right to self determination but as their personal property. They were not going to allow the escape of this source of exploitable riches. They were determined to keep the Southern people under their control. States' Rights had to be destroyed.

"To do this, the North marshaled a million bloody bayonets to make sure their property—the people of the South—did not escape. For Southerners who only wanted to live in a country of their own, who wanted to be free of Yankee-imposed rule, there would be no personal liberty laws. The South would become an occupied nation forced into the Federal Empire against its will. 'We the people' of the South would become the political, social, and economic slaves in the new United States of America—a post-constitutional empire.

"Today the Federal Empire has become what Gen. Robert E. Lee predicted it would become: 'aggressive abroad and despotic at home.' The only way to reclaim the original constitutionally limited Republic of Republics is for Americans to insist on a return to *real* States' Rights. When Americans begin to realize that home rule is better than Federal rule, that 'we the people' at the local level know how to use our money better than the ruling elite in Washington, DC, that the economics of home rule are better than the exploitation of Wall Street and political cronies in Washington, DC, then perhaps Americans will decide to once again claim the right to be the masters in their own homes. They can do this by enacting a constitutional amendment acknowledging the right of 'we the people' of the sovereign state to nullify oppressive federal acts or to secede if necessary to protect our personal liberties."

§ Deo Vindice §

On the Skirmish Line with Uncle Seth
"The use of force against a State, would look more like a declaration of war, than an infliction of punishment, and would probably be considered by the party attacked as a dissolution of all previous compacts by which it might be bound."

—James Madison, circa 1787

103

Confederate Rifles Against Yankee Gunboats

It was early morning a few days before Christmas. Uncle Seth and the boys were searching the bottomland next to the creek to find an appropriately shaped cedar tree to use as the family's Christmas tree. The boys had been asking Uncle Seth to go with them to get a tree, but the old Confederate veteran had told them over and over again that the time was not right. Finally they were on the search for the family's Christmas tree. The bottomland was mostly covered by standing water due to recent rains, and the below-freezing overnight temperatures had left a fair amount of ice covering the pools of water. Freezes are not very common in lower Mississippi, and what ice develops is very thin and usually melts when exposed to the mid-morning sun. The boys were dressed warmly with cotton socks and fine new brogans covering their feet. With a good coat of saddle soap the brogans would "turn the water."

"Look, boys," Uncle Seth called out, "there is just the tree we need. It is over there on the small rise of land surrounded by water and ice." As the boys gathered around they all agreed that the tree was perfect but for its position—guarded as it was by a moat of ice and water. The boys could not understand why Uncle Seth had waited until the coldest morning of the season to decide to get the tree.

"Carroll Ray," Uncle Seth began. The boy quietly let out a low moan anticipating the coming orders. "Take off your brogans and socks and roll up your trouser legs and go get our Christmas tree." The other boys began laughing at Carroll Ray's harsh assignment but stopped when Uncle Seth added, "And you other boys do the same thing because he'll need help cutting down the tree and getting it back across the ice and water."

There was no thought of ignoring Uncle Seth's orders. The boys waded across the icy moat, cut down the tree, and began dragging it to the dry land where Uncle Seth had a roaring fire waiting. The boys seemed especially proud of their adventure and especially appreciative of the warmth from Uncle Seth's fire. But they were surprised and a little bewildered when Uncle Seth told them that he had spotted this tree some time back and had been waiting for the correct time to bring them here and have them wade the icy waters.

"Now gather around the fire and get your dry socks and brogans on while I tell you about my Christmas back in 1862. It was cold just like this when a fellow from Louisville, Kentucky, by the name of Tom Hall, a bunch of good ole Rebels, and myself were fighting Yankee gunboats and the Yankee General Sherman near Deer Creek Pass north of Vicksburg, Mississippi. We were assigned to an area that was covered in icy water and spent most of the time in that icy water ankle to hip deep. As a matter of fact, that is where we spent most of Christmas week. We would position ourselves behind the levy and shoot at the Yankee gunboats as they came by. Any invader who exposed himself for even a moment would receive a Confederate greeting molded in lead. One of our favorite things to do was to wait until the sun glinted off the brass sights on the back of the gunboats cannons. We would then take turns shooting off these expensive aiming devices. The shots were usually between five hundred to one thousand yards, and we seldom missed! Just shows you what excellent marksmen we country boys were."

"And still are!" interrupted Carroll Ray.

"Oh yes, guns, hunting, and outdoor pleasures are still an important part of our Southern way of life," Uncle Seth agreed with the enthusiastic youth. "Well, there was a lot going on because this was the second attempt the Yankees had made to get into Vicksburg. But all we common soldiers knew was that we had an evil invader in front of our position and cold, wet ground behind. We were also all very hungry; for weeks all we had to eat was parched corn. We did not have any way to grind the corn into meal, nor did we have any pots or pans to cook it in even if we could have made it into cornmeal. Added to that was the fact that there were only a few spots of dry ground on which we could make a fire. Most of the time we just parched the dry corn still on the cob and tried our best to eat it.

"One day a fellow we called Swazey rushed down to where Tom and I were positioned and told us he had just spotted a young bear going into the brush on the island across the levee. Well the thought of fresh meat, even bear meat, was enough to call us to the hunt. We waded through the hip-deep, icy water to the island and began the hunt. Soon we heard the report of Tom's Enfield

A black sharpshooter (Courtesy Charles Hayes)

rifle. It was not long before we had the bear skinned and quartered, but we were forced to cut the meat into small strips, wrap it around our Enfield rifle ramrods, and roast the meat over an open fire.

"During this campaign, the Yankee gunboats would shell our position for hours every time our sharp-shooting boys would kill one of the Yankee sailors. We all looked forward to these bombardments because we knew that no enemy would be approaching us, which meant we could make ourselves comfortable behind the levee and take a well-deserved nap. It also meant that the Yankees were wasting hundreds of rounds of munitions and gunpowder. During the entire time that we were on that line, which was several weeks, the Yankee gunboats only caused one injury. That causality was the result of a tree limb that was cut through by a Yankee cannonball and fell on the soldier standing beneath the tree.

"This was about the same time that Yankee General Sherman was attempting to penetrate Vicksburg's defenses along the Chickasaw Bayou close to where we were stationed. He had declared that it would cost the United States military at least five thousand soldiers to take Vicksburg, and he was prepared to pay that price. He sent in six thousand well-provisioned Yankee invaders against less than half that number of ragged and starving Confederates. His troops were met by the 42nd Georgia and the 28th Louisiana—who handily repulsed the invading forces. Our fire was so severe and accurate that the Yankee invaders broke rank and lay down to avoid it. When our officers saw this they marched the 26th and part of the 17th Louisiana onto the battlefield and captured twenty-one Yankee officers and 311 non-commissioned officers and privates, giving us a resupply of brand new Yankee rifles and other military accouterments. As the battle ceased, we allowed the Yankee infirmary corps to carry their wounded off the battlefield. But as soon as the Yankees had removed their wounded their sharpshooters began shooting at our hospital personnel, which prevented many of our wounded from receiving the immediate care required to save their lives—just another example of Yankee honor!

"Sherman sacrificed 1,439 United States soldiers in his attack while we suffered only 124 causalities. After this defeat he gave up on his plan to enter Vicksburg from the north. As soon as our officers saw that the Yankees were withdrawing, they attacked! We followed the retreating Yankees up the Yazoo River while the 2nd Texas rushed up to within pistol shot of the Yankee transport boats on the Mississippi River. Those brave Texas Confederates poured rifle and pistol shots into the crowded transports, causing great loss of life on board. It is interesting that General Sherman did not mention this last encounter in his official report," Uncle Seth noted with a sense of pleasure in his voice.

"Uncle Seth, you said that the Yankee gunboats would spend hours firing at your position even though it produced very little result. But why would the Yankee gunboats waste so much ammunition firing aimlessly at you?" asked Carroll Ray.

"Well, they were—and still are—a part of a large industrial empire and they could afford to waste resources on foreign entanglements and imperialistic adventures—after all, the payback on imperialism is very handsome for the empire's ruling elite and those with close connections to the empire's ruling elite. And that is why 'we the people' of the South wanted no part of the Yankee's Hamiltonian dream of a large, powerful, commercial, and economic empire. We especially did not want to be ruled by the Yankee Empire. But boys, I want you all to understand just how much we suffered in our attempt to preserve your right to be left alone and to live under a government ordered upon the American principle of the consent of the governed. Tom and I, as well as all the other men who wore the gray in the War for Southern Independence, did not endure such unimaginable hardships in order to allow a few rich plantation owners to keep their slaves! We fought because we knew that the Yankee Empire wanted to make slaves of all Southerners—black and white!" Uncle Seth kicked dirt over the fire and began the trek back to the house. The boys took turns dragging the Christmas tree, but they did not try to engage Uncle Seth in conversation because they knew that the old Confederate veteran was thinking about his country's sad fate.

§ Deo Vindice §

ON THE SKIRMISH LINE WITH UNCLE SETH
"The brave Confederate soldier had lost his leg below the knee—shot away by a Yankee cannon ball—and was given a medical discharge and sent back home, a small cabin in the Southern hill country, to recover. After being home for a year the man had made a decent recovery and had learned to walk on his new 'peg' leg. He returned to his old unit and re-enlisted to fight for his country. During a prayer-meeting held by a local parson the minister attempted to close the meeting with his final prayer in which he prayed that God would send 'our Southern soldiers more zeal, more courage, and more fortitude' but the prayer was interrupted by the one legged Confederate soldier who told the minister, 'You got it all wrong preacher! You ask God to send us more ammunition and provisions and we will attend to the rest, thank you very much Lord!'"

—Gen. John B. Gordan

104

Southern Lady Rejects Yankee Soldier's Offer of Friendship

Billie Jean was reading an article in one of Uncle Seth's magazines that described how Winnie Davis, Pres. Jefferson Davis's youngest daughter, had refused an offer of marriage from an eligible young gentleman because he was from New York. Winnie explained, "It would grieve my father for me to marry a Yankee." Looking up at Uncle Seth, a perplexed Billie Jean asked, "Why would she refuse to marry someone just because he was a Yankee?"

Uncle Seth chuckled as he looked down at his great-granddaughter. The war was forty years in the past, long before Billie Jean was born. She had no way to understand unless Uncle Seth could explain, and hopefully she would then explain it to her children. Taking a while to decide on the best story to use, the old Confederate veteran took a deep breath and began his explanation.

"Let me tell you about what happened in Greenville, Alabama, in April of 1865. Despite years of war against an invader that outnumbered us four to one, the people of Greenville never lost hope of final victory and the ultimate independence of the South. But early one morning they were awakened by the celebratory firing of Yankee cannons—the Yankees had just received the news of General Lee's surrender. As their cannons ceased firing, their bands began playing the 'Star-Spangled Banner,' 'Hail Columbia,' and that most hated tune, 'Yankee Doodle.' But over it all could be heard pianos in hotels and private homes playing 'Dixie' and 'The Bonnie Blue Flag.' Our armies had been forced to surrender, but our spirits remained firm in dedication to the right of our people to be free.

"The town was occupied by Yankee troops, which made it hard for young ladies to venture out for fear of what might happen to a female surrounded by the troops of an invader. One day a Yankee officer passed a note to a young Southern lady who had attracted his attention. But she rebuffed the Yankee's entreaty and declared that she would never consent to socializing with a Yankee. The offended Yankee officer sent another note detailing his confusion as to why such a young and gentle girl would be full of so much hatred. This Southern lady returned the Yankee's note with the following poem penned on the back:

Hatred? Yes, I have learned to hate
Till my warm Southern blood
Runs madly in my slender frame,
A boundless, angry flood—
Wouldst thou know why? Look on The South,
Look over each blackened field;
This waste where our defenders stood,
In death alone to yield.

O, have you seen the burning homes,
The flames of sacrifice?
And have you known, as I have known,
The Northman's heart of ice?
Your homes are fair, and plenty stands
Laughing upon our woe;
How can we smile in this drear waste,
Still trampled by the foe?
Honor was more to us than life;
And thus, with aching heart,
We crushed the selfish, mortal cry
And bore diviner part.
Yes, still for my poor, stricken land
I'd lay earth's garments down,
Take death by famine, flame, or sword,
To win her freedom's crown.

Scorn? Yes, I am proud to scorn
Falsehood over all the world;
Your flag is the brightest painted lie
That ever was unfurled!
I hate—aye, hate—I loathe the name
Of Union. O, how base!
Enforced by strong-armed Tyranny,
That scorn is in my face.
Pull down Oppression's gaudy sign,
Usurping hands have hung;
I cannot walk beneath its folds,
To Southern breezes flung—
Mad? Mad were they who bore it here
With curses; faces bold
Mocked the black robes that faintly tell
Of sorrow in each fold.
Where'er I turn my restless feet,

The invader's bristling bayonets stand,
Enforcing petty tyrannies
In this our own fair land—
Home! Ah me, I am homesick too!
The dead on battle plain
Alone are free; survivors must
Still wear a galling chain.

But Dixie Land will blossom forth,
Her fertile valleys bloom;
Freedom will spring, reborn, from flame,
And garland every tomb
With amaranth, and Liberty
Will break her prison bars—
Or else, give me for winding sheet
Our hidden cross of stars.

"The Yankee officer was rebuked and was soon called off to fight the Indians in the West who were resisting the Federal Empire's efforts to remove them from their ancestral lands. After that successful campaign, the officer was eventually transferred to the Philippines, where he earned his general's stars fighting the local people who for some strange reason were not enamored with the idea of being ruled by the Yankee Empire.

"This young Southern girl had given her heart to a local lad who had joined the Confederate army at the outbreak of the war. He was at that time a prisoner of war held by the Yankees at Johnson's Island. They were married a year after the war ended and even many years later she maintained that she was as true to her dear Southland as ever. So you see, Billie Jean, there was a reason why Winnie Davis would not marry a Yankee. Even though the Yankee had not been a soldier during the war, he represented the nation that invaded, conquered, occupies, and oppresses our people." The old man looked down at Billie Jean, but the young child still did not completely understand. Uncle Seth often wondered if the South of the future would be able to recognize their situation or if they would, like serfs of old, meekly accept the South's assigned role to become an impoverished embarrassment to the Federal Empire.

§ Deo Vindice §

ON THE SKIRMISH LINE WITH UNCLE SETH
About fifteen years *before* the war, a prominent Yankee member of Congress was asked why Congressmen from the North insisted on

harassing the South about slavery. After considering the question for a moment he replied, "The real reason is that the South will not let us have a tariff, and we touch them where they will feel it." Northern motivation for supporting radical abolitionists was love of money, *not* love of African slaves in the South. Their motivation for invasion was love of money—their guiding policy is and always has been a policy promoting the pursuit of profit uninhibited by principles of morality or constitutional government.

105

The Confederate Soldier's Only Regret

Uncle Seth was sitting next to the open window. It was late evening; the sun's light had faded beneath the western horizon and the old Confederate veteran was enjoying the sounds of the whip-poor-wills off in the distance calling to each other. He was so deeply engrossed in the simple enjoyment of the moment that he had not noticed Carroll Ray standing next to him holding an open school textbook.

"Uncle Seth," the youngster spoke softly, "why are our soldiers so sad in this picture?"

Uncle Seth took the boy's book, looked down at the page, and paused for a long while before answering. Carroll Ray wondered why Uncle Seth didn't have a quick answer.

"Carroll Ray," the old Confederate veteran began, almost in a whisper, "this is a photograph of a very famous piece of post-war artwork. It is called *Furling the Flag*. It very artfully captures the emotions of the men who wore the gray in the War for Southern Independence at the moment when we were forced to surrender and demonstrates the love and devotion we had for our country, the Confederate States of America. But you cannot understand the emotion if you do not understand the truth about why we were fighting, and this is something that those who now occupy our country are determined to make sure your generation and future generations never learn!

"Let me tell you a story that will explain why we were fighting against such overwhelming odds, why many of us are still fighting, and why we hope that future generations of Southerners will also answer the call to resist being dominated by the Federal Empire's ruling elites in Washington, DC, and Wall Street. I met Mr. W. M. Long from Nashville, Tennessee, at the 1905 United Confederate Veteran Reunion and he told me this story about his brave Kentucky comrades. They were a part

Furling the Flag *by Richard Norris Brooke* (Courtesy West Point Museum Collection, United States Military Academy)

of Company D, 1st Regiment, Kentucky Cavalry. The incident occurred near Bentonville, North Carolina, in early March of 1865, when General Johnston drove the Yankee invaders, commanded by General Sherman, back almost four miles in hard fighting. Long and several other soldiers were detached and sent forward as scouts to find out where the Yankees were. They rode up a road toward an old-fashioned Southern home expecting to be fired on at any moment. All of a sudden five Yankees burst out of the house and ran towards the woods in back of the house. An elderly woman came running toward the Confederate soldiers crying and begging them to shoot the Yankees because they were 'outraging my young daughters'—and by that she obviously did not mean that the Northern invaders were tossing verbal insults at the young women of the house. I don't think I need to be any more graphic; you understand what I mean don't you?" Uncle Seth asked the young boy almost apologetically. Carroll Ray nodded and grunted affirmatively, too embarrassed to make eye contact.

"Well, our boys let loose a Rebel Yell and charged the Yankee villains, overtaking them before they reached the woods. With five well-aimed shots they denied these Yankees the privilege of any further pillaging and raping of our Southern homeland. Even though it was early March it was still bitterly cold and Long's coat and boots had long since been worn away, leaving him with very little protection from the elements. But one of the dead invaders was just about the same size as Long so he decided to relieve the villain of his boots and coat, knowing that the dead man would have little use for either (particularly considering the hot regions below where the Yankee villain was now residing). The next day the Confederate scouting party was captured and one of the Yankees recognized the coat and boots as belonging to one of their missing men. The Yankees immediately placed a rope around Long's neck and began looking for a tree from which to hang this prisoner of war. Luckily Long was saved by an order for the Yankee army to move out; but they did strip Long of all his clothes down to his bare feet and underwear. It was still bitterly cold, but Long was forced to march from Bentonville, North Carolina, to Savannah, Georgia, barefoot and with no trousers or coat. While passing through Cape Hatteras, Lt. G. R. Pope used his last fifty cents to purchase Long a coat and trousers. The Confederate prisoners were eventually sent to Hart's Island prison camp in New York harbor.

"Now why did these men willingly suffer such dangers and hardships? The Yankee propagandists tell the world that they were fighting to keep their slaves, but the truth is that we were fighting to keep the Yankees from making slaves out of the South. We were fighting to protect our wives, daughters, mothers, and children. We were fighting to protect the nation that we had freely consented to live under. We were fighting to protect the Confederate States of America.

"While at the 1905 reunion I heard a speech by the veteran Milford Overley from Flemingsburg, Kentucky, in which he described the attitude of his Kentuckians when they were forced to surrender. He said that it was a sad day for him and his men. These were hardened soldiers who had braved death and had seen many of their friends and kinsmen killed. Their home state of Kentucky had been overrun and occupied by the Federal Empire early in the war, and most had not been back to see their kin since the fighting began. But at the surrender there was not a dry eye among the survivors; these tough men wept like children. There was unbelievable sadness in their hearts—hearts that had been broken for the love of their lost country. In utter despondency someone lamented, 'I guess they will expect us to take the loyalty oath and pledge allegiance to the United States—our new masters.' Another determined Southern soldier declared in response, 'May God in Heaven damn me to the hottest and darkest pits of Hell if ever I love any country other than the South!' You see, Carroll Ray, these men were sad because they knew what has been lost: freedom and the right of our people to live under a government ordered upon the free and unfettered consent of the governed, the right to live under a government that will simply leave us alone.

"Carroll Ray," the old man said as he closed the book and handed it back to the young boy, "we need our country—the Confederate States of America. We need it today more than ever and I fear that when your grandchildren are grown they will need their country even more if they are to ever again be truly free." Uncle Seth knew that this was more than the young boy could understand. Indeed, the old Confederate veteran wondered, in light of all the anti-South propaganda that constantly issues forth from the Federal Empire, if future Southerners would even have the courage to understand.

§ Deo Vindice §

ON THE SKIRMISH LINE WITH UNCLE SETH

Miss Sue M. Bryant of Saline County, Missouri, was arrested by Federal authorities for flying a Confederate flag at her home and refusing to take the oath of allegiance to the United States of America. She was sentenced to Gratiot Street prison in St. Louis, where she remained for months refusing to pledge allegiance to the nation that invaded her country. Authorities reported to her that her father was ill and near to death and offered to release her if she would sign the Loyalty Oath—which she reluctantly did. It was a deception used by the invader to get her signature on a false document. Miss Bryant thenceforth assured her friends and eventually her children that she was yet true to the principles of the Confederacy for which she suffered.

106

General Sherman's Plan to Colonize the South with Yankees

Uncle Seth and three of his great-grandchildren had taken the train to Vicksburg, Mississippi. A member of the local Sons of Confederate Veterans (SCV) Camp had arranged to meet Uncle Seth at the train station. The young SCV member arrived driving a brand new 1928 Ford sedan; a walking tour of the Vicksburg Battlefield would have been too much for the old veteran. Uncle Seth knew that his time on this earth was getting shorter with the passing of each season and he wanted one last chance to show his descendants the battlefield on which he and so many of the young boys from their community had fought. But more than that he wanted to make sure the next generation of young Southerners understood why so many of their non-slave owning neighbors were willing to sacrifice all to protect the independence of their country, the Confederate States of America. The Vicksburg Battlefield would be the perfect place for him to make his point again. Now, Uncle Seth would rarely visit Yankee-controlled sites. He did not like such places because they were generally used as Yankee propaganda centers. Uncle Seth knew only too well that the victor in any war writes the history of the war and uses its power to enforce its own version while suppressing, if not extinguishing, the invaded country's history.

"OK, let's stop the car and get out here," Uncle Seth said. He opened the door while the car was rolling to a stop in front of the Alabama monument.[1] "Now, over on the northern side of the siege line was where our neighbor John Wesley Kennedy was stationed with the 38th Mississippi Volunteer Infantry. Here on the southern side the city was being protected by units from Alabama. Take a look at this monument; it shows men fighting as if surrounded on all sides. You see a soldier who has already given his life to defend his home. And in the center you see a woman representing all we

1. Through the license of fiction Uncle Seth is allowed to visit the Alabama monument in 1928, some twenty-three years before it was actually erected.

were fighting for—our homes, our families, our right to be left alone, our very right to exist as a people. And look, what is she holding up so proudly as her soldiers fight against overwhelming numbers of invaders?" The old man looked around searching for an answer from his great-grandchildren.

"She's holding up the Confederate Battle Flag," announced Joe William proudly.

"Yes, that's right, Joe William," Uncle Seth replied approvingly. "The Yankees who run this Federal battlefield will try to tell you that we were fighting to keep our slaves. They do that because if the truth were ever known they would be in danger of losing their empire. You all always remember that the current Federal Empire was built on the graves of many a brave Confederate soldier. In truth the Yankees would have exterminated us all and replaced Southerners with Yankees if they could have done so." Uncle Seth paused to see if anyone would challenge his estimation of the Northern invaders' villainy.

"Now, Uncle Seth, I have heard that said before. While I do not find it hard to believe, do you have any actual proof?" asked the SCV member.

"Well, it just so happens that I do," Uncle Seth said, so happy to accept the young man's challenge that it seemed almost as if it had been planned.

"I have here with me a copy of a letter written in 1862 by the Yankee General Sherman." Uncle Seth's explanation was interrupted by boos and hisses from his great-grandchildren. Uncle Seth turned to the SCV member and boastfully explained, "They've learned well!" After allowing an appropriate amount of time to pass he continued, "General Sherman wrote this letter to his brother, who was a senator from Ohio in the United States Congress. It speaks of how General Sherman had ordered the confiscation of all gold, silver, and salt from the citizens of Memphis, Tennessee. He notes that he has one citizen held under the penalty of death because that citizen violated an order. General Sherman then goes on to complain that Southerners are so determined to maintain their loyalty to the Confederacy that it will take 1,300,000 Yankee soldiers to maintain Northern rule over such people. Then he declares, 'Of course I approve the confiscation act, and would be willing to revolutionize the government so as to amend that article of the Constitution which

The Alabama State Monument (Courtesy Charles Hayes)

forbids the forfeiture of land to the heirs. My full belief is, we must colonize the country [the South], *de novo*, beginning with Kentucky and Tennessee, and should remove 4,000,000 of our people [Yankees] at once south of the Ohio River, taking the farms and plantations of the Rebels. . . . Don't expect to overrun such a country or subdue such a people in one, two years or five years. It is the task of half a century. . . . To attempt to hold the entire South would demand an army too large even to think of. We must colonize and settle as we go South. . . . Enemies [Southerners] must be killed or transported to some other country.' Children, now do you understand why these brave Alabamians and their other Southern comrades were so willing to fight even though they were surrounded on all sides by such overwhelming odds?" Uncle Seth turned to admire the monument.

"Yes, boys and girls, don't think this was the attitude of just one Yankee invader," declared the SCV member. "No, this was typical of the hatred those people had for us, our people, and our desire to live under a government of our own choosing—a government that would not be dominated by Yankees. Even after the end of the war the desire of the North to repopulate the South remained. One carpetbagger declared that he hoped a large part of the Yankee army would remain in the South and make it their home, that with additional immigration of Northerners they would remake the South after the Northern fashion. He declared that 'if the results of the war are to be secured, and the nation protected against the recurrence of such a calamity, these States must be rebuilt from the very ground-sill.' Then he warned that the South would rise again and that the only way to prevent it from doing so was through a massive immigration of Northerners into a depopulated South. And don't forget what Yankee General Grant said in an order to Yankee Maj. Gen. David Hunter: 'In pushing up the Shenandoah Valley . . . it is desirable that nothing should be left to invite the enemy to return . . . such as cannot be consumed destroy.' So you see, it was their desire—if not official policy—to eradicate the people of the South." The SCV member turned to look at Uncle Seth.

Uncle Seth began again, "It is now up to you to protect the honor of those of you kin who wore the gray in the War for Southern Independence. Our numbers are getting smaller each year; each year more of my comrades answer the final roll call and cross the river to rest in the shade of the trees; each year there are fewer of us who can bear witness to the righteousness of our Cause. It is now your Cause. Soon you will be old enough to join the Sons of Confederate Veterans and continue the fight. You must always remember Gen. Stephen D. Lee's orders given to the Sons of Confederate Veterans in New Orleans when the SCV was first organized:

> To you, Sons of Confederate Veterans, we will commit the vindication of the Cause for which we fought. To your strength will be given the defense of the Confederate soldier's good name, the guardianship of his history, the emulation of his virtues, the perpetuation of those principles which he loved and which you love also, and those ideals which made him glorious and which you also cherish. Remember, it is your duty to see that the true history of the South is presented to future generations.

"Well, it won't be long before I am gone, and then the world will see if your generation and generations following you will have the same courage that my generation had." The old Confederate veteran seemed to become fatigued quicker lately; every new battle left him still determined but more exhausted than ever before. The children followed him back to the car, each engrossed in his own thoughts.

§ Deo Vindice §

ON THE SKIRMISH LINE WITH UNCLE SETH
"I, Felix Motlow from Mulberry, Tennessee, personally witnessed the execution of three Confederate prisoners by the Yankee invaders—these Confederate soldiers' only crime was that they were defending their homes from an evil invader. The three men were W. T. 'Billy' Green, Tom Brown, and Bill Davis. They were captured about three miles outside of Lynchburg and shot without any evidence that they were conducting themselves as anything other than as soldiers of the Confederate States of America. They were not even shooting at the enemy but were attempting to get away from the advancing Federal forces. Davis and Green were riding the same horse while Brown had his own horse. Davis was shot shortly after he was captured. Green immediately surrendered but a United States military *officer* rode up shouting at his men, and demanding to know why they had not shot the second and third Southerner. The Yankee officer shouted, "Shoot the damn bushwhacker. Why did you let him surrender?' Upon hearing this Green jumped from his horse and like a lion in rage grabbed the Yankee officer's pistol and killed the Yankee with his own pistol. The Yankee troops immediately shot Green and Brown. Such is Yankee honor—glory, glory, hallelujah."

107

Tree Cut Down by Yankee Minie Balls

The boys had tacked a paper target on an oak tree behind the barn and were busy setting their sights and doing a little target practicing before the beginning of turkey-hunting season. "You boys could buy a turkey for the price of the powder and lead you are wasting on target practice," the old Confederate veteran teased as he approached the boys. "And if you keep shooting at that tree you will end up cutting it down with hot lead," he added.

"You can't cut a tree down with rifles!" exclaimed Barry.

"Oh, yes you can," countered Uncle Seth. "I have a friend in South Carolina who had an oak tree twenty-five inches in diameter fall on him during the Battle of Spotsylvania. It was cut down by Yankee minie balls—of course the Yankees were attempting to cut down my friend and his comrades, not the tree," Uncle Seth chuckled as he sat down on an oak stump next to the boys' 'firing range.' The boys momentarily ceased their practice and turned to hear what the old Confederate veteran had to say.

Not waiting for any additional encouragement, Uncle Seth began, "Mr. Henry M. Bradley of Saluda County, South Carolina, told me about his experience during the War for Southern Independence. He joined Hampton's Legion early in 1861 and fought for the Cause of Southern Freedom from First Manassas all the way to surrender at Appomattox. At First Manassas he was with Capt. M. W. Gary—who eventually achieved the rank of general. Well, Captain Gary pursued the stampeding Yankees all the way to Centreville. Henry said that the whole way was strewn with overturned carriages and buggies, discarded guns, and other military accouterments that the fleeing Yankees no longer had any use for and decided to leave for the Confederates. He told me that Hampton's Legion only lasted for eighteen months. It began with slightly over one thousand men, but within eighteen months of hard fighting their numbers had been reduced to ninety! When Hampton's Legion was disbanded, Private Bradley—Henry—joined A. P. Hill's Corps in the 1st South Carolina Regiment.

"It was when he was with the 1st South Carolina Regiment at the Battle of Spotsylvania that the Yankee minie balls cut down the big oak tree. Just prior to that event, his unit had dropped back to a prepared defensive position where they had built transverse breastworks. The Yankees charged the defensive line and pushed the Confederates out at one point of the line. McGowan's brigade was quickly given the order to retake the occupied portion. A fierce hand-to-hand struggle ensued, but the invaders were eventually driven back. During this entire time a terrible thunderstorm with incessant lightning and driving rain was adding its flavor to the scene of battle horror. The United States forces decided to attempt to retake the position and attacked with almost overwhelming numbers. Their troops came within a few feet of where Henry was loading and firing as fast as he could, three or four rounds a minute. His rifle was so hot that he had to hold it by its leather shoulder strap because his fingers would instantly fry when they touched the metal barrel.

"One of the Yankee officers—brave fellow, no doubt—mounted the top of the breastwork on Private Bradley's left and demanded that the Southern troops surrender themselves and their position. In an instant almost every Confederate rifle barrel was pointed at him and discharged! Now from a military point-of-view this was not a smart thing for the Confederates to do. One rifle shot would have dispatched the officer and his insulting demand, leaving the rest to tend to the approaching enemy. But as if by instinct, every man there ignored the pressing danger in front of him and burned with a manly desire to extract revenge for what they perceived as an insult to their honor. They fired and the Yankee officer flew off the breastwork as if he were a dry oak leaf being blown about by a harsh autumn wind. The poor Yankee officer, not knowing the mind of the average Southerner, did not likely intend to insult them but merely thought that as a practical matter the struggle should end; logically the small number of rebels had to give up to the overwhelming numbers of the better-equipped and morally superior Yankees. But those were different days, boys, before Southerners had learned to supplicate before their Yankee masters.

"Henry explained that the transverse breastworks were built with logs hewn and stacked at each flank to prevent the Yankees from establishing a direct line of fire into the Confederate defensive line. He told me that the tree that was cut down by Yankee minie balls was within arm's reach of where he was positioned. After their last disastrous charge, the Yankees pulled back to their position and began a non-stop rifle-firing exercise—like they were trying to see which Yankee could use up the most ammunition.

The enemy's fire was either passing harmlessly overhead, making impact on the breastwork, or striking the oak tree. Henry said that the enemy's rifle fire acted like a wood plane or wood chipper—before long he was covered in wood chips. The firing continued for almost twenty-four hours. It was as if a perfect sheet of hot Yankee lead was constantly flying over the Confederate breastwork, much of it pounding the oak tree. The mighty oak tree gradually lost its leaves and smaller limbs, and eventually it looked like a tree skeleton standing there in the middle of this horrific battle scene. Late the following evening the tree yielded to the overwhelming might of the Yankee Empire and fell to the ground. After the battle our men noticed the many acorns strewn across that blood-soaked ground where so many young Southern patriots sacrificed their lives in the defense of their country and where that once-mighty oak had stood for years. With each tiny acorn resided the promise, the hope, the prayer that one day yet another mighty oak shall rise again." Uncle Seth concluded and walked slowly back toward the barn.

§ Deo Vindice §

ON THE SKIRMISH LINE WITH UNCLE SETH
"The mercy of God did not bring independence. Nor was the war over. One phase was done. . . . The avowed purpose [of Northern policy] was the destruction of Southern Civilization."
—Andrew Nelson Lytle. The young girl shot by the Yankees in Uncle Seth's first story was Lytle's grandmother.